D0119866

THE PRETENDER

THE PRETENDER

Jane Stevenson

Jonathan Cape
London

Published by Jonathan Cape 2002

2 4 6 8 10 9 7 5 3 1

First published in Great Britain in 2002 by
Jonathan Cape
Random House, 20 Vauxhall Bridge Road,
London SW1V 2SA

The Random House Group Limited Reg. No. 954009

The Maps

Map of Middelburg (p. xi) by Cornelius Goliath, c. 1670; Map of London (p. 64) by
John Ogilby and William Morgan, *The City of London*, 1676; 'A New Map of Barbados'
(p. 165) by Richard Forde, 1672 (The British Library, London); Map of St James's
and Westminster, centring on Tuthill (Tothill) Street (p. 252), William Morgan,
London &c. Actually Survey'd, 1682 (Guildhall Library, Corporation of London). Grateful
acknowledgement is made for permission granted to reprint copyright material.

A CIP catalogue record for this book
is available from the British Library

ISBN 0-224-06141-0

Papers used by The Random House Group Limited are natural,
recyclable products made from wood grown in sustainable forests;
the manufacturing processes conform to the environmental
regulations of the country of origin

Typeset by Palimpsest Book Production Limited,
Polmont, Stirlingshire

Printed and bound in Great Britain by
Mackays of Chatham PLC, Chatham, Kent

For Peter

Acknowledgements

I have many friends to thank for help with this book. Peter Davidson, above all, and Jamie Reid Baxter. John and Marita Gilmore, dialect coaches extraordinaire, have kept me right on the history, language and flora of Barbados. I have made grateful use of James Knowles's research on Thomas Bushell, and Nigel Smith's on Thomas Tryon. Anne Lawrence and Frank Thackray have offered a variety of insights into the Puritan mentality, and for various reasons, I am also grateful to Arnold Hunt, Léon Lock, and Alison Shell. I owe a great deal to Janet Todd's work on the life of Aphra Behn, and the Zeeuws Archief in Middelburg has again been immensely helpful.

It may seem to some readers that I am very harsh in my representation of Aphra Behn. There is no indignity or accident which befalls her in this novel which is not securely based on known events in her life, which was a wretchedly hard one. It is not certain that she had syphilis, but she certainly suffered from some chronic ailment which caused periodic bouts of ill-health, and killed her when she was about fifty (in 1689). Nothing is known for certain of the true circumstances of her marriage. Her husband may have been the Johan Behn, a slaver since at least 1655, who was master of an elusive vessel, the *King David*, or *Coninck David*, captured by the English and rechristened *The Good Intent*, as Janet Todd has suggested.

Among my many debts to the scholars and writers of the later seventeenth century, I owe a particular debt to the mapmakers – in particular, to Cornelis Goliath's 1670s map of Middelburg, John Ogilby and William Morgan's 1676 map of the City of London,

William Morgan's 1682 map of St James's (which includes the Westminster area), and Richard Ford's 1674 map of Barbados. Thanks to their work, it is possible to walk in imagination along streets and across country which in many respects bears no resemblance whatsoever to the way it looked then. One place where the seventeenth century does still live is the 1675 Quaker Meeting-House at Brigflatts: I am grateful to the Friends who have cherished it without changing it, and who are generous enough to permit access to outsiders.

Jane Stevenson
Turriff

Hence oft I think, if in some happy Hour
High Grace should meet with one in highest Pow'r
And then a seasonable People still
Should bend to his, as he to Heaven's will,
What might we hope, what wonderful Effect
From such a wish'd Conjuncture might reflect.
Sure, the mysterious Work, where none withstand
Would forthwith finish under such a Hand;
Fore-shortened Time its useless course would stay
And soon precipitate the latest Day.

Andrew Marvell,
'The First Anniversary of the government under O.C.'

And though my father like a fool, with a hey, with a hey,
    Lost his life to save his soul, with a ho;
        I'll not quit my present love
        For a martyr's place above,
    With a hey tronny nonny nonny no.

A New Ballad, 1679

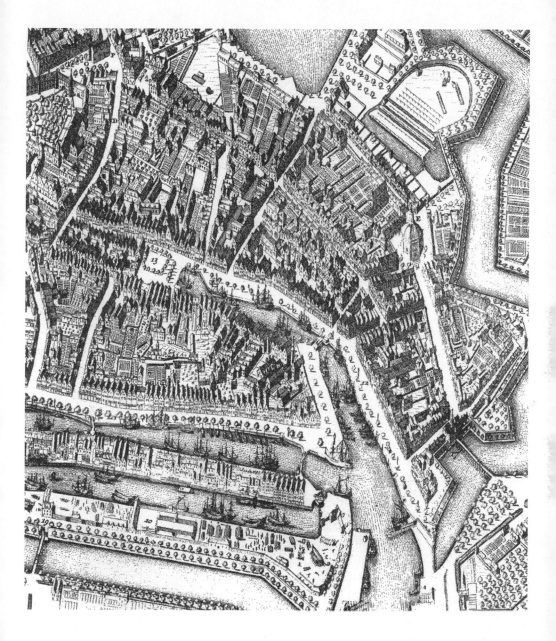

I

The mechanisms of our bodies are composed of strings, threads, beams, levers, cloth, flowing fluids, cisterns, ducts, filters, sieves, and other similar mechanisms. Through studying these parts with the help of Anatomy, Philosophy and Mechanics, man has discovered their structure and function . . . With this and the help of discourse, he apprehends the way nature acts and he lays the foundation of Physiology, Pathology, and eventually the art of Medicine.

Marcello Malpighi, *De Polypo Cordis* (1666)

February 1662

'And now we come to the heart of the mystery, gentlemen. Come forward a little, it is a sight you will seldom have an opportunity to see.' Delicately he traced the swollen, ripening curve with his forceps, as they all obediently craned their necks. 'About three months gravid, I should say. She should have pleaded her belly, poor wretch. But perhaps she did not know the signs.'

Putting down the forceps which he had been using as a pointer since laying aside the mass of the intestines, he picked up a scalpel, and began to cut. The thin, cold winter sun lanced down on the table, which was positioned to catch the best possible light. The room was completely silent, except for the precise, tearing sound of the blade sawing through tough muscle.

Balthasar leaned forward with the others, sweating with sickly fascination, breathing shallowly through his mouth. The meaty stink exhaling from the opened body was an almost solid thing, though the girl had been dead only forty-eight hours. Even though he was avoiding breathing through his nose, it seemed to have coated his whole mouth and throat with a layer of impalpable foulness. Incense burned in the room, but the delicate, musky sweetness only intensified the horror of the stench.

The sight before him was profoundly disturbing for a young man who had never before in his life seen a naked woman. The neck was of course damaged by the garotte, but since they were clustered about the lower part of the cadaver and the head was turned away from them it was not visible; he could only see the line of the cheekbone. The upper part of her body was pretty. She was very slight, bluish-white and waxen in death, with pale, maidenly nubbins of breasts that suggested extreme youth; if he had met her, perhaps carrying a pile of linen or a basket of eggs, he would have flirted with her, sought a glimpse of those little breasts now so pitilessly bare to his gaze. Yet the moment his eye strayed below the waist, he could no longer even think of the body as human, it was something worse than butcher's meat. The abdomen gaped open, omentum and bowels laid to one side to display the womb, like a terrible red egg in the nest of the pelvis. Both legs had been sawn away just below the point where they met the torso. The ends were dry and shiny like mahogany, with gleaming rings of paler fat and ivory bone, and between the great dark-red meaty ovals, her shameful parts were obscenely exposed in all their meagreness, adorned with a little tuft of blonde hair. He kept looking at her sex and away again, revolted and excited, and knew that his fellow students were doing the same. It was impossible for him to associate the dry and abject tags of flesh that he could see with what he had touched in his occasional fumblings beneath the skirts of whores, which had seemed, at the time, a slippery pit fit to swallow the world. Is this how all women are made? he wondered sickly, but was distracted from this train of thought by Professor van Horne.

Pinning back the two halves of the womb, now completely sectioned, he reached into it with the forceps, and brought forth a pale homunculus attached to a long, bluish cord. 'A male, I believe,' he announced, squinting at the tiny object expertly. 'Well, perhaps the law has spared him much suffering. He would not have amounted to much, with such a beginning.' Carefully, he laid the fetus down on a piece of white linen. 'Observe him well, gentlemen, so that his existence will not be absolutely in vain. The head is well developed, though the eyes are not open, and the heart is formed, as are the spine and the liver. We now know that his heart would already have been beating, and it may be that this little creature lived for some time after his mother met her end. He was not independent, as the cord which tethers him to the matrix bears witness, but neither was he wholly part of this wretched girl, any more than he was party to her sins. For all we know, he was already dreaming when death came quietly into his small world. So do we all begin.'

Turning to the anatomical atlas which lay open on a lectern beside the table, Professor van Horne began an exposition on the anatomy of the uterus. Balthasar and his fellow students took notes conscientiously; he was perhaps not the only one so disturbed by what he saw that he wrote mechanically and followed little of what the professor said.

At last, the lesson came to an end. Professor van Horne threw a sheet over the ruin of the girl and her child, while the students pocketed their notebooks and prepared to leave. Feet clattering, they trooped up the wooden stairs of the anatomy theatre, a precipitous, funnel-like oval of benches designed to give students the best possible view of the dissection table at its centre. Around the outermost set of seats articulated skeletons were placed, a horse and its rider, a cow; their delicate white bones arrested by an armature of wires and struts in postures which imitated their natural movements in life. There were also human skeletons carrying banners, the gonfaliere of Death: 'pulvis et umbra sumus', 'nosce teipsum', 'memento mori'.

'D'you know who she was?' Balthasar asked his friends as they emerged, shivering a little, into the raw air of February, hands deep in their pockets.

'I've no idea,' said Jan. 'Willem, you went to the execution, didn't you? Did anyone say?'

'Yes. Well, what she was, anyway. She was a country girl, she came to the city for work, and didn't find it. She scrounged and starved for a bit, maybe earned the odd stuiver on her back, the landlady got tired of waiting and tried to take her clothes. They had a fight, she pushed the old woman down the stairs and broke her neck, and the other lodgers caught her before she got to the end of the street. Lucky for us, really. It's my tenth dissection, and only the first woman. It's wonderful she was pregnant, I never thought I'd get to see that.'

'Luck indeed,' said Jan, with passion. 'Van Horne was right, calling it a miracle. It was beautiful. I've wanted to see inside a womb for a long time. He should've thrown the book away, sows and bitches are no guide at all. Hardly anything he told us was supported by what we saw. I was nearer than you, and I could see there wasn't the slightest trace of two chambers. The standard account needs complete revision, based on observation alone.'

'Was she pretty?' asked Balthasar suddenly.

The others looked at him, surprised. 'Who?' said Willem. 'Oh, yes. Pretty enough. Pale as a cheese, but she was on the gallows, wasn't she? She might've looked all right, smiling. It was just an ordinary face.'

Balthasar swallowed. Jan was incandescent with technical enthusiasm, but he could not help thinking of the girl. His mind was bumping around the unpalatable effort of imagining what it could be like to be so poor that one could die in defending two or three guilders' worth of old clothes. At the same time, he was uncomfortably aware that if his own ventures failed, there was nothing to keep him from such an end. The thought of her stirred in the pit of his stomach, and filled him with a strange nervous excitement.

Jan shook himself, as if shaking off a thought. 'Let's go for a borrel, jonges. That was wonderful, but I want to get the stink out of my throat. Anyone got a clove or anything?'

Balthasar had a paper of aniseed comfits, and passed them round. Chewing their sweets, the three students headed for a nearby inn, 't Zwarte Zwaan, their usual place of resort. It was not much of a place, but it was fairly cheap, and the landlord kept a good fire and the news.

'Oh, good,' said Balthasar as they pushed open the door, 'this week's *Courant*. I'd better take a look. I want to see if Thibault's been up to anything, back home.'

'You've had a lot of trouble down in Zeeland this last year,' observed Jan sympathetically. 'It's a long way away, when there's property to think about. Have you got family down there – maybe your mother's people?'

'No,' said Balthasar hastily. 'I've got no relatives. There's just a couple of old servants.'

'Tough luck, Blackie. Something more to worry about. What're you drinking?'

'Brantwijn, please.' They sat down together, Balthasar taking the seat nearest the window, the better to see the dirty, poorly printed pages. All three immediately began filling their pipes, and Willem began to tell Jan one of his long, rambling dirty stories, leaving Balthasar in peace to scan the paper. While his fingers filled and tamped the pipe with automatic skill, his eye, running down the columns, was alert for a few specific words, 'Middelburg', 'Zeeland', 'Thibault'. Thus, when his gaze passed over the words 'konigin van Bohemen', he did not at first register them; only a strange double-thump of his heart. He looked again, and this time, saw what was said. 'The queen of Bohemia is dead in London.' A strange, cold sensation began in his stomach and diffused through his body. His mother was dead, and he was completely numb.

'So, what d'you think of that, then, Blackie?' Willem's voice broke into his paralysis.

'Sorry?'

'You didn't hear a word, did you? Is there trouble at home? You're a funny colour – you look as if you'd have gone pale, if you could.'

'Oh, it's nothing.' Balthasar forced a smile. 'I'm tired, I think, I was working late last night.' He put the pipe down unlit, reached for his brandy, and gulped half of it in one swig. 'God. This is terrible stuff. What d'you think he puts in it?' As he had hoped, that turned the conversation.

Later, walking alone to his lodgings, he wondered what to do. The obvious answer was to stay where he was and get on with his degree, but he had an appallingly strong impulse to run for home which he knew to be futile: his father, the only person he could possibly have talked to, had been dead for five years. But he had brought none of his mother's letters with him, since he did not care to risk them outside the house, and he wanted very much to reread them.

Once he was in the privacy of his own room and his mind was working once more, he realised there was one thing he could usefully do, and that was to write to Cornelis Jonson van Ceulen, who, since his father's death, had been his only link with his mother. The old German had been a court painter in England under both James I and Charles I, but had fled in the early years of the Civil War, when Balthasar himself had been only a baby, and settled in Middelburg. Pelagius, Balthasar's father, always interested in English exiles, had become acquainted with him, and had secured him Elizabeth's patronage. The portrait he had painted of her, which Pelagius displayed in their small house in

Middelburg, had launched him on a second, modestly successful, career among Zeeland burghers and their wives, and Jonson had been duly grateful.

It was Jonson's image of a strong-featured, middle-aged woman with hazel eyes, fabulous pearls and a low-cut dress, holding a white rose, which was, to Balthasar, practically all that he knew by the name of mother. When she had come to Middelburg for a week of sittings, he had been only six, and he had not known anything of their relationship; try as he would, he could remember nothing she had said to him, and his memory of how she had looked was overlaid by the portrait itself. All he was sure of was the lustrous, rustling folds of her silken skirts, and the scent of amber and orris which they gave off; she had been exotic and awe-inspiring. His only real link with her was the letters, which had begun only after his father had told him who he was.

Due to the extreme secrecy of his birth and bringing-up, a discretion that his father had imposed upon him so strongly that it felt like a physical lock upon his tongue, when she wrote to him, as she occasionally did after Pelagius's death, the letters were sent under cover of notes to Mr Jonson, and his replies, brief as they were, went the same way. In the course of writing his letter to Jonson, he made up his mind. He would stay where he was; he had neither money nor time to spare.

September 1663

The packet-boat from Dordrecht was making its way up the Walcheren Canal towards Middleburg on the last leg of its journey, with the sun lying low on the horizon and making them all squint as they looked towards their first sight of the town. Balthasar, at last, was going home. Chilled from the long, cold journey threading through the islands of Zeeland, and uncertain in his mind, he looked up as the familiar defences of the Oostpoort came into view. He longed for home, and yet the thought of it appalled him. In the depths of the hold, roped and corded, were all his books and clothes from Leiden, together with his certificates of graduation as a doctor of medicine. His life as a student was now a thing of the past, before him was a house, and the two servants who had brought him up, Narcissus and Anna. All the security he had ever known. He longed to see them, and memories crowded in his head, Anna's warm lap, riding on Narcissus's shoulders, the alarms and excitements of childhood, how strong, wise and potent they had once seemed to him, especially Narcissus. Now, their dependence terrified him. He must succeed as a doctor to keep food in their mouths, coal in the cellar, linen in the press. The death of his mother, so far away, had removed his last point of resort beyond his own abilities, and she had left him nothing. The servants were his to command, but also his to care for, and he was infuriated by the assumption of helplessness in their confiding, painfully written letters. If he failed, he thought grimly, they would all three beg on the streets. Narcissus and Anna could, and would, do nothing to help him, or themselves.

The thought stayed with him through the protracted business of tying up at the Oostpunt, hiring a handcart and porter for his luggage, and the short walk home down the Spanjardstraat. When he came within sight of the small, rosy-brick house called De Derde Koninck, the sound of the porter's cart rattling on the cobbles alerted the household, and Narcissus looked out. In the slanting evening light, the round, dark head peering round the jamb of the door seemed strangely creased and distorted; the familiar keloid scars of ancient burns on Narcissus's cheek and neck, traces of an accident which had happened long before Balthasar was even born, seemed to pull his face into grotesque lopsided-ness; for a moment, he looked like a monster. The next second, he recognised his master, and his face split in a wide, white grin of delight: he flung wide the door, and hurried out to kiss Balthasar's hand.

Having exchanged the formal embrace of welcome, he did not relinquish his grasp, but peered up at his tall foster-son with anxious affection.

'You are well, dearest child? You look very well. You have eaten well, and been cared for?'

'Very well indeed. And how are things at home?'

Before Narcissus could reply, Anna emerged to make her curtsey, Balthasar remembered the porter, leaning patiently on his hand-cart, and between them, they got Balthasar's possessions off the cart and into the house.

Once over the threshold, the sense of familiarity was over whelming. The Queen, his mother, gazed down serenely from over the fireplace. The room was more cluttered than it had been in his father's day, when Elizabeth's portrait had been its only decoration. A picture of himself as a baby which he had found hidden in a cupboard now hung over the linen press, and there was a Venetian mirror bought in an auction the year after his father's death. Blue-and-white Chinese vases were symmetrically placed on the top of the press, and a small but good carpet adorned the table by the window where the big Bible lay in its place of honour. There were brass wall-sconces with small mirrors behind them to double the light they shed, and Anna had kept everything clean and polished like new. The room was full of reflections, points of light winking from gleaming metal and shining wood.

It filled him with ambivalent satisfaction. His father Pelagius had set his face absolutely against extravagance and superfluity; apart from books, he had bought nothing which was not strictly necessary. Balthasar, as he reached an age to notice such things, had longed for the tokens of an established, burgerlijk household, a desire which, tentatively voiced, had earned him the old man's devastating scorn.

'Balthasar my son, you are the descendant of kings, and a child marked by fate. I will not tell you more until you are older, but understand this for now. You are something far beyond these provincial bourgeois, and you have no need whatsoever to live by their lights. Let it pass.' The black eyes had flashed dangerously, and he had not dared to say more; his father's hand was a heavy one, and he required obedient respect from his son. All the same, he could still remember the suffocating frustration and resentment which rose in him at his father's wilful refusal to understand, even while he lowered his eyes like a good child and waited to be dismissed. It was all very well to talk of mighty destinies, but the world he lived in was a small one. He attended the Middelburg Latin school, like the sons of the other professional men in the town, and he was forced to see himself through the eyes of his schoolfellows. It was bad enough being black, with all the teasing and jeering it brought him, but the poverty and eccentricity of his home was a gratuitous extra source of torment, which rubbed him raw on a daily basis.

Then, when he was seventeen, he found himself the master of the house, and all that was in it, which included a gratifying quantity of gold. He had to be careful, and justify all his expenses to a trio of carefully selected guardians until he came of age, but it was with a mixture of pleasure and defiance that he had almost immediately set out to equip his home like the houses of his friends.

Narcissus and Anna had prepared his old room for him, of course. But in the morning, waking to the familiar sounds of the servants moving about, and the sounds of the street, the clip-clop of the first farmers driving in with milk, cart-wheels, voices and church bells, he wondered, as he lay in bed, whether he should signal his changed relationship to the household by moving to his father's quarters upstairs. He was now the master, after all.

Once he was up and dressed, rather than going straight down to breakfast, he mounted the steep stairs to the attic, with an automatic fluttering of the stomach which dated from the time his father was alive. His own books and papers from Leiden were piled in the middle of the floor. The rest of the room, from the plain bedstead at one end to the desk by the window at the other, was redolent of the presence of his father, austere, authoritative and demanding. The walls were lined with bookshelves; the theology Pelagius had read for choice, and a collection of works relating to his practice as a doctor and herbalist, all, from Balthasar's professional point of view, rather out of date. From the height of his own hard-won knowledge, Balthasar felt that he was entitled to begin to see his father in perspective. For all his success as a practitioner, the old man had been no more than an empiric, a quack of talent.

Also in the room, he knew, probably under the bed, was a large wooden box. Pelagius had always worn the key of that box on a chain round his neck. Balthasar vividly remembered his sense of transgression as he had finally slipped the chain over his father's dead and heavy head, gently, as if this last indignity might somehow waken him. At the time, he had not felt able to deal with the old man's private life: confused and frightened by his own freedom, he had shut the door to the attic, and hidden the key, chain and all, at the bottom of his own cabinet.

More than four years had passed since then. He had been away to University, and graduated as a fully trained doctor, something his father had never been. It was time to take possession, to replace the plain serge bed with the good red brocade hangings he had chosen for himself, the old rush chair with his new velvet-seated one, which was a little big for the room he now had, but would be perfect up here in the attic if they could get it up the stairs. He could make himself comfortable; perhaps use the first-floor room which had been his since his babyhood as a closet, or even a consulting room.

The decisions made, he turned and went down to the kitchen. Anna had made the milk-porridge with currants that had marked special occasions for as long as he could remember, and there was gingerbread, and buttermilk. He sat down at the kitchen table to be served, watching his erstwhile nurse as she bustled about. He had called her Nantje when he was little, he remembered suddenly; it was a long time since he had thought of her by that name. She could not be all that old, he perceived suddenly, she was perhaps in her mid-forties. But she could never have been good-looking, and now in her middle years, her pale, protuberant eyes, beaky nose and receding chin reminded him of an anxious little hen. Her movements were also hen-like, jerky and indecisive. She had always been a worrier: throughout his childhood, whenever he had run home in tears with a black eye, a bloody nose or bruised from a fall on the ice, he had always gone by preference to Narcissus – Sisi, as he had called him then. While Nantje wrung her hands and wailed, loving and ineffectual, Sisi would wipe his nose, cherish him in strong arms of unquestioning love, and tell him a story or sing him a song until the tears had dried.

Looking at Anna now as she moved about the kitchen, he assessed her in the light of his new knowledge of the body. The exophthalmia was perhaps goitrous, but probably no cause for anxiety. She showed some symptoms of arthritis: it was clear whenever she got to her feet that her knees were stiff. But she was thin and spare; all in all, there might be twenty or thirty years of useful life in her. It struck him as he sat idly watching her work and eating the porridge she had cooked to welcome him, that his medical knowledge was a sort of magic glass. One could no longer simply see the surface of a person, what she looked like, let alone what she hoped to show to the world. There was no escaping his cruel knowledge of the body beneath the clothes, all that people tried to keep secret, and beyond that, the things which were secret even from them: the workings of their inner organs, the track-marks of disease and future suffering. It was so easy to know more of people than they knew of themselves, it was saddening.

Narcissus came in with bread from the baker's and a basket of herrings and cabbage. Once he had set down his burden, Balthasar explained what he wanted. Together, they began to work out how it might be achieved. It took the rest of the morning to sort out the attic to his satisfaction, but when they had finished, it was all but unrecognisable. The books had been completely rearranged, and those which were of no use to him stored in a chest: he might even sell them. Once he was alone, he got his father's box out from under the newly rehung bed, and took it over to the table by the window. Sitting in his velvet-seated chair, he unlocked it, and raised the lid. It seemed to be half-full of small, rather dirty-looking packets, folded in eight, frayed and dirty at the seams from being long carried about.

It was with an odd reluctance that he unfolded the first of his mother's letters. It felt somehow as if he were uncovering her, exposing something which should remain hidden. The familiar, bold script gave him a pang which was in some shameful way sexual, but when he began to read, a flat sense of disappointment crept over him.

My dear Pelagius,

I am glad to hear so well of your ventures. There is no good news to be had here: my children have formed the habit of treating me as a fool. Timon continues to frown, and to tear the house down about my ears. I can easily believe he would prefer to have me at Heidelberg, but I cannot resolve upon it, his humour and mine being so diverse. When he was here I could not persuade him to anything, and now much less so – La Grecque takes his part in all things. I hope for your sake the bantling grows more dutiful than these froward children. I will be infinitely obliged if you can return to The Hague by May. Mr Mason will be in England, and I will have need of you. Your most constant affectionate friend to command in love –

Candace

The names did not puzzle him. He knew very well whom they referred to, but it was strange to read over old quarrels, and stranger still to know she had thought of him. In 1652, when this letter was written, he had been just beginning at the town Latin school, a little boy with a satchel on his back, paying the price of his obvious strangeness in daily persecution, unaware even that he had a living mother. Slowly, he laid the letter down beside the open box, and took out another. It did not take him very long to read them all. He had not uncovered his mother's nakedness, far from it. He could sense a communication between his parents, but it did not lie in the simple words before him, but rather in the spaces between, where he could not see it.

There were no more letters in the box, but it was not yet empty. There were a couple of books in it, and some oddments. His questing fingers met a little washleather package, and he unrolled it, to find a most peculiar object. A carved crystal, set in gold, and surmounted by a golden bird. A strange thing for his father to have owned, and he could not think what it was, though it was obviously rare and curious: for a moment, he wondered if it might be African, it seemed so unaccountable. Dismissing it as an insoluble problem, he rolled it up again, and laid it on top of the letters. He opened the first of the books, and found some pages of notes on Indian plants: he was briefly puzzled, until he realised that there was also writing at the other end. Turning it round, he found that two-thirds of the pages were filled with a Latin text in his father's hand, called 'The African Sibyl'. The old man must have had a reason for writing it out, but it meant nothing to him. He set it aside, and looked at the other volume. This was also in Latin, and turned out to be a private journal written by his father. It seemed, from its opening, that it must have dated from some time in the last years of his life.

Fascinated, he began to read. It was obviously an entirely private document which Pelagius had written in order to clarify his mind. It told him far more of his father's spiritual life than of the events which had shaped him: rather than expanding on the thing Balthasar most wanted to know, which was how on earth his parents had come to love one another and why he had been born, he had written a dissertation on earthly and heavenly love, in which he castigated himself for being a slave to his natural affections. The book also revealed, more fully than ever before, his uncomfortable belief that his son had somehow been born to set the world to rights.

Balthasar sat on, reading, while the sun went down the sky. The book brought his father so close to hand it was as if the old man were standing in the room with him. He did not even rouse himself when the bell of the nearby Oostkerk sounded for evening prayers, but stayed where he was, stirring only to light a candle, until he came to the final words: 'and thus I humbly resign myself to the dispositions of almighty God'. He got stiffly to his feet, cramped with long sitting, and noticed that the box was still not quite empty. At the very bottom, there was a sheet of paper folded in half, which turned out to be the certificate of his parents' marriage, another slip, which recorded his own baptism, and a small purse of Genoa velvet which looked as if it might contain jewels, though when he lifted it hopefully, it was far too light. When he opened the strings, it turned out to hold nothing but a handful of ancient hazelnuts, darkened by time and handling, the shrivelled kernels rattling loosely in the shells.

He looked at the sheet of paper before him which recorded his mother's marriage to his father, and a kind of terror overcame him. He crossed the room, and opened his doctor's bag to find a scalpel. His father's diary, which he had called *Notatitunculae*, was bound in ordinary vellum. Folding the papers in half again to make them smaller, he slit the binding carefully along the top of the front board, and slid the pages inside. Once he had made some glue and sealed up the slit, no one would be any the

15

wiser. The smell of food was coming up the stairs, and he could hear the clattering of delftware. Time for supper; the glue could wait. He piled everything back into the box, locked it, and went downstairs.

It took him a long time to get to sleep that night. The strangeness of his quarters oppressed him and made him restless. Opening his eyes in the grey half-light before dawn, he saw someone sitting in the chair by the window, on the far side of the room. Heart thumping, he slid cautiously out of bed, and approached soft-footed. The chair-legs scraped on the floor as the intruder turned to look at him. It was Pelagius, his dark face set in bitter lines of judgement, his eyes blazing with terrible, familiar anger.

'You're not here,' Balthasar shouted. 'Go away. I'm dreaming you.'

'Miserable child,' growled his father, the deep, well-remembered voice harsh with rejection. 'I am not your dream. You are mine.'

Balthasar lunged forwards, with what motive he did not know; he felt a sickening jolt, and found that he was sitting up in bed. It was indeed dawn, and the room of course was empty. Sweat was running down his chest, and his nightshirt was clammy and unpleasant against his skin.

The next morning, heavy-eyed and unrested, he walked into the town with Narcissus, who had errands to run, intending to visit Cornelis Jonson. Before they went their separate ways, they turned together into the Groote Kerk. On a modest slab by the west door was the memorial Balthasar had commissioned for his father. It was simple enough, the name and the date of death with a flourished cartouche around the letters; plain as it was, he remembered grimly, it had cost him a little over eighty guilders.

Narcissus startled him out of his thoughts. 'It was hard for him to be buried here,' he said softly.

'How do you know?' Balthasar demanded.

'He told me when he was very weak. Your father's people believe it is a hard fate to die in another country. And of course, those of the royal house of Oyo who are not buried in the Bara, which is the royal graveyard, are not remembered in the king-list, so their names are not kept alive. It disturbed his peace, at the last.'

'But he must have spent almost his whole life out of Africa,' objected Balthasar. 'I am surprised he still remembered such things. And they should not matter to a man who has found God.'

Narcissus smiled rather sadly. 'You are young, little master. When you are older, you will realise that the life you are brought up in will never truly leave you, no matter where you chance to go. And your father should have died a king. That is no small matter.'

'Do you think he would have gone back to Africa, if he had not been caring for me?'

Narcissus shook his head. 'No. Make yourself easy, my dear child. He could not have gone back, there was no place there for him. But it grieved him, all the same.'

Once they had parted, Balthasar went in search of Cornelis Jonson van Ceulen. He found the old painter at work, sitting at an easel and wearing a hempen smock over his shirt and breeches. A lustrous black brocade dress was seated on the model's dais, cunningly propped with an armature of wire and pillows, and an elegant, wire-stiffened lace ruff was pinned to the high chair-back so that it rose fanlike behind the empty neck of the dress.

Jonson was setting a highlight along the arm, with slithering, expert scribbles of a small brush, but he turned, hearing footsteps, to see Balthasar make his bow. He bowed in return, still seated, brush and palette in hand.

'Ah. Mynheer van Overmeer. I am very glad to see you.'

'A burgomeester's wife?' enquired Balthasar, smiling in acknowledgement, and indicating the work in progress.

'A wedding portrait. One of the Schot daughters is marrying a merchant of Vlissingen. All most appropriate. The bridegroom has commissioned a pair of portraits in their wedding clothes. Juffrouw Schot is exigeant, and fashionable. I trust her father has judged the depths of the young man's pockets aright, or there will be storms to come.' As he spoke, he was cleaning off his palette with a knife. The parsimonious, carefully arranged blobs of pigment smeared and blurred as the blade scraped across them: he finished the job with a turpentine-soaked rag and set the palette fastidiously to one side. 'I was most sorry to hear of the Queen's death, mynheer. I am sad to say that I do not have a message for you. I am sure you were not forgotten, but she died very suddenly, after only two days' illness.'

Balthasar was unsure how to reply. He had in truth never known how much the old painter knew. As he hesitated, he felt his face grow warm: Jonson was staring at him; his gaze dispassionate, measuring. His eyes were still very blue. 'There is no one to overhear us, young sir,' he said softly. 'I painted the late Queen of Bohemia, a good portrait, though I say so myself. She chose to interest herself in a young man, the son of a confidential servant, and when I came to meet the young man in question, I found that although he was a blackamoor, her lovely eyes were set in his young face. I deduce nothing, but I will not hide my own eyes from what I can plainly see. Have no fear. I spent twenty years in the English court, and a good many secrets have come my way in the course of my life. I do not betray confidences.'

Balthasar, naked before his kind, searching gaze, could only bow once more. He felt the blood mounting to his head, and knew his cheeks must be flaming. He felt literally tongue-tied, and enraged by his own ineptness.

'I had a great respect for your father,' remarked the old painter. 'He saved my life on more than one occasion, I believe. Be comforted. You will be alone with your knowledge soon enough, young sir. Few enough can have known anything of this business, and all of them are now old, if indeed they are still in life.'

'Did he tell you how it came about?' blurted Balthasar.

'Of course not. He told me nothing. As I said, I have eyes, and I know how to use them. He was right to be secret – I will own, I would have thought very ill of the matter if anyone had told me of it. But your father was not a toy for any woman's lickerish fancy. I conversed with him on many occasions, and he was a man of royal blood and royal nature. Whatever may have possessed them, I will swear that they were in their sober senses, and thought they acted for the best. But your father did say something to me once, which I did not understand, because I had not then seen you. He told me that you were the child of a dream.'

Again, Balthasar was at a loss for an answer. Cornelis Jonson waited politely for a few moments, then picked up his palette. 'I must bid you good morning, young sir. Morning light is not to be wasted at this time of year. I have some more information about the Queen's last weeks in letters from my friends in London, and I will be pleased to copy them for you. You are welcome to call again, but come when the sun is going down the sky.'

It was nearly a fortnight before he took up the invitation. He told himself he wished to allow Jonson time to make the promised copies, but in fact, he needed to get over feeling an ill-mannered fool for not realising a morning call would be unwelcome. When he finally brought himself to return, he was surprised, as the servant opened the door for him, to hear voices. He entered and made his bow, wondering what he might find. He was still more surprised, straightening up, to find a lady, rising in a rustle of skirts to make her curtsey. He approached, full of curiosity. He had never seen Cornelis bargaining with a client – the obvious explanation for her presence, since the painter had no relatives in the town – and he was most anxious to do so. The dignified negotiation of payment was one of the essential skills of the professional man, and he felt sure that Cornelis would have much to teach him.

'Mynheer van Overmeer, may I present Mevrouw Behn? Mevrouw, this is Mynheer Balthasar van Overmeer, a citizen of this town, and lately, a doctor.'

'Honoured, mevrouw,' he said politely. Once they were seated again, he looked at her with interest. She was a young woman of about his own age, attractive, well-built, with plump cheeks, and moist, heavy-lidded, protuberant eyes. He felt her glance darting all over his body in little stabs, and unconsciously straightened his back.

'A portrait, perhaps, mevrouw?' he asked politely.

'Mevrouw Behn is not a client,' explained Cornelis. 'She has come most kindly to bring me news out of England.' A little disappointed, he considered the woman more carefully. Her name and her clothes were Dutch, but once he looked again, he saw that there was much that was strange about her. The dress was not silk, as he had first thought, but a much cheaper camlet, a silk-and-wool mixture with the silk used for the weft so that it would show to best advantage. The toe of her shoe, peeping beneath the hem, was frayed. The linen collar was a little past its best, and not expensive, and she wore no lace – all in all, he realised, he had been misled by an un-Dutch showiness in her dress and mode of presenting herself. She was a good deal less prosperous than she sought to appear.

'Are you English, mevrouw?' he enquired.

'Yes, mynheer. Do you speak English?' she said eagerly. Her Dutch was fluent, but her accent was atrocious.

'I do, mevrouw. My father wished me to learn the language.'

'Oh, and why was that?' she asked, switching with obvious relief into English, and favouring him with a charming smile.

He hesitated. 'My mother's connections were with that country,' he said cautiously, 'and a teacher was to be had, an old Royalist exile in need of employment. If I may ask a question in return, what brings you to Middelburg?'

'I am married into Holland, Mynheer van Overmeer, and my husband's family is here. I have been here only a little while, and my husband is away. It is weakness, perhaps, but I found that I longed for the sound of an English voice. When I heard Mynheer Cornelis was an old courtier, I came at once to pay my respects.'

'Have you then connections with the court?'

'I am no courtier, sir, but I have some acquaintance with Whitehall and St James's. My father was a gentleman of Kent, and loyal in the late times, so he suffered for it like your late tutor, and we were bred in country simplicity. But once the King was returned, he resolved to mend his fortunes by taking office abroad, and was appointed Lieutenant-General of our possessions in the West Indies. Alas, he died at sea on our voyage there, so when opportunity allowed, I returned to England with my mother and brother.'

Her voice was pleasant to listen to; she rattled on, glib and charmingly confiding. 'But how did that bring you to court, mevrouw?' he asked.

'I was coming to that. When I was in Surinam, I met with some Indians, not the usual sort who lived around the settlement, but taller, and grim of aspect. They told me of a place in the mountains called Toomac-Hoomack, deep within the continent, where gold-dust streams in little channels, fetched down by the rains. I wished to acquaint his majesty privately with this tale, so I went to St James's, and sought the favour of an audience. He is a tall young man, very black and harsh-favoured, but most winning and gracious in his speech. My husband has an office in London, and when we lived there, we often walked in Pall Mall, or went to see his majesty dine.'

'Did you ever see the Queen of Bohemia?' he could not resist asking.

The lady's hands flew up, as if she had been asked to express the inexpressible. 'The Queen of Bohemia! Yes, indeed. She lived long in Holland, did she not, and came over when the King was crowned? I saw her at the playhouse. She was the very pattern of antique beauty, I remember, and most sweet and graceful in her mien. His majesty was very gallant to her, it was clear she had won his heart. Have you some knowledge of this lady?'

'I did not know her,' he explained stiffly, 'but my father did, I believe.'

Mevrouw Behn continued to make conversation for ten minutes or so, then smilingly made her curtsey, and took her leave.

Once the door was safely shut behind her, Jonson turned to Balthasar. 'Well, Mynheer Balthasar, and what do you think of Mevrouw Behn?'

'She seems to me a most witty and engaging lady, Mynheer Cornelis.'

'Engaging she is, and smooth, but be wary, my young friend. She is not a woman to be trusted. Observe. She speaks of her father, and of the court, as if she was quite the gentlewoman, but if she is so, then why is she the wife of a greasy Dutchman? I do not trust her tales of the Indies. I'll wager she went to find some rich planter, but she failed of her venture, and returned with nothing better than a Dutch cheeseworm. Mynheer Behn is not a man in a great way of business, I can assure you, and his brother is a printer, a man who works with his hands. We do not see such women in Middelburg, but my friends tell me there are town-misses in London now who give themselves out for gentlemen's daughters when they have nothing but their wits to give 'em the title, and I suspect she is one of them. I have been a servant to the Stuarts all my life, but I am glad I am not in England to see with my own eyes what the new King is making of his realm, if women like Mevrouw Behn are a sign of the times.

'Another thing. My London friends told me at the time that the

Queen of Bohemia had honoured the playhouse with her presence. She went to D'Avenant's opera with the King, and I rejoiced in the news, because it told me her health was improved. I was copying the passage out only the other day – I will give you a budget of papers to take with you, when you leave. But from what Mevrouw Behn was saying earlier, the visit took place when our fair guest was in the Indies. Your mother's life in England was sadly brief, and she was seldom very well, so I think she went only once to the playhouse. I deduce that one of the lady's stories may be true, or the other, or neither, but not both.'

II

Soldiers fight and hectors rant on
    Whilst poor wenches go to rack.
Who would be a wicked wanton
    Only for suppers, songs and sack?
To endure the alteration
    Of these times that are so dead –
Thus to lead a long vacation
    Without money, beer or bread.

Farewell Bloomsbury and Sodom,
    Lukeners-late and Turnbull-street.
Woe was me when first I trod 'em
    With my wild unwary feet!
I was bred a gentlewoman
    But our family did fall
When the gentry's coin grew common
    And the soldiers shared it all.
Thomas Jordan, 'Moll Medlar's Song', 1664

Mevrouw Behn picked her way over the cobbles, turning the encounter over in her mind. The painter was clearly a man of address and a gentleman with good connections in England, and she resolved to improve the acquaintance. She sensed his caution and reserve towards her, but she felt she could melt his resistance, given time. The blackamoor doctor was a puzzle. Everything in his dress and his mien suggested nothing more than a young Dutch burgher and a callow young cub at that. But Mr Jonson treated him as a person of some importance; and in any case, how came a man of his colour a doctor in Middelburg? He piqued her curiosity, and she tucked him away in the back of her mind.

Her steps unconsciously slowed as she turned the corner to Sint Janstraat and approached 't Schippershuis, her home. She surveyed it, as she came nearer, with settled detestation. From some distance away, she could hear the thumping of the press which accompanied so much of her waking life. It had come as a most disagreeable surprise to her to find herself living above a printworks in this fashion. It was not the life which her husband had led her to expect: he had given a very different impression of his circumstances before their marriage. She had met him as captain and owner of a vessel, *The Good Intent*; and as they voyaged home from the Indies, he had told her that in addition to being a shipowner, he was also a merchant in a good way of business, with offices in London. Although she knew he was from a German family settled in Holland, she had assumed as a matter of course that they would live in London. When subsequently this expectation had been disappointed and he had taken her to the Netherlands, she had thought at the very least that she would be mistress of the house to which he brought her; she had imagined, vaguely, something not unlike the tall house on the Dam which she had just left.

Instead, she had found herself once more living in two rooms: there was indeed a substantial house, it transpired, but it was shared with Johan's brother Petrus, his wife and their brats, and with Petrus's infernal printworks. Aphra slipped down the alley, hoping to enter unobtrusively by the kitchen courtyard, and return to her own room without anyone realising she had been out. She was irritated to observe when she came through the courtyard gate that the youngest of her three nieces was standing in the kitchen doorway, industriously picking her nose. The child stared at her, round-eyed, then turned and scuttled inside; Aphra could hear her shrill voice shouting, 'Papi! Papi! She's come home.'

Her heart jolted: had Johan arrived unexpectedly? Would he object to her excursion? She had found it difficult to reconcile herself to going out without a servant: no genteel Englishwoman would consider doing so, though bourgeois Dutchwomen, the class she most reluctantly found herself in, did so as a matter of course. But the house kept only one overworked maid, so there was no one with time to accompany her and she had begun to feel that if she did not escape for a little, she would run frantic and beat her head against the wall.

She stepped into the kitchen, greasily odorous with recent frying, took off her cloak, and began folding and smoothing it with scrupulous care, keeping herself busy until she found out what was towards. A moment later, she heard the sound of heavy, wooden-soled shoes, and Petrus appeared. He was the elder of the two brothers, a plain, heavy-set fellow, powerful-looking like his brother Johan, but graceless, with deep lines from nose to mouth.

'Where have you been, sister?' he demanded.

Aphra turned away, picking at a spot of mud on her cloak. 'Walking for my health, mynheer,' she said airily, hatefully.

'You would not need to walk, sister, if you worked as you should.'

'I was not brought up to drudge in kitchens, brother Petrus,' she retorted. She could feel the chagrin swelling her throat, choking her voice.

'You have two hands and five wits, sister Aphra. You could learn. But I do not want to speak of this now. It is for Johan to talk to you. Come. I have something to ask you, perhaps more to your mind.'

Intrigued, despite herself, Aphra followed him out of the kitchen and along the stone-flagged passage which led to his office.

'I have a difficulty, sister,' said Petrus heavily, once she was seated. 'I have a commission for work from England, and the manuscript has been sent. But something is missing. I can read it well enough, and it ends in the middle of a sentence. I do not want to offend this customer, so I have told off what there is, and three pages more of this size would make sixty-four pages octavo. Your tongue is ready enough, sister Aphra. Will you write an ending for me?'

'But I have never thought of doing such a thing,' she protested. 'It is one thing to write for my friends, but gentlewomen do not write for the press.'

Petrus shrugged. 'It may be so. But your name will not appear. You are the only English speaker in the family except Johan, and he is in London. My fee is thirty guilders, after paying for the paper, and the copies are wanted for Tuesday morning. I will give you four guilders if you will do this.'

Aphra opened her mouth to protest further, and shut it again. Money of her own ... it was too attractive a proposition to resist. 'I will take your manuscript, brother Petrus, and see what I can do.'

Safely upstairs in her own quarters, she lit two candles, and laid the manuscript of *Free Parliament Quaeries* down on Johan's desk. Despite the reluctance she had seen fit to show to Petrus, she was delighted by the prospect of writing. Over the months since her marriage, her sense that she had made a disastrous, irrevocable error committing her to a life she could not endure had gradually risen to such a pitch that she was beginning to wonder if she might turn frantic. Writing at least promised temporary escape into a world of her own devising.

Bitterly, her mind ran over the disastrous sequence of events which had brought her to 't Schippershuis. Johan, far handsomer than his brother, and with much more of the air of a gentleman, had wooed her assiduously during the voyage back from Surinam. Impressed by what he said, and hinted, of his circumstances, she had in turn given him the impression that she had both wealth and prospects; they had married in Barbados. After their return to England, he had brought her to a poky suite of rented rooms up three pair of stairs in Covent Garden, where her dreams had faded and died.

It had taken only a few short weeks for Johan to satisfy himself that her wealthy connections were chimeric, whereupon their relationship had abruptly changed. She had had real hopes of Sir Thomas Colepeper – the nearest thing she had to a patron, since her mother had been his childhood nurse – but he had sent a kindly letter wishing her well in her married life, and a promissory note for five pounds. A fortnight after the débâcle of Colepeper's letter, one of Johan's old business partners had called, and following a long evening of confidential discussion, Johan had paid off their landlady, left his London affairs in the charge of his confidential man, Mr Piers, and taken her across to Holland, where he had left her. She had not seen him since. He had, she knew, gone on a slaving voyage to Africa; once he had concluded his business there, he would have to cross the Atlantic to the Indies, then cross it again to get home. Perhaps she would never see him again. She remembered only too well what a mid-Atlantic storm could be like, and *The Good Intent* was a little ship which had seen hard service.

She sighed, and reached for a scarf. The room was getting cold. Apart from the practical problem which his death would represent for her, did she care in her heart, she wondered, if she ever did see him again? Something about his light eyes, his swagger, had turned her bowels to water when she was still a maiden. Watching him from under her eyelashes, as *The Good Intent* slogged through the Atlantic rollers day after day, it had been easier to imagine him rich than poor; he had so much the air of a man who would take what he wanted. In fact, he seemed almost the man that, as a child, she had once dreamed of becoming, before she was made to understand that a girl must grow up to be a woman.

Lying awake at night in her fetid cabin, she had imagined him as a lover until she had seduced herself with her own fantasies. The reality had disappointed her, once her curiosity was satisfied. He was powerful and lusty, and she enjoyed his performance after a fashion. But he was impatient; he liked to act at once upon his desires, while she found herself dreaming of quite other things; long glances, playful words gradually becoming more tender, light touches. A man who would come softly up behind her, and lift her hair to kiss her behind the ear. She could almost feel the light, moist lips, and the thought made her shiver and cross her legs. Johan, when he was moved to passion, simply opened her bodice, lifted her skirts and fell to; it was purest luck if she was able to adapt her mood to his. Moreover, marriage had put her under his hand, and what enjoyment could there be when a husband had the power to enforce his whim? How, without her own money, could a woman live in independence? Almost, she thought of running away, but no one could believe the life of a whore better than that of a wife; one would simply be at the beck of many men rather than one, with old age and unprotected poverty looming in the future. She thought momentarily of her brother, but though they were good friends, he was not in a position to keep her.

Tucking the scarf around her shoulders, she opened the bundle of papers, and began to read. After a while, she began to feel a hot blush rising up her neck, and flung the manuscript down. She was outraged that Petrus would think his brother's wife capable of writing such stuff; in his boorish coarseness, perhaps he thought it was all the same to her. She had a good mind to take the pages and throw them in his face; yet somehow she found herself picking them up again. As she read on avidly, her resolution began to weaken. No one need ever know. The Behns had formed a settled opinion of her uselessness and derided her pretensions to gentility. Her sister-in-law Maria, a fat and sour-faced vrouw with hands permanently reddened by lye, despised her for her idleness:

while her ill opinions would doubtless be quadrupled by the *Free Parliament Quaeries* were she to read them, she would never do so, because she understood not a word of English.

Usefulness might win her a measure of respect from the two brothers; it might even win her something like freedom. And bating his obscenity, she was at bottom broadly in sympathy with the author of the work in front of her, who passed for 'Tom Telltruth'. The *Quaeries* were aimed at the Whigs, and she shared Tom's dislike of them. Lord Ashley, the Chancellor of the Exchequer, came in for particularly harsh treatment, and in her view it was deserved. It was a matter of common gossip that the King distrusted him; the man had been a Parliamentarian throughout the Civil War, and had turned his coat at the most opportune moment. His addiction to whores was also widely known; she had heard stories enough, when Johan and Mr Piers and their cronies had been drinking by the fire in their cramped quarters in London, talking and laughing as if she did not exist.

She had got to the end of the manuscript. 'It was reported here, that Lord A——y was seen this sennight most strangely diverting himself at Jack-a-Newberry's Six Windmills in Upper Moorfields –' and there it stopped. Doing what? she asked herself. The Six Windmills she had heard of as an established house of ill-fame, presided over by a woman called Pris Fotheringham. Gradually, something half-overheard began to come back to her; Piers reporting Mrs Fotheringham's trick of exposing herself without shame, head downwards, and allowing the cullies to fill her *chose* with half-crowns. Piers had laughed as he told the story, the scornful, whinnying laughter which she most disliked, and he had made Johan laugh, but the notion made her sick. She suspected the author was hinting at this report, but she certainly could not write such a thing about another woman; it was too distasteful. Still, there was another story she had overheard, about Thomas Scot, but no matter; Johan, she dimly recalled, had spoken of an occasion when he had taken both his mistress and her maid to bed together. She could make something of that, perhaps, with Mrs Fotheringham, and another whore who need not have a name, though she would be safe enough if she called her Moll or Sukey or Betty. Her earlier meeting with van Overmeer came back to her. Perhaps the second woman might be black, for piquancy, then she could be called Moorea, or Mistress Sable. Or should she be blind? There might be something to be made of a blind whore, and the mistakes she could tumble into. She sat on for a while, revolving the possibilities in her mind, then reached for a pen.

In the event, Johan did not return until late November. Aphra returned from a morning stroll along the wharf of the West India Company where she had vaguely thought she might hear a little news of *The Good Intent*, and when she pushed open the door to her own quarters she found him standing in front of the fire reading the *London Post*. For a moment it seemed almost as if she had conjured him out of her own thoughts.

'Well, wife. You have been busy, I see.' Looking around, she saw the room through his eyes. What had once been a dressing-table was piled high with paper, the mirror relegated to the windowsill. Recent editions of London diurnals lay about, and books of various kinds: copies of the *Decameron* and the *Cent Nouvelle Novelles*, draft papers and notes. She felt herself beginning to blush. More than once in their London life Johan had struck her, to make quite certain she knew her position. He was cruelly strong, and it was impossible to know, as the blood mounted to her cheeks, giving her away, whether or not he was angry.

She threw her cloak onto the chair, and raised her eyebrows, pulling off her gloves. New and elegant gloves, blue dogskin, bought with her own money. She had been a fool, she thought bitterly, not to hoard every stuiver she had earned. 'I have spent much of my time in London of late,' she said as lightly as she could. 'Your brother has profited from it, I believe.'

'So he tells me. You have a certain gift for this trash.'

Her labouring heart began to slow towards a normal pace, though she continued to be tense and wary. When he had knocked her down in the spring, the blow had come without warning, his expression had remained affable till the moment he struck. 'It was none of my seeking, sir. I hope he told you that.'

Johan shrugged. 'It's all one. At least we've found a use for you, for all your missish ways. Petrus tells me you're earning your keep.'

'So you are not offended?' She hoped that she had kept any kind of pleading note out of her voice, but she could not be certain.

He tossed the diurnal aside and walked towards her. 'Write what you like. Think what you like. I care only for what you do.'

'And you know I have not betrayed you, I trust,' she retorted.

He smiled at her, almost gently. She had forgotten how expression-less his pale eyes could be. 'Oh, yes. This is a small town, and walls have ears. And if you did, Aphra, I would kill you.'

She thought he would strike her then, to make his point, and her eyes squeezed shut despite herself. But he did not; instead, she felt his hands at her neck, undoing her collar. 'Come, my wife. If you spend your days writing filth, you must have something to write about.' She did not consider resistance for a moment, it was far too dangerous, but as he pushed her ahead of him towards the bed, her mind was filled with shame and anger.

Johan stayed in Middelburg all winter. He spent much of his time drinking in taverns, or down on the Maisbaai, gossiping with West India Company officers. She gathered he had not been wholly displeased with the profit from his voyage, though she did not dare ask him what he had actually made. To her great relief, he made no attempt to stop her writing. Quite the opposite. He began speaking to her in Dutch rather than English, and insisted that she improve her command of the language: when she became more fluent, he brought her a sheaf of English books, and told her that when she was ready, she was to translate them. All talk of payment had ceased; or rather, as she was well aware, Johan had arranged with Petrus that he was to pocket a percentage of any profit his brother made from her work. She regretted it extremely, but she knew that as a married woman, she could hardly have expected anything else. And it gave her, at the very least, a cogent reason for avoiding housewifery.

Balthasar lingered unhappily in his room, still in his dressing-gown. He was conscious that time was passing all too swiftly, but he was paralysed by indecision. Certainly, he must wear his new suit, which, although it was the plain and sober black a doctor should affect – even the buttons were jet, not gold – was good silk, but he was in two minds about his beautiful new lace collar. It was certainly very fine, edged with two inches of point de Venise, and when he had been offered it, he had been unable to resist it. If he wore it, it would show him prosperous and substantial – or would the Regents think him profligate? He was in little doubt that they would offer him the position, which was, God knew, not one of great value or importance, beyond the fact that it would be his first civic appointment, and hence a sign of his rise in status. But two of the Regents were the guardians appointed for him by his father; he had been managing his own affairs for three years since he came of age, and he knew that they would be scrutinising him for any signs that he was insufficiently prudent. Reluctantly, he reached for the plain starched linen which he had known all along he would choose in the end. A few minutes later, he was dressed, just in time to get to morning prayers, though on an empty stomach.

The sun was shining brightly, but so early in the year it was a cold walk on the frozen cobbles up past the French church and the Schuttershof to the almshouses, especially for a fasting man;

he was glad of his cloak. The clock in the tall tower of the Nieuwe Kerk was striking nine as he knocked on the porter's door and told the man his business. The porter led him across the handsome quadrangle, lined on all sides with the little cell-like homes of the old men and women who had found safe haven there, and took him to the Regents' Chamber. He knocked, and opened the door, bowing with hat in hand. When he straightened up, he was relieved to feel he had made the right choice. Though the group before him included some of the most prosperous citizens of Middleburg, and their linen was of superlative quality, they all wore the plainest of flat collars, with the exception of old Aernout Schot, who was past eighty, and had never seen fit to discontinue the starched ruffs he had worn in his youth.

'Balthasar van Overmeer, Doctor and Surgeon of the University of Leiden, at your service,' he said.

'Doctor,' replied Joachim Everaerts, president of the committee, inclining himself a little in his seat in acknowledgement. 'You are fully qualified, and a man of good reputation in the town for your medical skills, your religion, and your habits of life. We are minded to appoint you doctor to the old people's almshouse. Your duties will be to attend the residents once a week, and alleviate their suffering, on the charge of the town. When God sees fit to take one to Himself, you will wait and watch with the dying, as you would for a private patient, and do all you can for him or her as part of your ordinary duties. However, if there is infectious disease or any such out-of-the-way call on your skills, you may submit an additional bill to the Regents, and we will consider the justice of your case. Do you agree to these conditions?'

'I do, and I am honoured to be chosen,' he replied very correctly, bowing again. He could feel Everaerts's eyes resting on him approvingly: he had been one of his guardians, in which capacity he had been honest, scrupulous and effective, and it was, Balthasar reflected, probably due to a lingering sense of responsibility in him that he had been asked to take this post.

'Well, that is settled then,' said Everaerts. The secretary of the committee reached for a pen and recorded the decision which had been reached in the big, leather-bound ledger. He beckoned Balthasar forward, turning the ledger so that it would be accessible to him. Balthasar stepped up, and after a moment's embarrassment wondering how to dispose of his hat, which he resolved by leaning it against his leg, he signed his name neatly in the designated space. Everaerts countersigned, the secretary witnessed the signatures, and the interview was over.

Balthasar bowed again and beat a retreat as rapidly as he could, conscious that his stomach was beginning to rumble. Ravenous, he made his escape from the almshouses and hurried to the Groote Markt where he would be able to get breakfast in a tavern. Pictures began to form in his mind as he made the best possible speed over the slippery cobbles; a nip of genever to keep out the cold, then beer, Deventer-cake if they had it, or honey-cake, something sweet any-way, cheese . . . he caught a welcoming whiff of cooking-fat on his left, and slipped gratefully into the first open tavern that he saw.

It was rather dark in the interior, since the shutters were mostly closed against the cold, and empty, so he was able to get a place by the fire. The tavern-wench came up, a slatternly figure with her kerchief coming untucked, exposing much of her bosom, and he gave her his order, averting his eyes as she stood before him. She slip-slopped away, and after a minute or two set a fine, well-aged cheese on the table before him, and a basket with some slices of Deventer-cake, dense, brownish stuff, strongly flavoured with honey, cinnamon, nutmeg and cloves. He stretched out his cold feet towards the blaze and swigged his genever, enjoying the warmth spreading through his body. He began to feel at peace with the world. The almshouse job was a fine step up for him, and things could hardly have gone better.

'Master Balthasar?'

He looked up, hearing his name, and for a long moment, looked without recognition at the man who addressed him: another tavern servant, he must be, since he was not dressed for outdoors. He was small and shabby, with wispy hair, colourless blond shading to grey. Something in the posture, slightly stooped forward so the arms seemed to hang in front of the body, the swimming, red-rimmed eyes, was familiar, but who was it? Then memory came to him with a rush; it was his old tutor's man. Sir Thomas Urquhart had been, like Jonson, one of the Royalist refugees who had ended up in Middelburg. He and Balthasar's father had had interests in common, and like many another refugee, he had been penniless; Pelagius, accordingly, had employed him to teach Balthasar English. By the greasy, shabby look of his servant – the name suddenly came back to him, he was Mr Monroe – he had not prospered since.

'Mr Monroe. How is your master? I have not seen him since I returned from Leiden.'

'He is dead, sir. I could find no other master, so I am working here.'

'Oh, I am most sorry to hear it. What ailed him?'

'He died of laughter, sir. The only man I ever knew to do such a thing. I heard at the Dam that the King was restored in London, and I ran home to tell him. He began to laugh at the news, and took a choking fit, and so he died, still with the smile on his face.'

'Curious indeed,' said Balthasar. 'Few men die happy.' As he said it, he was assailed by doubt. Had it, he wondered, been the laughter of simple rejoicing, or had it been a laugh of another kind? From what he remembered of Urquhart, there was no more loyal supporter of the Stuarts, but his temper was not a simple one. He suspected, rather, the laughter of a philosopher, which is close to despair; that at the end, Urquhart had choked to death over the fact that a cause which had consumed the lives and wealth of a generation could thus so simply be brought to an end.

'Master Balthasar,' continued Monroe in a rush, 'I have some books of my late master's. I can find no vent for them here in Middelburg, and I am in want, as you can see for yourself. There is Sir Thomas's book of the Battle of Worcester, and his book on the Universal Language.'

Balthasar considered the proposition. He was not sure how he felt about Urquhart, in retrospect, but the man had without doubt been interesting on almost any subject except genealogy, to which he was unfortunately addicted, and to read a little in English from time to time would help keep the language in repair. Since the restoration of the English King, there were few English speakers in Middelburg, and he seldom had occasion to use it. He had once read a tract of Urquhart's on the descent of his family from Adam, which the old Scot had given to Balthasar's father. He was aware, therefore, that Urquhart's style was prolix and ornate – however, since he preferred words derived from Latin and Greek to commoner forms, he was, paradoxically, rather easier to understand than many simpler English writers since Balthasar could easily guess at unknown words based on classical roots. 'I will give you sixteen guilders for them,' he said after a little thought. 'Bring them this evening to De Derde Coninck, in the Spanjardstraat.'

'God bless you, sir. I will bring them as soon as I can.' Monroe hesitated, then spoke again. 'Do you need a man, Master Balthasar?'

'I am sorry, Mr Monroe, my household is complete. But did you not say you have a place here?'

'It is no place for a respectable man, sir. This is a house of accommodation.'

Balthasar's heart gave a little leap, and he looked about him. There was nothing in the frowsty room to distinguish it from the taproom of an ordinary tavern, except its emptiness. The whores, poor wretches, would presumably be asleep at that hour of the morning, having worked all evening and most of the night. He knew nothing of Middelburg brothels: if they resembled those of Leiden, which he had visited a few times in his student days, they would be frequented chiefly by the riff-raff of the town and by sailors. A young professional man with his way to make in a small town such as Middelburg simply could not afford to acquire the reputation of a whoremaster. Monroe was still looking at him like a lost dog, but he hardened his heart. As soon as he had brought the promised books, all communication between them must cease, lest the many watchful eyes of the citizenry draw a false conclusion.

On the same January day on which Balthasar took up his new position as doctor to the almshouses, Aphra was sitting alone in her quarters in 't Schippershuis. It was like no married life she could have imagined, she thought to herself, stretching and rubbing her writing hand, which was beginning to cramp. She had nearly finished her first major translation, *The Accomplish'd Cook*, which had been far less difficult than she had feared. As she had begun to realise with relief a little way into the work, one recipe is at bottom very much like another. Once she had mastered key phrases – 'Take a —— and boil it in fair water', 'Mince them into collops', 'Dish it on a silver plate' – Robert May's book had presented almost no problems, except for some of the words for unusual foodstuffs. She knew very little about cookery, and could not make informed guesses, so she had sometimes solved the problem simply by substitution, translating 'lamprey' as 'eel', or she had left items out when she could not guess at them, and when absolutely necessary she had asked Johan. Her next task lay in the cabinet, a book called *The School of Venus*, which she feared would be far more difficult.

Curiously, she was beginning to be almost happy. She had not come to love Holland or her husband, and she was often bored and lonely, but the work she was doing had indeed gained her a kind of independence. If she chose to walk, play the flute, or visit one of her few acquaintances, she met with no objections. She could spend long hours reading undisturbed, and see the other members of the household only at mealtimes. Another thing she had come to be grateful for was that, while Johan had a formidable capacity for alcohol, and was frequently drunk, he never drank till he was spewing and incapable. Moreover, neither lust nor anger came uppermost when he was in his cups; he merely became morose and silent, sunk into his own dark thoughts, and asked no more than to be let alone.

Now that she had made herself into an asset, their relations were on the whole cordial. Sometimes, when the mood was on him, he was even good company, as he had been on the voyage home, and would tell her stories of Curaçao, Elmina and Virginia. Her principal fear was that he would get her with child. He had clearly no particular desire to do so; if he was sober enough, and thought of it, he would withdraw at the critical moment and spend on her thigh, but he was not always successful in controlling himself, or sober enough to try. She got up to put a little more coal on the fire, and as she did so, heard heavy feet on the stairs. Johan coming home.

He came into the room, face reddened with the cold, with frost sprinkling his thick sailor's coat, and went at once to the fire to warm himself. She sketched a curtsey, which went unacknowledged, and returned to her desk.

'What news, Johan?' she asked. Coming back in the middle of the day like this, he would not have been drinking. He had almost certainly been down at the Maisbaai.

He cocked an eyebrow at her as he stood chafing his cold fingers, still wearing his coat. 'Good for some, Aphra, and perhaps for us. Our West India Company has swept that pirate Holmes's garrisons from the coast of Africa, and the credit of the Royal Africa Company is ruined. There will be long faces in London, but they are reaping the rewards of their own folly. Holmes and his men took several of our forts on the Gold Coast, but the shareholders did not allow him the means to hold them, for fear of the expense. Yet they were taking four hundred thousand English pounds out of Africa in a year! You can trust a banker not to see further than the end of his nose.'

'The King had a share in the Royal Africa Company, did he not?' asked Aphra. She was downcast by the news; she remained entirely a partisan of England, and of the Stuarts in particular, though she knew better than to say so.

'Ja. The King, the Duke of York, the Queen and the Queen Mother, they tell me. So now he has less to spend on his whores and his horses. Or perhaps the ladies will get their diamonds and satin, but the navy will not get their new ships. And that is to the good, wife, because we are heading for war.'

'War!'

'Oh, yes indeed. Our interests are crossing so much, in the East and the West Indies, and now in Africa. They have not forgiven us for Amboyna, and we do not forgive them for seizing our ships. We will certainly be at war again before long.'

'But the Stadhouder is the King's own cousin,' said Aphra helplessly. 'How can he do such a thing?'

'Who cares a rush for the Stadhouder? What is he now, twelve? The House of Orange means nothing today, it is the States-General that rule. And I do not suppose that your Charles will trouble himself over the Stadhouder, when there is so much to be gained.'

'But Johan, I cannot see why you find this good news. Surely the seas will be closed, and your trade will suffer?'

Her husband snorted with derision. 'No such thing. Where there is war, there is paper. Petrus will be busy from morning to night. The English do not have a free press; so everyone with an opinion that does not suit the government will be slipping across to print their little tracts here in the Netherlands. The English navy is not so very vigilant, and in any case, we will be keeping them occupied. For my part, I see that it will be worth my while to go over as soon as possible. I have a status as a London resident, and there will be an embargo. But London will still want Dutch linen, and many a thing besides, embargo or no. I can give the traders a way round. The merchants will entrust their goods to me; I will declare that they are mine, sell them on, and take a percentage. Thus we profit without lifting a finger, and the world goes on.'

'Please take me with you, Johan.'

'Not yet. You have your uses, I agree, but I want to see how the land lies. I will send Mr Piers for you when I think the time is right.'

There were angry tears pricking at her eyes, but she knew better than to dispute with him. After his many years as a slaver, he would not tolerate any challenge to his authority. He turned away from her, shrugging at last out of his coat, and went into their bedroom to change his shoes. Aphra stayed where she was, brooding on all that he had said. Some time later, after Johan had gone out again, she wrote a brief note outlining the principal points of what he had told her and addressing it to the King. She signed it with the single word 'Astrea', slipped it into her pocket, and went out in her turn, to call on Cornelis Jonson. He exchanged regular letters with England, she knew, and she trusted she could persuade him to send it on her behalf.

Johan left a few days later, and she finished her Robert May translation. As Johan had predicted, Petrus found himself very busy with pamphlet work, but she began on *The School of Venus* anyway, so as to have it ready when business slackened off. She had made a private bargain with herself that once it was finished, she would return to the question of London. But it had turned very cold, and the prospect of crossing the Channel was not an agreeable one: anxious though she was to escape from Holland, she was prepared to admit that it would be prudent to stay till spring.

She found the work exhausting. It was dark for much of the time, and the cold, combined with peering by candlelight at her work, gave her eyestrain and a series of troublesome headaches. The book itself posed a considerable problem. It was lewd beyond belief – the subject was the instruction of the naïve Fanchon by her older confidante Susanne – and to her shame, she found it curiously affecting. Always more easily moved by her own imaginings than by actual feel, as she pictured the scenes in her mind, she began to experience a strange, constant heat in her *chose*, and to find her thighs continually wet. When she went down to eat with Petrus and his family, she found it hard to look at him, aware that he knew what she was working on. Besides the embarrassment of finding herself so vulnerable to bawdy writing, she was hard put to it to find words for all that the book described, and she dared not ask for help. She took refuge, instead, in metaphor, and the translation became increasingly flowery as a result.

One morning, she awoke very early, and found she was unable to open her eyes. The bones of her head seemed as if they would crack open, and she could not bear even the light that seeped through her bed-curtains. As she lay weeping in agony, she realised, shifting to ease her position, that her thighs were once more wet and slippery. Disjointedly, as her head throbbed with pain, the thought came to her that the warmness and wetness she had been feeling had nothing whatever to do with *The School of Venus*. Some time later, the maid Saartje came up to take her chamber-pot and rake out the fire, and found her still in bed. She clumped over with rough goodwill, pulled back the curtain, and asked her how she felt. Whispering and wincing, Aphra implored her to go and get a doctor.

Towards the end of the afternoon, she heard a knock on her door. By that time, the headache had abated a little, and she had found it possible to get up, change her smock, and comb her hair. She was unsurprised to see the dark face of her onetime acquaintance,

Balthasar van Overmeer, with Saartje bringing up the rear for the sake of propriety. After all, she reflected sardonically, he was the most recent doctor to be established in the town, and therefore almost certainly the cheapest. And she was valuable enough to the household to be worth treating, but not at any extravagant level. Johan, God be praised, had left her some money for her expenses, so she would not be reduced to begging from Petrus.

'Mevrouw Behn,' he said, surprised. 'I am sorry to see you unwell.'

'I hope you will soon see me better,' she retorted.

He moved a stool over to the bed and sat down, taking her wrist to feel her pulse. Once he had done so, examined the urine which Saartje had prudently set aside that morning, and ascertained that she was not feverish, he asked for her own account of the matter, then began to question her. 'The headache is worst when you are warm in bed?'

'Yes. It wakes me in the morning.'

'And . . . I am sorry to have to ask this, but have you had any pain or difficulty with making water?'

'Yes. For a few days at the end of last month, I felt a burning pain when I went to relieve myself, but it passed off.'

The young doctor's warm brown skin grew visibly warmer. 'And have you experienced leucorrhea?'

'What?'

'Er . . . "the whites", you might call it? Or "the white flowers"? A discharge of a womanly kind, but not at the proper time, and white?'

'Yes.' She spoke curtly, furious with herself. She could see all too well where his questions were leading, and she was chagrined and humiliated that she should have made such a mistake. If she had understood her own body aright, she might have nipped this in the bud, before it took hold.

'And have you noticed anything else in your privities, which was not as it should be? A swelling of some kind, or a sort of ulcer with hard edges?'

'Certainly not,' she replied with hauteur.

Van Overmeer sighed, looking at her apologetically. 'Mevrouw Behn, I think you may have guessed what the trouble is. Your husband has given you an infection. It is not so troublesome to the fair sex as it is to ours, and it seems that you have been spared the worst. But you need a course of mercury to remove the disease lest it bring you grief in the future.'

'What do you mean?' she asked, beginning to be frightened. Mercury was the subject of coarse jokes among Johan's friends, and she had formed a vague impression it was painful and unpleasant.

'Once a disease is in the body, mevrouw, it must be purged. For the *lues*, we have found that the best evacuation is in the saliva, and to some extent, in purging and sweating. I will bleed you now from the right arm, which should take away some of the corrupted blood and give you ease, then I will bring you a purge, and a box of *unguentum Saracenum*, which is a mercury liniment. You yourself must rub it on your arms, thighs and calves for three nights running, and towards the end of this time, salivation will set in. Keep the vessel which you use for spitting, and do not pour it away. We hope to produce four pints of saliva in twenty-four hours, so I will need to see how it progresses, and if I need to give calomel also. Once the purgation has ceased, you are to spend a few days on a dry diet of biscuit, or nuts and raisins. You will not find that you want much, I think.'

There was clearly no help for it. The prospect before her was repellent, but that the condition could not be left to get worse she knew only too well. Hovering in the back of her mind were unspeakable visions of misshapen, ulcerated faces with gaping holes where their noses had been, foul figures creeping in the dark like wounded spiders, rotten before they were dead. Setting her teeth, she pushed the sleeve of her smock up above her elbow, and held out her arm for the knife.

The treatment was quite as unpleasant as it had sounded. For the first couple of days, nothing much happened, apart from the twice-daily ordeal of an emetic. Saartje, rather to her surprise, tended her briskly but kindly, and was assiduous in making up the fire – van Overmeer had been insistent that she be kept warm, to bring out the sweat. She soon began to perspire, and since she was not permitted to change her smock, both her clothes and her bed became sour and frowsty. But after this initial period of respite, in which the headache mercifully abated to some extent, the salivation began. Her gums began to ache, ulcerate and stink, and her mouth filled with an endless welling of foul, sweetish saliva. She sat up in bed for hour after tedious hour, spitting it out as fast as she could. She was anxious not to swallow any, lest she retard the cure, but even if she had been less conscientious, she was quite unable to lie down – her only attempt to do so had produced an almost immediate fit of choking, and she feared that if she persisted she might drown in her own fluids. Exhausted, and nauseated by her own foulness, she sat wearily holding the wooden bowl she was using as a spittoon, enduring as best she might.

Van Overmeer, who called every day, was pleased with her progress. He bled her once more, and gave her a little calomel and a course of enemas, but merely by way of perfecting the cure. Five days after taking to her bed, she was able to get up, weak and shaky, and sit in a wooden chair while Saartje gave her a sponge-bath in front of the fire and changed her smock and her bed-linen. Gradually, she began to take a little more interest in her food, and to regain her strength. After another week, Van Overmeer called to find her considerably thinner than when he had first seen her, but with bright eyes and a more natural colour in her cheeks, and pronounced her entirely cured.

III

Certainly either historians have been much to blame in recommending to us a pompous name of virtue, glory and renown, acquired by our ancestors, making that appear noble and useful to mankind, which was dull and rude, or else their children have nothing in them worthy of their fathers.

S. L., *Remarques on the humours and conversations of the gallants of the town*, 1673

Balthasar pushed open the door and went into the bookseller's. He had had a depressing morning at the almshouse. The spring sun had brought the old people to the doors of their tiny dwellings, where they sat in the sun, looking in front of them, silent for the most part, waiting to die. He did what he could for them, but it was endlessly frustrating to witness their slow degeneration. He tended useless feet and hands so twisted by disease they looked like wax left near the fire, and prescribed warming liniments for the pain, knowing he could offer nothing but useless palliatives. That morning he had seen an old man so short of breath he had hardly the strength to move himself, though there was no catarrh or other obvious cause; looking into that grey-tinged, wrinkled face with its ever-open mouth gaping desperately for life-giving air, he cursed his own lack of knowledge. What would one find if one opened up the chest, he wondered. Was there a growth impeding the action of the lungs, were they somehow adhering to the rib-cage? There was no way of finding out: the almshouse patients were respectable, if relatively poor, citizens, and he would not be permitted to open

his patient when the man died, as he soon would. In any case, even
if he knew what the trouble was, he had nothing but palliatives to
offer. Later, emerging from that suffocating atmosphere of stoic
endurance into the town street, he looked up at the blue spring sky
and racing mares'-tail clouds, and decided to go and buy himself a
book. A small indulgence, something purely for entertainment.

His heart gave a little leap as he shut the door behind him.
Mevrouw Behn was standing by the window with the bright
sunlight flooding in on her, gilding her brown hair and falling
on the pages as she turned them. He should not be surprised, he
told himself. When he had attended her at the beginning of the
year, he had noticed that her rooms were full of books and paper;
what more natural place to find her? She was looking through
one of the display books with great concentration, and had not
noticed him. He observed her covertly. She had not regained all
of the weight she had lost during her illness, and she was still a
little pale. The loss of flesh had brought out the pretty moulding
of her cheek and chin, and she looked, if anything, a trifle younger.
There was something childish in her absorption. All around her,
men darted sly glances, appraising her face and figure, but she was,
or affected to be, unconscious. He came closer, rather tentatively,
uncertain if she would like him to greet her, until she turned and
smiled, addressing him in English.

'Doctor van Overmeer. This is a merry meeting. It is good to
see you, but are you neglecting your duties?'

He grinned shyly. 'I spent the morning at the almshouse,
Mevrouw Behn. I thought I would allow myself a little respite
before I go to my afternoon's work. You are in good health,
I hope?'

'As you can see, Doctor. I am an advertisement for your
skills.' Indeed she was, he thought, self-approvingly. As they
stood together talking by the window, he was near enough to
her to tell that the stinking humours had gone from her mouth,

which gratified him. Capitein Behn would doubtless have sought treatment in London: while a modest woman, he knew, could easily fail to notice the tell-tale chancre, her husband would certainly have observed what was amiss, and taken steps to remedy it. When he returned, they should be able to have a normal life together. In ten years' time, if God willed it, he might see her in church, plump and happy, with a bonny flock of curly-headed children about her skirts. After the hopelessness of his morning's work, it was good to see so striking an instance of the triumph of skill and knowledge over nature; it gave him a sort of proprietorial affection for her.

She closed the books she had been looking at, and smiled at him sidelong. Her hands were small and plump, blue-veined, with rather tapering fingers. 'I am also allowing myself a respite, Doctor. I have worked hard, these last weeks.'

'What at, mevrouw?' he asked politely.

Her smile broadened. 'That, I fear, is not something I care to speak of.'

'Well, Mevrouw Behn, I do not seek to pry,' he answered, confused. She looked as if she wanted to tell him; did she want him to press her? On the whole, it seemed best not to. 'Good day to you,' he said, bowing politely. He thought she looked a little disappointed, as he turned away. He left the shop without making a purchase: the meeting had been enough in itself to lighten his mood, so he prudently left his money snug in his purse.

But when he got home twenty minutes later, Narcissus met him on the doorstep with news which sent Mevrouw Behn and everything else out of his head. Cornelis Jonson was seriously ill. Without pausing even for a draught of beer, Balthasar turned, bag in hand, and went straight to the Dam, where the maid let him in and took him through to the bedroom.

He found the old painter propped on a pile of pillows, purple with the effort of drawing breath. Even without putting his ear to the old man's chest, Balthasar could hear the catarrh bubbling

and crepitating in his lungs. Daniel, his assistant, knelt by the
bed, holding a basin of hot water in hands ineradicably stained
by years of grinding pigments, trying to ease his breathing with
the steam. A beaker of warm brantwijn with cloves and ginger in
it steamed on a trivet by the hearth; Balthasar could smell the rich,
spicy reek of it.

'Take the brantwijn away,' he ordered. 'Spirituous liquor and
hot cordials will send your master to his grave. They might seem
to bring him ease, but they entangle and harden the matter of the
cough, and delay the cure.'

'Balthasar,' said Jonson faintly. His eyes were shut and sunken;
the whole of his vital energies concentrated on the next breath.

'Have no fear, sir. I came as soon as I heard, and I will do all I
can to ease you. You need to be bled, first of all, and I will apply
a blister to the nape of the neck. Do you feel pain in your side?'

Jonson shook his head. 'Just . . .' Unable to finish the sentence,
he waved his hand. Just the cough, which leaves your body as sore
as if you had been beaten, thought Balthasar sympathetically.

'Excellent,' he said soothingly. 'This is all very bad, Mynheer
Cornelis, but if there is no pain in the side, there is no pleurisy,
and no real danger. Now I must examine you.' He knelt by the bed,
and lifted Jonson's bedgown and shirt, and put his ear to the thin,
pale-skinned chest thus exposed, listening carefully to the squeaks
and bubbles within. What he heard on the whole reassured him.
The catarrh was at the top of the lungs, sticky and difficult, to be
sure, but not malignant: with help, it could be cast up.

'Here is a receipt for a cooling pectoral ptisan,' he said, subsiding
onto a stool and scribbling busily while the assistant settled his
master's clothes around him once more. Syrup of sugar, with
liquorice, elecampane, aniseed, angelica, orris-powder and flowers
of brimstone; it would cool and soothe. 'I will give it to the maid
to fetch for you. This should check the cough, and prevent fever.
Take it when you will, and abstain from meat, wine and spirits.

I do not recommend a narcotic, which may impede expectoration. If you can, get up and move around for a little in the middle of the day. The exercise will open the pores of your skin, and supply a natural and easy passage for the exhalations of your catarrh.'

Jonson nodded; he looked exhausted.

'I am very sorry to see you in this case,' said Balthasar. 'I have seen several instances of this cough in the last few weeks, and although it is very unpleasant, it seems not to be dangerous. We will have you well again very soon, I hope.' He bent down to open his bag, and found his scalpel. Twenty ounces of blood from the right arm should bring some ease, he thought, ordering the assistant to fetch him a basin.

Once the old painter had been bled, bandaged and blistered, Balthasar took his leave. 'I will return this evening, just before prayers, to see how you are faring,' he promised. He gave his prescription to the maid, who was hovering anxiously outside her master's bedroom, and told her to make what haste she could to the apothecary. He was a little less sanguine than he had intended to sound. True, the cough was not a malignant one, but the victim it had seized upon was elderly and frail. It would take careful nursing to bring him back to full health.

Things were no better in the evening, though the cough syrup he had prescribed seemed to bring some relief. But as he found on his next day's visit, Jonson had had a better night, and the cough seemed to be loosening. Jonson was able to talk through his wheezing, though in a whisper, and was pleased to see him.

'Balthasar,' he said, once professional questions had been asked and answered, and they were able to converse, 'I have a favour to ask of you.'

'Of course, Mynheer Cornelis. What is it?'

'Here is the key to the box on my dressing-table. You will find a letter in it, addressed to Mevrouw Behn. I want you to keep it for her, in case I take a turn for the worse, and I would like it to reach her as discreetly as might be, so I do not want to send Trijn or Wouter.'

Balthasar rose obediently, taking the key, but he could not quite keep the surprise from his face. He found the letter easily enough, and pocketed it, observing as he did so that it was not in the painter's own hand. 'Have you revised your opinions of the lady?' he asked mildly, trying not to sound curious.

'My dear Balthasar. Mevrouw Behn is a woman of great charm and few scruples, and I would say, dangerous company for a young man. But for all that, she has some countervailing virtues, not least, philopatriotism. This is not a clandestine correspondence of the usual kind, I do assure you. Her Dutch captain need have no fear.'

'But if she has friends in England, why does she not write to them in the usual way?' persisted Balthasar, and realised at once that he had gone too far.

'Young sir,' Jonson rebuked him. 'Yours are not the only secrets I keep, or have kept.'

'I am sorry,' he said humbly. 'I will not enquire again.' He took the letter home, and put it in a safe place, wondering what he should do about it.

When he visited again during his evening round, he was distressed to find Jonson flushed, shivering, and complaining of chills. He laid his hand on the damp, hot forehead, and his heart sank. Fever. The catarrh had become malignant and turned to bronchitis.

He prescribed a cooling julep of borage and citron, warned Wouter and Trijn to keep the fires up, and went to look in on another patient, more worried than he cared to admit.

The next day, he purposely kept his call on Cornelis Jonson for the end of his midday round of home-visits. As he feared, the fever had taken hold. The old man lay propped up on his pillows, glassy-eyed and unresponsive, and his breathing was distressing to hear. Balthasar sent Wouter scurrying for a stronger cordial of hyacinth, Venice treacle and pearls, and drew up a chair to Jonson's bedside, dabbing the old man's brow and hands with a handkerchief wetted in rosewater.

He had sat for perhaps twenty minutes, wondering if the old man were strong enough to tolerate a clyster, when he heard footsteps behind him. He turned, thinking it was Wouter returned with the cordial, and found Aphra Behn standing there, clasping her hands and looking pale and distressed.

'How is he, Doctor?' she asked.

'If I can break the fever, he will be well enough,' replied Balthasar, aware that he did not sound hopeful.

'Mynheer,' said the painter with sudden urgency, surprising them both. His voice was hoarse with phlegm.

'Yes, Mynheer Cornelis?'

'You have the letter?'

'Yes, of course, mynheer. You gave it to me yesterday.'

'You have the letter?' he said again, and Balthasar realised the fever had sent his mind astray. 'My lord, the Queen has sent you a letter. I have kept it safe for you.'

'I have got the letter,' said Balthasar soothingly.

Jonson's wandering eyes focused on him, in senile confusion. 'Who are you? Where is the Black King? I have a letter for the Black King.'

'There is no black king, mynheer,' said Balthasar firmly. 'That was long ago.'

'Are you Pelagius?'

'Pelagius is dead, Mynheer Cornelis. Rest now.'

Jonson struggled to a more upright position. 'But if he is dead, who has got the letter? Have you stolen the Queen's letter, damn you?'

'I have not got the Queen's letter.'

'Liar. You took the letter.'

'That was a different letter,' said Balthasar through his teeth, completely exasperated.

'Do not argue with him,' said Mevrouw Behn from behind him. He had forgotten she was there. She moved forward in a swish of skirts and sat down on the edge of the bed, leaning forward to lay a hand on Jonson's brow and looking into his eyes.

'My poor old friend. You have done your duty. All the letters are in the right hands. All is well. Sleep now.'

For a moment, it seemed as if he might accept her words, but after a moment of relaxation, he tensed once more. 'Have you got the King's letter?' he demanded.

'Yes, yes, yes,' she soothed.

'Thief. Harlot. Deceiver. Give it to the King.' Her bewilderment was written on her face as she sat back.

'What king?'

'Pelagius ... where is Pelagius? Have they captured him and sent him overseas?'

'Pelagius is coming,' said Balthasar. 'Drink this. It will help you to rest a little, and you will see him when he comes.'

'They caught him once,' explained Jonson, swallowing obediently. 'He told me.'

Balthasar mopped his brow again. For some minutes, Cornelis continued to mumble disjointedly about his letters, but in the end his eyelids began to close and his face went slack.

'What did you give him?' whispered Aphra.

'I added some poppy syrup to his draught,' said Balthasar. 'I will have to watch him now, lest I need to take other measures. Narcotics are dangerous in a case of fever, but he was heating himself so much with his own imaginings, I thought he would do himself harm.' He turned to Aphra, who was still sitting on the bed. 'Mevrouw, I hardly dare say it after these last minutes, but I have a letter he asked me to give to you. It must have been the last anxiety in his mind, hence this babbling of letters.'

'Where is it?'

'Unfortunately, I have left it at home. You know where I live, I think, De Derde Koninck, in the Spanjardstraat. Call whenever it is convenient. I will tell my servants to admit you, if I am not there, and you will find it in a box on the writing desk in my room.'

'Thank you, Doctor.' She was silent for a moment, looking thoughtfully at Cornelis's sleeping face. 'Doctor van Overmeer . . . who was Pelagius?'

'My father,' said Balthasar shortly.

'But why did Mynheer Jonson speak of him as a king? At first, I thought when he said the King's letter, he meant a letter from the King, but that was wrong, was it not?'

'My father was a king in Africa.'

'Then how came he here?'

'He was taken as a slave. But he was a free man by the time he came to Holland.'

Her face was avid with interest, and it made him uncomfortable. 'It must be dreadful for a man of wit and genius to become a slave, and still worse for a king. I cannot imagine anything more tragic.'

'Yes, indeed. He spoke little of it.'

'Did they make him work in the fields with a hoe? I saw poor wretches working thus, in Surinam, and pitied them.'

'By no means,' said Balthasar, somewhat irritated. 'He was servant to a scholar, and became a scholar himself.'

'It is as I thought,' she said at once. 'True rank makes its own recognition.'

'Not necessarily,' said Balthasar. He was infuriated by her glibness, and the whole conversation was making him acutely nervous. 'Our Lord was despised of the people, spat upon and neglected, and no man on earth was more noble than he.'

'Touché. But you have made a parallel. Your father the King was rejected by his own, or he would not have been enslaved, and it is clear that he was recognised by those with eyes to see. Our Lord was scorned by the Jews, and yet the Three Kings came from afar to fall at his feet. You of all people should know that, since you live at the sign of the Kings.'

'Mevrouw, you come near to jesting upon sacred subjects,' he said, trying to control his temper.

'You misunderstand me, Doctor van Overmeer,' said Aphra with dignity. 'I am no Dutchwoman, to scramble for petty gain and despise my natural rulers. There is nothing but God more sacred to me than a king.' In the silence following her words, they listened together to Jonson's painful, rasping breaths. She stood up with care, so that her movement did not disturb him, and looked down on Balthasar. 'I will bid you good day, sir, and go to pray for our good old friend's recovery.'

Aphra went home, trying to work out her best course of action, and thinking to herself that it was typical of the design of her life that, at a moment when she should have been dancing in the streets for very joy, she was embroiled in complications. Mr Piers was at Sint Janstraat, Johan's right-hand man, ready and waiting to take her to London. Yet it was vital that she recover the letter she had gone to Jonson's house to collect. Why, she asked herself bitterly, need everything be so difficult? Back in the New Year, it had seemed an excellent idea to activate her old identity as an informer – she had done good service in Surinam, she knew, and when she was back in England something might come of it: she intended never to return to Holland, and if she were to leave Johan, she would need patrons. The response of Thom Killigrew, the King's spymaster, had been encouraging; she had been recognised, and had even been able to supply one or two items of information specifically requested.

Jonson had rapidly grasped the situation, and had been helpful. 'No less a painter than my great predecessor Mynheer Rubens involved himself in the business of intelligence,' he had observed, with his pleasant smile. 'I have painted three generations of the Stuarts, and though I am too old now to remove to London, I am happy to assist them as best I may.' And now the old fool was dying of a rheum, just when she needed him to write her letters of introduction, and a potentially incriminating letter from Thom Killigrew was lying in the hands of a witless young doctor, from whom it must be recovered, come what might. Johan was no great patriot, but if van Overmeer naïvely gave him the letter to give to her, she feared at the very least a beating which would leave her bedridden for days, and she well knew that there was little of the stoic in her constitution.

Brooding thus fruitlessly, she turned the corner of Sint Janstraat, and went into 't Schippershuis. She found Mr Piers in her work-room.

'Madam,' he said, rising and bowing very correctly. She curtseyed in return, noting that he had been going through her papers. How right she had been to burn all the London correspondence. Piers was tall and slender, with blinking, white-lashed eyes which made her think of pigs, though in other respects he was a handsome enough fellow, and gentlemanlike. He had none of Johan's obvious dangerousness; indeed, Johan's contempt for him as a man was made clear by the freedom he allowed him in associating with his wife, as if he were an eunuch. Aphra had been nonplussed at first, though Piers himself seemed content to fall in with his master's requirements. She had gradually become aware that he was a more formidable person than he seemed. Since he was not a gentleman, he did not wear a sword, but she knew that he carried a concealed stiletto, and suspected that he had used it more than once. He was sharply observant in an almost feminine manner, which made her wary, since she had no way of gauging the nature of his loyalty to Johan. She smiled at him engagingly, what she thought of as her innocent smile.

'My poor old friend is very ill,' she announced. 'It is very sad. I had gone only to take my congé, but now I fear I may never see him again in this world. He has a malignant catarrh of the chest, and alas, I have found that if these ailments seize on a body out of season, they come with an especial violence. He caught it, I think, in the downpour of last week.'

'Poor fellow,' said Piers carelessly. 'This was Jonson of Cologne, the face-painter?'

'Yes, indeed. I had hoped he might be useful to us, when we go over. He painted King James and King Charles, you know, and he had a great practice with the English court, so I had thought his name might serve us, but alas, it is not to be. He was delirious when I called, with his physician in attendance.'

'Well, he would have served us little, in this present world,' commented Piers. 'His acquaintance will now be antique dowagers and down-at-heel notables of the last age. The first Charles had an unaccountable taste for prosy bores and virtuous women, but they are little heeded at court today. The friendship of Lady Castlemaine would serve us better than anything, and I fear your Jonson was not so prescient as to paint her in her cradle.'

'Does old loyalty count for nothing, then?' countered Aphra, a little annoyed. She went over to the table, and began sorting the piles of paper on it, while Piers lounged by the fire.

'Nothing whatever, madam. Who is such a looby as to expect anything else? When our Black Prince returned from France, he must needs reward those who held the power, so how, then, was he to find purses for all those who suffered in his cause? That is the way of the world, and well have we learned it. My family have been court musicians since Elizabeth's time, but it is Captain Cock and not I who sings in the Chapel Royal.' His voice had thickened from its usual light, indifferent drawl, and Aphra opened her mouth, but he forestalled her. 'This is from our purpose. How soon can you be ready? I would as lief sail in the morning, if your affairs are in a posture for leaving.'

'Not so soon, Mr Piers,' she replied gratefully. 'I have a little more business in the town. I have been ill, and I need a strengthening cordial which my doctor has prescribed, so I needs must visit the apothecary. But my clothes will be soon enough put up, and this mess of paper is little enough to detain us. I must have my notes on politicians, for I think Mr Behn and his brother may wish me to go on writing for the *Parliament Quaeries*, but my Dutch translations are finished, thank God. All that matters has been printed, so consign 'em to Hell by way of the fireplace. Of private correspondence, I have none but these few letters from my brother. Mr Behn is not in the way of writing.'

'Mr Behn is a wise man,' replied Piers dryly. 'No man but a fool sets his mind down on paper, and none but a lunatic, his heart.'

'There are many lunatics, then, in the world ... or so I have heard,' she added prudently, though belatedly.

'Truly. And not one but thinks himself the emperor of the moon.'

She shot a glance at him; had that been a note of sadness? He was not an easy man to read, for all the swiftness of his tongue. 'Have no fear, Mr Piers. I need but two hours to parcel up my traps, such as they are, and an hour for my business in the town. If you bespeak us places for the afternoon tide, then I can undertake to be ready well in time.' She brushed past him and went into her bedroom. When she emerged, she was carrying her flute. 'It wants an hour yet to supper. Shall we beguile the time with a little music?'

He blinked at her rapidly with his weak eyes; she had touched his softest spot, she knew. They had often made music in London, when Johan had no call on either of them. He shrugged with a pretence of unconcern. 'Let us surprise these two-legged cheeseworms, then, madam.'

She sat down on her writing chair, and raised the flute to her lips, blowing a couple of soft notes to check that the tone was true and clean.

'Do you know "Captain Digby's Farewell", madam?'

She nodded. 'I have it in my songbook. I have only the bass and the air, so you must forgive me if I make the best shift I can to accompany you.' She reached for the book and found the page. Raising her eyebrows, she began to play, swaying a little in her seat. Piers stepped away from the fire and stood upright, head well balanced, hands loose by his sides, like the singing-boy he had once been, and waited for his cue. Her lip curled when he began to sing, almost spoiling her note, as she wondered what the Behns might make of it. Piers was a male alto, the voice completely true, but astonishingly high and very loud, with an almost brassy quality like a human trumpet.

> 'And I'll go to my Love where he lies in the deep,
> And in my embraces my dearest shall sleep:
> When we wake, the kind dolphins together shall throng
> And in chariots of shells shall draw us along.'

He was, thought Aphra critically, a very fine singer indeed. His phrasing was clean and precise, and every note was accurately hit. He seemed almost possessed by the song; his usual faintly mocking expression had vanished, and his eyes were half shut, while the fingers of the hands hanging correctly by his sides curled and clenched.

> 'For my Love sleeps now in a watery grave,
> And has nothing to show for his Tomb but a wave,
> I'll kiss his dear lips than the coral more red,
> That grows where he lies in his watery bed.
> Ah, Ah! Ah, my Love's dead! That was not a bell,
> But a Triton's shell, to ring, to ring out his knell.'

Aphra brought the accompaniment to a conclusion, and lowered the flute. 'Bravo, Mr Piers,' she said. He looked at her as if he was bewildered, still caught in the meshes of the song. The bell for evening prayers sounded from the Nieuwe Kerk. Let them jangle, she thought, leafing through her songbook. 'Do you know "I saw fair Chloris walk alone, when feathered rain came softly down"?'

He sucked in his breath, and nodded. 'Not too fast.'

'No, indeed. One . . . two . . . three . . .'

That had all gone very well, she thought judiciously, as she left the house late the following morning. All her belongings were packed, while she and Mr Piers had spent most of the evening making music together, a pleasure for both, sweetened additionally for Aphra by her delicious sense of the bewilderment this outlandish noise must be causing in the Behn household. And that afternoon she would leave for England, perhaps for ever. She fervently hoped that, if she continued to make tales of London bawdy, supplied by Johan, perhaps, and certainly by Mr Piers, who was no mean gossip, she would make herself so useful there would be no talk of her returning to Middelburg.

When she had looked for perhaps the last time around her room at the top of 't Schippershuis, her heart had been singing. All that she wished to take was boxed and bundled in the middle of the floor, while Mr Piers was out looking for a carrier. As her gaze swept round the room, checking to see if anything had been forgotten to which she attached the slightest value, her eye fell on a copy of *Fanchon en Susanna*, her Dutch translation of *The School of Venus*. She would take it, she decided in a breath. She was most unlikely to meet Doctor van Overmeer, who would be out on his morning calls. She remembered his blushes as he attempted to question her about her privy parts; a virgin, or all but, she concluded, with a touch of genial contempt shading the thought. A timid fellow, he must be; some women were mad for blacks, it was hard to believe he had not had his opportunities. She was not ungrateful to him, and they would never meet again: perhaps she would leave him the book to surprise him, and perhaps in time his wife would be grateful.

When she reached his house in the Spanjardstraat, she found, as she had expected, that he was out. There was nobody at home, in fact, but a goggle-eyed, thin little woman who seemed almost half-witted. But she was brought successfully to understand why Mevrouw had come, and conducted her self-importantly into the house. Aphra cast a critical glance around her. Prosperous enough, and well appointed, though small, she noted. The portrait over the mantelpiece struck her at once; the pearls alone told her the subject was royal. The Queen of Bohemia, it must be, from what he had said; and a hard-faced old trot she was, for all the jewels. She noticed another picture out of the corner of her eye, as the maid conducted her up the stairs. A negro baby, in a dress of fine, cream-coloured silk. He was holding a stem with two roses, a red and a white. The infant Balthasar, she presumed, but why was he holding the roses of England? Perhaps they held another meaning, though she could not think what it might be.

'The master's room is at the top of the stairs,' said the maid, having brought her to the first-floor landing. 'Find what's yours, I'll be in the kitchen.'

She whisked off down the stairs, leaving Aphra to climb thoughtfully. The room she entered, a spacious attic, was legible enough. He slept at the back, and worked at a table set under the window in the front gable. She went straight to the window end, and found her letter at once, lying on the table. She pocketed it gratefully and considered what else was before her. A box; locked, but the key stood in the lock. How very confiding. As a matter of principle, she opened it. It seemed to contain a drift of young man's treasures, nothing of any significance, except for a fair amount of gold. She took a single thaler on principle; more, and there might be an alarm, but when a single coin was missing, men generally assumed they had miscounted. Ah. Something else. A worn and ancient silk ribbon, and on it, a key. Aphra looked around her. The maid was safely downstairs, and a second level of concealment, even at this naïve level, was always interesting. And Balthasar was interesting to her; he posed a series of unanswered questions, and Jonson obviously thought him a person of importance.

Nine times out of ten, a man who thinks his desk is private will put what is most private under his pillow or under his bed. No sooner thought than acted on; she moved swiftly on tiptoe to the far end of the room. Under the bed it was. She lugged out the second box and tried the key in the lock, with success. Sitting back on her heels, she contemplated the papers within. They meant nothing to her. Two manuscript books in Latin; and she could not read a word of them. A thought suddenly struck her. The two volumes of *Fanchon en Susanna* were much of a size, small quarto, and in similar plain vellum bindings. On an impulse, she exchanged the two books for the ones she had brought, and took two or three letters – the same hand as the letters in van Overmeer's first box, she noted – for future perusal. Piers could read Latin; and a secret was a secret; the fates had put the books in her hands, and at the least, if they turned out to be of no advantage to her, nothing had been lost. Meanwhile, time was of the essence, though she judged she had been alone in the room for less than three minutes. She relocked the box, shoved it back under the bed, and softly tiptoed to the far end of the room, where she put the key on its ribbon back in the box on the desk. It was a well-made house, she noted approvingly; not a single board creaked. Then, moving decisively, allowing her heels to clip firmly on the floor, she returned to the door.

'Mevrouw! I have found what I came for, thank you,' she called. She made a fair amount of noise, descending the stairs. Though she did not expect the doctor to be back for an hour or so, her pulse was beating in her temples, and she felt dizzy.

The maid seemed to see nothing strange, however, and conducted her politely to the door. She was just about to open it, when it opened of its own accord; her heart leapt into her throat. But it was not Balthasar; it was, or seemed to be, Caliban; a plainly dressed creature of indeterminate age; its skin was as dark as pitch, with black, glittering eyes, and all up one side of the round, bullet head, seamed with hideous scars. She looked at the creature in horror, until it bowed to her. Nothing but a black man, a victim of some long-ago accident which had defaced him. 'Good day to you, mevrouw,' he said politely. If he was Caliban, he was a gentle enough monster, she thought, as he stood aside to let her by. Curtseying a farewell, she fled towards Sint Janstraat. Three short hours, then she would be out of this cursed country.

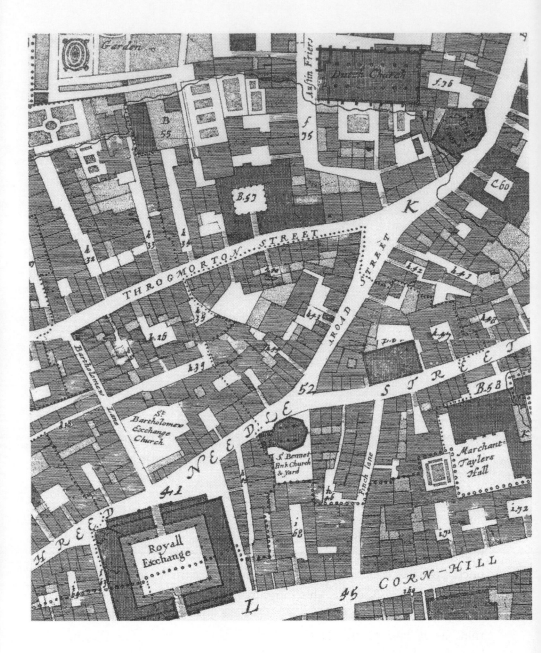

IV

What life can compare with the jolly town rake's
When in his full swing of all pleasure he takes!
At noon he gets up for a whet and to dine,
And wings the swift hours with mirth, music and wine,
Then jogs to the playhouse and chats with the masques,
And thence to the Rose, where he takes his three flasks.
Thus in Covent Garden he makes his campaigns,
And no coffee-house haunts but to settle his brains.
He laughs at dry morals, and never does think
Unless 'tis to get the best wenches and drink.
He dwells in a tavern, and lives everywhere,
And improving his hours, lives an age in a year.
For as life is uncertain, he loves to make haste.
And thus he lives longest, because he lives fast.

Peter Motteaux, 'The Town Rake', 1696

May 1672

Riding east towards Austin Friars, Balthasar reflected on how much, in so short a time, he had come to loathe London. It had once, perhaps, been a great city, but six years after the great fire, it made him think of Isaiah's judgement on the ruins of Babylon. The population had been winnowed thin by death even before that, as it had in the Netherlands, but here, what the Plague had spared, the fire had taken. Everywhere stood the burned corpses of buildings destroyed in the fire, their blackened spars still pointing towards Heaven like the despairing arms of wretches burned alive. The sites where new structures were going up were still sparsely scattered in the townscape, and most of them were still half-built piles of masonry, cut stone and brick surrounded by rickety scaffolding. Here and there a great new building rose from the ashes, flat-fronted rosy brick for the most part, with big, Dutch-fashion windows; he had passed the new Royal Exchange – for London bought and sold, when it would not house its citizens, or God – similarly, the Guildhall, the Customs House, and most of the livery companies' halls had been rebuilt. The city was a strange motley of the rich and new and the desolate. It seemed almost as if the sour black ash which lay as a visible layer in any disturbed ground still scented the air with the smell of the vanity of human wishes, taking the cheer out of the spring sunshine. Here and there, thin on the air, came the sound of bells. Not many. The city had boasted more than a hundred churches before the Fire, and after only six years, few of the intended replacements had been completed. But some there were, a reminder that even in this abomination of desolation, it was Ascension Day, and people were going to church.

Was it the city he hated, he asked himself, guiding his gentle old horse up Threadneedle Street, or himself, and the continuous state of quiet, abject terror which was the condition of his life? Composing his mind to self-examination, he recognised in himself a growing self-disgust and loss of professional confidence which made him prey to melancholic imaginings. Patiently, he set himself to unravelling the problem of his own state of mind, as he had been taught to do, so that he could lay it before God. Fear: one entirely alone and friendless in an alien city might well feel fear. It was wrong, and he should try to trust more in the mercy of God; his father would certainly have told him that. His fear of London itself, as a massive, inimical presence, an entity as blindly threatening as a cancer, was no more than childish terror in

66

the face of the unknown. He must strive, with God's help, to overcome it.

The self-disgust ... ah, there was a problem indeed. It went back, he well knew, to the deaths of Narcissus and Anna. Plague had come to Middelburg in 1665. It had appeared in Amsterdam in '63, carried from Smyrna in a Levant trader, or so men said, and had broken out at intervals here and there in Holland thereafter. He had seen his share of it and done all that he could, in common with the other town physicians, but when it came to De Derde Koninck, it took away with it his beloved old servants and friends, and all the confidence he had had in his profession. He had thought of them as burdens, he remembered with bitter self-recrimination; he had, in a childish way, never truly believed in his heart that they could leave him. Once they were dead, once it was too late, he began to realise how dear they were to him, and how irreplaceable.

Narcissus had died quietly; he had come in complaining of a headache, sat down, and fainted where he sat. Half an hour later, he sighed out his last breath without even waking. While Anna clung to her unconscious husband, shaking him, kissing his slack mouth, frantically calling his name, Balthasar had applied cantharides, the strongest stimulant at his command, then as a last, desperate measure, he had bled him. Kneeling on the floor at the feet of his lifelong companion and second father, he had watched tensely as the bright red blood spurted from the dark arm, and then, in despair, he had seen the spurt die into a trickle and cease, and known that his Sisi was dead.

Anna, by contrast, had died hard. He had helplessly witnessed the nearest to a mother that he had ever known delirious with pain and fever, vomiting uncontrollably, and badged with the crimson blotches which marked her for death. The utter uselessness of all that he did to heal, or even to alleviate her progress towards her end, had been hideously borne in on him. He had studied for four years at Leiden, and practised, not without success, for eight. And at the end of it, he felt, he knew nothing; when he most wanted to help, he was helpless. And how could he hope to make his name in London, if he did not even believe in himself?

Well. Time to lay the whole problem of his life before God. He jumped neatly from his horse, a dapple-grey called Dowsabell, tied her to a stanchion by the reins alongside many another respectable nag, and went into the church. There had been a Dutch Reformed church in London for more than a hundred years. They used part of an ancient building, once a Catholic church, miraculously preserved on the very edge of the fire-zone. The Powlett family, who had built themselves a great house on the site of the actual canonry in Queen Elizabeth's time, had made the east end where Mass had once been said into a warehouse where they stored corn, coal and suchlike stuffs on and around the high altar, while the nave of the original structure had been given to the Dutch for their church.

The building gave him, as always, a degree of comfort. It was long and spacious, like the Abdij at home, and properly plain as a church should be, the walls whitewashed, showing here and there in the plaster the scars where Papist monuments had been removed, the floor bare and clean, and clear glass in the windows, the only touch of pomp the great brass chandeliers hung on long chains from the high ceiling and the carved wooden preaching-place. He walked in, unconsciously relaxing a little as he walked forward into the soberly dressed assembly of men and women like himself, hearing the familiar sound of Dutch as the far-flung little community met before the service began to exchange news. He lived from week to week in a state of permanent exhaustion caused by the effort of speaking English: it was a blessed relief to him to relapse back into dear, familiar Dutch.

News would not be good, that was certain. He could see that the little knots of worshippers were poring over courants and broadsheets of one kind or another, faces drawn, and brows anxiously knitted. The French King, master of the biggest and most efficient army in Europe, had declared a quarrel with the Netherlands on the thinnest of grounds, then early in April, he had declared war, and that army was now inexorably advancing on the Netherlands.

Balthasar, as so often now, felt like a traitor. He had left Holland for London before the trouble had really started. Listening to the news from the skippers on the Dam in the first months of the year, reading the diurnals, sick and tired of his lonely life in de Derde Koninck, he had come to a sudden and radical decision in March, sold up everything he owned in Middelburg, and with only a few valued possessions and a precious wallet of promissory notes drawn on the Amsterdam Wisselbank sewn inside the waistband of his breeches, he had emigrated to try his fortune in his mother's country. Every word out of the Netherlands since he had left confirmed the wisdom of this decision, but the fact did not comfort him.

Looking around, he saw a familiar face, long-nosed, with heavy cheeks and a comfortable double chin set off by a small pointed beard: Daniel Everaerts, the head of a cadet branch of one of Middelburg's oldest and most established families, long settled in London. Heavy and florid in prosperous late middle age, he held court beneath the central window, the light pouring down on the heavy curls of his fashionable full wig, the shoulders of his dove-grey velvet coat, and the *Zeeuwse Courant* which he held in his hands. Balthasar approached, and bowed. It was Everaerts who had taken pity on a fellow townsman and given him his first opening; after these few short weeks, his clientèle was drawn almost exclusively from members of the Dutch Reformed Church, apart from a few of his immediate neighbours in Westminster. The older man acknowledged his low bow with a courteous nod.

'What news of the French, Mynheer Everaerts?' he asked.

'King Louis will soon reach the Maas, and there is nothing whatever to stand in his way when he gets there,' declared

Everaerts heavily. 'But that is not the end of it. The prince-bishop of Münster declared war on the Republic a few days since, and so has the Elector of Cologne. So there are troops advancing on the country from north-east and east, as well as from the south, and we were ill enough prepared to face even the French. Thank God that the Stadhouder has taken the reins of power. I am a merchant and a man of peace, but I freely admit that trusting the country to the States-General has been a great mistake, perhaps our last. They have thought only of peace and the saving of guilders, and the army has been starved of men and equipment. No voice has been raised to prevent them since the death of Fredrik Hendrik. And now, the enemies gather along our borders, and the wealth so prudently husbanded in Amsterdam is no comfort to the citizens who must face them.'

It was a nightmarish vision which he offered, of a country beset on all sides – for the English ships to the west were enemies as well. Looking at the strained, pale faces on every side, Balthasar knew that all of them, each to the best of his or her ability, were grappling with the same unthinkable idea which possessed his own mind. That their country, the youngest in Europe, might yet be overlaid like an unwanted child, and snuffed out as if it had never been. The people round about him were a community of exiles, for one reason or another, but it is one thing to be an exile, another to be a person without a country. He could not imagine the idea of the Netherlands not existing; yet, he thought, what did he have on the other side of the Narrow Seas that he could ever go back to?

All around, the quiet conferences began to break up as people drifted into their places for the beginning of the service. The predikant announced psalm 18, and with sober fervour, they sang, 'The Lord is my rock, and my fortress, and my deliverer'. They sang unaccompanied, in the Dutch fashion, and more than in any service Balthasar could remember, one could hear that they were praying as they sang, as he was himself. 'The sorrows of hell compassed me about: the snares of death prevented me. In my distress, I cried unto my God.'

When the service was over, he thrust his worries out of his mind, and dutifully made himself available, lingering at the end of the nave looking pleasant and approachable. Most of his income, such as it was, was garnered through approaches after the service from people who preferred to recount their symptoms in Dutch, or, simply, trusted a Leiden-trained doctor more than a licensee of the College of Physicians – though some day, he reflected distractedly, as he nodded and smiled, he must scrape acquaintance with that august body, and gain their countenance for his work. But even on this day of grief, there were plenty of folk still whose private miseries outweighed their common anxiety for the fate of the Netherlands. Before he went out to the patiently waiting Dowsabell, he had garnered a probable hernia, a scald-head, a case of what was almost certainly worms, and a possible consumption to add to his current case-list. The College could wait.

Balthasar was living in Tothill Street in Westminster, on the advice of Everaerts, who lived there himself in one of the big, old noblemen's houses strangely built of wood and plaster which still survived there among a greater number of smaller brick houses no more than ten or fifteen years old. His reason for settling there was simple: the church roll showed Westminster to boast a larger Dutch Reformed community than any other parish, hence, it was the easiest place for a Dutch doctor to build up a practice.

Westminster was a great contrast to the City, since it had escaped the fire, and was, in itself, an area of great and strange contrasts, beyond anything he had known. The vast, ancient bulks of Parliament House, Westminster Hall and St Peter's Abbey loomed over the streets, as the Abdij did in Middelburg. But around them was a rookery of narrow, twisting streets fouler and more dangerous than anything he had ever known; and to the north of the Abbey was the Sanctuary, an area beyond the law, where fugitives and criminals were free to do as they pleased. However, away from the Abbey, towards the Park, were streets of respectable houses, both great and small, such as Tothill Street. If God had been minded to strike this city, thought Balthasar censoriously, looking towards the dark kennels of the Sanctuary as he trotted homewards down Bow Street, it was hard to see why He had withheld His cleansing fire from this den of iniquity. But perhaps the old city had been still worse, though it was hard to imagine how.

His own house was a small, plain affair, with no name, just a number, in the English style. It had been chosen with care, as a highly respectable address; the grandeur of Lincoln House, the Lord Chamberlain's residence, and the few surviving mansions such as the one Everaerts and his family lived in lent countenance to the smaller and more recent houses in the street. In his choice of dwelling and way of life, he had been anxious to strike a balance between a degree of show which would bear witness to a decent and gentlemanlike prosperity, and the prudent conservation of his resources against future difficulties, so he had asked for, and followed, Everaerts's advice in setting up his new establishment.

The English fashion was for more servants than at home; he kept three, Bessy, a bouncing, red-armed woman who presided inside, taciturn James, whose duties included the care of the horse, and a boy called Jacob, a runtish little creature with a perpetual sniff who did the roughest of the work. He was not yet comfortable or at home, either with the house itself, or with the servants. The house made him unhappy, because it seemed to him fusty and dirty. The sea-coal they burned left films of gritty dust on every surface. He was used to Dutch housewifery, to scrubbing, soaping, polishing and sweeping from morning to night. He had thought Bessy a slattern at first, until he realised, as he visited patient after patient, that the English were simply indifferent to a level of dirt which would have had Anna reaching for mop and broom. It still made him uncomfortable, and he missed Anna, and indeed Betsy, the capable soul who had looked after De Derde Koninck in the six years since Anna's death.

He walked the horse to the Tothill Street mews, and called up as he dismounted. The window of the loft over his stable opened, and James's head popped out: a moment later he had swung himself down the ladder, and come out to take Dowsabell's bridle. The man slept at one end of the loft which was otherwise used for hay and tack, partly for the sake of security, partly for decency, lest in that mistressless household he become over-familiar with Bessy. Having surrendered the horse, Balthasar went back up the street on foot, and in to his noon meal.

After he had eaten, he decided to go out again, on foot this time. He had only one or two evening visits to make, so he had some free time before him, and the sun was shining. With no particular end in view, he bade Bessy farewell and told her he might not be in to supper, reached for his good beaver hat and his green silk Sunday coat which had cost (as he thought every time he donned it), an obscene amount of money, and sauntered out into the street.

Few people were about, on this holiday, but as he left Westminster, strolling up the Long Ditch towards St James's Park, he heard a confused, shrill hubbub ahead of him. Coming round the corner of the street, he saw a curious procession; a black-clad minister flanked by churchwardens with their staves of office and followed by a motley procession of children walking two by two, chattering and carrying sticks. Curious, he tagged along in their wake; when they reached the boundary marker, the churchwardens raised their staves, and all of them, adults and children together, roared or shrieked their loudest, clattering their sticks against the walls, or one another. Balthasar watched them as they formed once again into their crocodile and marched on, and when he saw a respectable-looking fellow on the other side of the street, he crossed to accost him, removing his hat politely.

'Can you tell me, sir, what these children are doing?'

The man looked at him with the faint hostility he was accustomed to; neither a dark skin nor a Dutch accent was liked in London. 'Ascension Day. They're beating the bounds.' He saw the incomprehension on Balthasar's face, and condescended to explain further. 'They go round the whole parish to make sure of the bounds. The children do it, so they'll remember. They raise a cheer at each marker, to fix it in their minds.'

Balthasar bowed politely. 'Thank you, sir. The custom is strange to me.'

The man gave him a curt nod, and walked away without acknowledging his reply. Well, thought Balthasar, perhaps he should think himself lucky the man had done him the courtesy of an answer. The practice pleased him: London was a formless place of endless flux and change in which new building was going up on every side in hectic confusion without any visible plan. It was somehow reassuring to know that through all this alteration, the officers of the churches were keeping hold on the extent of their responsibilities, and that the sparrowlike children of the city would grow up understanding the streets where they lived.

St James's Park was an occasional resort of his, though not a favourite one; he generally preferred Tothill Fields, south of the Abbey, for his walks. Like much else of London, the park was poised between past and future magnificence. The stumps of great trees felled for fuel in the dark days of the Commonwealth, half-hidden in the grass, bore witness to its glories before the war. The groves of young trees, few more than fifteen feet high, promised pleasant promenades for future generations. But even in its half-grown state, it was trim and charming in the daylight, whatever it might be as the light began to fade. Cows grazed at their ease, and milk warm from the udder could be bought noon and evening from the milkmaids who set up their stools by the Whitehall gate. It was also stocked with exotic deer, including an elk, a huge, shy beast, which he had once glimpsed in the distance, moving through the sheltering shrubbery with a curious, rocking gait like a monster from another age. People strolled here and there chatting and flirting; citizens and their families, prostitutes, thieves and actors, the court and its hangers-on, met, and yet did not meet. Balthasar, walking by himself and watching, saw the way people looked at one another; the ease with which they identified their own kind, and he apprehended once more how foreign he was. Two women were walking ahead of him, elegantly clad in satin, and trailed by a black child in a livery coat: two prostitutes, or a fashionable lady with her maid and her boy? No true Londoner would be confused, but how did one tell? Vizard masks were worn by virtuous and vicious alike; respectable ladies followed fashions set by courtesans. There were clues, there must be; but what were they? Musing thus, he walked towards the avenues which lined the King's new canal, a long, straight stretch of water lined with four rows of trees, which he liked, because it reminded him a little of home. He passed the ladies, and saw their eyes glittering through their masks as they looked sidelong at him; should he bow? The black child was looking at him; and Balthasar was sickened to observe that he wore a silver collar about his neck, as if he were a dog. He looked away, pretending his eye had been taken by a pelican, another of the Park's exotic inhabitants. It was flying overhead, the wind whistling in its great white pinions, and as he watched, it set its wings cleverly at an angle, and arrowed down towards the water.

As he strolled along the south bank of the canal where the pelican now contentedly swam among the ducks and swans, his eye was caught by a group on the far side of the water. An immensely tall man who wore a heavy, full-bottomed wig, nearly as dark of complexion as Balthasar himself, was striding out with a pack of small dogs foaming about his heels. A well-dressed group trailed behind him, but the great length of his legs gave him the advantage, and he had forged well ahead. It was the King, Balthasar realised suddenly, walking among his subjects, quite at his ease, with no fear of assassination or even insult, though little more than a decade since, England had been a republic. Balthasar continued walking, hastening his steps a little, his pulse quickening. If the King meant to circle round the canal, then they would meet. He looked cautiously to see what other pleasure-seekers did when he passed – they stood respectfully, doffing their hats and bowing low, while the women curtseyed, and that was all the ceremony that was used. Heart hammering, he walked on, and a few minutes later, they met. Balthasar caught a brief glimpse of the King's black eyes, thin, heavily lined cheeks and strong nose before he inclined his head and pointed his toe in a formal bow. Straightening up, he gazed after the tall figure until the group of courtiers who panted in his wake passed him where he stood and cut off his view. And what would you have said, your majesty, he asked himself wryly, if I had hailed you as 'cousin', and told you my mother was sister to your father? I am less of a beggar than you were when you were my age, my skin is no darker, and by God, I am a prettier fellow.

An old chagrin stirred beneath his breastbone as the thought of his incredible stupidity moved through his mind; his foolish trust in the honour of Mevrouw Behn, which had lost him his father's books, and the precious certificate of his parents' marriage. He knew who was to blame; the lewd books so impudently left in the place of the cherished manuscripts told a simple enough tale. But he had not had occasion to open one of the books for weeks after his last meeting with her; when he ran to Sint Janstraat, wildly hoping that he could ransom his father's papers, he had been told she was long since departed to England. He might meet her here, he thought suddenly. She was probably still in London; she certainly had not returned to Middelburg. But how could he find her in this city of tens of thousands, when wives and whores alike went masked in public? She might be in this very park, and he would not know her. Eight years had passed; she might have caught smallpox, or another clap, or lost all her teeth: even if she went barefaced, she might be unrecognisable. A noseless, faceless whore, creeping out after dark. It gave him a little comfort, to think of her come to such an end. His pleasure in walking had entirely ceased; he felt tired and depressed. He would walk slowly homewards, he decided, make an early supper at The Cock, off Tothill Street, a respectable establishment which was near to home and kept a good table, and then read quietly for the remainder of the evening after he had done his rounds.

The Cock, late on this holiday afternoon, was not crowded. There was no difficulty in finding a table to himself; there was one by a window, overlooking the courtyard, which would suit him very well, since he could entertain himself by watching the comings and goings. One of the tapsters came up once he had settled himself, wiping his hands on his apron, a decent, sober black man, who knew him.

'What's your will, Doctor?'

'A pint of small beer, John. Later, I will bespeak a supper.'

John Timothy bowed, and went to draw the beer. Balthasar sat for some time, sipping his beer and listening idly to the hubbub of the taproom while the spring sunshine slanted down the sky and evening approached, letting the unmelodious English voices fall into no more than a pattern of sound. He was thinking about the King and his father, and the books which Aphra had stolen. With them had gone all the evidence which proved who he was; if his father had ever imagined that somehow he could declare himself as a royal child, he could no longer do so. But, he very much feared, his father had meant nothing of the kind. It was his personal qualities which the old man had had hopes of, and he had made no secret of his disappointment at finding his child so commonplace. In a way, it occurred to him, losing the books had been something of a mercy. His failure of nerve as a scientist and physician was enough for any man to struggle with. Without the books at hand to remind him of Pelagius's dreams, his failure as a son could be laid decently to rest in the past.

Suddenly, the tapster appeared once more at his side, looking a little ruffled.

'Sir, will you come? A gentleman has had an accident.'

'Surely,' said Balthasar, getting up, and following John as he slipped expertly through the knots of early evening drinkers. 'What has happened?'

'He has cut himself on a broken bottle, though how it came about, I do not know.'

John Timothy pushed open the door of one of the private rooms, and called, as a voice answered faintly from within, 'Sir, I have brought you a surgeon.'

Balthasar entered the room, to find it stinking of spilt wine. The shards of the bottle still lay under the table. His patient was in a chair by the fire, a handsome fellow with notably wide-set grey eyes, though at that moment, very white in the face, and holding a handkerchief tightly round his left hand; Balthasar could see it was already sodden with blood. The light was beginning to fade; he took a candlestick from the mantelpiece, and gave it to the tapster, who lit it, and knelt by the side of the chair holding it so as to give him a good light. The cut, when he unwrapped it, was in the ham of the hand, deep, but not complex, and missing the sinew of the thumb. He sent John Timothy running for brandy, clean rags, a needle and some linen thread, and within a few minutes, the wound was searched, cleaned, stitched and bandaged.

'I thank you, sir,' said his patient, leaning back in his chair and drinking the last of the brandy. 'And your fee?'

'Four shillings, sir. I am Doctor van Overmeer, and you will find me at seventeen Tothill Street if the wound gives further trouble.'

'It will not, I am sure,' said his patient carelessly. 'I have well-healing flesh.' Turning aside, he fished in the pocket of the coat which hung over the back of his chair; a most handsome coat, Balthasar noted rather enviously, with silver lace on the sleeves and fronts, though no longer in its first freshness. Onehandedly, he fumbled with the strings of the purse, and shook out what it contained. When he had handed Balthasar his four shillings, there was not much left.

'I must owe our landlord this reckoning, alas,' he observed.

'I am sorry to have discommoded you,' said Balthasar courteously.

'It is no matter. I have owed him often enough, and he knows he is safe for his money. It is an actor's lot, Doctor Overmeer, to starve between engagements. But we are opening a new play on Wednesday, and I will have money enough, for a while.'

'I have never seen a play,' confessed Balthasar, looking at his patient with renewed interest.

'Come, then. I am with the Duke's Theatre in Dorset Gardens. Go along Fleet Street, then turn down Salisbury Court, or still better, get a waterman to bring you – the theatre fronts onto the river, just after the Temple, and before Blackfriars Stairs. We have been open there for a year, and all the boats know it by now. Bring the half-crown you must lay out for a seat, and some money, perhaps, for entertainment, but leave your purse and your watch at home. The pit is alive with whores and pickpockets, what one does not get from you, t'other will. Let us transport you to a new world, but leave yourself the shillings you need to get home.'

'When does the play begin?'

'Half past three. Come earlier, if you can. The best seats in the pit are on the upper bench at the back, next the boxes, and they are soon taken. If you sit there, you have the support of the boxes at your back, and the advantage of seeing and hearing the great ones round about, if the play is not to your liking, though I hope you will be well pleased.'

As Balthasar approached the theatre shortly after three on the following Wednesday, he surprised himself with his mood of childishly excited anticipation. It was easy to hire a waterman at Parliament Stairs but he seldom allowed himself the extravagance, not only because of the cost, but because the river presented a social challenge to which he felt unequal. It was the custom for oarsmen and their passengers to exchange insults from boat to boat, and his English was still too slow and too literary to let him play the game. All the same, it struck him suddenly, once they were on the water, that for the first time since his arrival in London, he was happy. The May sun warmed him and gilded the buildings fronting the river, and there was much of interest in the journey, sitting at his ease in the stern of the wherry as the oars dipped and creaked and the man shouted back all but incomprehensible responses to his challengers. There was the multitudinous life of the river, where boatmen swarmed like insects; and, slowly passing like a pageant, a sequence of palaces, noble gardens formally laid out with parterres and statues which were seen at their best from the water, the wharves and water-stairs fronting the Thames. The theatre itself was visible from a considerable distance, a stately building of classical form, with columns. It had its own landing-stage, and a good deal of ill-tempered dispute was taking place around it, as each boatman tried to set down his fare. He paid off his own man and mounted the steps to terra firma. Remembering the advice of his erstwhile patient, he did not join the crowd that sauntered in the sun, eyeing one another and gossiping, but went straight into the theatre, and paid down his money. The theatre terrace was self-evidently a promenade for the fashionable, and he had no aspirations to that status.

There were bills stuck on the columns of the theatre, from which he learned that the play was to be *The Citizen turned Gentleman*. The upper bench which the actor had recommended was filling up already, but he was able to get a very good seat. The theatre was as splendid within as it was without, the stage ornately framed in gold like an enormous picture, with a huge panache of arms at the top, whose, he did not know. Elaborate chandeliers, blazing with candles, hung above the forestage, and a row of little dip-lights flickered along the very edge of the actors' space.

The pit gradually filled with a malodorous, chattering crowd – men and women both; most of the women, he suspected, whores, and for the most part, wearing vizard-masks. The audience in the boxes, entering more slowly, was notably better dressed, and there were more women. Many of them seemed to have come to be seen, rather than to view the play. He saw men removing their wigs and combing them, then sauntering from box to box to bow to, or flirt with, acquaintances, ladies sitting shamelessly peering into pocket-mirrors, fiddling with their hair, their rouge, their beauty-spots, and settling with a great deal of complacency to be admired.

When he judged it was perhaps time for the play to begin (following his patient's advice, he had left his watch at home), he saw musicians filing into the gallery, where they began to tune up. An air of expectancy slowly began to rise in the building, though, for the present, nothing was happening. He caught a movement in the largest box, the one immediately on the right of the stage, and then, with a great scraping of chairs and benches, the whole audience rose, and bowed or curtseyed. The King came to the front of the box, and acknowledged the courtesy, then took his seat. He was surrounded by a group of courtiers; on his left, a buxom lady with sleepy eyes and white, voluptuous skin, fabulously bejewelled; on his right, the only man Balthasar had seen as tall and dark as Charles was himself, though considerably older.

He turned to his neighbour on the right, who, like the rest of the audience, was looking at the royal party. 'Excuse me, sir. Who are the man and woman with the King?'

The man looked at him in astonishment. 'Where are you from, cully? Greenland? That is Lady Castlemaine, the King's whore, and his royal cousin, Rupert of the Rhine. I wonder what the Prince is doing here?' the fellow went on, with an insolent familiarity which seemed intended not to inform, but to impress the stranger with his knowledge. 'He is Commander of the Fleet, he should be at sea, sinking hogen-mogens. Perhaps he is come to beg more money for his ships, though if he wants money, he should send Peggy Hughes to wheedle it for him.'

Balthasar realised that he was looking at one of his half-brothers; a strange thought, since it was the first time he had seen one of them in the flesh. One of the oldest of his mother's children by the Elector. He looked a grim old warrior beside the King's urbanity and the lady's luxurious softness. A disappointed man, from the way his mouth was set. A few moments later, Balthasar was distracted from his contemplations; an actor had appeared on the stage, coming forward to speak a prologue, so he settled down to give his attention to the play.

To his great regret, after his eager anticipation, he was profoundly bored and disappointed. The actresses were pretty, in the main; the audience around him was enjoying it, and commenting freely; the party in the royal box could be seen laughing heartily. But for a man with an uncertain grasp upon the English class system, it was impossibly obscure; he could not understand why those around him thought it was funny. Grasping for understanding, he formed the impression that the writer thought it contemptible that a man who had earned money by his own efforts should seek to be respected. Furthermore, as the play progressed, Balthasar began to evolve a lively contempt of his own for the citizen turned gentleman, on account of his aping of the manners of another class, but still more, he heartily despised the sneering wits who assumed that anyone not of their kind was a hypocrite. The pursuit of pleasure and liberty which they seemed to hold up as the best of human goals repelled him. It seemed to him only the pursuit of interest in another guise, and he could not begin to imagine why a man should pride himself on being useless, or why the hero had aspired to so ridiculous a status.

The one aspect of the entertainment which pleased and impressed him was the singing. When the singers and dancers dressed as chemists entered to cure Sir Simon of melancholy, he was greatly struck by one man in particular, a tall fellow, whose voice was quite extraordinary; almost a woman's in pitch, but with a force and timbre no woman could possess. Once the performance was over, he wondered if it might be possible to go behind, and congratulate his acquaintance, for the sake of courtesy. The theatre was not for him, but since he had been personally invited, he thought he should try to speak to the man.

Nothing could be easier, he discovered: fashionably dressed young men were wandering freely behind the scenes. The actors were evidently prepared for this invasion; the ladies, still in their paint and costumes, were each surrounded with a court of admirers, oafish young lawyers and town sparks for the most part, while the men lounged and chatted, their eyes flicking rapidly to either side of their interlocutors lest some grandee should appear. The atmosphere was frenetic, hectic, but cheerful, it was clear that the play was a success, and though Balthasar knew little or nothing about the theatre, he could readily guess that their livelihoods must depend on bringing this fickle crowd back for night after night, since it was obvious to a man trained to observe that the company was working as hard at entertaining the audience in their own persons as they had when in character.

He spotted his patient, whom he now knew to be called Mr Harris, since he had pronounced the epilogue, holding forth with a bottle of sherry in one hand, and a glass in the other. His hand was obviously completely usable, Balthasar was gratified to note, though he still wore a discreet plaster across the wound.

'Ah, the Dutch doctor,' cried Mr Harris, gesturing magniloquently with his glass. 'I hope you have enjoyed our poor best.'

'Very much,' he said politely, bowing, and searching for a compliment which he could deliver with reasonable conviction. 'I very much enjoyed the music, also. I wonder, might I present my compliments to the man who sang so high in the second act?'

'So-ho', said Harris, smirking, 'You are an admirer of the other sweetness, the *mollitudo* of the ancients? Well, I can certainly present you to Mr Piers, nothing is easier.' Taking Balthasar's arm in a familiar fashion, he advanced with him into the next room, where Balthasar immediately saw the singer, leaning negligently against a wall.

'Endymion, sweet soul, I have here an admirer, and perhaps a votary.' Balthasar repossessed his arm, and made his bow, feeling himself assessed from head to toe by the mocking gaze of Endymion Piers. 'A Doctor Overmeer, he cured my hand to a miracle.'

'Enchanted, Doctor.' Mr Piers returned his bow. '"Overmeer"?'

'Balthasar van Overmeer, at your service.'

Piers raised an elegant eyebrow. 'And what sea have you come over, mijnheer, to give you so dark an aspect?'

'You speak Dutch?' said Balthasar, delighted.

'A little.' Piers did not elaborate, but stood looking expectant: Balthasar realised with some surprise that he seemed genuinely to desire an answer.

'I am a citizen of Middelburg, in Zeeland, Mr Piers, but my father was African.'

The singer's lips parted; it seemed for a moment as if he would speak, but a most peculiar expression crossed his face, which Balthasar was quite unable to interpret, and he shut them again firmly. When he next spoke, it was to change the subject. 'You are fond of music, Mijnheer Doctor? You might care to know that Mr Banister, who is the King's Musician, holds musical meetings in his rooms in Whitefriars. These are mostly of new music, sometimes his own compositions, or perhaps the airs of the day. A shilling, a few pence for refreshment, and the best voices in London. Fridays, at five in the evening.'

'Thank you, Mr Piers.' Balthasar was truly interested. He did not himself sing or play an instrument – his father had seen only vanity in such accomplishments – but he dearly loved to hear good singing. The play had been dull, but a musical evening sounded much to his taste. 'I will try to come, if my duties permit.'

Mr Piers bowed courteously. 'And I will hope to see you.' Someone else was at his elbow; he turned away to speak to the newcomer, and Balthasar slipped quietly out of the room. He desired no further entertainment. Though he was conscious of the meaning looks of a number of well-dressed and attractive women, he was shy of whores – and if by any chance the women were not whores, their amateur status was hardly a defence against disease, if they ogled strangers in the playhouse. As a doctor, he knew only too well what such an encounter might bring with it, and as a man, he was not prepared to submit to the drawling impertinence with which town-misses disciplined the insufficiently fashionable; he had heard quite enough of their habits of patronage, quietly listening to what went on around him.

As far as alternative sports went, though he was not wholly averse to an evening's drinking, he preferred to do it within walking distance of Tothill Street; the thought of being alone in the city, fuddled and helpless, frightened him. So, content with his afternoon's pleasures, he left the theatre, and went to look for a boat to take him home.

It was three weeks before he felt justified in allowing himself an evening's recreation. His practice was beginning to build up, and his English was improving to the point where he could comprehend the slipshod speech of poorer folk; he was increasingly a busy man, and perhaps in consequence, was beginning to emerge from the depression and sense of his own fraudulence which had dogged his first months in London.

In his dealings beyond the Dutch community, he had decided to describe himself as a surgeon, even though in England surgeons were of considerably lower status than doctors. This had the incidental advantage of putting him beyond the College of Physicians' monopoly, but more importantly, in his own mind – since he could perfectly easily have sought incorporation into the College if he had chosen to – because after his careful and thorough education at Leiden, he knew he was more competent in that respect than almost any other practitioner in London. His doubts about the value of his work did not extend to surgery: he could set a fracture, reduce a dislocation, or sew a hare-lip to the highest professional standard: the results were immediate and obvious, and he could trust his knowledge and skill. Of course, he treated medical problems, when people chose to bring them to him; and for all his intellectual doubts, his modest success in this field gradually brought him the recognition that in this sphere also, he was doing more good than harm. Further than that, he could not in conscience go.

On the Friday in question, he decided that, since it was a beautiful June day and he was walking into Whitefriars, he would give himself an additional pleasure, and go by the booksellers in Paternoster Row, hard by the ruin of St Paul's. He did not often go that way, since he knew how hard he found it to resist a purchase, or more than one. When he reached the booksellers, he entered a shop at random – he had never been sure if there was any kind of organisation. All the sellers set out much of their wares as unbound sheets on tables, and even where there were bound copies, they were plain-bound in brown calf, so the books could not readily be distinguished from one another – more elaborate bindings were made to order. It made it difficult to judge the character of a book, or even a shop, without looking at it more closely. Turning over a few pages here and there, he found he was looking at play-texts, of no interest to him. A book with verses caught his eye, as another customer glanced at it; alas, it turned out to be verse of the slightest and most trivial kind, the book was called *Covent-Garden Drolery*, a title which, he thought as he dropped it disdainfully, said all that a man of sense would need to know about it. He asked the bookseller to direct him towards colleagues who dealt in more serious works, preferably with a medical interest, and was duly pointed along the row.

'This is new over from Holland, sir,' said the bookseller, once he had explained what he wanted. He turned over the title-page of the book thus indicated, and stopped at the author's name, astonished. Johannes van Swammerdam: Jan, his old university friend, whom he had not seen or thought of in ten years; and the book was called *Miraculum naturae sive uteri muliebris fabrica*, the miracle of nature, or, the construction of the uterus in women. Fascinated, he leafed slowly through the exquisite plates, and as he did so, a long-forgotten afternoon returned to his mind; the only dissection of the female organs he had ever seen. He remembered that Jan had been at his side, and his own depression, though the reason for it now escaped him; Jan's interest and enthusiasm also came back to him, fresh in his memory. How very strange. For him, the afternoon was only a dim and unpleasant memory, but for Jan, it must have been the beginning of a ten-years' work.

There was no doubt in his mind as he looked at the result; he would have to buy it, whatever the cost. He had never been asked to perform a caesarian section, but surgeons were very occasionally called upon to do so by a desperate midwife when the woman's life was already deemed lost, and an heir was in question. He dreaded such an approach, but this book was by far the best he had ever seen on the anatomy involved, and would do all that could be done to prepare him, should be ever find himself faced with the dreadful task. *Miraculum naturae* was expensive enough to make him blink, but he paid the price without demur, and left orders for a plain calf binding. The

bell of Christ's Hospital sounded the half-hour as he was con-
cluding his bargain, and made him jump. Time to move on to
Whitefriars.

The evening which followed repaid his most sanguine expec-
tations. It was a gathering of very gentlemanlike fellows in a
panelled room of some elegance, with small groups of chairs and
little tables here and there about the floor, and a collation of
cakes, wine and ale on a sideboard with a servant in attendance.
At the far end of the room, a harpsichord stood waiting, with
a man in a dark coat standing by it, who was presumably Mr
Banister. Mr Piers greeted him courteously when he entered,
and introduced him to James Nokes, another actor of the company whom he vaguely remembered having seen on stage. Nokes
greeted him with a sort of grave, childish simplicity, standing a little too close, and looking up into his face in a way
which gave him pause. The man had been like that on stage,
he remembered, and for no reason he could see, had set the
pit in a roar. He suspected a shrewd mind behind the simple,
almost helpless air, and was duly on his guard. Mr Nokes clearly
found his response in some way unsatisfactory, and turned away,
leaving him to find a seat on his own, as Mr Banister stepped
forward to begin the first song. His voice was a full, sweet tenor,
perfectly trained, expertly ornamenting the notes with shakes and
flourishes.

> 'Drest Seraphins, put on your softest wings,
> Glide eas'ly from above:
> With blisses Heaven's fruition brings
> Refresh the panting hopes of Love.'

The alto Mr Piers and a third singer, another tenor, joined him in
the chorus, in a harmony so exquisite it was almost painful. 'Charm
him, charm him,' they sang;

'Then with a bee-like hum
Gently wake,
For Hero's sake
Leander from Elizium.'

Balthasar felt that he had been transported to Elisium as he sat; never had he heard such singing. Between airs, he was perfectly content to sit on his own and look about him. There were interesting people in the room: his eye was particularly caught by the group nearest to him, a dark man with a remarkably brilliant and piercing gaze, notable for his air of suppressed energy, for all that he was lounging at ease in his chair. He was sitting with a younger man, very fair and girlish in the face, whose expression was closed and secretive. He spoke to his dark friend from time to time in a confidential monotone, while his *vis-à-vis* replied in grunts, or not at all.

Another very striking individual was sitting by himself, notably upright, with his long white hands clasped together over the gold head of his cane. He was old and beautiful. He wore his own hair in the old-fashioned way: it had receded a little at the front, leaving him with a high and noble forehead, but it swept down over his shoulders, snow white and plentiful. He had a hawk nose, and a ruddy, healthy complexion; his eyebrows were finely arched, and he looked the picture of placid, antique dignity: his expression was quizzical and kindly.

When the music had at last come to an end, Mr Piers came over once more. 'You are a man of science, Doctor van Overmeer. Let me introduce you to Mr Bushell.' To Balthasar's great pleasure, his discreetly pointing finger was indicating the elderly man who had excited his interest. Piers saw his expression, and continued without waiting for his assent. 'Mr Bushell has much to commend him in his own right, as you will find, but he is also a link with a greater past. As a young man, he was servant to the wonder of the age, Sir Francis Bacon, Lord Verulam.'

Balthasar was almost overwhelmed by the thought. The author of the *Advancement of Learning* and *The New Atlantis* was to him, a fabulous figure. All his professors at Leiden had reverenced the name of Bacon; men of science, Dutch as well as English, were content to acknowledge that they lived in a Baconian world. And the man before him had worked with him, perhaps, even, touched him! Reverently, he scrambled to his feet, and crossed the room, hat in hand, behind Mr Piers.

Mr Bushell was as gracious as his kindly expression had led Balthasar to expect. 'You are a surgeon, Piers tells me. Leiden, or Amsterdam?' His voice was low, and very sweet, it seemed to caress the ear.

'Leiden, sir.'

'Excellent. As good a medical school as the world affords, outside Italy. Well, Doctor van Overmeer, I am pleased to make your acquaintance. I live in Lambeth Marsh, a little out of the way, I fear, but it suits me well enough, and I have been there this twenty year. If you cared to attend me there, I would be pleased to receive you.'

'Mr Bushell,' blurted Balthasar, 'I would be honoured to attend you in Lambeth.'

'Sunday, then. You will attend church in the forenoon, no doubt, so perhaps you will take your dinner with me. You will find my house by the pointed pyramis, as you come from Southwark. Expect no Lucullan feast. My meals are simple, but I enjoy a little company on occasion, and I hope to see you on Sunday.'

V

Love a woman! You're an Ass
   'Tis a most insipid passion
To choose out for your Happiness
   The silliest part of God's Creation.

Let the Porter and the Groom,
   Things design'd for dirty slaves
Drudge in fair *Aurelia*'s womb
   To get supplies for Age and Graves.

Farewell *Woman* – I intend
   Henceforth every Night to sit
With my lewd well natur'd friend
   Drinking to engender wit.

Then give me health, wealth, mirth, and wine,
   And, if busy Love entrenches,
There's a sweet soft Page of mine
   Does the trick worth Forty wenches.
   John Wilmot, Earl of Rochester, 'Song', September 1680

'Thank you, Kit. A dish of anchovies, a neat's tongue, two dozen of oysters, and a bottle of claret. And we do not wish to be disturbed.'

The tapster bowed correctly, and left them to themselves. Mr Bushell and Endymion Piers were sitting together in a private room in the Blue Boar, off the Whitechapel Road; an inn well known to them both, since it was one of London's molly-houses: that is, a place where men with an interest in their own sex discreetly foregathered.

'Well, Dim,' began Mr Bushell. 'Why have you attracted my attention to this blackavised herring-eater? He is not, I think, a ganymede, or even one with an interest that way. I observed his speech with Mr Nokes, and he was deaf to all that was said to him.'

Piers shrugged delicately. 'To be sure, it is but a poor, staring hogen-mogen, fresh from Hog-land. But I know something of the creature, and I think he may yet serve some turn or another. It is also possible that he commands wealth far beyond anything he seems to be, though of this I am not certain.'

'You are mysterious, Dim.'

'It is something of a tale. Listen, here comes Kit with our little supper. Once he has gone, I will tell it you.'

A moment later, the tapster entered, with napkins over his arm, and a tray in his hands. He arranged their dishes on the round table between them, poured two glasses of wine, bowed again, and left them.

Endymion Piers held his glass up to the light, swirling the wine, took a draught from it, and began. 'You know, I think, that before my engagement with the Duke's Company, I was for some years secretary to one Johan Behn, a merchant in a small way of business, and a rogue and cheat on a somewhat larger scale?'

'A connection of the bouncing Astrea, was he not?'

'Her husband. He was a handsome fellow, but a boor, and a man of violence – she is a woman of no judgement. However. When that prince of commerce still adorned this sublunary world, he sent me to Holland on one occasion, where he had left the fair Astrea to rusticate most unwillingly among the butter-boxes. While she was there, by some means known only to herself, she purloined two books from this little Dutch doctor, and showed 'em to me when we returned to London. She was an intelligencer for the King, not paid at that time, but a useful informer, as I found out later from Thom Killigrew, so doubtless she had her methods. But alas for her, the books were in Latin, you see, so she needs must come to me for a version. As it turned out, the one was not worth the paper, some species of vapouring divination, but the other was a diary of a kind, and hinted at a most interesting tale. The writer was an African, a prince by his way of it, and in his latter years, when he wrote this account, a psalm-singing Puritan, driven mad by dreams and prophecies. The substance of his story was that, after many adventures too tedious to recall, he became secretly the husband of a lady of quality. Our doctor, I think, is the son of that marriage. He is a mulatto, beyond doubt.'

'And the lady? Have you any clue?'

'Mrs Behn believes, and I think she has reason, that the African we speak of was the confidential servant of the Queen of Bohemia – confidential enough, perhaps, to creep into the royal bed. Recall our young doctor's face, Mr Bushell, bating the tawny skin; it is a long oval, and think how his eyes are set. He is not like his majesty, who is Medici to the core, but he has a look of the Duke of York, who favours the Danish line. So did the Queen of Bohemia.'

'Well, well, well. So, so. The Mystical Lady of the Rosy Cross had a tooth for dark meat in her latter years. Other women of quality have had a taste that way – it was whispered in 'sixty-four, I recall, that the Queen of France gave birth to a blackamoor, though I'd not vouch for the truth of it. Pour me another glass, Dim. This is a strange tale indeed, and needs consideration. This diary that you saw. Do you have it to hand, and are you sure it spoke of a marriage? Our van Henk is not a by-blow?'

'I have not the diary, alas. Mrs Astrea took it back, and I have not thought of it from that day to this. I do not know where it is gone. The African wrote in clouded terms, and perhaps thought he concealed all, but he wrote of marriage, without a doubt. In any case, the man was a canting precisian, and not, I would guess, an hypocrite; he would not have recorded fornications without groans of penitence and cries for divine forgiveness. How her majesty found herself a black of this kind, when there are grinning ostlers and broad-backed footmen to be had for a shilling, I cannot imagine.'

Mr Bushell shrugged, and took a silver toothpick-case from his pocket. He attended to his teeth with slow deliberation, while Piers sipped his wine and watched him, content to wait. 'And what earthly use is this information, Dim? *Cui bono?* There is no evidence that I can see.'

Piers spread his hands. 'I cannot tell as yet, but surely there is something. When we know a little more of this doctor, perhaps we will have a better idea. In any case, who knows what he inherited from the lady, his mother? Surely the doting Queen loaded her Ethiop with diamond collars, and set pearls a-gleam in his sooty ears, as Titania adorned her ass-headed love. The town misses do as much for their negro pages, and they have not the jewels of a queen at their disposal. The doctor will have reaped the benefit, no doubt, and he is mightily impressed with you; so you may yet draw the Queen's moneys to your ends. What do you owe? A hundred thousand? More?'

Bushell sipped his wine. 'My dear Dim, I have been in debt so many years, I am a veritable master of the art, and I make myself very easy on the subject. I truly think that it is the great-grandchildren of my creditors who must pursue me, and many of them have forgot I am still breathing. So; what do you think we should do?'

'I think I had better try to ensure that he does not meet with Mrs Aphra. I have some regard for the woman; she plays the flute to perfection and writes most wittily, and I fear that he might be quite unreasonable. It was the purest luck she was not there this evening – where frowning Jack Hoyle goes, these last weeks, you will find the fair Astrea, making eyes like a lovestruck milkmaid.'

Mr Bushell tittered, a soft, not altogether pleasing sound. 'The dark fellow, little Ned Bedford's particular friend?'

'That is he.'

'Well, Mrs Aphra is wasting her sighs, I should say. He was not made for the use of women, or I mistake myself.'

'Molly he is, sir, and no doubt of it. I have taken a turn with Madam Jacky myself, on occasion. But the Dutch widow has a great taste for dabbling in mysteries properly closed to her sex, whether wit, scribbling, man's-flesh, or secrets, she has been thus since I first knew her. Indeed, she is something of a female Rosicrucian in herself — she refuses to comprehend that there are mysteries not to be attempted or attained by the fair sex. But in any case, I think her fancy for Jack is no great mystery. He is a violent man and ruthless, in some respects not unlike the late Captain Behn, though dark where he was blond. She must have a liking for the type, and I think sometimes there are those of the sex who positively prefer to sigh over what they cannot have.'

'You may be right, Dim,' said Mr Bushell dismissively. 'I have not made them my study.'

'I thought I would find you here,' said Endymion Piers, dropping carelessly onto the bench beside her. The coffee-house was well frequented, even at that early hour. It had long been one of the principal meeting-points for the many actors, town-misses and men of fashion who lived in Covent Garden, a number of whom spent much of the day there, using it as something between a club and a place of business. Aphra was one of them; snugly settled in a corner by a window, she had papers and a notebook spread on the table before her, and was writing with fluent, practised ease.

Aphra raised her mug to him, and took a swallow of her ale. 'And where should I be, but Chatelin's, to watch the world go by?'

she asked, laying down her pen and shuffling the papers before her into a rough pile. 'It saves on coals, and I hear the news. Have you taken your morning-draught, or would you care for coffee or chocolata?'

'I have breakfasted, thank you.'

'How goes *The Citizen*?'

'Very well. The King and the court are pleased, and the cits come in their droves to see if they can fathom what the jest is. Your young friend Ned Ravenscroft has made fifty or sixty pound by it, with his third-night's fees, and it will be printed. Prince Rupert has agreed to accept the dedication.'

'Oh, I must write to Ned. It is matter for congratulation.'

'Indeed.' He seemed about to say something else, then changed the subject. 'I believe I will take a glass with you after all. Hey, potboy! A pint of your London ale, an't please you.'

While he waited for his drink, staring out impatiently into the room, Aphra watched him carefully. The years were being kind to him. He was better dressed than he had been in the days when he had been Johan's man, but he was still lanky, still in possession of a misleadingly youthful complexion, and he wore his clothes with the same casual air. She understood him, she felt, a great deal better than she had in the old days. Johan, sarcastically amazed at her obtuseness, had eventually told her bluntly that he was a sodomite, and once she had got over the shock and her chagrin at her own naïveté, she had realised that the fact dramatically simplified their relations. They had associated for some time after Johan's disappearance, in a joint effort to rescue something from the wreck of his fortunes, but since he had found a place in the Duke's Company, they had seen far less of one another. It pleased her that he still remembered that she liked to drink in Chatelin's coffee-house.

The potboy came by with Mr Piers's ale. 'Here's to old friends,' she said, pledging him, as he picked it up.

He clinked cans with her, and drank. 'Some old friends are more welcome than others,' he observed.

'You are cynical, Mr Piers. There is no old friend I would not welcome, ay, with open arms, however poor he had become. We children of liberty must stand as one another's allies.'

'Balthasar van Overmeer?'

For a moment, the name meant nothing to her, then the memory connected. She felt the blood draining from her face, and wondered momentarily if she might faint.

'He is not so very poor, I am pleased to say,' Mr Piers continued, affecting to misinterpret her. 'He is a doctor in Westminster, in quite a prosperous way of business, or so it would appear.'

'What is he doing in London?' she croaked. Something seemed to have happened to her voice.

'What does anyone in London? It is the great mart of the world, and draws men to it like the Charybdis of the ancients. He is here, and there's an end to't. Mrs Aphra, I have a memory of a book we read together, eight years ago. It was a spiritual journal in the Latin tongue, and it belonged to a certain van Overmeer, did it not?'

'Yes,' she managed, with her tongue trying to stick to the roof of her mouth.

Mr Piers pounced on the admission; she had always been a little afraid of him in these moods. 'Aphra, what has happened to the book? What use have you made of it? I want the whole story, and none of your cogging.'

She drank some of her ale with a show of indifference, but her heart was pounding. 'Piers, you are not my keeper. What right have you to question me?'

He put his hand on her wrist; his grip was moist, cold and strong and made her shudder. 'Aphra. I have the right of a man who knows where you both live. I have an interest in this information, and you will give it to me. Where is the book?'

'I have lost it,' she confessed.

His breath hissed through his teeth, and she doubted very much whether he believed her. 'Truly, Mr Piers,' she hurried to say, 'I would not lie to you. I had it for the rest of that year – it inspired me to begin to think of a play, one of the first I ever essayed – *The Female Rosicrucian*, do you remember? I told you about it, at the time. It was to be about a woman, the Lady Bianca, and how she was cozened by Rosicrucian adepts into marrying a blackamoor. Johan was going between England and Zeeland that spring, you were often in Harwich, and I was left much to myself. I had my draft and the book and some private papers in a wallet, and one day, he came into our lodgings in a great hurry, and set the place by the ears looking for clean linen and certain papers of his own. In his haste, he took my wallet in mistake for his – that was the end of May, and that was the last time I saw him, as you very well know. The book may be in Middelburg, if it is anywhere. It was you who made enquiries afterwards, and you told me Petrus had said that he had got safely over, and it was on the way back that *The Good Intent* was caught up into the Battle of Lowestoft and sunk. This is all true, upon my honour.'

'Honour? Honour is a word. A man must eat, and words are an ill diet for a man – or a woman. I have a friend who has need of this book, and I ask you to remember it. Oh – and Aphra,' he added carelessly. 'If I were you, I would avoid John Banister's. The black doctor has a taste for music.'

'Thank you,' she said humbly, alert and on her guard. 'Mr Piers, if you know or discover anything of van Overmeer and his haunts, can I trust you to let me know?'

'My dear Mrs Aphra. You can trust me, as I trust you.' The pale, blinking eyes mocked her, as he raised his can, and swallowed the last of his beer.

On Sunday morning, Balthasar put back the shutters of his room and let the June sun pour in on him. He had awoken full of excited anticipation, and looked forward greatly to the day's adventures. Standing in his shirt with the sun warming his breast, he scratched his head and felt his scalp prickling under his fingers. Time to get his head shaved again. He took his wig from its block, and turned it around, looking at it critically, letting the heavy curls fall through his hands. It was in passable condition, and he could improve it with a combing, but it would benefit from professional attention. For today, it would have to do.

On an impulse, he sat down in his shirt before the mirror, and settled the wig on his head. Whose hair had it been, he wondered for a moment. He had heard tales that unscrupulous wigmakers had bought the hair of men and women dead of the plague, though he did not think this wig was such a one. Good hair was taken from the living head, since it rapidly lost its lustre if it came from the dead, and this was a good wig. But it was so unlike his natural hair, he had taken some time to accustom himself to the way the curls moved about on his back and shoulders as he turned his head. Looking at his face framed in English hair, the question came into his mind: could he pass for a white man?

He stared into the mirror, and considered his face as if it belonged to a stranger. The skin was dark, a warm brown, especially against the white of his shirt, but much lighter than that of true negroes like his father and Narcissus. His eyes were brown-black, but so were many another's, including the King's. The nose was long and decently prominent, even inclined to the Roman, with nostrils not notably expanded, and though the lips were strongly cut, the mouth was not very African. On the whole, the shape of his face was more like his mother's than his father's, especially in the upper part. With his dear-bought curls tumbling about his shoulders, he asked himself the crucial question: if an Englishman saw this face, would he necessarily see a mulatto, or might he be taken for a sun-scorched East-Indiaman? His anxious gaze gave him no clear answer, and abruptly he stood up, disgusted with himself. It was all one, anyway. He was the son of a king, and he had no desire to deceive any man.

He dressed himself with care; his best shirt with the lace wristbands, which annoyed him by never being as well cared for as the linen Anna used to get up for him, his best breeches, and his one pair of silk stockings. With the green silk coat and his good, red-heeled shoes, he hoped that he looked the gentleman, but not over-fine. He played momentarily with the notion of buying a cane, such as Mr Bushell had wielded so elegantly, but he doubted his ability to handle it with grace and ease. Time was getting on; soon he must go to church. As he clattered down the stairs, it struck him suddenly that it was the first Sunday since his arrival that he had gone to Austin Friars thinking of anything other than the plight of his country.

The journey to Lambeth was a complex one. Once the service was over, he rode down to London Bridge from Austin Friars, and crossed for the first time into Southwark. It was almost more like riding along a street than a bridge, because of the tall houses on either side, though the roaring of the water through the narrow arches below remained as a constant assertion of the river and its force. He looked up curiously as he came to the gatehouse on the south side. Yes, as he had been told, high above him were stakes, leaning at angles from the gatehouse roof, each tipped with a roundish object: the heads of the regicides Cromwell, Ireton and Bradshaw were there, and had been for ten years, tarred to preserve them from the weather, lest their ill fame fade from the memory of man. At that distance, they were dark, irregular oval masses. He could not tell which was which.

Once across the bridge, he was in unknown territory. Between Southwark and Lambeth, houses stood one or two deep along the bank of the Thames, but as soon as he ventured inland, he found himself in a mysterious landscape of marshlands, fields and polders, crossed by a few causeways raised against the floods; not unlike parts of Walcheren. The fields were lined with rows of willow and alder, obscuring the houses and the river, and flocks of wild duck flew up from among the reeds, quacking in alarm as he trotted past. It was hard to believe he was little more than a mile from London.

He was approaching Lambeth itself, having not yet passed anything which could be taken for a gentleman's residence, and was beginning to worry: he had ridden in a straight line while the river bent in a great bow, and the castellated towers of the Archbishop's palace were distantly visible beyond the embosoming trees. But there was a copse over to the left, and within it, some sign of masonry. A branch of the road went that way, and he followed it; approaching nearer, he was delighted to observe the steep sides of a tall structure, and knew he had found out the place. Bushell's house was curiously retired behind a screen of trees and the 'pyramis', which stood in front of it. It was what Balthasar would have called an obelisk, some twenty feet high, with no obvious purpose, and heavily overgrown with ivy. The house itself was a gentlemanly lodging, of three bays on three floors, thus very nearly a cube of red brick trimmed with white stone. He left Dowsabell in the stable, where a slouching boy came forth to receive her, and Mr Bushell met him on the steps.

'My dear Doctor. As you can see, I live very privately, but it is a great pleasure when true seekers after knowledge disturb my solitude.' As on their previous meeting, Bushell was quietly dressed in a plain, rather old-fashioned black coat and breeches, but his linen, though it boasted no ruffles or lace, was of immaculate whiteness, challenging comparison with his snowy mane of hair. With a courteous gesture, he welcomed Balthasar into the house.

Balthasar stepped in, passing beneath an inscription which read 'INSTAURARE ET PERFICERE', and looked about him in admiration. The hall where he stood was hung with black baize, and floored with chequered black and white marble: it went back the entire depth of the house, thirty feet or more. The oaken staircase was adorned with carved balusters, each with an ambiguously smiling head set upon an intricately carved narrow pillar, like a classical herm, gleaming with polish. As Balthasar stood, hat in hand, admiring the fineness of the work, the row of dark faces marching up to the first floor seemed all to be looking at him as if they knew something which he did not.

A grey-clad, elderly man came from the back of the house, and made his bow.

'My servant Jack Sydenham,' said Bushell, 'and indeed, my friend and coadjutor, as I was my Lord Bacon, Lord Verulam's. In the 'fifties, I became obnoxious to the Parliament, sir, for my loyalty to the late king, and if I had been taken, I was to be hanged, but all the same, for several years before the glorious restoration of his son, I lived here where you now find me, going out only at night to walk in my garden. Only Jack knew I was even in England, and he lied most nobly on my behalf, whenever enquiries were made.'

'You are both to be congratulated, Mr Bushell,' said Balthasar politely. 'You for inspiring loyalty, and Mr Sydenham for showing it.'

Mr Bushell bowed in response to the compliment, and touched Balthasar's elbow with his long, white fingers. 'Let us go to the parlour, mynheer. Jack has a little collation for us, I think.'

Mr Bushell's eating-chamber was at the back of the house, overlooking the garden. This was a somewhat unusual one: there were yew-trees of many years' growth, clipped into cones and leading the eye towards a curious grotto, edged with pendant, icicle-like stones, presumably natural formations of some kind, though Balthasar had never seen the like. They gave the arched opening the look of the mouth of a giant fish, he thought, or Hell-mouth in a picture of the Last Judgement; and he thought further that he would not care to enter the darkness beyond and look out through those teeth. The room itself was not hung with pictures but decorated with mottoes painted onto the panelling of the walls: 'IN GEHENNA NOSTRAE IGNIS SCIENTIAE', 'DE CAVERNIS METALLORUM OCCULTUS EST, QUI LAPIS EST VENERABILIS', 'HAEC OPERATIONEM NATURAE SECRETAM CONFORTAT', and many more; they meant nothing to him, though they suggested strongly that Mr Bushell actively continued the work of his late master.

The table was set with a somewhat meagre meal; there was salad, bread, a dish of eggs and a dish of herrings, but no meat. Mr Bushell himself ate only dry biscuit and a dish of green herbs: lovage, lettuce, purslane, and others Balthasar could not readily identify, dressed with a little oil, mustard and honey. He drank water, though there was wine for the guest. 'This is the diet for a philosopher,' said he, smiling gently, 'most like to that of our long-lived fathers before the Flood. The fumes from the decoction of wine and meat, ay, and even white-meats such as I have set before you, depress the aerial and Heaven-tending aspects of soul and body, and clog the brain with particles of crude matter. He who aspires to become an adept and to reach beyond the sublunary sphere must first master his diet, as a step towards mastery over himself.' Balthasar swallowed what was in his mouth, and laid down his fork, discountenanced. 'No, no, continue,' urged Bushell hospitably, 'you are young and strong. The fires of the body burn brighter in one of your years, and you may eat these simple foods without harm.'

But for all that he could say by way of encouragement, the meal was swiftly over. Sydenham brought nuts, Malaga raisins and gooseberries for a dessert, but when Bushell waved them away, Balthasar was too diffident to fill his plate; on his host's insistence, he took one or two of each, and a little more wine. Bushell, meanwhile, leaned back in his chair, sipping his glass of water, and discoursed brilliantly on his memories of Bacon, and his own adventures in natural philosophy, most particularly, in mining and metallurgy.

'I mined lead and silver in Cardiganshire at the beginning of the late war,' he said, 'greatly to the benefit of his sacred majesty at a time of direst need – the metal was known of, but it lay deeper than any had dared go. I devised a method of driving in fresh air to the mine, and improved the adits so that the poor Welshmen could go with safety down to the deepest veins. The ore was refined there and then, and both silver and lead sent in secrecy to Oxford, where the late King Charles had his capital, until at length Cromwell came to hear of it, and set a guard upon the road. I received a warning in time, and was at pains to conceal where we had worked and to destroy the ventilation I had devised, so he got no benefit from it, but alas, neither did his majesty from that time onwards, greatly to his hurt. I have some more silver mines in view now, in the Mendip hills, and now that the times are more settled, I hope to make them a true benefit to the King and the nation.' Bushell drew back his chair. 'Well, sir, if you have dined, let me take you to the Long Gallery. I walk there always after meat, to compose my mind.'

Balthasar obediently followed his host up two flights of stairs, to the attic floor. The Long Gallery was, in the nature of things, not very long, perhaps forty feet, since the house was a small one; it stretched the entire length of the frontage. However, it was perhaps the strangest room he had ever entered. It was entirely hung with black baize and pedestals mounted with arrangements of skulls and bones were regularly disposed along the wall, while further mottoes hung about the walls. At the one end was a niche in the Gothic style, perhaps taken from an old church, and painted on the wall within the space thus defined, so as almost to deceive the eye, was a skeleton lying on a mat. The opposite end had an answering painting of an emaciated cadaver, which reminded Balthasar of the shrivelled, wind-dried relics of pirates and murderers which hung on the town gallows in Middelburg. By one of the windows was a telescope mounted on a stand, and a collection of instruments for measuring the position of stars: he recognised a sextant and a quadrant among them. The motto over the astronomy window was 'COELUM PENETRAVIT ACUMINE MENTIS': he recognised it after a moment's thought as a quotation from Lucretius, the atheist philosopher of antiquity. Bushell's voice broke into his inspection. 'This is my spiritual chamber, mynheer, where I meditate upon the stars, the supralunar spheres, the heavenly kingdom, and the journey we will take there. I disposed the room in this fashion, when the King met his martyr's end. We now have the satisfaction of seeing his son restored to the throne, but long before that day, I consecrated this room to his sacred memory, and so it will remain, while I am in life. I come here every day and think of him.'

Between the central windows, with a skull-topped pedestal on either side, was a black curtain; as he spoke, Bushell pulled the tasselled cord, and revealed a half-length portrait of a sad-eyed man with a lace collar and a pointed beard, his slender hand resting on the head of a large dog.

'Is this the first King Charles?' asked Balthasar.

'Of course. But I thought you would know that, Doctor van Overmeer? It touches you more than most, after all.'

Balthasar's heart gave an unpleasant lurch: he stared at Bushell in astonishment, while the older man looked back at him, with the hint of a smile in the corner of his mouth and eyes. 'You have no resemblance to his present majesty,' continued Bushell placidly. 'He favours the mother's side; it is the Italian strain which has come out in him. But the late King Charles and his sister the Queen of Bohemia were very like in the upper part of the face, and they had the same speaking eyes.'

Balthasar remained silent, hoping that his confusion was not apparent, determined to say nothing either to confirm or deny. Had Bushell some secret source of knowledge, some form of divination or celestial monition, or was this a lucky guess? 'It is a handsome face,' he said neutrally, 'and of a most sweet and Christlike patience.

It is easy to see why his people loved him, and why so many cherish his memory.'

'Ay, he could draw men to him,' said Bushell softly, 'and so could his sister. They called her the Queen of Hearts. I saw her, you know, before she left England.'

'Did you so?' He spoke before he could stop himself.

'My lord Bacon was the chief contriver of the masque presented by the gentlemen of Gray's Inn and the Inner Temple, on the occasion of her marriage. Her marriage to the Elector, you understand. My lord devised a most beautiful conceit of the marriage of the Thames and the Rhine, with infinite store of lights very curiously set and placed, and many boats and barges with devices of light and lamps. I was but a younker of seventeen or eighteen, hardly three years into my lord's service, and I was one of those charged with the lighting of the lamps at the due moment. I saw the Princess coming into the hall, shining like a star wrapt in a cloud. She wore white, and there were diamonds in her hair, and spangling her dress, but the cloud was her amber hair, hanging loose in those the last days of her maidenhood, and the stars were her topaz eyes, which outshone her diamonds. She was a nonpareil, the pearl of Britain, and all who saw her, loved her.'

Balthasar swallowed. He did not know how he could possibly reply. 'I would like to have seen her,' he managed.

Mr Bushell gazed at him, with eyes which seemed to pierce through to his inmost heart: he hoped they did not. The moment prolonged itself; then, mercifully, Bushell changed the subject.

'This room is for spiritual, astronomic and spagyric works,' he announced. 'As you will have observed, my house is arranged according to the order of the cosmos. Whereas this floor signifies Heaven, I designate the first floor *Terra*, the floor of the earth, where I think about the world, and matters which concern it. I attend to my mining and alchemical concerns on the ground floor, since they are subterranean, and concerned with the elements. The stair of wisdom links one with the next. Come, Mynheer Doctor. Let us descend to the earth, which is to say, my great room on the floor below.'

Thankfully, Balthasar followed him down the stairs, and into the room designated *Terra*, immediately below the so-called Long Gallery. Unlike the room above, it contained a number of presses with books, and a desk littered with papers of all kinds. Bushell gestured towards it. 'I have given my life to completing my master's work in the world. My lord Bacon had no son of his body, but I was his chosen disciple, and to the best of my poor ability, I have been his son in art. I claim nothing on my own account, as the emblem before the house will have told you; the pyramis grown up with ivy stands for a loyal servant who looks only to his master for support. What you see before you, mynheer, is the first fruit of my lord's hopes for the Great Instauration. This house is itself a building designed for the first stage of execution of my lord Bacon's *New Atlantis*, as its inscriptions show, and when I have opened the mines in the Mendips which I mentioned earlier, I intend to build Solomon's House, an invisible college of true wisdom, philosophy, and the love of God, either here, or more probably, in Wells, where I own land: in God's good time, I trust that it will lead to a reformation of morals and of the world. But as matters now stand, I cannot look to the King; I must be my own Maecenas – so if I build the New Jerusalem, as I hope, its walls will be of silver from my own mines.'

'Did you discover these mines, sir?'

'Ay, I did indeed. I have, I think, given you reason to suspect, Mynheer Doctor, that I can see a little further than most men. My eyes have been washed clean by the dew of heaven, by long waking, light diet, and many weary hours with the *arcana* of this world and the next. I have waked and studied and prayed for many an hour when my fellow man has allowed himself the refreshment of sleep, and I have gone up and down in England for many years looking at the rocks and the earth and reading their secrets. My spagyric enquiries directed me towards Somerset, and when I walked in the wild country of the Mendip hills to see why I had been thus led, I saw in the folds of the rocks the selfsame argentiferous formations I had seen in Cardiganshire long ago. If I can but attract some men of faith and vision and open this mine, we will have our own, native Potosi: the wealth of Peru will lie open for the taking here in England, without the dangers that attend the Atlantic voyage.'

Balthasar was fascinated. 'But can you not get the help of the King?' he asked. 'His majesty is a friend to the sciences, or so I have heard. And so loyal a follower of his father, the servant of so great a man, will surely get a hearing?'

Bushell smiled very kindly, shaking his head a little in fatherly regret. 'My dear young man, you betray your years. All good men should think so, when they are your age, but though Heaven send it is not so, you may find when your hair is as white as mine, that sad experience has taught you otherwise. My lord was disgraced, as many a great man has been; it was a shameful busines, so shameful he scorned even to make a defence. His memory is stained, and his servants have no honour. And I am stained further in my own right; was I not arraigned for treason? It is true that in this age of the world, what passed for treason then is loyalty today, but the memory of man is short, and the name of traitor sticks to a man like a brand. Furthermore, the world forgets that when I opened the mines in Wales, I poured silver into his majesty's coffers, and sent him a hundred tons of lead to make bullets. Much of that was necessarily secret, and the spending of moneys in wartime is like the pouring of water on sand, which leaves nothing to show for the labour. But, for that Cromwell could get nothing from 'em thereafter, it is bruited about now that I deceived them all, and cried up a mine where nothing was to be had. I am not bitter, my dear young sir. I have endured the reproaches of malicious minds, and worn a fool's coat in the repute of men more ready to condemn than to examine. You may judge for yourself what I am worth; look into my face, or look around you, examine any book or paper in the house that you have a curiosity towards. I have no secrets. I conceal myself only from those whose minds are made up before they come upon me. I will die, or I will finish my lord's work; whether it is the one or the other is in the hands of God.'

His simplicity and resignation were powerfully impressive. Balthasar made no move to examine the papers on the desk, which seemed to him intolerably rude, but looked reverently around the room. He had seldom wished for princely status since the time when he had outgrown childish fancies of infinite power and riches, but at that moment, listening to Mr Bushell, he wished passionately that he commanded royal wealth. It was absurd, and worse than absurd, that the King's whore should wear thousands upon thousands of pounds in gems in her ears and on her breast, while men such as Bushell were poor and neglected, though they were struggling to do the work of God and benefit their fellow creatures. 'I must go, I think,' he said after a while. 'It is a long way to London Bridge, and back along the other side to Westminster, and there are one or two professional calls I should pay this evening. I am most deeply honoured that you have shown me your work, and I shall pray for your good success.'

'The prayers of an honest man are always grateful. Come again, if you wish, and perhaps I will entertain you further. You have the makings of a true adept, sir, and it may be that I can teach you much you would find useful. I seldom stir abroad, but there are times when I must watch over a long experiment, perhaps for days and nights, and at such times, I am not to be seen. Write me a letter when you have a mind to see me again. My direction is not well known, and my name, alas, known to many of the ignorant and vicious, so if you will, address your letter to Mr Brown, and send it to the Seven Stars inn by St Mary's Church, Lambeth. Jack

Sydenham will collect it – he runs errands in Lambeth two or three times in the week.'

Balthasar jogged bridgewards across Lambeth Marsh, excited and with much to think about. Evening was starting to come down as he reached Southwark. The sky was still light, but pink and gold threads of cloud were beginning to drift among the summer blue. He was wary of Southwark itself; from what he had seen on the way out, a lone, well-dressed man was hardly safe in such an area. Once he got into the patchwork of gardens and huts on the outskirts of the settlement, he turned down towards Bankside as soon as he could, thinking that the river path would be better frequented and hence safer, but he still found he was looking nervously about him. It was not the custom for a doctor to carry a sword – indeed, if he had, he would hardly have known how to use it – but he began to long for a good, stout cudgel. Lurkers there were, shabby figures in twos and threes, plodding indifferently about their business, but none offered to molest him.

Mr Bushell's words were much in his mind. They resonated curiously with things he had heard long ago, in ways that Bushell could hardly have guessed at unless he truly did consort with spirits; he had been brought up among dreams. But Bushell's practical Baconianism, his projects for the scientific amelioration of mankind, seemed to Balthasar to rest on sounder, more empiric, foundations than his own father's hopes of a Just King and the rule of the saints, which had left the hows and whys of the longed-for revolution entirely to inscrutable workings of God.

Coming along Bankside towards the bridge-foot, he was some distance from the landing-stage by the Old Swan when he heard a confused shouting. Instantly on his guard, he approached warily until the situation became clearer. A group of hulking, ill-clad men were standing on the towpath, yelling abuse at a wherry, in which a gentleman was taking his passage across the river. The boatman was leaning on his oars, in fits of laughter, sculling a little to keep the boat on the spot against the tidal downrush from London Bridge. The passenger, a well-made young gentleman, perhaps in his late twenties, was standing up in the stern with his hands on his hips and flinging back insult for insult with great good humour, in the voice of Stentor. He had an olive complexion, an aquiline nose, and black eyes and hair, and he wore a small, pointed beard; he was keeping his balance against the motion of the boat as easily as a bird on a swaying bough. Balthasar realised his initial impression had been quite false; for all the yelling and the savagery of the language, both sides were more in jest than earnest, merely trading insults according to the custom of the river.

One of the men on the bank stepped forward and shouted, 'Yer ugly, funking son of a Bridewell bitch! Pimp to yer mother, stallion to yer sister, cock-bawd to the rest of yer relations! How dare ye show yer face upon the river, and fright the King's swans from holding their heads above water!' His cronies roared, and nudged one another with their elbows in appreciation, as the man in the boat digested the words; Balthasar could see his chest swelling, gathering air for his reply, which came ringing clearly across the water:

'Son of a mangy nightwalker! Y'are so like a monkey in the face, it's known the length of the river that an indictment is preferred against your wife at the Old-Bailey for bestiality, where you are to be arraigned to prove your species!'

Balthasar could not help but snort with involuntary laughter. To his relief, the group on the towpath ignored him. The lout's face reddened, and he stepped back, while another barged forward, hastily saying, 'Let me at him, I have one,' then shouting, 'Cuckoldly ninny-hammer! You were born to be hanged, travel where you will by water, for you need not fear drowning!'

'You parcel of rogues, what care I for your words? If all had their rights, I would be emperor of the world, and set you a-rowing in the galleys like stinking Turks!'

'Emperor of my arse!' a man roared back. Balthasar, who being on horseback had a five-foot advantage in height, was horrified to observe from the corner of his eye that a sizeable vessel, lent impetus by the ebbtide, which had just shot the rapids under London Bridge, was bearing down on the little wherry with terrifying speed: the men on land and the men on the boat were so absorbed in their combat that they had failed to observe it.

'Look out, sir!' he yelled, as loudly as he could, setting Dowsabell plunging in fright.

The man's face changed, and he looked swiftly round. He shouted at the waterman, who bent to his oars with a will, sitting down quickly as the boat spun about and was gradually clawed free of danger. The louts and Balthasar watched anxiously until they saw it emerge clear of the wash of the larger craft, which seemed to be some kind of lighter, perhaps carrying coal, and saw the waterman pulling strongly for the Salisbury Court Stairs with his passenger seated in the stern.

The group before him broke up in perfectly good humour, shaking their heads a little in reluctant admiration. 'He'll be a naval man,' Balthasar heard one say. ''Tis only the navy can cuss like that. I'll remember that one, about the monkey.'

He rode on, mulling over the incident. The man's ready wit and address represented so much of everything that he was not; he could not but feel a pang of envy. The words which stuck in his mind, though, were 'emperor of the world'. How, in what way, was an English gentleman the emperor of the world, or had it merely been a jest? Yet if it was a jest, the other men had not understood it. Strange, and in all probability, he would never get to the bottom of it.

Mr Bushell watched his guest out of sight. 'We will see that young man again, Jack,' he said to Mr Sydenham, who was standing behind, watching with him. 'I do not know when it will be, but the gudgeon is nibbling; he is not yet on the hook, but I think I will have him. Bring a piece of toasted cheese and a bottle of claret to me in *Terra*, my dinner was of the most subtle and philosophical, and I am sharp-set. I must recruit my strength a little, before my evening's work.'

'At least he will not come upon us without warning,' commented Mr Sydenham, 'you have seen to that.'

'Aye. The accommodation address is a thing of many uses. Well, Jack, my dear. Let us go about our business.'

In the days that followed, Mr Bushell made his preparations with some care. He had a number of projects in hand: he was trying to establish a system whereby prospectors would bring specimens to him for free assaying, thus providing him with useful information about mineral resources through the country, and this required a good deal of letter-writing. The best venture he had on hand himself was the Mendip one, which was extremely uncertain, and would require many thousands of pounds' investment before anything came of it. However, if he could but establish himself as a central clearing house for information, then there might be something better to be had. Meanwhile, all possible sources of backing for the Mendip project must be canvassed, including the somewhat uncertain one of Mynheer Overmeer.

The first step was to secure a picture of Elizabeth of Bohemia. There were many such; after Jack Sydenham and he had made discreet enquiry, he was pleased to find a print after Mierevelt of the Queen as a young matron, in the printseller's by the Exchange. She was wearing a ruff like a millstone, and if Overmeer had any memories of his mother, they would be in clothes of a later date, the ruff would have to go. He cut out the head, and glued it with white-of-egg to the back of a piece of glass; then once it had dried, he began delicately rubbing at the reverse of the image in tiny, circular movements with a piece of moistened sponge until he had removed virtually all of the paper, and the lines of the engraving could be seen glimmering through from the back. When it was completely dry again, he ground some pigments in linseed oil; lead white, lamp black, red and yellow ochre, with a touch of vermilion. He mixed a series of flesh-tints and applied them to the back of the paper: the oil, soaking into what remained of the paper, rendered it transparent. It needed no great skill to sketch a swanlike neck below the face, an expanse of bosom, a twist of dark, gauzy material over the breasts, to scumble the edges of her hair and the bodice of her dress into stygian darkness, and coat the rest of the slide in opaque black. It took most of an afternoon to complete the work to his satisfaction, and when he had finished, he held it up to the westering sun, and smiled. The Queen's face and bosom leaped out from the glass, strangely lively, due to the transparency of the colours. He put it carefully to dry, and went to write letters.

In addition to the principal chamber, *Terra* contained two back rooms; one was Mr Bushell's own bedroom, the other a study or closet, which could be entered from the main room, which on the following day, he did, taking with him a candle. It was tight shuttered, and like most of the rooms in the house it was hung with black baize. The wall to the left of the door was not simply black-hung, in fact, though this was not apparent to a casual eye, a section of the thick, matte fabric was a curtain, and at a discreet tug from a cord, it whispered aside, revealing a small area of bare, white plaster wall, little more than a foot square. On the opposite wall, the black baize was hung some way out from the actual plaster; Mr Bushell pushed the curtains open, and revealed behind them a strange device; a box containing a brass tube fitted with a convex lens. Opening the box, he fitted his glass-painting into a frame within the structure which had been made for its reception. Deftly, he lit a stub of candle which stood behind the tube and in front of a hemispheric mirror reflector, set so as to concentrate the light and funnel it towards the lens. Mr Bushell shut the curtain before his

magic lantern, making sure that the hole for the mouth of the lens
was correctly placed. A moment later, the grave face of the Queen of
Bohemia sprang to life on the patch of white plaster of the opposite
wall, and he adjusted the focus until it was sharp. He pulled the cord
of the other curtain; between the dense, unreflective texture of the
baize and the feebleness of the candle, he was pleased to observe the
picture was not visible, though the cone of light emanating from
the hole in the curtain opposite was dimly to be seen. He opened
the box, and lit his own candle once more: with a stronger light
in the room, the cone disappeared. He blew out the candle in the
magic lantern, well pleased. He was a careful man; he would never
risk such a show without a careful testing of the perfection of all
elements. There was a connecting door between his bedroom and
the closet; Jack knew very well how to take a cue, and could be
relied on to slip through and light the lantern at a point when the
gull had his back to the curtain and was sure not to observe the
gleam of the lens.

VI

Love is now become a trade,
All its joys are bought and sold.
Money is a feature made
And beauty is confined to gold.

Courtship is but terms of art:
Portion, settlement and dower
Softens the most obdurate heart.
The lawyer is the only wooer.

My stock can never reach a wife;
It may a small retaining whore.
Let men of fortune buy for life:
A night a purchase for the poor.
Henry Playford, *The Theater of Music*, 1685

A week or two later, towards the end of June, Balthasar was summoned to the bedside of his friend and patron, Daniel Everaerts. Full of concern, he reached for his bag and hurried up the road to see what the problem might be. He was under no illusions: so young a man as he had been sent for simply because he was living in the same street, whereas Everaerts's usual doctor must live further afield. The case, therefore, was a very urgent one. He found Everaerts in bed, in an immaculate white gown, with a handsome red velvet nightcap to protect his shaven head from the draught. His wife, buxom and still handsome, hovered anxiously by the bedside, together with Everaerts's confidential servant, who had brought him. It was a very well-appointed and elegant room which he thus entered for the first time: it had good oak panelling, and was hung with pictures which caught at him even in the moment he could spare to look around: there was a portrait of a younger Daniel Everaerts which could only have come from the hand of his own old friend, Cornelis Jonson, and several pictures of Middelburg which gave him an immediate pang of homesickness. But Everaerts was breathless and bluish in the face, with sunken eyes; there was no time for gaping around.

'Have you had pains in the right arm, sir?' he asked at once.

'Yes, he has,' replied his wife; Everaerts himself merely nodded, barely moving his head. It hardly needed his taking the pulse to confirm that the action of the heart was gravely impaired. He scribbled down a prescription for a strong cordial containing the most efficacious ingredients he knew for the strengthening of the action of the heart, Venice treacle, bezoar, gold-leaf and prepared pearls in a vehicle of syrup of cloves, and sent the man off with it at once; while waiting anxiously for his return, he asked Madam Everaerts to send to the kitchen for hot bricks, wrap them in wool, and put them by her husband's feet, under the covers. She moved quickly and quietly to do as he said: he watched her speaking to her gentlewoman, a competent-looking girl with squarish, rather masculine hands and auburn hair, and took note of the manifest concern and affection for their master which was written on the faces of all the servants in the room, male and female alike.

'Warmth and quiet are the key,' he directed. 'He must be watched, of course, but for now, he should be left to himself.' He looked across significantly at Madam Everaerts, who took his meaning: in an undertone, she directed the gentlewoman who had brought the bricks to take her place by the bed, and led the way out of the bedroom to her husband's closet, shutting the door behind her.

'Madam,' said Balthasar quietly, so as not to disturb the sick man, 'what brought this onset about, do you know?'

She looked up from her hands, which she had clasped together in her lap. Her large grey eyes were still pretty, though they were shiny with unshed tears. She was English, he knew, and considerably younger than her husband, and she might reasonably hope to marry again, so Balthasar was moved by her concern for him. 'Grief, Doctor. He has been wearing out his heart over the news.'

'What is the news, madam? I have been busy with my patients, and I have had no time to make enquiries. I have heard nothing since the news of de Ruyter's success against the English fleet. I thought we were in better case?'

'The English are held off, indeed, but we are assailed from all points on land, and compassed by our enemies. The French have taken the south, the Bishop's troops have taken the north. Only Holland and Zeeland are still free. Mynheer Everaerts collapsed when he heard the news of Utrecht.'

'Dear God,' said Balthasar, dry-mouthed. 'What has happened to Utrecht?' He could hardly believe what he was hearing. Utrecht was in the very centre of the country! he wanted to protest; feeling how his own heart was beating, he well understood how an older man might have been overset.

'The city surrendered. There was not even a siege, they opened their gates to the French. There will be Catholic Mass sung in the cathedral. Mynheer Everaerts has held up his head well enough in the face of disaster, but dishonour has brought him low.'

Black, burning shame filled him. 'And how did this come about – I am sorry to cross-question you, madam.'

'Oh, I do not mind speaking of it. The citizens were wild with fear. They thought no defence could be made, so they made none.'

Balthasar sat in silence, almost stunned by what she had said.

'We must all pray for better news,' he said finally. 'Let the secretary seek news each day, and if there is any amelioration in the fate of the Netherlands, make sure your husband knows at once. Hope is the best medicine for a condition brought on by despair.' Madam Everaerts nodded, pale and serious.

Balthasar turned to questioning her about her husband's medical history, and took notes on his tablets of all that she said. It sounded to him as if a weakness in the action of the heart was a problem of long standing, which the shock of the news had thrown into an acute form. There was a knock at the door: the secretary had returned with the cordial. Balthasar and his hostess returned to the bedroom, and he carefully administered a dose. It was hard for Everarts to swallow, and Balthasar retired, full of doubt as to the outcome.

When he returned home, it was to read everything he had about the action of the heart, and how to strengthen it. His books left him in worse perplexity than before; they seemed to contradict each other at every turn. Warmth and rest were easy recommendations, all were agreed on their benefit. Many authorities recommended purges and cathartics, variously administered; it seemed to him that his patron's life flickered so low that to attempt a cure by such means was to risk its complete extinction. There was a stoppage of urine, perhaps a byproduct of the oppression of the heart, but a diuretic might cause further strain . . . He feared to do nothing, but feared equally to do too much. In his great difficulty and perplexity, a thread of memory came to him; his father, for dropsies and weaknesses of the heart, had often used a tincture of foxglove. Foxglove was not even part of the English pharmacopoeia, there was no mention of it, except in the older herbals, and there was no scientific basis for its use – though it was true that his father's experience, insofar as he remembered it, suggested that in cases of dropsy, it seemed to procure some kind of purgation – but it was gentle. He could be seen to be doing something and not sitting with folded hands to watch Everaerts die, but he would not be taking the risk implicit in heroic intervention. There was no point in trying a pharmacist, since it was not a plant in any kind of use, so taking the boy Jacob for the sake of speed, he set off for Tothill Fields, where in this late June, foxgloves were almost certainly to be found.

Even in his mood of anxiety, he enjoyed Tothill Fields, a pleasant, open area of rising ground, with good views down to the river and across Westminster to London: there were patches of vegetable gardening, fenced with quickset to protect them from marauding cows, and open areas where cattle wandered freely. There were also areas set aside for horse racing and other sports, and as a single gesture towards elegance, a maze. It was too countrified an area to attract the smart whores and idlers who frequented St James's, and for that among other reasons, he liked it. It was a place frequented by gardeners, milkmaids and cowmen, decent folk, and people with some good reason to be there. He was looking for barren, sandy ground, which he would certainly find towards the highest point of the Fields if he needed to go so far, or for hedges, either of which might yield a stand of foxglove.

It was a hedge he came upon first; on the far side were comely rows of summer cabbage, and in the shade of the thorny barrier were the serried, pink-and-white ranks of foxgloves, their witchy towers of soft, tubular, freckled blossoms moving a little in the breeze. He shouted for Jacob, who was searching in a different direction, and between them they filled a wicker basket with the flowers and leaves, which the lad carried home. A dislikeable plant, he thought to himself; there was something distasteful in the way the texture seemed wilted even while the plant was still growing. All the same, he borrowed a pipkin from Betty, and made a decoction: when he called again in the evening, he took it with him.

The cordial had done nothing to help. With great misgivings, he persuaded a little of the foxglove tea into Everaerts's slack mouth; after half an hour's anxious watching, he was convinced that it was doing no harm, so he gave him some more before he went on the round of his other visits. He found his patron very considerably better the following morning. Madam Everaerts, tearful with relief, was able to show him a full chamber-pot after days of stoppage; the man's face was a much better colour, and the beat of the heart undeniably improved. But with his natural delight in success was mingled a sort of chagrin: there was no classical warrant for employing foxglove, which the herbals described as bitter, hot and dry, and useless. The cure, for such it seemed to be, was an offence against science. He hated to find himself a mere empiric, such as his father had been, applying specifics ignorantly with no theory; as the thought crossed his mind, he seemed to hear his father speaking: do you value your pride, my son, if there is hope of a cure? Yes, said the other side of his mind, stubbornly at war with himself. It is not personal pride, Father, it is faith in system and the integrity of knowledge. But for all that, he decided, he would trust in foxglove, which seemed, by contrast with what he had learned, both gentle and efficacious. A useful first line of defence, indeed, though it seemed like a kind of surrender. He promised himself a series of animal experiments, which might at least give him more security on the question of quantities, and bring his practice more within the realm of science.

Everaerts, on a regular dosing of foxglove, continued to improve. Madam Everaerts cried Balthasar up as a miracle-worker, greatly improving his practice, though in Balthasar's own opinion, it was the news, in the first week of July, that William III had been made Perpetual Stadhouder of Zeeland and Holland which had truly set his patron on the path to recovery. Everaerts had been profoundly relieved. 'He will turn the tide,' he declared from his sickbed. 'A state does well enough with a mercenary army, but it must be led by a noble. Pray God that the young man can take control of our stiff-necked people.'

Once Everaerts was out of danger, it was possible for Balthasar to give a little time to his own concerns: with one thing and another, he had hardly left Westminster in a fortnight. He would have enjoyed another evening at Mr Banister's, though for a young doctor still building up his practice, an evening away was decidedly an extravagance. Bushell was also on his mind; but on a more purely mundane and immediate level, he was anxious to visit a good tobacconist. While he was not a great smoker by Dutch standards, he liked his pipe, especially in the evening, and he was fastidious about tobacco. What he had was running low, and also becoming a little dry. Lonely as he was, and his regular visits to Everaerts's well-ordered household had brought home to him powerfully how much he wanted the wife he could not yet quite afford to keep, he was determined to enjoy such pleasures as his life permitted him.

Accordingly, having finished his morning visits one Tuesday, he turned Dowsabell's head towards London rather than returning home. He would visit Mr Howes of Fleet Street, the best tobacconist in London, and take his dinner in town. He was in cheerful mood as he rode east. Everaerts was almost better, and the whole affair, though sad enough, had undoubtedly served his own professional advancement. Furthermore, bating purely selfish concerns, if there was a thread of hope for the survival of the Netherlands, it was undoubtedly in the Stadhouder, now firmly in command of the parts of the country which remained free.

He found his visit to Mr Bushell very much in his mind as he trotted sedately past Scotland Yard. The bulk of his practice was in Westminster and the area immediately contiguous; there was another Dutch doctor in Spitalfields, a Deventer man from Overijssel who, though he was a specialist in cutting for the stone, was skilful enough in general practice: the Dutch community of the

City tended to give him their custom. Few occasions, therefore, apart from the Sunday journey to church, found him riding east beyond St James's, in the last two or three weeks, there had been none. He must write to Mr Bushell soon, he vowed to himself; Everaerts was clearly out of danger, and his time was more his own.

The idea of the Invisible College moved him profoundly, and he longed to be part of it; it occurred to him that it might even in some way be the fruition of his father's hopes for him: certainly, it was the only idea which had come his way which carried any possibility of his being anything other than a very ordinary fellow. He knew himself humbly as no manner of genius or virtuoso, no innovator like his erstwhile friend Swammerdam, who had approached his studies with a level of passionate intellectual interest which Balthasar knew that he himself could not command. On the other hand, there must be a place for doctors in the Great Instauration: even men new-made would not have bodies of light. And if improved diet and the practice of virtue made illness a thing of the past for the fortunate philosophers, there would always be a place for a surgeon, for accidents there would surely be from time to time, and a man cannot reduce a dislocated hip by philosophy alone. He could not, to his regret, help Bushell with his projected silver mines, but he wanted seriously to discuss with him the possibility of offering his services to the Invisible College itself, once it began to take shape. Perhaps he should drop into a scrivener's and buy paper and a pen; the General Letter Office was in Bishopsgate, a good way beyond where he was going, but he began to wonder if he should take advantage of being more than halfway there, and send Mr Bushell a note.

These thoughts took him most of the way along the Strand, and almost to Fleet Street, but once in Fleet Street itself, his mind began drifting into reflections about tobacco. A song which Mr Piers had sung in the play came back to him: 'Naught is so sure, and perfect a cure, as wine, as mirth, and good company, and if aught doth lack, 'tis a pipe of tobac – coco – coco – coco'. Unlike almost everything else he had heard in the theatre that afternoon, it seemed to him perfectly true. But the tobaccoes available in London were naturally different from what he was used to; while the common folk of the Netherlands smoked coarse, home-grown stuff which was produced in Utrecht and Gelderland, often flavoured with spices to disguise its rankness, he had always favoured a plain blend of fine-quality imported leaf from Brazil and Venezuela. On his last visit to Mr Howes's shop, he had plumped for Oroonoko, thinking that it would be a South American leaf such as he was used to, and had found it rather disappointing.

Benjamin Howes's establishment was a dim and unprepossessing shop at the corner of Shoe Lane. He handed his mare's bridle to one of the ragged wretches who had started up on seeing him dismount, pushed the door open, and walked into the dim interior. The shop was full of drifting wreaths of bluish smoke, enough to make him cough: there were benches around the walls, and on them, a group of elderly men were whiling away their time smoking and exchanging desultory conversation. A figure of a very different kind was standing by the counter.

'A roll of best Spanish chewing-baccy, sirra,' he said sharply. 'I'll have none of your funking mundungus.' The voice was pleasant, but remarkably clear and penetrating; after a moment, Balthasar, with a shock of pleasure, recognised the young gentleman he had seen in the wherry.

A roll of tobacco was produced; and the other first smelt it carefully, then taking out a clasp-knife, he cut a little and put it in his mouth. Observing Balthasar watching him, he raised an eyebrow humorously. 'If a man is being asked to pay eight shilling a pound, it behoves him to make sure he gets what he pays for, lest roguery flourish for want of a check,' he observed.

Balthasar was somewhat shocked. Eight shillings seemed to him a colossal sum for a pound of tobacco. 'Perhaps you could advise me, sir?' he said tentatively. 'It is clear you are an amateur of tobaccoes. I am used to best Brazil, and I would like something of the same kind.'

'Virginia,' said his acquaintance promptly and with decision, while the spotty youth behind the counter nodded his agreement. 'Give this gentleman your best old, mild, sweet Virginia, small cut. It is pipe, not chewing tobacco you want, I imagine?'

Balthasar nodded, and the assistant weighed out a pound of Virginia, and showed it to him in the scales. It was loose, unlike the tight, sticky roll the other man had bought, and looked and felt more like tobacco as he knew it. The smell was very agreeable, and he nodded. 'Twenty pence, sir.'

Balthasar fumbled in his purse and produced a shilling, a sixpence, and the two odd pennies, relieved that it was no more, while the youth shot his tobacco into a paper cone, which he secured at the top with sealing-wax. The other man pushed two half-crowns and three shillings across the counter, and they both pocketed their purchases, and walked out together into the sunlight. He wanted to say something, but he was too bashful to scrape an acquaintance.

'I have seen you before,' said the other man suddenly, as they stood blinking together in the doorway while Balthasar fished in his pocket for a penny for the horse-holder. 'On that horse . . . You were on Bankside, were you not, when the lighter came within a touch of running me down? I believe I owe you my life.'

'You have a ready memory, sir,' said Balthasar, surprised and gratified. 'As ready as your tongue. It is something indeed to hear a gentleman outswear a riverside lout.'

The other man shrugged. 'It is but a trick of the mind. I seldom forget a face, and yours is a little out of the common. Tell me, if you will. Are you a Dutchman? You speak good English, but I hear Holland in your voice. And do I not also hear a touch of Scotch?'

Balthasar bowed politely. 'I am Dutch, sir, brought up in Zeeland, but I was taught English by Sir Thomas Urquhart, a Scot, and a friend of my father's, who was settled in our town. He has perhaps left me with a tincture of Scots in my speech. My ear for your language is not good enough to detect it. My name is Balthasar van Overmeer, and I am a doctor in Westminster.' He hesitated a little, out of shyness. 'Sir, it is coming on to dinner-time. If you have no other business to prevent you, may I ask you to bear me company?'

The other bowed in return. 'Lieutenant Theodore Palaeologue, at your service. I will dispute your right to the reckoning though. I owe you rather more than the cost of an ordinary already. I am an officer in his majesty's navy, but I do not pursue my quarrel with your countrymen on the level of the individual. I have a great admiration for your de Ruyter. He was outnumbered and outgunned at Sole Bay last month, but for all that, he made a pretty hash of the Frenchmen, and sent our first-raters limping home in such a style that all an honest man can say is to regret that he is Dutch and not English. With such an admiral, we would have been docked in the Great Harbour at Amsterdam a fortnight since.'

They began walking back towards the Temple together, Balthasar on the outside, leading Dowsabell, who plodded patiently after them like a dog. 'I am glad, then, that you have not,' he said frankly.

Palaeologue laughed. 'Spoken like a good fellow. This is not a war of principle, which should make us enemies at heart. Though as a matter of honour, I must do my duty when I am called upon, this is naught but piracy on a national scale. The pretext for war is of the scantiest; and it is only too clear that his majesty is but acting as the jackal of French Louis. Speaking as a private citizen, I have little stomach for seeing a Protestant nation swallowed up by France, merely because your merchants and ours are quarrelling in the Indies.'

St Dunstan's was coming into view; it had had a lucky escape from the fire, and had been ornamented as a thank-offering with a new clock-tower containing a remarkable device, two figures with clubs, who struck the bell which hung between them every fifteen minutes. They were at work as Balthasar and Lieutenant Palaeologue approached; the clock said half past one. A little way beyond the church was the Cock and Bottle; they turned in there, and Balthasar committed Dowsabell to the care of an ostler. He asked for, and was shown, a private room, and ordered a dinner; the tapster offered them a capon, a dish of hog's puddings, a salad, a barrel of oysters and a dish of curd-cakes, and Lieutenant Palaeologue declared himself well content with the fare. They settled down comfortably to await their meal, and Balthasar, who had insisted on his right to play host, poured wine for them both.

When they were finished with their food and were onto the second bottle, Balthasar broached the question which he had wanted to ask from the beginning. He was greatly taken with his guest, and very much wanted to know more about him.

'Lieutenant Palaeologue, something has been running in my mind. When you routed those lubbers on Bankside, you said you were the emperor of the world, or should be so, if all had their rights, did you not? Why did you so, may I ask?'

Palaeologue smiled. 'Does my name mean anything to you?'

'It is "ancient word" in the Greek tongue. Beyond that, nothing.'

'Well, sir. The Palaeologi were the last emperors of Christian Greece. I am directly descended from the brother of Constantine XI, who lost the throne of Byzantium when Constantinople fell to the Turks. The family settled in Pesaro, and became subjects of the Medici. My grandfather Theodore served the House of Orange as a soldier of fortune in the Low Countries, so I can say that my family has trailed a pike on behalf of your countrymen. He came to England after that, and was gentleman rider to the Earl of Lincoln. My father Ferdinando fought for Charles I at the Battle of Naseby, and like many another follower of the King, fled to Barbados, where he has recently died. I am his only surviving child, and as you already know, I am seeking to make my fortune in the navy, though with the present retrenchments, I see little chance of doing so.'

'So you are the last Roman emperor,' said Balthasar slowly. The thought was dizzying.

'It is all one. That was another age of the world. I am proud of my descent, which is no common one, but I said it only to puzzle those loobies. I do not dream over what might have been.'

'I commend your good sense sir,' said Balthasar, then in a rush, added, 'I am in somewhat of a like case.'

'Well, sir,' said Palaeologue, his eyebrows rising, 'I think you must be the first man who has ever responded thus to my tale. How so?'

'My father was a king in Africa. He was dispossessed, and sold as a slave, though he was afterwards made free. I am his only child. My given name, as you know, is Balthasar, but I also carry the name Oranyan. My descent goes back to the founder of the kingdom, who bore that name. His sword is carried by each king of Oyo in turn.'

'So, Doctor van Overmeer. Do you dream of returning to Oyo, and wielding the sword of your royal ancestor?'

'I do not,' Balthasar confessed. 'What would I do in Africa? I would not know how to begin unseating the usurper Egonoju, or more like his son, from a throne he has held for fifty years. The Oyo are a great nation, I believe, but I know little of their ways, and nothing of their tongue.'

'We are of a mind, then. I have no stomach for driving the Turk from Stamboul. Descent is a tale for a winter's evening. A man's life is his own. I do not contemn pride of blood, of course. When all is said and done, to be the shadow of a Caesar — or of a king of Oyo — is to be a little more than a poor Christian gentleman, but we are men, and not walking ghosts or the dreams of our ancestors. As mere men, we must do our duty in the station to which God has called us.'

There was, to Balthasar, something extraordinarily liberating in Palaeologue's attitude. He had been so used to thinking of his life as his father had presented it to him, as one which was necessarily in thrall to his ancestry; the notion that he could simply be himself was profoundly appealing. Palaeologue's words seemed to justify the mute rebellion against his father's dreams which had been gathering in his mind for years. True, Pelagius had never implied that he should storm the throne of Oyo, while the notion that he should dispute the throne of England with King Charles was obviously absurd. But he carried a burden of his father's expectation all the same, which was related in some way to his birth: yet, he thought suddenly, that did not mean he himself need seek to be king of anything, literally or metaphorically. Palaeologue had somehow made himself at ease with his ancestors; could not he do the same?

He enjoyed the dinner more than he had any meal since his arrival in London. Palaeologue was well read without affectation, a sincere Christian, and an entertaining conversationalist with a knack for evoking wit. Their talk ranged over many subjects, but for much of the evening they discussed the Bible, and the relationship between its revelations and the discoveries of modern times. In particular, Palaeologue proposed the topic of Africa: if the peoples of Africa were descended from Ham, son of Noah, and therefore laboured under a primal curse, did this justify their enslavement in modern times? Such debates had been meat and drink to his father Pelagius, and he found himself well able to hold up his end of the argument.

Balthasar knew himself generally shy and dull with strangers, yet he realised that he was talking to this man with an ease which he seldom felt. He had been crushingly lonely since Narcissus and Anna had died, brought up in a terrible awareness of lineage, but as a man alone and apart. In the strangeness of his inheritance, the Lieutenant was something more like a brother of the spirit than he had ever before attained to, even as a student in Leiden.

It seemed strange in a way to be talking so readily with a man who had compassed the death of Dutch sailors, but as Palaeologue himself had implied, he was the most honourable of enemies. He also insisted on paying the bill; when they parted, it was with the assurance that he would dine at Balthasar's house the next Sunday but one and allow him to make due reparation.

In the interim, he decided, as he reclaimed his horse and mounted, he must see Bushell again. He would ride to Bishopsgate and leave a letter for him, as they had determined. He had an inkling that the old scientist was perhaps the man to show him the proper course of his life – at any rate, he was the only man he had ever encountered who gave him the faintest hope that he might in any fashion realise his father's dreams.

Mr Bushell received him on the steps with the same courtly simplicity as on his previous visit. 'Welcome, Doctor van Overmeer, I am so glad you could come,' he said smilingly, as Balthasar doffed his hat and bowed. He stood to one side, and ushered his guest into the house. 'Perhaps today you would care to visit the *Mundus Subterraneus*? You did not see it when you were first here, that I recall.'

'I should be delighted,' said Balthasar. Bushell led the way to the room to the right of the staircase, which had DOMUS PLUTONIS over the door, and stood back courteously to let Balthasar enter first.

'This is the domain of the metals and of fire, hence, the house of Pluto,' he explained.

It seemed at first to be no such thing. A number of plain cabinets with drawers stood around the walls, together with a bookpress. There were several tables, including a large oak one, positioned to catch the light and covered in a variety of scientific instruments:

Balthasar recognised one of the new 'microscopes', the finest he had ever seen, set behind a complicated device for concentrating light, such as he had heard of, but not seen, and there were also a number of instruments for weighing, bottles and flasks of different kinds, and several mortars. The hearth was a complex structure which included something like a bread-oven, while a brazier and a number of crucibles stood ready on the hearthstone.

'The table of touchstone belonged to my lord Bacon himself,' said Bushell, indicating a small table with a matte black top, 'It came to me as part of my salvage from the wreck of my lord's fortunes.' He indicated the instruments on the table. 'These are the tools of assaying.' Pulling open a drawer, he removed a lump of blackish rock and handed it to Balthasar. 'Here, for example, we have galena, metal-bearing ore from my silver mine in Wales. This is my *prima materia*. We may examine it, in the fashion of the Royal Society, with a microscope: here before the window is an instrument made by Richard Reeve, the best maker of such things that this or any land affords. If we remove a shaving from the ore and put it beneath the lens, we will learn nothing whatever. It is formless to the eye, and no less formless when we examine it more closely. It cannot be weighed, numbered, or measured to any great effect. For it to yield its secrets, it must be subjected to fire, closely covered away from the influence of the air. The correct application of heat and pressure will yield the noble metals. Lead, copper, silver and gold are latent within this black stone, and the art of the metallurgist, as Lord Bacon taught it me, is to nourish and bring forth these precious metals from the dross which cumbers them. Gold, being the noblest and most subtle, is the hardest to coax forth, second comes silver, third copper, then lead. How they appear, and in what proportion, depends on the skill of the operative.'

Balthasar turned the stone over in his fingers, looking at it with interest, and realising that he had never thought about where metals came from – the Netherlands surely imported most if not all of what they used; certainly, there were no mines in Walcheren that he knew of. The stone told him nothing, even on closer examination. 'Is not the proportion of metals within the stone a quantity fixed by nature?' he asked.

'By no means. The man of knowledge can increase the metals he desires by providing due nourishment for them, though gold, because of its subtlety, is very difficult to increase. The alchemists of old gave their attention to gold, which represents, both philosophically and practically, the pursuit of an ideal, and hardly any were successful, though we hear that the finest of them, Doctor Dee and Sir Michael Scot among others, were able to breed gold to their desire. It seemed more practical to my lord Bacon that humbler practitioners should instead pursue the lesser metals, which require a less high-tempered heart in the adept, and less subtle instruments in the extraction, and are therefore amenable to an industrial scale of production. I took these precepts and put them into practice in Cardiganshire, and hope to do so again before I die.'

'I thought metals simply lay in the ground,' confessed Balthasar.

'Sometimes they do.' Bushell opened another cabinet, and handed him a piece of rock brightly veined with copper. 'The task is easy, when the metal lies so patent. It can simply be melted out. This copper has come into being through a natural decoction and refinement within the bosom of the earth itself. Gold itself also sometimes appears in pure veins, most notably in the Americas, or so we are told.'

'Someone once told me that there are mountains in the Americas where gold runs down with the rivers,' said Balthasar.

'It was likely true. Gold is peculiarly heavy. When the rock around it is disturbed by the action of frost, the water, as it melts, will tumble the exposed metal down with the stream, so that it lies like gravel in its bed, or is moved along by the current. I have never seen this, though I have often read of it – if there were ever golden rivers here in England, they are long since exhausted. But it is only the noblest metals which the earth can purify and refine without human aid. Baser metals, such as iron and tin, are never found in pure form. Here, also, are metals,' he continued, handing his guest further samples, 'though they do not seem it. This redness indicates iron, either in a latent or a corrupted form – you will know the corrupted form as ordinary rust. This green, similarly, indicates the presence of copper. You will have observed, I think, that the action of air on copper causes the surface to become green. For the most part, as the samples I have shown you will have indicated, certain earths, or certain varieties of rock, can be identified as the matrix which will give birth to a particular metal, or very often, more than one. It has been my life's study, one which I consider a sacred trust.'

Bushell paused a moment, looking at Balthasar very soberly. 'I came into my lord Bacon's service when I was only a lad of fifteen, and for all that remained of his life, I was his assistant. He made me privy to his knowledge of mineral philosophy and his secrets for the trial and assay of metallic ores. When his enemies brought him down, I became the heir of his knowledge. So obliged a servant would be prodigiously ungrateful if he did not, with all zeal and faithfulness, discharge the duty laid upon him. My mineral designs are but the expression and realisation of my lord Bacon's knowledge. Since they bring wealth, they are also *in potentia*, the foundation for Solomon's House, and the fulfilment of his conception of the Great Instauration of Learning. My lord had no more than the means to subsist according to his degree, and he was much taken up with the King's business, as lawyer, judge, and at the last, as Lord Chancellor of England, but in my hearing, he often regretted that he had not made mineral philosophy the darling study of his youth. Now, to the best of my poor ability, I am living out his dream. The fruits of my first mining enterprise went to the support of King Charles, and I do not grudge that it was so, but now, if I can set men to raising silver from the Mendips, in the fulness of time, that silver in turn will raise the walls of the New Jerusalem.'

Balthasar received this long speech in awed silence. The room, with its abundant evidence of esoteric knowledge, impressed him, and the charming quality of Bushell's voice seemed gently to bind him in silver chains. Bushell ceased speaking, and walked over to the bookcase, from which he removed a small volume. 'Here is the basis for my work,' he said, holding it out to Balthasar, who opened it curiously. The title page declared it to be *Mr Bushell's Abridgement of the Lord Chancellor Bacon's Philosophical Theory in Mineral Prosecutions.*

'This was published in 'fifty-nine,' he commented. 'Were you not proscribed?'

'Ay, and it was put forth with great difficulty. I was a man much under suspicion, as you will have gathered, and living clandestinely. But I wished to share my knowledge with those who had ears to hear, lest, if the Parliament men should catch me and hang me for a traitor, my lord's knowledge should perish as if it had never been. My lord Bacon published very little during his lifetime, he was too taken up with public affairs. It was left to Mr Rowley and myself, his faithful servants, to rescue his work from oblivion. It was a risk indeed, but a worthy one. Cromwell was dead, which emboldened me, and as it turned out, the Commonwealth itself was approaching its dissolution, so I was not pursued with great vigour.'

There was a knock at the door: Mr Sydenham opened it, and put his head into the room. Mr Bushell took the book from him, and laid it on the table. 'Come, sir. If you have done here, let us to our dinner.'

Balthasar, his head swimming with visions of metals, philosophers and the New Jerusalem, followed his host meekly along the hall and into the dining-room.

After dinner, at which Mr Bushell, as on the previous occasion, talked much more than he ate and confined himself to the simplest nourishment, he led the way up to *Terra*.

'My lord Bacon was a man of the most esoteric learning,' Bushell resumed, once they were seated. 'He was the greatest philosopher of this age of the world, and his eye pierced through the coverture of nature to what lies concealed. Nothing could resist his gaze: I will never forget his eyes, which were a delicate, lively hazel in colour, clear to admiration, and pierced like those of a basilisk. The veins and secret places of the earth were open to him, and the subtle currents of the air.'

'I am not sure that I follow your meaning, Mr Bushell,' said Balthasar cautiously.

'Do you not? Well, perhaps I can make it clearer. I am to my lord Bacon no more than the least of his disciples, a moth who aspired to the company of a star, but he was graciously pleased to teach me a little of what he knew, and not merely in the field of minerals. Take yourself. Any man can see that you are young, and well favoured, and a mulatto. If you open your mouth, it is also obvious that you are a Dutchman by origin, who perhaps spent time in Scotland, or among Scots. By your dress, looks and manner, the keen-sighted might learn that you are a man who goes for one in the middle rank of life, and perhaps, that you are a doctor, since your dress is sober, and you carry no sword, though you have the air of a gentleman. But with the inner eye which my lord opened for me, I can see more than that.'

'What do you see?' whispered Balthasar, staring hypnotised into the eyes of Mr Bushell, which seemed larger and more luminous than before, like the eyes of an owl. He felt helpless to resist the older man's will.

'I see that you are a man who is guarded, though you know it not. Good spirits are about you.' Bushell's gaze shifted; he seemed to be looking over Balthasar's right shoulder at someone who was standing there, which made the skin on his back crawl: he could feel sweat trickling down his spine. 'I can see two faces,' continued Bushell. 'A black face, stern and noble of aspect, and a white face, of great beauty.'

'But how can this be?' croaked Balthasar.

'There are many subtle influences companying each one of us, my dear young man,' said Bushell gently. 'Remember, if you need an example from Scripture, that Saul saw and spoke with the spirit of Samuel. There have always been men and women with eyes that could see beyond the common. Yet I think I could show you one of these spirits. You are a young man of pure life, are you not? Not a toper, a man of violence, a blasphemer, or a whoremaster?'

'I am,' said Balthasar reluctantly, deeply troubled. The little he had eaten at dinner lay uneasily on his stomach.

Bushell rose and took flint and steel, and used them to light a candle. 'Come with me into my closet,' he commanded. 'Spirits are subtle; I cannot make anything visible to you in the light of day. In the darkness of the closet, with the air still about us, and evil influences excluded, it may be that I can share my vision, as Lord Bacon taught me.'

They went together into a small room opening off *Terra*, hung completely with black cloth, so that the light of the candle seemed to faint and die. Bushell pulled shut black curtains over the closed shutters, taking time to adjust them to his satisfaction. He turned to the door, and pulled the portière curtain across it, reducing the room to a black cube of fabric. 'We must have complete stillness,' he explained. 'For a spirit to take on even a body of light, and show itself to you, it must have no interference from random draughts in the air. Sit you here, and make no sudden movements – if we are privileged to see aught, then you must keep very still.' He took a pastille from a small silver box, and set it alight in a small metal cup set on the room's only table. Balthasar sniffed, as smoke began to curl up. 'Frankincense, musk, and storax,' said Bushell. 'Sweet scents are favoured by virtuous spirits, and dispel harmful ones.

The incense serves another purpose; the smoke will tell us of any draught there may be.'

They sat for a time in silence, watching the smoke. In the airless little room, it rose but did not disperse; instead, it seemed to form a series of insubstantial layers. The perfume was dizzying, almost intoxicating, in so confined a space, and Balthasar began to feel slightly ill. Bushell sat quiet and relaxed, looking at nothing, holding the candlestick in his hand. The light fell unevenly on the folds and hollows of his face, making it look much older, almost like a death's head.

'By the living God that made you,' said Bushell suddenly, not loudly, but with immense force, 'I charge you, appear to us in a form that we can see.'

There was a moment's sickeningly prolonged pause, then Bushell blew out the candle. Dry-mouthed, his eyes stinging from the smoke, Balthasar saw a coloured, oval spot on the black wall in front of him, which gradually resolved itself into the face of his mother, younger and lovelier than in Jonson's portrait, gazing directly at him with what seemed loving interest.

All at once, the extreme discomfort which Balthasar was experiencing hardened into something definite; complete intel-lectual rejection. According to all that he had been taught and sincerely believed, the virtuous dead slept in the Lord. How, then, could this be the spirit of his mother? 'No,' he blurted, struggling to his feet. At once, with his movement, the image winked out, but not before he had seen something absolutely revelatory; the shadow of his hand, falling across the beautiful face. With the blood roaring in his ears, he plunged across the room, and wrenched open the curtains. He yanked at the bar of the shutters, and it yielded, bringing a flood of light into the room.

Bushell had not moved, apparently taken aback by the speed of Balthasar's reaction; he sat on, candle in hand, with complete astonishment written on his face. Balthasar seemed to himself possessed by decision and purpose, so that he hardly recognised himself; his mind was functioning with swift clarity, and he understood what he had seen. If his fingers had cast a shadow on the image, the source of light was behind him. He whirled round, putting his hand out towards the black hangings, and was far from surprised to find that, instead of his fingers meeting solid plaster behind it, his lunge carried him into void. He wrenched the curtain, for such it clearly was, to one side, and stood looking at the ingenious apparatus which had brought his vision about. The old servant, Mr Sydenham, was standing frozen and stony-faced in the little space.

Breathing hard, Balthasar looked from one to the other. Mr Bushell met his eyes expressionlessly, and said nothing at all. 'I will respect your white hairs, sir,' Balthasar said coldly. 'You will meet no reprisal at my hands, greatly though you deserve it.' He turned away from Bushell and looked into the apparatus. Despite himself, he was moved by its practical ingenuity and beauty. A marvellous device, fit for the purposes of science and art, betrayed by a self-serving quack magician. He reached inside, and removed what stood in the frame before the light and the mirror; it was the face he had seen, in miniature. He cast it to the floor, hearing a satisfying crack as it fell, and ground it under his heel.

VII

Here's that will challenge all the Fair:
Come buy my nuts and damsons, my Burgamy pear.
Here's the *Whore of Babylon*, the *Devil and the Pope*:
The girl is just going on the rope.
Here's *Dives and Lazarus*, and the *World's Creation*:
Here's the *Dutch Woman*, the like's not in the nation.
Here is the booth where the tall *Dutch Maid* is,
Here are the *bears* that dance like any ladies.
Tota, tota, tot goes the little *penny trumpet*,
Here's your *Jacob Hall*, that can jump it, jump it.
Sound trumpet: a silver spoon and fork;
Come here's your dainty *Pig and Pork*.

The Humours of Bartholomew Fair, c. 1680

It would be his first entertainment in his own house, so Balthasar made extensive preparations. He was a man who generally contented himself with ale, but for Lieutenant Palaeologue he bought a small rundlet of Bordeaux wine and two bottles of old brandy, and he went to the best pastrycook's in Westminster to bespeak manchet bread and, on the cook's advice, a batalia pie, full of interesting titbits which included sweetbread, cocks-combs, ox-palates, marrow, pistachios and artichokes. Betty was an indifferent cook: she was to roast a chicken and a shoulder of mutton and make an oyster sauce and a dish of boiled cauliflower, all of which she could do, though he did not care to trust her for anything more elaborate. With almonds, strawberries set forth on a cool green cabbage-leaf, and candied apricots, also from the pastrycook's, it made a dinner he was not ashamed to set out.

He missed the linen and delftware he had had in Middelburg – of the plenishings of De Derde Koninck he had brought only his pictures and silver, thinking that anything else would likely be spoiled on the voyage. He now had barely enough dishes to garnish forth the table, and their forms and glaze, coarser than the Dutch makers', did not please him.

But all in all, he thought finally, surveying the room with satisfaction on his return from church, it made a fine show. The hot dishes were still to come up, but the pie gleamed like a plump toy castle, gilded with egg-yolk, the apricots and strawberries lent a touch of brilliant colour, and the house smelt enticingly of roasting meat. Gib, the kitchen cat, had prudently been shut out of the house for the day.

When Lieutenant Palaeologue arrived, they made a cheerful meal. The pie was a great success, and while the left-over chicken, mutton and so forth would furnish the kitchen generally, he hoped to reserve its remains for his own consumption. He and Palaeologue were unable to avoid discussion of the political situation: he had feared it would be embarrassing, either to his guest or himself, but on the whole, it turned out to be comforting.

'We have not broken you,' observed Palaeologue, sipping brandy, 'and now, we will not. The moment is past, since we have lost the element of surprise, you have broken the dikes and flooded the country, and the nation has plucked up its courage to rally behind the Stadhouder. Though your de Ruyter may yet send me to the bottom of the Channel, I am truly glad that we have not. I do not know if there are many who think as I do – I am loyal to King Charles, since I have taken his shilling, but at heart I am a soldier of fortune and not a trueborn Englishman. As such, and as a Protestant gentleman, I value the Netherlands. For all that it is so small, it has been a powerful check to the ambitions of France and

Spain. Both countries have poured men and millions into the Dutch bogs which might otherwise have been spent harrassing England, or building up their resources in some other way to the hurt of the free nations. As far as may be seen, all the great wealth in silver which the King of Spain has taken from Peru this hundred years has been squandered on men and *matériel*, and vanished into the mud of Flanders. For a country with the wealth of the Indies behind it, Spain is a poor, starved, beggarly place, and as a Protestant, I am glad of it.'

The mention of the mines of Peru struck an unpleasant chord in Balthasar's mind, and he shifted uneasily.

'I have raised a sad thought, sir,' said Palaeologue, watching his face.

'It was the word "silver",' explained Balthasar. 'I fell in lately with a projector, a man who was trying to raise Solomon's House in the Mendips, or so he claimed. I do not know what I believe of him any more. He is a great man of science, and a most subtle and crafty person. I think I believe him about the silver, and perhaps I believe him about his design for an Invisible College, and that he has given his life to these matters, I have no doubt at all. But he attempted to lay an imposture upon me through conjuration, to put me in awe of him and bind me to his will, and that I could not bear.'

'What was the imposture?'

Balthasar took a deep breath. 'He conjured an apparition of my mother's face. It was a trick, an image painted upon glass and thrown upon the wall by the light of a candle.'

'A brave trick, though, and worthy of better uses,' commented Palaeologue.

'I thought so too. The apparatus was a most cunning one, and excellently made.' He took a draught of his wine; determined, for once, to speak out. 'No, I confess what truly troubles me is not the trick, which I fathomed, or even the knavishness of it, but the fact that he knew my mother, and for that, it seems to me that he must truly be the magus he pretends.'

'Are you sure, sir?' asked Palaeologue gently. 'Did you not see what you expected? A woman's sweet face, and you, perhaps, blinded with tears – a man has a way of conniving with his own cozenage, at such a moment.'

'No, sir, I am very sure.' He took a deep breath; the thought that he was about to reveal the great secret of his life seemed to be making his tongue thick and unwieldy in his mouth, but how could he explain, if he did not reveal it? And after all these years, with his mother long dead, what could it possibly matter? 'Lieutenant Palaeologue, I think you a man of honour, and I will tell you a secret I thought would go with me to my grave, if you swear on your honour to keep it.'

'I do swear, an't does not touch the security of his majesty's kingdom or navy.'

'My mother was the late Queen of Bohemia. She took my father to her in holy wedlock, how and why I know not. I saw her but once, and my father did not speak of it. He brought me up removed from the court, and I know he had a hope for me as Shiloh, the child born to renew nations. It may be that they shared this dream.'

'What you say is passing strange,' commented Palaeologue. 'So, you could salute his majesty as cousin.'

'I could, but I would do no such thing. I know no good of kings and courts. My mother and my father both lived their lives as exiles. My uncle lost his head, not half a mile from where we sit. The Stadhouder at home was set aside in contempt by de Witt and the States-General, though in the last few weeks, he bids fair to regain his power – but all in all, sir, I have no envy for the life of a prince in these our times.'

'Spoken like a wise man,' said Palaeologue. 'I agree, though, that your magus should know or guess this is strange indeed. You have a great look of the Duke of York, now I come to think of it – since he is Admiral of the Fleet, I have often seen him – but I would not have thought to set you beside him in my mind's eye. Tell me, though. Has no one ever known, or guessed?'

'One man guessed. A face-painter in Middelburg, who had made her portrait. That is the picture, over the chimneypiece. He saw her face in mine, and told me so, but he is long dead.'

'And did he have connections in England?'

'Yes,' admitted Balthasar, 'but he was the most discreet and secret of men.'

'Were there any others?'

'Perhaps. There was an Englishwoman married to a Dutch captain who stole my father's private journal. I know not if she ever read it, it was in Latin, and perhaps the theft was a wanton one. But the book made some allusion to these matters in veiled words, so there may be one who knows of it.'

'Well then,' said Palaeologue. 'That is sufficient. You will recall the story of King Midas and his barber. A secret confided to one may become known to another. Perhaps your projector was acquainted with the painter, or with the woman, or the diary was bought and sold and came into his hands. Any of these things could have happened, so do not torment your mind with thoughts of wizardry. The means for a natural explanation are to hand.'

Balthasar, as he listened, was impressed by Palaeologue's reasoning. He seemed a man made to dispel shadows.

'You set my mind at rest,' he said. 'But it has made me very sick of the follies and vanities of England. I am tired of the false faces of smiling harlots, and men who say things in doubled words. This white-haired, saintlike old deceiver is but the worst of what has befallen me. I am not at home here, and I think I never will be.'

Palaeologue nodded soberly. 'A little more wine, sir? I have sympathy for what you say. I came from the Indies to seek my fortune in the navy, and entered the service as a King's Letter boy, when I was fourteen. I did my seven years' service as midshipman, and was posted Lieutenant in the year seventy. But what has happened to the navy in my time would sicken any man of sense. For the last five years – ten years, more like – we have been fighting a war not hand to hand, but hand to mouth, while the Admiralty sells off ships, leaves the poor devils of tars unpaid for years on end, and skimps on food, water, timber, and even powder for the guns. Even such *matériel* as we have is bought with other men's money – the King stopped the Exchequer in January, so it is the bankers who pay all.

'Given that the Duke of York has been deprived of office for popery, and the King, who is perfectly indifferent to the sea, is now Lord High Admiral, that there are men with connections who stand ahead of me, and that de Ruyter is sending the actual vessels to the bottom of the sea at a great rate, I do not think I will ever captain an English ship of the line. In any case, it is not the prospect it was when I first dreamed of the sea-service. The English built the finest ships in the world, in the time of the first Charles. Under his son, the practice of mean economy means that the new men-o'-war are outweighed, outgunned and outmanoeuvred not only by the Dutch, but even by the French. The old *Sovereign of the Seas* is still afloat after nigh on forty years' service, and the contrast is painful. She is old-fashioned, but she is weatherly, and she makes many of the new vessels look like toys.

'Doctor van Overmeer, I have a proposition to lay before you. My father died two years ago, and my mother is alone and in poor health. I am minded to throw up my commission, at least for a time, and cheer her steps toward the grave. There are more lieutenants now than ships to put them in, and I doubt my superiors will make any difficulty. My mother is a woman of notably masculine mind – my father was a scholar and a dreamer, and left much business in her hands, so I do not fear greatly for her, but I own, I should like to be sure I have done my duty by her. Barbados is a land with more diseases than doctors – it is a rough, young colony, but it is something very different from London. If you came out with me, I would be grateful on my mother's account, and I am sure you would find patients aplenty. Being a mulatto, you might find the climate endurable, though I cannot pretend that the planters will make you welcome.'

'It is something I have not thought of,' said Balthasar slowly. 'Are you sure I would be able to work there? I have found it hard in Europe to be black, but I think it would be no better in America, and perhaps worse.'

'On the other hand,' said Palaeologue, 'a man of your breeding must surely make himself respected anywhere. There are few professional men on the island, and you would start with a recommendation; my father was well thought of, the churchwarden of his parish, and my mother has a good name throughout the island as a woman of sense. She will receive you kindly, I know, because of the little matter of saving my life, and also because you are a person of distinguished ancestry. I am sure that with her countenance, your knowledge and ability would make their mark.'

'Well, I shall give the question my consideration. Your mother's welfare weighs with me, I assure you. I think perhaps the answer will be no, but let me have a little time.'

'Oh, six months, a year,' Palaeologue said airily. 'It will be some time before I can honourably resign my commission, in the present state of things, though I think that now the Duke is set aside, the King will huddle up a peace soon enough, and they will be pleased to be rid of me. My honoured mother is by no means on her deathbed – *absit omen* – but she begins to complain of poor health, and I should like be certain she is happy and well accommodated in her widowhood. And I confess, I should like to see her before we meet at the Last Judgement. It is more than twelve years since I left the island, so she has never seen me with a beard.'

'Well, sir. I will think about what you suggest.'

*   *   *

By August, Balthasar was down to two visits a week to the Everaerts household, and with a less important patient who lived less close to hand, it would have been one, or perhaps even none. The old gentleman was getting on very well. But on one such visit, Balthasar was shown up to the closet by Everaerts's confidential servant. He found the old man snug in a loose morning gown, fur-trimmed despite the balmy summer air, his thick-veined hands folded on his broad stomach. Balthasar regarded him with approval, noting his patient's healthy colour as he straightened up from his bow, and sensed approval in return. Unusually, Madam Everaerts was sitting with him, a piece of embroidery in her hand: she might just have been keeping him company, but it crossed his mind to wonder if her presence meant anything.

'Doctor van Overmeer,' commanded Everaerts, once his pulse had been taken and all other preliminaries concluded, 'I have made a number of enquiries about you, both in Middelburg and here in London, and there is none with a word to speak against you in either city. There is a question I would like to open with you.'

'I am at your service, mynheer.'

'What think you of my wife's gentlewoman?'

'Why, nothing,' replied Balthasar in confusion. 'She is not a proper person for me to think of. All I can say is that she always seems bonny and blooming – have you reason to be concerned about her?'

Husband and wife looked at each other; they seemed to exchange a smile of indulgent complicity. 'Let me tell you a little of her history,' said Madam Everaerts. 'Please sit down, if you will.'

Balthasar sat, his hat on his knee, while she began her tale.

'Sibella is the daughter of a kinswoman of mine, my second cousin Margaret Lane. My family were loyal to the King, and accordingly, when she took a husband, her choice fixed upon an officer in his majesty's army, Simon Carteret. He fought bravely at Marston Moor under Prince Rupert in 'forty-four, and in the years that followed that great defeat, both the Lane family and the Carterets became greatly impoverished. He and his wife saw little of one another, since he was much on campaign, but it must be confessed that when he did return, he was far from what might have been desired in a husband. In 1651, he went with Prince Rupert privateering to the West Indies, and never returned. We had word after that he had lost a foot in an action at sea, and so he had been invalided out of the Prince's service and bought an estate in Barbados. When he went, Margaret Carteret had a child at the breast, a daughter. None of their previous children had lived beyond infancy, and perhaps he thought this one would not, but she lived and flourished. She was bred up according to the strictest principles and as a gentlewoman, though very poor. When her mother died, I took in and trained her up as my waiting woman. That, I think, is all her little history. She is a good girl, and I love her dearly.'

'God will reward those who protect the widow and the orphan,' said Balthasar politely. 'You are laying up treasure in Heaven.'

'I have laid up a treasure on earth,' Madam Everaerts replied, 'for she is that.'

'Doctor van Overmeer,' interrupted Everaerts. 'You are a young man of excellent reputation, in a good way to make your living. We have been very taken with you over the course of these long weeks; my wife thinks you a veritable Aesculepius, and I am, at the least, convinced of your knowledge and skill. Mistress Sibella is twenty-one years old, and we would like to see her settled. The character of her family you can guess at from the many excellences of my dearest Sarah, the household she has been bred up in, you can see for yourself. Could you find it in you to fancy the girl as a wife?'

Balthasar gaped at him, unable to formulate an answer. 'Mynheer Everaerts, it would be the greatest honour in the world to be connected with your family,' he said eventually. 'I have had no such thought or design, but any man can see that the maiden is modest and comely.'

'I could give very little with her,' warned Everaerts, 'and all the property she has of herself, is in Barbados, and we do not know what state it may be in, or what it is worth. Her father is dead, of that I am sure. We have our own children to provide for, and with the present state of uncertainty in Middelburg, I must hold myself in readiness to give aid to my kinsmen in Zeeland, and even, perhaps, to the Stadhouder if it is required. She has her wages put by, and we can give her good store of linen and plenishings, and perhaps fifty pounds in money for a nest-egg, but that is all I can do.'

Balthasar considered the question. Certainly, the girl's connections and family were all he could reasonably want in a wife, and far better than a man such as himself could expect. 'My mind is in a maze,' he said slowly. 'I had not yet thought it prudent to take a wife, though if the gentlewoman has a liking to me, I would be greatly honoured by her good esteem. But I confess, mynheer, there is one point which I stick at: I will never marry a woman who mislikes me, and the idea of a husband who is of another race may be repugnant to her. I can trust you, I know, not to force her inclination.'

'Very well, Doctor. I respect your position. She is a modest girl, and I think, has no more thought of you, than you of her. Look well at her, when you come again, and my wife will open the matter with her. If you have a distaste for her, or she for you, then no harm is done, but if you think you might find it in your hearts to agree, then perhaps you can make one another's acquaintance.'

'I was truly fond of Sibella's mother,' added Madam Everaerts. 'Her life was not a happy one. I promised myself, that when I came to look about for a husband for her child, I would try to find a man who was honourable, and of kindly nature, above all other considerations. Blackamoor you may be, but we know how you have lived your life, both here and in Zeeland, and in that respect, you are all that we could want for her. You have a good heart, Doctor van Overmeer, and you are honest. A dowerless maiden cannot look very high, and I think I can answer for it that she will frame her fancy to her fortune. I would also say, that from what I know of you both, I think that you and she could find contentment together. She knows from her childhood what it is to live in poverty, so she would be able to keep house economically, but if you prosper, as with the help of God you surely will, she has the education and the skills to be a dainty enough gentlewoman, when circumstances permit, and she will not disgrace her station.'

'I am truly honoured that you have thought of me in this connection,' said Balthasar again, helplessly.

'Go to, then, Doctor. We will see you on Friday, and I hope you will find your affairs to prosper.'

Balthasar walked the short distance down Tothill Street, his thoughts in turmoil. The comfort of a wife was something which he longed for; and if children did not come too often, he had begun to hope he might soon be in a posture to keep one. But he did not know to rank himself in the marriage-market: on the one hand, he was of good estate and prospects, on the other, he was a mulatto – he feared to look either too high or too low, and had, indeed, had it in mind to confide his problem to Everaerts in due course, and take his advice. The idea of a girl reared in a Dutch household appealed to him greatly. She would clean properly, which Betty did not, and since her prosperity was necessarily related to his own, she would not be wasteful, which Betty was. He was well aware that without a mistress, his household was no household. She would be a companion, sitting with him in his lonely evenings – his thoughts hardly dared run so far as to think of the solace of her company in his lonely bed, things were as yet so uncertain.

On his next visit to the Everaerts house, Madam Everaerts was again in the room, with a lapful of wool and her hands up before her, shackled with blue yarn. Mistress Sibella sat with her, winding it off her hands into balls. While Everaerts engaged him in conversation, he covertly watched her; she was looking at what she was doing, but he could see her profile, which was strong, with a well-shaped nose. Her skin was pale, and mostly clear; the light fell on her face, and he could see a few small, silvery pits and hollows on her forehead and around her chin – she had had the smallpox, and got away very lightly. All to the good, the devastation the disease could wreak on a fair face was sadly well known to him, but it struck only once in a lifetime. There were some large, patchy freckles across her nose, and on the upper part of the cheeks, a blemish, but not a serious one. Her eyes were grey, the brows straight, and rather thick. He liked her ear, exposed by the little cap she wore; it was pale and prettily shaped, like a shell. Her mouth was somewhat too large, but the lips were tucked together firmly as if she was in the habit of self-control. She was unfashionably thin, but her posture was good ... He became aware of three things, belatedly. First, that he was answering the worthy Everaerts more or less at random, second, that a suppressed smile was beginning to quirk at the corners of the older man's well-disciplined mouth, and third, that Mistress Sibella was beginning to blush, the colour rising up her neck as if her face and head were a transparent vessel swiftly filling up with blood. He averted his eyes, conscious that her entire face was flaming scarlet, even to the pretty ear, and tried to collect his scattered wits. A moment later, Madam Everaerts had mercy on the girl and him, and swept her off about some other household task.

'Well, Doctor. You have seen her, and do you like what you see?'

'I like her very well,' he said awkwardly. He hardly dared ask if she had given any judgement on him.

'My wife put the matter to her,' said Everaerts. 'She said as you did, that she had not thought of it. But she approved your professional skill, and the care that you showed, and said she would be ready to be guided by us.'

'I could ask for no more,' he said, though the coldness of the response was depressing.

'No, indeed. The girl you would want to marry would not show herself too ready. Our Sibella has always shown herself chaste in mind, as she is in body. She has not been a hoyting girl, or run loose at fairs and playhouses. I think she is shocked to think of this match, since it has not been in her mind, but she is not displeased, though devil a word Madame can get from her – at least, there have been no tears, or maidenly megrims. Bartholomew Fair falls later this month; if you would like to squire Mistress Sibella to the fair, you have our permission.'

'I would be honoured,' he said, dry-mouthed.

He decided to take her on the second of the fair's three days, when perhaps the most determined pleasure-seekers would have exhausted themselves, and the performers not yet gone stale. He called for her after dinner; she was ready in what must be her best dress, plain blue stuff, but new, and set off with good lace cuffs and pinner. Her auburn hair was smoothly combed back, and her face was completely unreadable. He was wearing his green silk coat, and the point-lace collar he had bought in his extravagant twenties, and had hardly ever dared to wear.

He had hired a hackney-coach to take them to Smithfield: he handed the silent Mistress Sibella in first, then jumped in beside her. After ten minutes of joggling and swaying in the rattling vehicle, which threw them against one another at every turn, he could feel the warmth of her thigh striking through her petticoats. She must surely also feel his leg? He was physically moved by her proximity, by the thought of her; but for all he could tell, she was as calm and cold as a bowl of cream in a dairy.

The coach-driver let them off at the entrance to the fair, and he gave the man his eighteen-pence. Within was Bedlam. The crowds surged and swirled, and a confused babble arose; among the sounds which met his ear he recognised the shouting of the crowd, many of whom were drunk, wailing children, the screams and cries of the barkers and vendors, drums, cat-calls, penny trumpets, fifes, trombones and hautboys. The smell of the fair came out to meet them, as complex as its sound; over all the manifold odours of spilled wine and beer, sweat, urine, vomit and horse-manure drifted the scent of roast pork, greasy and enticing. Somewhat repelled, he looked at her sideways: she was wide-eyed and her lips were slightly parted, whether with interest, excitement or disgust, he could not tell.

'Have a care, Mistress Sibella,' he said politely. 'Make sure your pocket is buttoned up securely, this will be an Alsatia for pickpockets and petty thieves.'

'Thank you,' she said, her voice so low he could hardly hear it. 'I am taking good care.' He gave her his arm, and after a moment's hesitation, she took it, and they walked together into the yelling multitude. The fair was intensely confusing, though Balthasar knew, having made enquiries, that it was to some extent divided into regions. The avenue they were walking down was the place for actors' booths; on the platforms outside, blue-clad merry-andrews shouted, mimed, joked, gesticulated, and when they had attracted sufficient audience, tried to persuade their watchers to come inside and pay. Actors displayed themselves, lounging in tinsel and tawdry finery; he recognised the costumes of kings, queens, buffoons, priests and devils, and could guess at the wretched shows they would present. Meanwhile, once they had escaped the actors, he knew that they would find other areas of the fair which were devoted to music and dancing, rarey-shows, miscellaneous entertainments, tricks of one kind or another, and above all, food, most notably the roast pork for which the fair was famous, which was cooked and served at Pie Corner, by Giltspur Street.

The word 'Bacon' caught his ear, confusing him, since his mind was running on pork; he turned to see what it was, while Sibella fell in obediently with his change of direction. One of the leather-lunged merry-andrews was shouting, 'Walk up, walk up, ladies and gentlemen, sirs and princes! See Friar Bacon and his brazen head, which told him the past, present and future! Hear the Friar at his conjurations, and the tale of how he offered to wall the kingdom with that same metal, and how the devil caught him napping! Walk up, walk up!'

He realised Sibella was speaking, though her voice was inaudible in the general din, and bent so that she could speak into his ear. 'Do you want to see it?' she asked. Her breath tickled him. He looked at her, and she did not seem eager, so he shook his head, and they moved on. He knew nothing of Friar Bacon, and the story of another projectionist was the last thing he wished to hear. Perhaps the devil would catch Bushell, one fine day.

The fair was so crowded that he and Sibella were buffeted against one another, and she kept a close grip on his arm. They attracted hostile looks from time to time as they walked, which he devoutly hoped she did not observe. And once he heard, though at a distance, 'Why black men should feel they can make sport with our English maids, I do not know.' He looked round, but no challenger presented himself; the speaker was lost in the crowd.

They moved together out of the street of booths, and found themselves facing a larger structure, set at the top of the row. The barker was shouting, 'Walk up, walk up, sirs and gentles, the girls are just going on the rope! Walk up, and see the famous German maid perform side-capers, upright-capers, cross-capers and back-capers, on the tight-rope!' He was interested, and raised his eyebrows interrogatively at Sibella, who nodded, so he paid sixpence apiece, and they went in. Inside the house, they found a ring scattered with bran. People were standing around it, there was a little group of musicians in a sort of loosebox, and two structures of scaffolding which supported the high rope. There were crosspoles at either end, and on them, two women were sitting. One was black and one white; both were slim and rather handsome, and to Balthasar's horrified amazement, both were wearing close-fitting, greasy velvet doublets and short silk drawers coming to just above the knee.

Balthasar received a hefty nudge in the ribs from the man to his left, who leaned towards him familiarly, enveloping him in a fug of stale gin and decaying teeth, and pointed up at the black woman. 'Look there, master. I often heard tell of the devil on two sticks, but I never saw it before.' Balthasar turned to stare at him coldly, and had the satisfaction of seeing the loutish grin freeze on his face.

The head of the troupe came forward into the ring, bowed, as the musicians struck up an air, and announced, 'My lords, ladies and gentlemen, Black Molly and the German Maid will show forth their skills for your pleasure.' He retired again to the ringside, and ten feet above their heads, first one woman, then the other, slowly traversed the rope. Balthasar, along with everyone else, avidly watched the flexing play of the muscles in their well-turned legs and, since the drawers were not tight, their thighs; a woman's leg above the ankle was no common sight to him, or to any other man. The black and the white woman then came back onto the rope together, and passed one another in the middle, a graceful and intricate manoeuvre which set the crowd roaring. Black Molly then retired, and the German Maid took a balance-pole and danced alone on the rope, skipping, and even leaping, with miraculous art. Sibella clutched his arm hard: he realised she must be afraid for the German woman, which he found touching. It was hard not to fear for her, whatever one told oneself, she seemed so ready to break her neck.

When she had finished, and bowed to much applause, Black Molly climbed to the very top of the booth, where other ropes hung, two of them joined with a cross-bar, and swung herself onto them. Far overhead, she seemed supported by the air itself: at one moment, she was hanging by her hands, then somehow she had a purchase on nothing at all, and was somersaulting in the air. He felt his mouth hanging open, as he gaped upwards, and knew those around him were in no better case. At the last, she seemed to slip – but the universal gasp of horror turned to relieved laughter and applause when a moment later they saw her smiling and blowing kisses, swinging lazily back and forth as she hung upside-down on the trapeze by her feet.

Balthasar looked at Sibella, who was looking rather pale and shocked. Though Molly had come safely to the ground, and the next phase of the act had begun, tumbling and acrobatics on the floor of the ring, when he asked if she wanted to leave, she nodded.

After they had walked out, he looked around. He wanted a place apart. In the main thoroughfare between the places of entertainment was the mindlessly swaying crowd, much of it drunk. Behind the booths, between them and the walls of the permanent buildings that surrounded Smithfield itself, it was easy to see, and smell, that men and women were taking advantage of the relative privacy to urinate, that sweethearts, or perhaps prostitutes and their clients, were kissing and fumbling there, in the universal licence of the fair – what else might be going on, he did not know, but he did not want Sibella to see it.

For want of anything better, he settled for guiding her to the head of an alleyway between two booths. People brushed past them, on their way to, or from, the area behind, but guarded by the corner of the building, they were comparatively quiet and unmolested, and able to hear one another speak.

He looked down at her: she was only half a head shorter than he, and he was a tall man. She met his eyes unflinchingly. 'Mistress Sibella, an't please you, will you answer me this? Does my blackness offend you?' Emboldened by Everaerts's implied permission, he took her hand, and tried to gauge whether it stiffened in protest at his touch. It lay limp and passive in his; he turned it this way and that, and they looked together at the conjoined fingers, white and brown.

She did not reply at once. He began to think she would keep silence, and became more and more disheartened, but at last she swallowed nervously and began to speak.

'Mynheer van Overmeer, I am a dowerless maiden, and dependent on the goodwill of my kin. I will have no jointure of my own, to protect me if my husband is unkind. The only protection I have is the love of my mistress. I promised myself, when I began to grow to woman's estate, that I would marry where she wished, and not seek to form any inclination of my own. My mother married for love, mynheer, and she got no joy of it.'

'Mistress Sibella, you have not answered my question.'

'I am trying to explain, sir,' she said doggedly. 'Please understand me. I want my own establishment. I want my independence, and a house where I am the mistress, even if it is a very small one. I have allowed myself to hope I will not die a grey old maiden, winding my lady's wool, and tending her grandchildren. But when I dreamed of a house of my own, what was I to hope for? Most men in the middle rank of life want a dowry with their wife. So, what I thought, when I thought about it, was that often an old man will take a second or third wife, and will be willing to bate a dowry if she be young, gently bred, and of good conversation. I have thought long about old men. Look about you, sir, and see them. Think what they are like. Gor-bellied or scrawny, and if they are neither, they are palsied, gouty, ptisicky, halt, or blear-eyed. But I told myself that if such a one approached my mistress, if he were a good man and kind, I would take him. You are none of these things, mynheer, but you are something I have not prepared my mind for. If I am coy, do not fear for me. I will do my duty, and

I have learned to be guided by my will, not by girlish qualms and shrinkings.'

Balthasar looked down at her, and let go of her hand. He had seldom been so angry, or so insulted, yet he saw the justice of what she said. As he recovered his equilibrium, he recognised that she had stated fairly and honestly her present state of mind. The strength of her character chilled him, but he had to admit that although he felt rejected, she had not, in fact, rejected him. In fact, she had implicitly accepted him, or at least, the station in life he offered her, because she seemed to think he was the best bargain she was likely to get, a conclusion which he had reached, on his own side, some days before. The thought of her by his side, bending that clear, powerful will to the service of their common interests, was something indeed. She would be loyal, she would be a helpmate, for that was the nature of the bond, and she was proud. He could only hope devoutly that her coldness was maidenly, and not the permanent bent of her nature.

'Well, mistress,' he said, as pleasantly as he could, suppressing any note of discouragement. 'I am no coxcomb to think I can compel a woman's love in half an hour's acquaintance, and I am no rake, to force myself upon you. Let us make up a bargain then. Will you be pleased to walk on? We might dance, if you cared to, or eat pork, or ride in the flying-coaches on the great wheel. There are puppet shows, Polchinello and Patient Grizill, if you have a mind to them.'

'Let us walk,' she said. They moved aimlessly through the fair, but he felt a certain satisfaction. She thought she had discountenanced him, he felt, but he had turned the tables. He bought some filberts and bergamot pears, and they cracked the nuts and ate them as they walked, as people were doing all around them. They visited the learned mare, who nodded out the answers to the questions she was set, and the waxworks show at the Temple of Diana, by the hospital gate, speaking little, but on the whole, in friendly fashion. They went to Pie Corner, attracted by the shouts of 'Here's your delicate pig and pork!' and were both so repelled by the black carpet of flies around the sizzling carcases on the spit that they came away without a dish of meat. He persuaded her to take a slice of cake and a glass of Malaga wine at another, cleanlier, booth where they could sit in comfort and watch a woman who danced with full wineglasses balanced on the backs of her hands, and spilled never a drop.

While they were sitting together, after the dancer had elicited one of Sibella's rare smiles, he asked her without preamble, 'Mistress Sibella. Have you ever felt desire?'

'Only the desire to be what I am not.' It was impossible to question her further. She looked away from him composedly, and sipped at her wine, and he saw very well how a man could be undone by passion for this woman who was as closed as an egg.

The clock on St Bartholomew's chimed four while they were still sitting in the booth. Balthasar felt as exhausted as if he had done a hard day's work. When he asked her if she wanted further entertainment, she seemed eager to go home. He bought her a pair of embroidered kid gloves as a fairing, and then they left Smithfield and went to look for a hackney-coach.

He took her home, paid off the coach, and walked slowly back to his own house. What was to be done with this bleak integrity? He was not greatly experienced with women. The whores he had met in his long-ago student days had made much of his prowess, but everyone knew whores lied, and as a grown man, he had never kept a miss. Could he melt such coldness? He had tamed a starling once, hoping to teach it to speak, which it did not. But with long patience, and slow, smooth movements, he had won its confidence, until it bounced about him as confidently as if he were a tree, and ate from his fingers. He would have to trust to the same weapons, he thought. Patience, proximity.

Preparations for the marriage went forward swiftly. When he

told Bessy of it, she gave in her notice, saying she preferred not to work under a mistress, which left him wondering whether she had expected more of him than ordinary usage. The thought disquieted him; he would never have considered making advances to the maid, since it insulted the dignity of honest labour, and moreover, it was a clear recipe for disorder and insolence: what did it tell him about London, that she seemed almost contemptuous that he had not? He was glad to be rid of her; especially since she agreed to stay until the wedding, and then depart with a present. When he told Sibella of her departure, she said she would prefer to engage her own kitchen-woman, so he left the matter with her. James and the boy Jacob seemed unmoved by the news, though James wished him joy, rather awkwardly.

They married at the beginning of October; Everaerts acted as sponsor, and hosted the wedding breakfast. Balthasar had a new tabby suit made, which cost him twenty pounds, the most expensive he had ever had, and Madam Everaerts gave Sibella her first silk gown. It was a very fashionable orange-tawny taffeta which brought out the mahogany tint of her hair, and he thought her beautiful, though she was pale and her expression was sombre, perhaps apprehensive. Lieutenant Palaeologue was among the guests, and wished them joy with obvious sincerity. Balthasar was glad to have him there. They had spoken often of the match, in the weeks since it was set on foot, and he had confided his anxieties: Palaeologue had been bracing.

'Never fear, my friend. There is no image in her mind you are to displace, and that is excellent. She is cold because she is ignorant, and you are a comely fellow, in good health. You will thaw her, never fear. But you are right in what you say. She must not be hurried, if you are to become friends.'

'Have you ever married, sir?' asked Balthasar a little tentatively.

'I have not had that honour. I confess to a certain pride of blood.

My mother counselled me that when I had a mind to marry, I should do it in England, not in Barbados. So few women come over to the Indies that even a whore if she is handsome and of good address may end as the wife of a rich planter, and I have a certain distaste for the notion of a wife taken from the kennels of London. When I went into the navy, it was with the hope that, if I was posted Captain and luck came my way in the form of prize-money, I might aspire to the hand of a gentlewoman no worse than my mother, or even better. But it has not come about, though I rub along well enough for a single man. But marry, Balthasar, and be glad of it. Luck and your own virtues have thrown you a chaste and well-schooled wench, and such a one is a prize above rubies.'

The conversation came back to him, as he watched Palaeologue drinking and chatting with Madam Everaerts, his easy charm conquering her reserved, old-fashioned manner so that as she looked up at him, she was laughing like a girl. Not for the first time, he envied his friend's social gifts. He looked across at Sibella, slightly hoping she was not watching the interchange; she was not. Eyes downcast, she was playing with her wineglass in apparent concentration, fitting the foot carefully into one or another of the rings it had made on the white linen cloth. She looked up, feeling his eyes upon her, and swiftly looked down again.

The interminable feast dragged on, and finally, with much joking and well-wishing, the party saw them to bed, scrambled for the bride's garter, and left them, at last, to themselves.

She lay in the bed in her smock, looking at him, unmoving: the candles were still lit, and the fire, so he could see the glitter of her eyes. He did not know what to do. With no particular premeditation, he sat up beside her, not too fast; he could sense the wariness in her as he moved. It seemed to him she was thinking of him as a kind of wild beast, and it made him angry. He swung his legs out of the bed, and stood up in the middle of the floor. 'What are you doing?' she whispered, when he made no further move.

He did not reply, but moving slowly and deliberately, he pulled his nightgown off, and dropped it on the floor, followed by his nightcap. She sat up, huddled with her knees to her chin, watching him warily. Balthasar spread his arms, and slowly, slowly, turned on the spot. He was in no state where he might fear frightening her; enjoyment was the last thing on his mind. Once he had turned himself completely round three times, he stooped for his nightgown, and put it back on, and sat down on the end of the bed, regarding her soberly.

'What are you doing?' she asked again, a note of honest bewilderment creeping into her voice.

He looked down at his loosely clasped hands, and up again. 'My dear wife, I am showing you your bargain. I think I am a handsome enough fellow, do you not agree?'

'Do you want me to do the same?' she asked; he could hear the nervousness in her voice. She thought him mad, perhaps. The thought stirred him, despite himself, but he said merely:

'No. I will take you on trust.' He could feel the night air on his shaven skull; it felt strangely exposed.

'Will you come back into the bed, sir?' she asked, when he showed no signs of moving.

'Thank you, Sibella.' He got into bed, and lay flat, staring up at the tester. She was up on her elbow, he knew, looking down at him, though he did not look at her.

'Sir . . . Balthasar. I am ready.'

He turned his head at last, and looked at her. 'Sibella, I truly do not think so.' He sat up again, and blew out the candles. He was beginning to enjoy himself; he could feel her irritation at the postponement of whatever ordeal she was expecting, but he was determined. He would have no truck with a virgin martyr, the notion insulted him. He shut his eyes, and pretended to sleep; after a time, rather to his surprise, he did so.

He awoke in the dawn; there was a little grey light seeping into the room, and Sibella was using it to look at his face at close quarters. He could feel her breath, and the soft weight of her breast against his arm. Still pretending sleep, he shifted a little, then rolled over, flinging out an arm, and bringing her down beside him. Grunting a little, he settled again, relaxed, feeling her lying along the length of his side. After a first startlement, her body was soft against his.

'I know you are not asleep,' she whispered. She rolled onto her back, and it was his turn to rise on one elbow and look down at her. There was an expression on her face he had never seen before. She was looking at him; not as an object, a problem or a threat, but for the first time, as if she hoped to know or understand him.

'Good.' She put up her mouth to be kissed, then rather tentatively, put her arm around his back, and pulled him down.

They had been married for a month. In that time, Sibella had conducted a rigorous inquisition of Betty's housekeeping, and had hired another woman called Esther as kitchen-maid. She had disposed the new plenishings she had brought with her to her own satisfaction, sent every stitch of linen which had been in the house to the whitster's, and cleaned it from top to bottom. Relations between them were reserved but affectionate; to his infinite relief, she was showing no distaste for him as a man, far from it. They were getting along very well. A few nights after their marriage, he had confided his ancestry to her; he was sure it had raised him in her eyes, not least because he had forborne from using it as a bargaining counter in their courtship. Still more importantly, she was beginning, he was sure, to take real pleasure in their nightly embraces, though she kept him at arm's length during the day; she was too dignified a woman for kissing and towsing. Once dressed, she set herself seriously to work, conscious of setting an example to the servants; he would not see her softer side again until her bodice was unlaced. She was a taciturn woman, on the whole, and she had been so busy taking control of her new household, that they had had hardly a minute together to converse.

But at last, they were reaching a point where a routine could be established. When he came in from his evening round of visits, she had a simple supper, bread and cheese, perhaps apples or nuts, and a pottle of ale awaiting him. Since he could never give her a precise time for his return, these preparations were not elaborate: their main meal was in the middle of the day.

He ate his supper, drank his ale, lit his pipe, and looked across at his new wife with deep pleasure and satisfaction. She was sitting by a candle, the light shining on her hands and catching the line of her brow and cheek, and was making an edging strip of fine crocheted lace, which was not to be mistaken for true point-lace but made a goodly show in its own way. She seemed to him entirely beautiful, though she was biting her underlip, and frowning down at her work in concentration. Even the freckles he had once despised now seemed an adornment, setting off the fairness of her skin.

'Sibella,' he said. At once, she put her work down, and looked across at him enquiringly. 'When I was coming home this evening, I found myself thinking there was a question I wanted to ask you. You have all the keys of the house, and you know what we have here. I have a small store of gold safe in the Bank, and between your earnings and Mynheer Everaerts's present, you have brought nearly a hundred pounds with you. So we are not poor, and I am in a good way of making our living, if God wills it. I am content with my lot, now that I have found you, and it begins to seem that we agree. But a few months ago, in the summer, my friend Lieutenant Palaeologue put a proposition to me. His mother is in Barbados, and he suggested that I go out with him next year, attend his mother, who lives on a plantation in the parish of St John, and re-establish my practice in the island. I was all but resolved to turn him down, because of the risk which attends this removal. But your father left you property. I care not a whit for this; when I took you, I counted only on what I had fair and square in my hand. This property may now be worthless, or in the hands of others, but it is yours. It seems to me that you have a voice in this, before I carry a final answer to Lieutenant Palaeologue.'

Her eyes dilated, and her mouth hardened in a way that he was beginning to know. 'I want to go to Barbados, though I have never been able to think how it could be encompassed. I want what is mine. What is ours, I should say. When God gives us a son, we could make a gentleman of him.'

'Sibella, I do not think that an estate in Barbados is the same thing as an estate in England, and in any case, I do not aspire to make any child of ours a gentleman. I cannot see that they come to much good, in this world or the next. Do not pout, my wife, and do not build your hopes too high – if we go, I will go as a doctor, and if there is anything to be salvaged of your property, we will sell it.'

Her face had closed again. She never disagreed with him, but he was perfectly well aware that her lapses into silence might conceal anything, consent, indifference, even stubborn opposition. He suspected the latter, in the present instance. He was beginning to know her, and he feared that he was talking not to her clear-eyed, adult sense, but to the dreams she had cherished in her years of dependency. Well, they would find what they would find, he thought. If by some miracle, the property was what she obviously wanted it to be, perhaps she would get her way; if it was not, he hoped she was intelligent enough to cut her losses.

'Remember, this will be no very pleasant journey,' he warned. 'I do not know if we will be able to stand the tropics – the climate is a risk, from what the Lieutenant says, even more for you than for me, and it is difficult to rear children. There may be losses as well as gains, of a kind we may regret most bitterly.'

'That is in the hand of God,' said Sibella simply. 'But I want to go.'

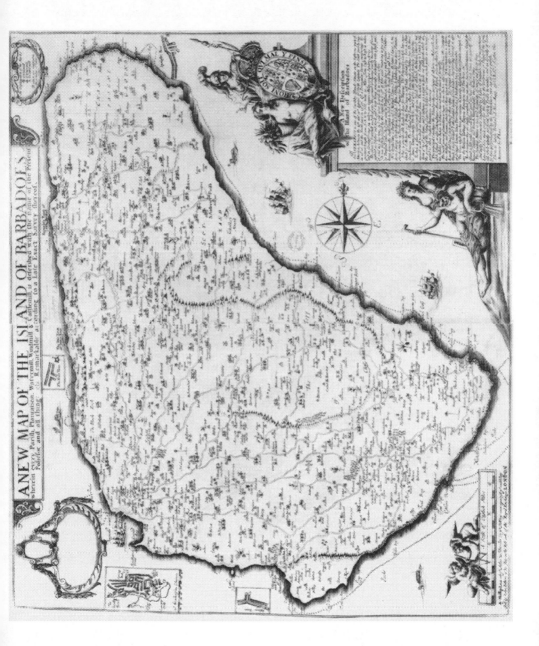

VIII

Birds feed on Birds, Beasts on each other prey,
But savage Man, alone does Man betray.
Pressed by necessity, they kill for food;
Man undoes man to do himself no good.
With Teeth and Claws by Nature arm'd, they hunt
Nature's allowance, to supply their want.
But Man with smiles, embraces, Friendship, Praise,
Most humanely his fellows Life betrays.
With voluntary pains works his Distress
Not through necessity, but wantonness.

John Wilmot, Earl of Rochester,
A Satyr against Reason and Mankind, 1675/6

'Mrs Behn. Or do you prefer Astrea? Well met. What are you working on?' Piers looked down at her, wineglass in hand, as she sat in her usual corner of Chatelin's. She had been working hard, and failed to notice his unobtrusive approach.

Aphra pushed the papers aside dismissively, and smiled up at him. She was looking tired, he thought not unsympathetically, and her complexion had lost its youthful bloom; she was not quite bedraggled, but she did not have an air of prosperity.

'Copying,' she replied, corking her inkwell and wiping the pen. 'When times are hard, it is my good Italic script which stands between me and worse things. All of us must sell something of ourselves if we are to live, and I have been glad enough to find a market for my hand. You may call me Astrea if you wish. I meant it for a nom-de-plume or an alias in my romantical youth, but now I publish as Mrs Behn, and half London calls me Astrea to my face.'

'What have you here?' he asked, drawing up a chair and stirring her loose papers.

'A pasquil of mad Charles Sedley's. All the town rake-hells must see it, and no one dares to print, so Robert Julian has sent it me for copying. Alas, the jest loses its freshness by the twelfth time of writing.'

Piers took up a page, looked at it, and read aloud in a schoolboy singsong,

> '"Portsmouth, the incestuous Punk
> Made our most gracious Sov'raign drunk.
> And drunk she made him give that Buss
> That all the Kingdom's bound to curse,
> And so red hot with Wine and Whore,
> He kickt the Commons out of door"

— ay, 'tis sad, ill-natured doggerel, nothing but spleen and bad rhymes, and without even the merit of truth, I should say. You could write better yourself.'

'I would do so, if I had a market for 'em,' she said, a little grimly.

'*The Dutch Lover* did not mend your fortunes, then? I feared it had not.'

She shrugged. 'It was thirty pound in all, for my third-night's fee, and that was two months ago. When I am in funds, I must treat the good fellows who treated me when I was poor, I must pay my landlord, and a woman must dress, if she is to be seen at all. Thirty pound does not go far, as you know yourself.'

'Well, I am sorry for it,' he said.

'It was not the best of notions, perhaps,' Aphra confessed. 'I thought the name would bring 'em in to jeer at Mynheer Haunce, but the war is gone on too long, I think. He was but a small part of the plot, but the people do not even want to hear the name of a Dutchman – they think only of taxes when the word comes to their ears.'

'A lesson, my dear Astrea. Put your faith in the poinarding Spaniards and Venetian courtesans that have peopled the stage this hundred years. Give the people cruel fathers, nunneries, incest, revenge, sequestered daughters, and poisoning Jesuits, and you will fill the theatre. The Dutch are dull, as you know to your cost.'

He paused, and sipped deliberately at his wine. 'Speaking of the Dutch and their dullness, I have news of your own Mynheer Haunce which will please you, I think. The doctor. Did you not fear, when the playbills went up, that he would present himself at Dorset Gardens, vowing revenge?'

'Oh. What have you heard of him?' She tried to match his unconcern, but he could hear a tremor in her voice.

'He is gone to Barbados. He lived in Tothill Street, hard by the Lord Chamberlain's office. Harris met him first in The Cock there, and it was easy enough to find out his direction once I made enquiries in the tavern. Who knows why he is gone – to minister to his fellow negroes, perhaps. But you need have no more fear of him.'

She let out a deep breath, relief visible on her face. 'Thank you, Mr Piers. I am more grateful than I can say.'

Balthasar never forgot his first sight of Barbados. The *Penelope* had been out of sight of land since they left the Canaries behind; a month of mid-Atlantic waves, with nothing to look at but the sea and its gradually changing life. As they travelled south and west, they had begun to see porpoise and grampus, then, one exciting day, flying fish and dolphins. Beyond the Tropic of Cancer, they

168

began to see albatross, like huge white crosses hanging in the air, their wings unmoving. They were gliding on the Trades, as the *Penelope* itself was doing, far beneath them. His eyes were so used to the sea and the sky, when he saw a little hummock of something towards the horizon, he thought at first it must be a whale.

Palaeologue came up beside him. 'There it is,' he said. 'I applaud the captain's skill. They say that because it lies so low, it is like trying to find a sixpence thrown down on Newmarket Heath. The Trades blow you faithfully to this latitude, but finding the island is not easy once you are here.'

'I must go and tell Sibella,' said Balthasar. He climbed down the companionway and entered the tiny cabin he shared with his wife. It was as hot as an oven, and it stank, of sweat, vomit and other human odours, and of the musty cockroaches that came out at night in a rustling mass and were bold enough even to bite at their feet as they lay attempting to sleep. Sibella was lying on the bed, as usual, her face glistening with sweat. She found the shipboard food nauseating, especially now that the water had staled and developed an unpleasant, stagnant flavour. She had got very thin on it, and lost much of her comeliness. The cockroaches sickened her, as did her own uncleanness; there was no water to spare for washing but what was dipped up from the sea, and they had found that soap in sea-water had no effect. Even the foul-clouts from Sibella's monthly courses could be no more than rinsed in salty water. She had looked at the stiff, repellent rags, defeated, and decreed that they were to be thrown away.

'Sibella, I have seen Barbados on the horizon. We will soon be off this ship.'

'Thank God.' She looked as if she wanted to say more, but did not. Balthasar was aware that she had made it a point of private principle not to complain of the hardships of the voyage since it was she who had cast the decisive vote for coming, but he could see for himself that she had found shipboard life very difficult, even once the seasickness had worn off. As soon as he had realised how badly she was taking the journey, he had braved the fetid horror of below-decks, where the wretches who were travelling to a life as indentured servants were carried all together with no privacy whatsoever, and had found there a reasonably genteel and well-spoken Irishwoman called Bridget Burnell, who had agreed to come up and care for her for a fee of ten shillings. So Sibella had not lacked a woman about her, but all the same, she had suffered greatly.

'Balthasar,' Sibella said suddenly. 'Bridget and I have agreed well enough this last month, and she is kind. Can we buy her?'

'I do not see why not. We must have a cookmaid, and she is for you to choose. But would you not rather make your choice once we are ashore? Have you asked Bridget if she can cook?'

'I would rather someone I know, Balthasar. If she cannot cook, she can learn.'

'Have you thought why she is on this ship? You know that nothing but dire necessity compels these poor people to sign away seven years of their lives. Many of the women are whores.'

'Well, and what would you?' said Sibella rather sharply. 'We must have a woman, and here in the colonies she must be either the scourings of London or a slave. Bridget at least speaks English, so I can teach her what else she needs to know. She has begged me to take her, Balthasar.'

'Very well, Sibella. Tell her she is of our family, but if she is idle or of bad conduct, we can sell on her indenture, and if she has a bad name as a servant, she will end in a field gang. She must not think that she has acquired the right to our protection or she may become proud.'

They were all on the deck when the ship came into Carlisle Bay and entered the harbour at Bridgetown. He had bought Bridget's indenture from the captain, so for the next seven years he owned her: when he told her as much, she had thanked him too fulsomely, and embarrassed him by trying to kiss his hands. She was much shorter than Sibella, a little, broad-set woman who seemed somehow formed by nature to be stout, though she was lean enough after the privations of the voyage: her face was also broad, with narrow eyes, a long upper lip, and a wide mouth. He thought her sly-looking and not altogether prepossessing, but Sibella had clearly become fond of her, and self-interest, he hoped, would make her loyal.

A goodly number of ships rode at anchor in the Bay, and behind the forest of masts and spars, he could see the town sprawled around the port, an undisciplined huddle of tall, narrow, gable-fronted buildings of English type, pressing almost up to the edge of the wharves. Behind it, the land climbed in terraces to the island's central plateau: here and there in the landscape stood windmills, a sight at once familiar and, in this context, surprising. Every inch seemed under cultivation; for the first time in his life, Balthasar saw the exuberant, deep, fresh green of sugar-cane marching up the slopes, and guessed what it was. The sun beat down on them and dazzled up from the water as they moved slowly into the noise and smell of Bridgetown; they could smell strong, ripe odours of fish-guts and sewage, and through it, somehow perceptible to their salt-caked, starved nostrils, the dry sweetness of the breeze from the land.

Balthasar saw his gold safely deposited in a bank, then he and Palaeologue set about hiring horses and pack-mules. Once the ship was unloaded, they formed up in a long procession, and he, Lieutenant Palaeologue, Sibella and Bridget set off up-country followed by a train of laden mules and their drivers. On the invitation of Lady Mary Palaeologue, Theodore's mother, they were to begin their sojourn on the island as her guests.

The narrow, red, dusty track wound up between the fields, edged with thick barriers of khus-khus grass. The cane was high behind it, a stiff, rustling mass as high as their heads, even on

171

horseback. It cut off their view entirely: Balthasar felt as if they were riding down a green tunnel. It was intensely hot, and in the impenetrable depths of the cane-fields, unknown creatures sang and rustled.

It was no great distance to St John. The whole island was, he knew, little more than twenty miles long, and from Bridgetown to the Palaeologue plantation was perhaps eight or ten miles, but they were all tired, unwell, and unused to the heat. As their caravan plodded slowly between the inimical green walls of cane, and sweat trickled down their backs, the journey seemed interminable.

At last, they came to a pair of coral-limestone pillars, and Palaeologue reined in his horse. 'We are here,' he announced. 'Welcome to Logue Hall. We surrendered the first part of our name, for the ease of our neighbours.' The road before them was the same soft red dust as the public thoroughfare, but it was edged with a stately avenue of palm-trees, their dead-straight trunks rising to a great height, then exploding in a tuft of feathery leaves far overhead. To left and right, between the palms, Balthasar glimpsed fields with orderly rows of savagely spiky growth, hard, serrated leaves, set in a crown. 'Pineapples,' said Palaeologue, seeing Balthasar looking at them curiously. 'My father did not venture on cane.'

The house was now visible, a white, coral-limestone structure, surrounded by a colonnade of pillars. 'My father had the builders make the house something after the Italian fashion,' explained Palaeologue. 'He thought it would suit the climate.'

As they approached the house, Lady Palaeologue came out into the loggia to meet them. She was an elderly woman, well past fifty, and sparely built, with white hair and an air of command; even in this moment of joy, she was sternly self-controlled, though he could see her lips quivering where they were pressed firmly together, and tears were running down her face. The slaves had assembled to greet their mistress's son, and they cheered as Lieutenant Palaeologue swept off his hat to salute them.

Balthasar dismounted, while his friend went to greet his mother, and went to assist Sibella and Bridget. Neither woman was accustomed to riding, and he knew they would be very stiff and sore. Sibella's face was tight with exhaustion, and the bodice of her dress was soaked through with great patches of sweat, while the skirt was covered in soft red dust up to knee level. Bridget was, if anything, in worse case. By the time she was steady on her feet, a slave had come forward to lead away the horses, and mother and son had emerged from their first embrace, though Lady Palaeologue kept tight hold of her son's hand as if she feared he might evaporate. Balthasar led his wife forward, feeling her lean her weight on his arm like an old woman, and watched with pride as she made her curtsey with a dignity which resulted solely from her iron will.

'Doctor van Overmeer,' said Lady Palaeologue, 'Welcome to Logue Hall. Make no ceremony, my dear,' she added, disengaging from her son and taking Sibella's hand as she rose from her curtsey. 'You are weary with travel. Rest now and refresh yourselves, and I will see you at supper. Quashie, Isaiah and Cleopatra will show you your quarters.' She bowed and turned away, and he observed that she was walking with difficulty, and leaning heavily on a cane. Theodore went to his mother, and as he took her arm affectionately, Balthasar saw that they were much of a height. They disappeared together into the dim depths of the house.

'Come wid me, sir an' madam,' said the oldest of the three slaves who had come forward: Quashie. Both men were dressed in coarse osnaburg linen trousers and shirts, the natural colour of the flax, while the woman Cleopatra wore a full skirt of indigo blue and a simple, round-necked bodice with sleeves to the elbow. All three had bare feet and legs; and Balthasar noticed that their feet and ankles were a mass of little scars and bites.

They were conducted to a high, airy room with shutters that

kept out the worst of the sun. It was blessedly cool, and contained little furniture. There was a clothes-press by the wall, set out from the wall with its feet standing in saucers of water, a table and washstand, and a shelf hung from the ceiling by tarred ropes. The bedstead was simple, hung with plain dornix, but as well as the woollen tester and side-curtains, the whole structure was shrouded in white gauze, which gave it a ghostly look.

'For de merrywings an' de skeeters,' said Quashie. 'When you get in de bed, you mek sure yuh got dem tight tight 'round, or you have dem in wid you an' dem does bite too bad.'

Balthasar nodded uncomprehendingly. A confused noise at the door heralded the arrival of their possessions: the barrels containing his precious books packed in straw were taken to another room to be unpacked later, along with the other barrels containing such household goods as they had brought. The chests containing their clothes were brought into the room, and Quashie took over and began to direct the unpacking, while Isaiah went for water, towels and washballs.

'Oh, the heat of this place,' exclaimed Bridget. 'The ship was bad enough, but 'tis like going to Purgatory while a body's still quick.'

'Bridget, are you a Catholic?' asked Balthasar sharply, disagreeably surprised.

'I am, sir.'

Balthasar absorbed the information in silence, angrily aware of his own obtuseness. He should have realised that an Irishwoman was probably Catholic, and he would certainly not have chosen to have a Catholic servant. But she was theirs now; Sibella had forced his hand. He looked at his wife: she had certainly known it from the mulish look on her face, which dared him to comment.

'You will find no priest in the island, Bridget,' he warned. 'And while you are with us, I will expect you to attend the household prayers in decent reverence.'

The woman's exhausted, travel-stained face flushed unbecomingly, a dark stain rising from the neck of her dress. She seemed about to speak, perhaps angrily, when she was interrupted. 'Come, Bridget,' said the slave Cleopatra: Balthasar noted that she was better spoken than Quashie, with a much less marked accent. She was a very dark-skinned black woman, perhaps thirty years of age, with a graceful carriage, a long neck, and a distinguished, almond-eyed face. 'I will show you where you sleep.'

'Rest now, Bridget,' said Sibella. 'Cleopatra will help me.' The moment passed, and Bridget went off tractably enough. Balthasar looked after her with misgiving. The Irishwoman was voluble and affectionate, she had won Sibella over with her caressing ways, but since they had first made acquaintance, he had detected a note of falsity in her chatter to which his wife seemed oblivious. He was inclined now to put it down to Papistry, but it worried him nonetheless. Had he not been certain that Bridget's self-interest lay in giving them good service, he would have dismissed her, for all Sibella might have to say about it.

When the black woman came back from wherever they had gone, she and Sibella closeted themselves in another room with water, soap and towels, so that his wife could do everything possible to cleanse herself from the long journey. Meanwhile, Isaiah brought more water for Balthasar, and he too removed filthy, sweat-soaked garments and began to wash himself. Quashie put out fresh clothes for him, which he had found in one of the chests following directions; plain russet breeches, yarn stockings, a linen shirt and waistcoat, a little fusty-smelling, but clean. Not as he would have chosen to appear; but with many a pang, he and Sibella had sold all their finery, her cherished wedding-dress and lace cuffs, his lace collar, and his good coats. Lieutenant Palaeologue, once they had determined on the journey, had warned them that silk was liable to mould, rot, and attack by insects; and their best clothes would very likely be spoiled on the ship. 'Buy anew, if you

175

will, in the island,' he advised. 'We import such stuffs, though it is hard enough to keep them in wearable condition, but let some other fellow bear the risk of the carriage.' They had seen the sense of that, though it had brought home to Sibella, he rather thought for the first time, something of the difficulties they would face: he had not himself been greatly surprised, having been brought up by Pelagius and Narcissus on tales of the tropics. But he had bought Sibella a pearl necklace with the proceeds, so that she would have a little finery to show she was a gentleman's wife, even if for the moment, she must dress like a servant-maid. However, he resolved that whatever it cost, he himself must have a gentleman's clothes. Their brief sojourn in Bridgetown had brought it home to him how completely dependent on his clothes he was, in this land of dark faces, to establish his status as a free and independent individual. He had agreed to the venture for Sibella's sake, but all that they had experienced since their arrival set qualms of misgiving in his bowels: it struck him suddenly that Palaeologue's respect for ancient lineage might have fatally misled him, and that the people of Barbados might see him very differently.

As he stripped and began to soap himself, standing in a basin of blessedly cool, fresh water, he became aware that Quashie and Isaiah were watching him intently. He could feel their curiosity, though they said nothing until he had finished washing.

'Master van Overmeer . . . you is a Dutchman?' asked Quashie, handing him a towel.

'Yes, I am,' he replied, briskly rubbing himself dry.

'An' dey say you is a doctor.'

'I am.'

'You nuh look like nuh Dutchman I did ever see,' said Isaiah so quietly he could pretend not to have heard it, but he was not minded to pretend any such thing. He knotted the towel round his waist, stepped out of the basin, and turned to face them.

'My father was African,' he said firmly.

The two slaves exchanged glances; the whites of their eyes flashing in the dark faces as they looked towards one another and did not speak.

'He was king of Oyo. I am Balthasar Oranyan, son of Omoloju, son of Onfinran, son of Onigbogi, son of Oluaso, son of Kori, son of Aganju, son of Ajaka, son of Shango, son of Oranyan, the first king of Oyo.' They looked completely blank, and he felt a jolt of disappointment; it was the first occasion he had ever recited the names memorised so long ago, and he had hoped for some response; information, admiration, even.

'Wheh' Oyo?' asked Quashie.

'I do not know. Somewhere in the West of Africa.'

'I is a Africa man,' said Quashie. 'Coromantee. But I never did hear 'bout Oyo.'

Sibella and Cleopatra returned while he was finishing dressing. His wife was looking greatly refreshed and much more like herself in a clean linsey-woolsey dress. It still showed the creases from its long sojourn in a chest, but she was wearing her pearl necklace, her hair was newly dressed, and her head was held high. Cleopatra came behind her, the filthy, discarded clothes over one arm.

'Well, my dear,' he said, 'Let us go and pay our respects to our hostess.'

After the preliminary courtesies were over, Sibella asked a question which Balthasar had also wanted to raise.

'Lady Palaeologue, I saw cane-fields everywhere along our way. It seemed as if the whole island was sugar. Is this so, or are we in an area peculiar to it?'

The old woman nodded, smiling at her benignly. 'It is. Sugar is now king,' she explained. 'It makes fortunes, and this island is very well suited to the cane.'

'But then, if I may ask, why did your husband not grow it?' she asked simply.

A shadow crossed their hostess's face. 'To a great extent, it is a question of scale, my dear,' she explained. 'When Sir Ferdinando first came to Barbados, the best profit to be had was in cotton and indigo. He was fleeing the wreck of the King's fortunes, and like many a gentleman in those times, he was not a man of great wealth. He could afford this estate of twenty-five acres, which was thought ample enough at that time, but he was good for very little more. Indigo requires investment in building: one must have great stone tanks, for rotting the leaves, and such building was beyond his means. The house he first brought me to was wooden, and it remained wooden for its first two decades, until his fortunes had mended a little. It was only late in the 'sixties that we replaced it with the house we now sit in. I suppose he might have set about growing cotton which also suits the climate well, but although it needs little equipment, the cotton-grower must have many hands to pick the bolls and gin them, and slaves are fifteen pound a head. So, to make no more of the tale, Sir Ferdinando decided not to risk taking on a debt which would perhaps destroy us, we cut our coat according to our cloth, and grew ginger and pineapples. They need little in the way of husbandry, and thus, it has been possible to content ourselves with a small establishment. I have four house-slaves now, the three you have met, with Quashie's wife Nanny in the kitchen, six field hands, and some dependants of the house, and this number has been quite sufficient – the family has been about this size for many years.

'When sugar came in, in order to turn this estate over to cane, Sir Ferdinando would have had to be in a position to make a very substantial investment, which we were not, without hazarding all we owned.' Her tone was scrupulously neutral, but all the same, Balthasar gathered a clear impression that she had argued for a more venturesome course. 'A sugar-grower needs a great estate. Fifty acres at the least, and perhaps a hundred slaves, though more is better – two men to the acre is the minimum rule, and three to two is preferable. Erecting a boiling-house, mills, and the

other necessaries is not economic on a small scale, and even if Sir
Ferdinando had cared to risk making himself dependent on another
man's mills, we would have needed to go deep into debt for fifteen
or twenty more hands, and carry the debt for at least a year and
a half, since cane takes more than a year to come to harvest. This
island is no Paradise, Mistress Sibella. In all the time we have been
here, near enough one year in three has been a year of disaster:
there have been four droughts, three years of tempestuous rain, and
a hurricane, which is a wind-storm beyond anything an English
person can imagine. A hurricane or a drought in a year when one
is deep in debt can damage a planter's credit beyond recovery.

'So, all in all, sugar is vastly profitable, but only the wealthy or
the well-connected can begin on it. Planters are fewer, and very
much richer, than they were when first I came here: for the last
twenty years, the wealthier men have been engrossing the estates
of their neighbours. In any case, Sir Ferdinando was content to
lead his life in gentlemanly leisure with his books and his music,
and I have come to find charm in the retiredness of this life. The
pines and the ginger have answered our simple needs. There is
good market for both, and since the island is now mostly sugar,
I sell much of my produce in Barbados itself.'

Sibella digested this lengthy speech. Her expression was carefully blank, but, Balthasar felt, if she had understood it at all,
she would surely have understood that her dreams were vain.
'Is Cleopatra the wife of Isaiah?' asked Sibella inconsequentially,
leading him to fear that she had allowed her mind to wander: the
innocence of the question was heartwarming, but embarrassing,
and on both counts, he hoped devoutly that their hostess would
not choose to be offended.

'Yes,' said Lady Palaeologue, with a certain emphasis, 'she is.'

Balthasar was immediately confirmed in his guess at island
manners, a surmise that the girl had in earlier days been the
old master's concubine, when he caught a half-corner of a smile

on the mouth of his friend. It seemed to him absolutely necessary to change the subject, and he immediately did so. 'Lady Palaeologue, we need to ask your advice, I think,' he said. 'My wife is the heir to a plantation in St George. Her father was, like your husband, an exile in the late times, a servant of Prince Rupert, and he died here, perhaps ten years ago. What should we do?'

'Have you a direction for the property?' asked their hostess with interest.

Sibella nodded. 'I have a letter which my father wrote to my mother,' she said.

'Well then, my dear. The first step is to look at it. We will do that, once you have recruited your strength. But I would advise you not to hope for much. The law here is that a man must maintain, at a minimum, one servant for every ten acres to cultivate the ground, otherwise he forfeits his property for non-management. In any case, a plantation left deserted is ruinated, lest it become a sanctuary for fugitives.' Balthasar was watching his wife's face as Lady Palaeologue spoke, and saw her expression close down in a familiar fashion as she absorbed this blow to her hopes.

Quashie came into the room, almost silent on bare feet. 'Dinner is served, my lady,' he said.

The food was strange to them; there was an excellent loin of pork, and a dish of chicken cooked with marjoram, red pepper and lime-juice, which was not unpleasant, once one became accustomed to the burning sensation left in the mouth. What surprised him most – and Sibella too, to judge by her expression – was that there was no bread, but only flat, rather dry and tasteless cakes, some curious roots, which Balthasar thought were somewhat like parsnip, but sweeter and redder, and a strange, slimy green vegetable, which he tasted and found repellent.

'You will learn to relish pork,' said Palaeologue, watching them cautiously experimenting with the food before them. 'Swine fatten here better than in England, but our beef is very poor. We keep a cow or two for milk, but beef cattle are not worth the ground they take up. It is better husbandry to buy salt beef. We cannot grow wheat in the West Indies, and the flour we import is often spoiled or stale, so when we have none that is good, the household follows the custom of the Caribs, and we stay our stomachs with cassava by way of bread-kind.'

'And these other things?' asked Balthasar.

'Those are batatas, or as some call them, sweet-potatoes. They grow plentifully here, and we also grow yams and India corn, which the slaves make the main part of their diet. Neither my mother nor I care greatly for them, so we rely on cassava when there is no good flour to be had. The long green pods are ochroes, which flourish here. We are too far inland for fish, alas; in this climate, it spoils in hours. Mistress Sibella, can I help you to a little of the fowl?'

'No thank you, sir,' she said, almost inaudibly. She had made a pretence of disturbing the food on her plate, but had eaten almost nothing.

'Sibella,' said Balthasar. 'You must eat. You have lost too much flesh already. If you find the pork heavy, you must take some chicken.'

He could see the resistance in her, but she obediently accepted a little chicken, and having cut it into the smallest possible fragments, began to swallow them like boluses. Balthasar sensed storms ahead, and hoped profoundly that she would not starve herself out of sheer obstinacy. His own life had left him adaptable, but Sibella was very young, and she was also narrow and tenacious. He feared for her.

At the end of the day, they returned back to their room. The dessert, sweet oranges, water-melons, musk-melons, guavas, papayas, custard-apples and of course, pineapple, had been a taste of earthly Paradise, especially after the dried, salt food of their dreary months at sea, even Sibella had clearly enjoyed the melting, succulent fruit. As night fell, the air was filled with noises, chief above all a monotonous calling like tiny silver bells endlessly shaken, and liquid whistles, whoops and gurgles which he could not recognise or associate with any living thing. During dinner itself, they had found out about 'merrywings'; he heard a thin, sweet, high note, like a bugle heard at a distance; and a moment after he had registered the curious, even beautiful sound, he found a lump on the side of his hand which itched infernally.

'They have found us,' said Lady Palaeologue resignedly. 'To your pipes, gentlemen, smoke is the only sanctuary.' At last, he understood the shrouding round their bed.

Once they had said goodnight, he and Sibella undressed as rapidly as possible in the strangeness of the high, square room lit by a single flickering candle. In the dim light which radiated from it, he saw a mazy, jumbling dance of tiny insect bodies; he was already covered with itchy lumps on all exposed surfaces. He watched his wife squat over the chamber-pot in her shift, then as she made for the bed, he warned, 'Disturb the hangings as little as you can, my sweetheart. We must keep the insects out.'

She slipped into bed; he used the pot after her, blew out the candle, and joined her cautiously. The intense velvet of the tropic night folded down round them. He put his arm across her, feeling the sweat start wherever the heat of their bodies met. It was, to him, erotic; the slippery, hot, saltiness of their flesh aroused him, but he controlled his excitement, aware of her distress and also that she was determined to suffer alone. He gathered her to him, and began to kiss her neck and ears with intent to comfort, just permitting his lips to graze her damp skin. As his mouth moved up her cheekbone, he became aware that she was lying on her back with tears leaking helplessly from the corners of her eyes.

'Oh, sweetheart. Darling Sibella. Tell me.'

He felt her body stiffen; then she capitulated. 'I wanted to bring you something,' she said, her voice small and bleak. 'I brought us here, because I thought I could make our heir a gentleman like his grandfather. And I have failed you.'

'But my dearest dear, we have not even seen the situation for ourselves,' he protested.

'It is all one. Lady Palaeologue has told us I no longer have a plantation.'

Though he was anxious to be tender of her and of her feelings, he began to feel a stirring of temper of his own.

'Sibella, I told you that if you had a plantation, we must sell it.'

She turned to him; in the absolute blackness of the tropical night, he could see nothing, but he felt the vigour of her movement.

'But that was before we were here.'

'Sibella, my darling little mouse, are you mad? I am a mulatto, Sibella, I am a man of royal blood on both sides, but I cannot set up as a planter! Did you not realise that?'

She was weeping against his shoulder, hot, bitter tears of humiliation; he could only hope they were not because she was married to a black. The thought sharpened his tongue, and he spoke to her as he had very seldom done.

'Recognise this, my wife. I have no reason in the world to be ashamed of my birth, but here in the colonies, blacks are slaves, whites are masters. I am neither. I hope and trust that I can practise my trade here, but I cannot ape the master and make myself a gentleman. They will not permit it.'

'Then I have brought you to this Hell for nothing,' she whispered.

'Sibella! I came because you wished it. I came because Lieutenant Palaeologue wished it, and damned if I did not come because I wished it myself. I have no love for London, you may be sure. But my dearest one, do not *posture*. It suits you very ill.' He put his arm round her, and shook her gently. 'My darling. I honour your wish to better us. But you know I am constrained. A coloured man is not fully a man, here in Barbados.'

She burrowed her head against his neck, and he felt her tears soaking his shirt. 'I did not know it, Balthasar. I did not think of you in that way. I think I have made a dreadful mistake.'

He comforted her as best he might, and even in the damp, tropical heat, she eventually fell asleep. He remained stiff and angry for long enough. The sense that she had blinded herself to the reality of him was a hard one to tolerate, though even he had not truly comprehended how much the colour of his skin would govern how he was perceived until they reached Bridgetown. Lady Palaeologue's relations with her slaves were personal and domestic, because the household was a small one. But it was clear that the usual state of affairs in Barbados was the big plantation, with a hundred or more slaves; he had known that abstractly from conversation with Lieutenant Palaeologue, but now that they were in the island, its full meaning began to come home to him. In such a plantation, the distance between white and black must be absolute.

In the morning, they both felt a little better. A night's sleep, however broken by heat and itch, had plainly done Sibella good. She was subdued and sad-looking, but the hysteria had gone from her voice and manner. Bridget knocked on the door as they were dressing. Her hands and face were swollen and lumpy with bites, and her eyes were red. Sibella asked her anxiously if she had been crying, but she explained curtly that her eyes were sore because the slaves purposely kept smoking fires going at night to discourage flying insects.

After breakfast, Balthasar examined Lady Palaeologue, and was on the whole reassured. His hostess was subject to gout, which accounted for the difficulty she had in walking. She was in recovery from a major bout, and her urine still showed the characteristic chalky precipitate. The action of the heart was a little disturbed, but otherwise, she seemed in good enough health for her time of life, though she evidently suffered a great deal when a fit was on her.

'If we were in England,' said Balthasar frankly when he had finished his examination, 'I would prescribe you a regimen with confidence, but not here. Until I understand a little more of Barbados, I am afraid of doing you more harm than good. When people born and bred in colder latitudes move to the tropics, they experience a general debility and failure of vigour: the blood, too, becomes thinner and paler. I do not yet know what allowance to make for the different air, water and climate of Barbados; and I do not know the virtues of indigenous foodstuffs. My father taught me, my lady, that what is beneficial in one place is not always so in another.'

'I commend your father's wisdom, and yours, Doctor,' said Lady Palaeologue, as Cleopatra knelt before her and deftly rewrapped the bandage on her foot. 'It is a rare physician who knows his own ignorance.'

'All I will say, until I am better informed, is that your diet should be light and moderate, but you observe this rule already, I think. Madeira-and-water is a safe drink for you, and I would advise a digestive, to strengthen the body and aid it in driving off the peccant humours. What this should be, I will try to discover as soon as may be. Chocolata is well spoken of on all hands; it should be ground and decocted in water, with only so little sugar as to preserve some of the natural bitterness, and perhaps you should try it. It is very easy of digestion. You should take a little candied fruit with your wine-and-water, lest it chill the stomach, and you will also find that ambergris is a great friend to nature, if it is to be had. Meanwhile, is there anyone else on the plantation who needs a doctor's attention?'

'All is well, I think. There is a good negro-doctor a mile or two from here, on Baxter's plantation, who looks after my slaves with success when they are afflicted. Yambo is a shrewd fellow, with a good knowledge of the herbs and simples this land affords, which I think he learned from the Caribs. My hands are not worked as hard as they are on a sugar plantation, and they have time to tend their gardens, so they are in the main, hearty. I am of opinion that half the disease we see among the negroes stems from poor victuals. Negroes, for some reason, are prone to sore eyes and night blindness, and we have our share of this affliction, but that is all at the moment, except for Cudjoe. Look at him, if you will. He is one of the two slaves here who are past work. Quibba stirs about a little, she sweeps the yards and mends the fires, but Cudjoe is entirely useless. His complaint is one peculiar to these parts, I believe, and it is found among both negroes and whites, so you may be interested by it. Whenever I am disposed to impatience under a fit of the gout,' added Lady Palaeologue a little grimly, 'I think of old Cudjoe.'

Balthasar took his leave, and followed Cleopatra across the stable-court to the negro yard. It presented an orderly spectacle; two rows of one-roomed, thatched, wooden huts, standing face to face, curiously reminiscent of the Middelburg almshouses. Ashy firepits fumed at either end of the 'street', and shade-trees stood around. They were orchard-trees too, he observed: he saw limes on a small, thorny bush near him, a papaya with its fruit hung round the stem like the many breasts of Diana of the Ephesians, and, squinting up at a nearby tree, he recognised the previous night's custard-apples hanging among the sparse, narrow leaves. Interspersed among the trees were tall patches of Indian corn and irregular plantings of leafy crops, strange to him. Chickens scratched and pecked about the huts, under the desultory supervision of a naked child of six or so who was playing a mysterious and private game with pebbles in the white dust and a wizened, ancient-looking woman sitting in a doorway smoking a pipe of coarse tobacco. She was wearing only a skirt, and Balthasar observed with distaste that her breasts had collapsed until they hung below her waist. Quibba, for so she must be, watched his approach with Cleopatra, but offered no greeting. The child ignored him completely.

'Is Bridget accommodated here?' he asked.

'She is, sir.' Balthasar looked about him; he did not like the woman, but he could not help thinking of what it might mean to someone who had clearly begun life as a person of some consequence to be living in a hut among black slaves, without so much as a screen against the mosquitoes. The effort of imagination was beyond him, but he felt a measure of sympathy for her surliness. Cleopatra stopped outside one of the huts, and knocked politely on the jamb of the door; a faint voice answered from within.

They entered the hut, and as his eyes adjusted to the darkness within, he saw that the room was small and neat, with a bare earth floor, a straw mat for a bed, and a few possessions stowed on a shelf. It stank of sweat and suffering. On a rough stool in the middle of the floor sat an elderly man, so positioned that he could look out of his door. His eyes were hollowed by prolonged pain, and rested on Balthasar without curiosity. He wore only a loincloth, and from the knees downwards, his legs bulged like bladders, with obscene, bloated folds at the ankle, perhaps five or six times their natural size. No trace remained of the natural shape of the limb, which seemed somehow to have melted like tallow. The skin was dry-looking, with a chalky whiteness on the surface.

'I am Doctor van Overmeer, Cudjoe,' he said. 'Let me examine your legs.'

The old slave looked at him, moving little more than his eyes. 'Nuttin' can cure dat, massa,' he said wearily.

Balthasar knelt and examined the swollen flesh, which was strangely textured, like a leather bottle full of water. His mind was buzzing, searching frantically for any kind of explanation, and he could think of nothing at all. It was as if the luxuriant propensity for growth, seen in everything around them, had somehow seized

187

on the limbs of this unfortunate man to produce this wild, unnatural expansion. He got slowly to his feet, entirely helpless. He could feel Cleopatra watching him, and wondered what she was thinking.

When he returned to the house, he met Sibella and Lieutenant Palaeologue in the hall.

'My dear sir,' said Palaeologue. 'I believe you have finished with my mother for the moment. I was proposing to your wife that we take a turn up to St George's. The plantation in question is somewhere in the environs of St George's Church, and I think that you should see what is there.'

The little expedition set off perhaps half an hour later, wearing broad-brimmed hats; Sibella additionally tied a veil over her face and neck to protect her complexion from the sun. It was a far pleasanter ride than the one which had brought them to Logue Hall. They were less tired, and it was a matter of two or three miles only. Simon Carteret's last letter to his wife had been explicit, and was easily interpreted by Lady Palaeologue. Sibella had the letter in the bosom of her dress, but the words played in Balthasar's head; like his wife, he knew it off by heart, having read it again and again on ship-board. 'Madam,' it began:

we will not meet again in this world. Our tempers were diverse, and the badness of the times laid stumbling-blocks in the path of our agreement, but for all that, I most freely forgive your all and several faults towards me, which were but droplets beside the crimson ocean of my sins. Do you so forgive me; and be it known to you and to all men that I, Simon Carteret, writing with my own hand, and sound of mind though weak in body, devise and bequeath all that I die possessed of here in the island of Barbados to you, my wife Margaret Carteret, and if Margaret Carteret be dead and another is reading this, to our daughter Sibella, if she is in life. I send this to you now, and I advise you furthermore, if proof be needed, that a copy is lodged with Gurney's Bank in Bridgetown.

The plantation where I now lie bears the name Mount Pleasant, and is situate in the east of the parish of St George. Approaching from Bridgetown, turn due east at the Quaker Meeting-House, and take the road that goeth up to rising ground, for a matter of a mile or less. You will see the peaks of the Scotland district, but before you climb so high, you will come to a great stone Cistern, this marks the north-west corner of the estate, which is the pleasant hill now stretching before you, while the boundary to the south-west is at the three old sandbox trees growing together.

Now, at last, the road before them was going up rising ground. Before them and on either side stretched an endless vista of cane-fields. Lieutenant Palaeologue reined in his horse.

'We have come about a mile, my friends,' he said. 'I would guess that the estate is hereabouts.'

Before they could move off again, a gang of slaves appeared round a bend in the road, men and women together, carrying hoes and bill-hooks, with a driver bringing up the rear. They were a wild-looking crew, dressed only in loincloths or breeches, and Balthasar noticed that of the dozen or so figures, two were white, their hair and beards matted into hanks, their skins reddened and coarsened by exposure to the sun. 'Good day to you, sirra,' shouted Palaeologue. 'What is this place?' The slaves came to a halt, and the driver walked across to them, surveying them with no friendly eye.

'This is Fosters Plantation. You are out of your way, sir.'

'And this ground before us?'

'Mount Pleasant Field.'

'Well, you are answered, Mistress Sibella. The estate is engrossed in the neighbour plantation.' She bowed her head; her expression was unreadable through her veil. 'Thank you, my man. We will not trouble your master, but I am Lieutenant Palaeologue of Logue Hall in St John, if he should enquire.' He turned his horse as the man bowed, a little more civilly, and Sibella and Balthasar followed suit, plodding down the road side by side. Dejection showed in every line of Sibella's body. As they went, the skies began to darken, as if picking up her mood.

'Hurry,' said Palaeologue urgently. 'We should try to reach the Quakers' house before the storm breaks.'

They stirred up their horses, and cantered down the road. As they came up to the meeting-house, the first drops of abrupt, drenching tropical rain were beginning to fall, heavy and, to Balthasar, astonishingly warm on the back of his neck and hands. They tied the horses outside, and hurried into the unlocked meeting-house as the rain began coming down in earnest. It was a shed-like, thatched building, and when they went inside they found it was bare and very clean, with whitewashed walls and a gallery running round two sides of the room, accessed by a staircase. There were plain benches standing round the four sides of the room, facing in to a central, square space, and all the furnishings were of plain, dark wood, lovingly polished. There was nothing like an altar, and no decoration of any kind, not even a cross or texts painted on the wall: he wondered momentarily how the Quakers' worship was conducted. The rain hissed and thudded down outside, the ground visibly steaming as it landed, but inside the little building there was a sense of intense, concentrated calm which seemed as much part of its nature as the shelter afforded by its roof. One by one, they sat down, each busy with his or her own thoughts. Sibella was sitting very upright, her hands clasped loosely in her lap; gradually the tense line of her mouth relaxed, leaving her face young and sad. He was reminded of how she had looked on her wedding day.

'Mistress Sibella, do not lose heart,' said Palaeologue, after an interval of silence. Even over the racket of the rain, his voice was clearly audible. 'I must own, the situation here is what I had expected. When I was a boy, much of St George's was still forest and wild hogs, but you heard my mother saying that the sugar-men have been extending their lands by all means that they could in the last twenty years. The estate would have been forfeit once it passed out of cultivation, as she told you, and Foster will have snapped at the chance to bring it under his hand.'

'Then we are here on a fool's errand,' she said shortly, almost rudely – though perhaps she was striving to make herself heard.

'By no means. With a will and a named heir to consider, your father's executor will surely have *sold* the land and slaves before the property was forfeited. There are scoundrels aplenty in the world who will rob the widow and the orphan, but your father dealt with Gurney's Bank and they are Quakers, which is to say, queer folk in the main, but honourable to quixotry. You must go to Bridgetown.'

IX

B arbadoes Isle inhabited by Slaves,
A nd for one honest man, ten thousand knaves:
R eligion to thee's a Romantick story,
B arbarity and ill got wealth thy glory.
A ll Sodom's Sins are Centred in thy heart,
D eath is thy look, and Death in every part.
O h! Glorious Isle, in Villany Excell.
S in to the Height – thy fate is Hell.
Thomas Walduck, a Barbadian, verse in a letter to a friend, 1710

'I have good news for thee, friend,' said Mr Fisher, looking up from his ledger. Sibella's letter lay open on the desk before him, together with the bank's copy of Carteret's will; after careful enquiry, he had expressed himself satisfied that the legitimate heir had finally presented herself. 'The estate was sold on the death of thy wife's father, lest it be sequestered. He will have bought for ten shilling the acre, but since the man Charles Stuart was restored, the rate has gone to twenty pound. Thus, the Lord has given thee an increase of fortyfold on his twenty acres. Adding to this the profits from the sale of slaves, beasts and other chattels, and subtracting the fees for overseeing the sale, the total value is six hundred and eight pounds, ten shillings and fourpence. The books are here, and you will find them well in order.'

'Thank you, sir,' said Balthasar. 'I am happy to leave these moneys in your safe hands, and I thank you for your honourable care of my wife's estate. I deposited our savings in another bank when we arrived, because it was the first that I saw – with your permission, I will withdraw it, and add the two sums together.'

'As thou wishest, friend.' Composedly, Fisher shut his ledger, and extended his hand. 'I shall hope to see thee in due course of time.'

Balthasar left the bank, barely able to understand what had been said. He had heard of the Quaker absence of ceremony, but the peculiar baldness of the banker's address was bewildering to him: even Sibella did not address him as 'thou', a form which seemed to be going out of use in England (though its equivalent in Holland was perfectly normal) and to hear the King of England referred to merely as 'the man Charles Stuart' was a jolt to his whole perception of the world.

The whole episode was so hard for him to grasp it seemed almost dreamlike. Apart from the oddities of Quaker manners, the transaction itself had astonished him. He had resolved before they left England to expect nothing, thinking it better to assume from the start that the Carteret legacy would be as worthless as the man himself, but after so much hope, false hope, and unnecessary despair on Sibella's part, this quiet upshot of sudden wealth was hard to take in. Cautiously, his mind began to play with the notion of possessing more than a thousand pounds, which with his own and Sibella's moneys, and now this estate, they did. It was a pleasant thought, and made them as secure as any could hope to be in this world, but he was well aware that the sum would not please Sibella. Where the devil lay, he well knew, was in the idea of an estate. Before they came to Barbados, she would have thought twenty acres' estate enough for anyone, and rejoiced beyond measure in six hundred pounds; but she had been infected by the madness of sugar. Having learned that an estate as Barbados now reckoned it was a hundred acres, and needed a clear three thousand pounds, two for the land, one for the slaves to work it, her notion of what would make her a gentlewoman had undergone an occult, mushroom-like expansion.

He was under no illusions about his wife. She was cherishing a dream of returning to London as a person so unquestionably wealthy, powerful and established that her years as a poor relation would seem as if they had never been; she also cherished the very English ambition, which he did not share, of re-establishing her family as gentry. Having chafed under the kindly patronage of the chief men of Middelburg in his younger days, he was not unsympathetic to the emotions that possessed her, nor was he wholly immune to the seductive dream of great wealth, but he was enough of a realist to know, as she must be made to know, that she was a child crying for the moon. Money was almost visibly being made around them, wealth rubbed and rustled along the roads as the cane-stalks swayed in the breeze, but it was made by men already rich, and no amount of will and determination would change that essential fact. They must take a house in Bridgetown, though his heart qualied at the thought, and he would begin to practise as soon as he might.

As the bank's doors closed behind him, one of his recent purchases came forward to assist him onto his horse. The first thing he had done on arriving in Bridgetown was to buy a silk coat and a wig, the second, to buy a horse, a mule and a slave. Palaeologue had ridden into Bridgetown with him, and he perceived, as men's eyes passed indifferently over him, that he was taken for the Lieutenant's house-slave. Lady Palaeologue had advised him before they left the Hall that when he went abroad, it must be on horseback, no matter how short the journey, well dressed, and with a servant riding behind him: thus, and only thus, could he hold up his head in this land of slaves where all men judged on appearance, and the journey to town was sufficient to prove the truth of her advice. But wherever he looked, there were difficulties. There were white slaves, as he had seen for himself; but could there be a mulatto master? It would be a difficult point to carry, as he was well aware from standing in church with Sibella alongside the Palaeologues on Sundays. Though he kept his eyes on his book, he observed of the suspicion and dislike in the planters' faces as they covertly assessed him, and even the minister had only spoken to him, briefly and coldly, once Lady Palaeologue had blandly forced them into conversation.

So: if he was going to defy the most basic tenet of Barbadian society, he must support his dignity as a professional man according to the customs of the place, whatever the expense. Accordingly, the slave-market was their first port of call after the warehouse where he bought his coat and wig. He was looking for a likely boy who could, with training, help him in his practice as well as lending him consequence, and found what he hoped would be a lucky bargain; an Ibo youth of fifteen or sixteen with a look of intelligence, who had lingered several months in the barracoon because he had a slightly clubbed and inturned right foot. The resultant limp was not marked, but he could not move very fast, which had discouraged the planters' agents. Balthasar, as he spoke with the boy, was struck by his capacity for observation, and the way he had put the time to good account in learning English, and bought him for fourteen pounds. Lieutenant Palaeologue then went about his own business, leaving Balthasar to go to the Bank: they were to meet later in a tavern in Cheapside. The short ride to Gurney's Bank without his friend had been an ordeal. He could feel hostile looks boring into his back, making him self-conscious, though his clothes were a protection: the watchers more likely took him for the favoured house-slave of some lord of the island than for what he was, but fear of offending such a grandee kept them at bay; still, he felt as if he were going unarmed among dangerous dogs.

For a moment, riding along the stinking street with Caesar bringing up the rear on the mule, sweating profusely into his wig while the sun beat down on his broad-brimmed hat and reflected up from the white, sandy dust, he glimpsed tall masts between two of the harbour buildings, and considered simply taking the next ship back to England. An unworthy impulse, probably, when Sibella was not even recovered from the voyage out, but he had a dark presentiment that Barbados would never have any more to offer him than it had already yielded.

'Master van Overmeer, Yambo is here,' announced Cleopatra, coming silently into their quarters on her bare feet. Preparations for the move to Bridgetown were well advanced. Sibella had taken the news better than he feared; a settled depression seemed to have come over her. She had been apathetic towards his plans for settling in Bridgetown, and even towards his purchase of a newly built, ten-roomed stone house on Swan Street, near the new cathedral, though now the move drew near, she was getting more interested, and appeared even to be getting some enjoyment out of planning what they would need: she spent long hours in consultation with Cleopatra and Bridget. Idleness did not suit her, and she had had little enough to do as a guest in Lady Palaeologue's well-run household. Meanwhile, Balthasar spent most of his time with Caesar, acquainting the boy with the rudiments of medical theory and teaching him to read. To his delight, once they became better acquainted, Caesar had confessed a little knowledge of Arabic script. In consequence, he had no difficulty at all with the principle of writing, and his practical knowledge came on by leaps and bounds. They were sitting together as Cleopatra made her entrance, looking at the Gospel According to St Matthew, which seemed to him more suitable than anything else they had to hand to use as a primer, and the boy had just gravelled on the word 'notwithstanding'.

'Thank you, Cleopatra. Run away now, boy – no, on second thoughts, follow me. I want you to hear this, and remember it.' He took his hat, his small memorandum book and a silver pencil, and with the sound of Caesar's irregular footsteps echoing behind him, went out to the courtyard.

He had mistrusted his father's wisdom, back in England. Here in the Antilles, it was all he had to sustain him. Pelagius had seldom spoken of the past, but once his son had settled on medicine, he had vouchsafed a few words on medical practice in the tropics. Trust hunters, he had advised, and trust peasants, they are the people who truly observe the conditions of the world they live in. Europe is but one part of the world, and as Hippocrates and the ancients tell us, man's constitution is affected by different airs, waters and places. Nature is universal, but medicine is not. Learn from those who know, and do not blind yourself to the value of what they have to tell you – but principles are constant, his own mind insisted in refutation, cutting off the memory of his father's voice, though he was happy to concede that, to achieve a given end, different methods might be needed. He hoped that he was about to find out what those methods might be, though no hunters, and no peasants, were to be found, but only slaves, who were strangers and sojourners like himself.

Yambo was waiting in the shade by the porch, squatting easily, and resting his arms on his knees. He stood up as Balthasar approached, and bowed. He was wearing only a pair of ragged trousers, though he had a linen bag slung across his back, and he was middle-aged, even elderly, but his figure was spare and powerful. His face, which was broad-nosed, high-cheekboned, and authoritative, was marked with regular, parallel cicatrices, indicating that he must have been born in Africa; his sides and arms, and doubtless also his back, were marked by the irregular scars of at least one terrible lashing, and he carried a branded B on his upper arm.

'You are the negro-doctor?' asked Balthasar.

'Da' is so, massa,' the man replied.

'I am Doctor van Overmeer, and this is my assistant, Caesar.

Lady Palaeologue tells me you have a great reputation for curing your fellow negroes. I would like to talk with you about the plants we see around us, your practice, the ailments you see, and the herbs and simples you use.'

Yambo nodded. 'Come wid me, massa, an' I gwine show yuh.' They followed him out of the stable-court, and into the negro yard. 'Aloe, now. Da' is a good plant,' indicating a crown of fleshy, spiky leaves by the corner of a hut. 'Yuh cut dem, so,' he continued, taking a knife from his bag and cutting a leaf. As he held it out towards Balthasar, a mucilaginous sap began to drip from the wound. 'Yuh does put de leaf in a bowl, stanning up so, an' when de juice collec', you boil dem down, and it wuk de bowels like gunpowder.'

Balthasar was fascinated. Purges were an essential part of medicine as he understood it, and a reliable local product would be a great asset. Taking the leaf, already beginning to soften under the ferocious sun, he touched his finger to the sap, then to his mouth; and tears came to his eyes at its bitterness.

Yambo's eyes creased; he was clearly amused, though he very properly did not laugh. 'It bitta, but it good,' he commented tactfully. 'An' if yuh catch de sun, or bun yuh hand, mebbe, slit de leaf, and lay it pon de sore place, it heal good good, an' draw out de pain.'

'Are there any other plants which procure a purge?' asked Balthasar.

'Physic-nut does be good for de bowels, for a vomit, belly-ache bush. Dere be physic-nut in de lower field.'

'Can you take me there?'

For the next two hours, he wandered the plantation with Yambo and Caesar, writing down what was said, drawing plants he hoped to identify again. Yambo was a mine of information. He treated fevers by wrapping the head of the patient in leaves of wild pine or of a plant he called dog-dumpling, while fit-weed was good for children who suffered convulsions. Gripes and colics were treated with ginger tea, catarrh with cerasee, worms with artemisia, the familiar wormwood of Europe, which flourished in the island. Indian root, the use of which had been discovered by the Caribs, was another standby, while a decoction of candleweed cured some skin complaints, and duppy basil made a cooling tea, or if hung in the house, discouraged mosquitoes. Balthasar had noticed the leaves hanging here and there in the negro yard, and now made a note to try it in his own house, once they had moved from Logue Hall. At last, Yambo excused himself, since he would have to get back to his own plantation before dusk, and Balthasar returned to the big house, sweat-soaked and racked with headache from squinting at plants in the sun, but triumphant, his mind alive with new knowledge.

In the weeks that followed, he saw Yambo whenever the latter could be spared, particularly on Sundays. Yambo's reputation as a healer was such that he was allowed a certain amount of licence, especially since Lady Palaeologue had explained the situation to Mr Betterton, his owner, who had passed on the information to his overseer. Together, they visited the negro yards of neighbouring plantations, and Balthasar saw for himself that the little gardens, fruit-trees and chickens of the Palaeologue estate, Spartan as it had seemed to him, represented luxury by the ordinary standard of slave life.

With Yambo as his guide, a Virgil to conduct him through the circles of Hell which constituted the world of sugar plantations, he saw sufferers from yaws, made hideous by repellent red eruptions bursting through the skin, and in the more developed cases, afflicted by ulceration, bone-ache and the destruction of noses, hands and feet. The disease seemed so like syphilis in its final and most repulsive stages that he began to wonder whether it could not usefully be treated with mercury, but he soon realised that the expense of the drug would not permit it, and the momentary hope he had had of being of use flickered and died. He saw dirt-eaters, listless, emaciated figures with a compulsive craving to eat earth, which he could not diagnose at all, further cases of Barbados leg, various forms of leprosy and a similar disease called coco-bays, each more hideous than the last.

He also saw less disabling illnesses, and a variety of other afflictions, the familiar hollow eyes and protruding stomachs of acute worm infestation, and other scourges which were new to him. There were insects called chigoes which burrowed into the skin between the toes, or under the toenails, and had to be dug out with a needle: the barefoot slaves were painfully vulnerable to them – Palaeologue had warned him about chigoes, and told him never to go out without shoes and stockings. He was further intrigued and sickened by a bizarre creature, which Yambo told him was called Guinea worm; it burrowed under the skin of the leg, most painfully, and could only be controlled by catching the head and winding the creature out onto a stick, a fraction of an inch at a time, a process which might take days or even weeks – an experience which Balthasar devoutly hoped, for his own part, to avoid.

The more he saw, the more he came to feel that although the island afforded visible pests such as the Guinea worm, and frightful visitations such as yaws and leprosy in which the flesh seemed to have turned upon itself, otherwise, Lady Palaeologue had been right. Most of the disease he saw would have yielded to rest, quiet, a gentle purging of troublesome humours, and better diet. The horror of plantation slavery came home to him as he pursued this thought to its logical conclusion. One could not rest a slave as one would rest a horse, since they were human and aware. If illness became more attractive than health, the healthy would inevitably observe it. Therefore, since nothing could be done to improve general conditions, the sick must be left to suffer. Sugar was terrible, backbreaking work, and could not be made easier or more pleasant without destroying its profitability. It never occurred to him to question the institution of slavery, a structural part of the world as he knew it in Europe, Asia and Africa alike, but he was depressed by the terrible arbitrariness of the plantation system which assigned almost all Africans to the same oppressive and menial labour simply on grounds of race, making no distinction of rank or ability.

One Sunday, he met Yambo, by arrangement, at the negro yard of Baxter's, the nearest sugar plantation to the Palaeologues' modest estate. Coming into the yard and swinging down from his horse, he found it full of people going about their own affairs; resting, working on their garden-plots, making, mending and contriving. His eye fell on two men squatting in the shade of a hut, their attention fixed on the ground between them. There were six regular pits excavated in the dirt, arranged two by two, some containing seeds. They were playing warri, he realised suddenly. The sight moved him strangely. It was an African game, his father had played it with Narcissus on occasion; if he strained his memory, he thought he could probably remember the rules. It was the first thing he had seen in this overwhelmingly strange place which made a connection with his past.

Yambo came forward to meet him while a little girl took his horse, and they went together to the sick-hut. There were several dirt-eaters on the plantation, far advanced in suffering, beginning to show the swelling of the extremities and unnatural bloating of the face which marked the beginning of the final phase.

'What causes it, Yambo?' Balthasar asked, over the indifferent heads of the victims, who were lying on their sides as unresponsive as a row of logs.

The other man shrugged. 'Could be a something de obeah-man do dem. Could be poison.' It was an answer, and no answer, Balthasar thought. Poison was very possible though, something, perhaps, like lead-poisoning.

'Have these poor wretches had any unusual tasks?' he asked. 'Have they worked in a different place from other slaves?'

'No, massa. Dem just in de gang.'

Frustrated, he let the question go. Perhaps these unfortunates were just particularly sensitive to a general contagion which might have seized any one individual: he was disinclined to accept the notion that witchcraft entered into the question. Bidding farewell to the sick slaves, who seemed hardly to have noticed he was there, he left the hut and went out into the sunshine. There was a man standing in the shade of a genipa-tree, looking at him so intently that even with Yambo beside him, Balthasar felt a cold prickle of alarm in his belly.

'How can I serve you, fellow?' he asked, keeping his voice calm and level. The stranger stepped forward. He was very dark-skinned, a man perhaps in his thirties, with a faintly familiar appearance.

Abruptly, he spoke, staring into Balthasar's eyes. '*Fo si mi, kimi fo si O, ohun lafi nmo ara eni ninu Òkùnkùn.*'

'I do not understand you,' said Balthasar. Was the man, perhaps, mad? But he seemed perfectly in command of his faculties. The people in the negro yard had for the most part laid aside what they were doing, and drifted within earshot: Balthasar was keenly aware of watching eyes.

'He is Oyo man,' explained Yambo, 'he come fuh see you,' and suddenly Balthasar understood.

'I am sorry, fellow,' he said honestly. 'I do not speak my father's tongue.'

The stranger nodded. '*Eemo Òkùnkùn. Omo kole gbaimo Baba k'ayé gun,*' he said more quietly, apparently to himself.

'Do you speak English?' asked Balthasar. 'What is your name?'

'Lil' bit. My name Aluko, dem does call me Pompey.'

'You were born in Oyo, Aluko?'

'Yes, massa. I been here t'ree year now.'

'How did you know to come here?' he demanded.

'Yuh did tell Quashie at Logue Hall you son of Oyo. He ask 'bout, if any Oyo man in St John, an' it come to me. He seh you son of Omoloju.'

'I am the son of the *aremo* Omoloju, and the grandson of Onfinran, who was *alafin*,' Balthasar confirmed, and Aluko covered his eyes with his hands, a formal gesture, presumably a token of respect.

Balthasar was deeply intrigued. His father had told him stories of Oyo, when he was a child, tales now dim and half forgotten, of a world entirely lost. Unexpectedly, a freak of chance had given him news of it. He remembered suddenly that in Oyo, kings veiled their faces. Aluko was refusing to look on him – was he, for the first time, being addressed as a king? 'Tell me, Aluko,' he said, speaking slowly and as clearly as he could. 'What has happened in Oyo, since Onfinran was killed and my father was captured?'

Aluko, eyes on the ground, answered him respectfully. 'Egonoju be *alafin* after Onfinran, he rule in Igboho. Abipa he son be *aremo*. Egonoju die when I did small-small chile, an' den Abipa did be *alafin*.'

'So Abipa was ruling, when you were taken captive?'

Aluko nodded. 'Abipa did be *alafin* in Oyo Ile.'

'Do you mean he has reconquered the old capital from the Tapa?' exclaimed Balthasar.

'Yes, massa. Abipa did strong, strong *alafin*. Oyo did great, Tapa did slave.'

When Balthasar went back to Logue Hall, it was in a very sober frame of mind. In a few stumbling words, the man Aluko had taken his universe and overset it. All his life, he had known that his father had been enslaved following the usurpation of his cousin; but the divine purpose underlying this calamity, the old man had believed, was to bring him to Europe to meet Elizabeth, and thereby to beget Balthasar. Suddenly, a completely different way of looking at the story was inescapably before him. Had his grandfather been an African Saul, swept aside by God to make straight the path for His chosen one – Egonoju, an African David, and his still greater son, Abipa? From what his father had told him, it was no small matter for Abipa to have recaptured Oyo Ile, the great ceremonial and religious centre of his people. Had his father been a mere irrelevance, swept aside in order that God might have mercy on His people of Oyo and restore the kingdom?

A couple of evenings later, Lady Palaeologue said suddenly:

'Doctor van Overmeer. I have been thinking. I will come to Bridgetown with you, and present you to Governor Atkins. You will need his countenance, if you are to establish your practice.'

'But, Lady Palaeologue,' he protested uncomfortably, 'it is too much to ask. You will tire yourself. And surely I can make my way by my own skill?'

'My dear Doctor,' she said firmly, 'no. I fear you cannot. No trouble is too much for a man who saved my son's life, but in any case, I can use the time in doing my year's provisioning for the Hall. I must confess, I would not have advised you to come, if Theodore had thought to ask my opinion. He grew to manhood away from the island, and I think he forgot what the planters are like. You well know you have met with cold faces at church, and for all your skill, things will go no better for you in Bridgetown, if the Governor does not recognise you.'

Balthasar, burning with humiliation, demurred as long as he could, but she was not to be moved. Four days later, after letters had been exchanged with the Residency, a stately procession set forth: Lady Palaeologue and Sibella in an elderly two-horse chaise with Bridget and Cleopatra on the servants' seats behind, and the two men following on horseback. They took rooms at the Royal Charles, one of the largest of the town's taverns, and once the ladies had rested and refreshed themselves, they set out for the Residency.

'Leiden, hey?' said Governor Atkins, turning over Balthasar's papers. He was a smallish man, thin-limbed but with a belly that strained his waistcoat, his face deeply creased by fatigue and responsibility. He had the yellowed eyeballs and peevish air of the malaria sufferer, and his ankles were swollen; for all that, the dominant impression was of forceful intelligence.

'Yes, sir. I received my degree in the year 'sixty-two, and I have practised ever since, first in Middelburg, then in London.'

'And your father was African?'

Balthasar tried to conceal his irritation. 'Yes, sir. He was physician in ordinary to the Queen of Bohemia.'

'Was he, now?' It was hard to tell if Atkins was interested or not. 'Well, then. You have greatly relieved my old friend, she tells me. What could you do, do you think, to keep me from my grave a little longer?'

'May we retire to a more private place, sir, so that I can take your pulse and ask some questions?' The Governor, it rapidly transpired, had a weak heart, some tendency towards dropsy, and was a long-term sufferer from malaria; all conditions which could to some extent be alleviated. Balthasar sent a cordial based on foxglove (which he had brought with him) and a hepatic draught the next day, with some notes on regimen, and a week later he was gratified by a brief note signed in the Governor's own hand which said that his health was considerably improved and he would be glad to receive the doctor at Government House once he had removed to Bridgetown.

'That is that,' said Lady Palaeologue with satisfaction. 'He will receive you, and then all Bridgetown will know you have his countenance. I hoped this would happen. He is a man of consummate loyalty, and the Queen of Bohemia's name will have weighed with him. Though many citizens murmured at it, he gave the King's commission as Governor of Dominica to a man who is half Carib, because he was loyal to the cause, and suffered imprisonment in the late times for the King's sake. I so hoped he would see the good in you, even if there are those who do not.'

They moved to Bridgetown soon after. Lady Palaeologue had been kindness itself, but neither of them enjoyed living under patronage: Sibella, in particular, had suffered from a return to something like her status before the marriage. They had both enjoyed furnishing the new house, and the adventure of choosing plenishings had made her almost cheerful. He was satisfied with his choice. It was a more pretentious house than he had ever had before, but he had never had such a need to demonstrate his status. Compared to the houses of the great men of Barbados, it was still modest enough. The residences of the sugar-refiners and distillers, the agents of the Royal African Company, and the town-houses of Codringtons, Colletons and the other chief planters were on quite another scale, sumptuous, even grandiose, buildings in sparkling coral-limestone and imported brick, glittering with glass windows, every pane of which had come four thousand miles bedded in straw, with a constant coming and going of liveried slaves at their doors.

Like the city of London, the city of Bridgetown was staringly new, and for a similar reason; in 1668, a domestic fire had accidentally touched off a hundred and seventy barrels of gunpowder in the island's magazine, unluckily next door to the blazing building. Apart from the destruction wreaked by the blast itself, fire had raced though the thatched wooden buildings of the old Bridgetown, and the inhabitants, when they began the work of reconstruction, had heeded the warning and rebuilt in stone, brick and tile. New streets of more modest, yet still substantial houses had arisen, belonging to the prosperous middling sort, the bankers and chief merchants, very like the new houses of London in appearance.

They increased their family; with so large a house to care for, Sibella wanted another woman to help with the inside work, so they bought a girl called Adjaba, and they needed a man as groom, so they bought one who went by the name of Mandingo Jack. With Caesar and Bridget already with them, Sibella found herself presiding over a substantial household.

It took some time to establish Balthasar's practice. Even with the good word of Governor Atkins to straighten his path, it was clear that there were many people in Bridgetown who would not trust themselves to a mulatto. But his Leiden degree, on the other hand, spoke for him; and so did his skill. There was no other university-trained surgeon on the island, and as his success in dealing with fractures, dislocations, hernias and the like passed by word of mouth from his first patients to their friends and relations, he found his days becoming gratifyingly full. Beyond his surgical practice, he discovered a whole new set of ailments: if the black population, on the one hand, suffered preponderantly from overwork and poor diet, the whites had their own alarming diseases, which he suspected arose from superfluity. Fevers of all kinds, quartan, intermittent, fluctuant, were rife, leading him to conclude that European constitutions under tropical conditions generated vastly excessive amounts of choler. He treated these patients, after purging, with a regimen based on chocolata, known to be a sovereign specific against choler, and controlled the immediate symptoms with Jesuit's bark, a regimen which met with a measure of success.

Other local diseases were less tractable. His first encounter with 'the dry belly-ache' was a nightmarish experience of watching over a patient writhing in the grip of an excruciating internal pain which had him begging for death, and which could not be reduced by any purges or emetics whatever, not even the recommended clyster of molasses and milk. Subsequently, after an urgent consultation with Yambo, he found that snakeweed powdered in rum had some effect, and also that opium acted as a palliative if the dose were high enough.

The amount that the white population drank seemed to Balthasar to account for a good deal of illness in itself: gout and dropsy were common among the planters, and their conviction that rum in prodigious quantities protected them from the ill effects of the climate, while possibly true, seemed to him to have run them headlong into a whole other set of self-generated problems. He was struck, as he became more inward with the white community, by their anxiety to distance themselves, not merely from their slaves, but from the island they lived on. He was certain of a basic principle, articulated by no less a man than the Surgeon-General of the East India Company, as well as by his own father, that wherever a disease was endemic, God set the best remedies to hand, but his white patients clamoured for imported drugs. The expensiveness of Jesuit's bark spoke more for it, in their view, than its efficacy, and they demanded to be purged with senna and rhubarb when he would rather have prescribed aloes. Yambo had shown him that a decoction of the big seeds called cavally or horse-eye was wonderfully efficacious in relieving dropsical swelling, which was common among the planters, but the people of Bridgetown could not, or would not, believe it, and were even insulted by the proposition that he prescribe a medicine which might be used for a slave. He was forced to introduce the treatment by subterfuge and charge as if for a European medicine. It went against his conscience, but it was forced upon him by the blind prejudice of his patients.

Within a few months of setting up in practice, he found that he was busy, but he was not happy. He had toyed with the notion of writing a book, based on his own knowledge and Yambo's, but had given it up: it was clear enough already no one would want to hear what he would tell them. Still worse, Lady Palaeologue, coming upon the boy Caesar laboriously spelling his way through the Gospel, had warned Balthasar in no uncertain terms that it was against the law to Christianise slaves: Balthasar might teach his boy to read if he wished, but he would be well advised to choose another primer.

He acquiesced, as he had to, but it made him profoundly uncomfortable not to lead his household in morning and evening prayers, a cornerstone of the right and natural order of things. The woman Bridget bowed her head correctly enough beside Sibella, but he knew that since she was a Papist, she was obeying in form only; there was no priest on the island, so she was obedient to his direct orders in the matter, but that there were reservations in her heart was beyond any possible doubt. He detested the thought that his other servants were pagans, but when he broached the subject with a patient, a cruelly afflicted woman of exemplary piety whom he seldom saw without a Bible in her hand, she shocked him to the core by declaring that there was no more purpose in baptising a negro than a puppy. Balthasar remembered his father, remembered also the grave and reverend band of Ethiopian theologians who had been one of the sights of Leiden in his youth, and felt his guts clench with fury, but he kept his reactions to himself. The woman was dying, and in any case, no doctor would argue with a patient, but after that, he resigned himself to silence.

Though he had dropped the question, he did not forget it. He was more than interested, therefore, to discover that he was not alone in his private convictions on the question; he heard from several sources, as he went up and down the town, that the Quakers did not exclude slaves from their meetings: his chief informant on the subject, the pious lady with the cancered breast, spoke of this with horror. She predicted imminent danger of insurrection: as she explained, trembling with weakness and indignation, several Quakers owned substantial plantations, which compounded the problem. Wilfully blind to their own danger, they obstinately put the safety and security of the colony at risk for the sake of a principle. It gave Balthasar much to think about. He had not been attracted to the curious manners of the Quaker banker, and he had been actively repelled by his lack of respect for rank and degree, but he was more and more interested by the almost unnatural consistency of the position which the Friends, as they preferred to call themselves, contrived to maintain, opposed as it was to the general current of life in the colony.

He was accordingly more than a little intrigued to be summoned one day by a civilly spoken black man whose bearing and approach, though courteous, had nothing servile about them. His master, he explained, had stood on a stool, attempting to reach goods from a high shelf, and had slipped; he believed the leg was broken. Balthasar took his bag, summoned Caesar from the dispensary, where he was making diachylon from powdered lead, olive oil and lard to replenish their stock, and bade him to bring all he had finished. The three then set forth together. Given the servant's manners, he was not in the least surprised to find that the victim, no whit disconcerted to be found supine on the floor of his shop with a cushion under his head, raised himself on an elbow and addressed him as 'Friend'. He was a man of perhaps forty, spare of figure and vigorous-looking, though at that moment he was pale and sweating with the pain of his injured leg. Balthasar noted as he entered that the shop was a hatter's, and he resolved that once the proprietor was recovered, he would return to look at the stock.

'I am grateful for your attention, friend,' the man said: the voice was nasal, but pleasant. 'My name is Thomas Tryon.'

Balthasar knelt beside him, and began to examine the injured leg, which turned out to have suffered a fracture of the tibia: the man was notably stoic as he prodded the wound.

'The bone is broken in the upper part, Mr Tryon,' he said, 'It will need careful management if you are to regain use of the leg. We must immobilise it, before we move you to your bed, lest it sustain further injury.'

'I am in your hands, friend Doctor,' said the other, and closed his eyes. Between them, Balthasar and Caesar removed the patient's shoes, stockings and breeches: the site of the injury was beginning to swell, but the breeches, fortunately, were loose enough to come off without needing to be cut. The diachylon was brought into play to secure the bindings of the leg and keep it straight, and while they worked, Tryon's man went to take a shutter from its hinges, and stood in readiness until they finished the bandage.

They succeeded in loading and tying Tryon onto the shutter, though for all the care they took, the man fainted when he was lifted. Balthasar immediately directed that they should take advantage of his unconsciousness and get him to his bed as fast as possible, before he came to; the unavoidable jolting as they negotiated the stairs would be agony for him. He had done his best to correct Caesar's inturned foot surgically, and had somewhat improved his gait and stance, but it was not to be trusted, so Balthasar took one end of the shutter himself, while the manservant took the other. They shuffled out of the shop as expeditiously as possible and went through the store- and work-room, up a steep pair of stairs, to the bedroom. Balthasar was struck by a certain Spartan quality: Barbadian rooms tended to be a little sparse, except in the grandest houses, and Tryon was not wealthy, but the private quarters bespoke something more like a positive objection to ornament. The bedroom was limewashed and scrupulously clean, with no matting of any kind on the bare floorboards; the bed was narrow and severe, with a thin flock mattress and a mosquito-curtain, but no other hangings at all; it looked bare and draughty to Balthasar, who had slept in curtained beds all his life. There were no pictures, and the only relief to the eye was provided by a shelf of books. They got Tryon into his bed, stripped to his shirt, and laid a sheet carefully over him. He was beginning to recover from the faint, so once he had regained his senses, Balthasar encouraged him to swallow a draught of opium, and watched him until he fell into a healing sleep.

Once Tryon was safely resting, he went across to look at his books, all in poor, plain bindings, wondering what clues they would give to the man. There was a Bible, of course, much-thumbed, and a book he immediately resolved to borrow or buy when opportunity arose, *A True and Exact History of the Island of Barbados*. Beside it stood some octavos; he pulled the first two off the shelf, and found that he had *An Introduction to the Teutonick Philosophy* and a pamphlet called *Strange and wonderful newes from Whitehall: or, the mighty vision proceeding from Mistris A. Trapnel concerning the Government of the Commonwealth and her revelations touching the Lord Protector and the Army*. He opened Mistress Trapnel at random, and found a barely literate outpouring of religious feeling, combined with a dogged, even fanatical determination to live by her own tenets, which struck him as admirable, or, from some points of view, even alarming. He put the book back on the shelf, and looked at the others, which turned out to be old friends, Culpeper's *Herbal* and Monardes's *Joyful Newes out of the Newe Founde World*, together with a book he had heard of but not read, Thomas Hobbes's *Leviathan*. He straightened them on the shelf, and went on his way, eager to speak to Tryon as soon as it was possible to do so.

When he called the next day, he found Tryon awake, and in a very good way of recovery.

'I have taken no infection, friend Doctor,' he said, when Balthasar congratulated him. 'There is little in my fleshly body for corruption to seize on. I had not expected to trouble any of your profession. I live by regimen: if the citizens of Barbados followed my plan of temperance, cleanness and innocency of life, sustained themselves on a vegetable diet, and avoided alcohol, tobacco and all other stimulants, I fear you and your fellows would soon be put to shifts. Foods are a thing of greater moment than the world generally imagines.'

'There are always accidents, Mr Tryon,' said Balthasar, smiling. The man's voice and manner could have been offensive, but he was so obviously innocent of any such intention that it seemed churlish to stand on professional dignity. 'Even flesh nourished by the principles of the angels would still be flesh. A man's foot can slip, a wound, especially in this climate, is the better for being probed and stitched.'

'To be sure, friend Doctor, and I am grateful for your skill. You may rest easy, I judge. The chance of the people of Barbados reforming their manners in this age of the world is as slight as that of a sinner coming to repentance. You have many laborious days before you.'

'I am sure of it also, Mr Tryon. I respect your views, and to some extent, I share them. The last man that I met who lived on a diet of vegetables was a charlatan, a magician, and I suspect, a thief, but his reasons, I think, were very different from yours – he claimed to live like Pythagoras in order to confound and amaze his gulls, but I see nothing of that spirit in you.' If Tryon could speak with ill-mannered frankness, he thought, he was owed frankness in reply.

'It is against the principle of truth,' said Tryon, simply.

'That is what I thought,' said Balthasar. 'Constitutions vary, and I would not recommend a meatless diet to invalids or persons of delicate habit, but all doctors of any sense at all recommend a spare diet, and most would agree that temperance is more healthful than over-indulgence. I dislike drunkenness, and I confess, I see far too much of it in this island.'

'That is so. It is no surprise that when the master decrees a holiday, the slaves, poor creatures, drink till they fall insensible. Their lives are wretchedly hard, they seize the chance for a moment's respite. But the great men of the place seldom draw a sober breath, and that is a different matter. Many of them believe it is a question of health, but here I stand – or lie, rather – ocular proof that a man will take no hurt from drinking pure rainwater, if it be fresh-caught and not left to breed corruption.'

'Mr Tryon, you mentioned the slaves. I wanted to ask you about the Quakers' views on Christianising them – I have heard much of this from other quarters, and I have meant to ask someone from your community.'

'Reach me down that box on the bookshelf, if you will,' replied Tryon. Balthasar rose from the stool where he had been sitting beside Tryon's bed and obediently went to fetch the box. Tryon balanced it on his lean stomach, and riffled through the papers within.

'Ah, I have it,' he said. 'I am not a Quaker myself, by the by, though I share many of their tenets, I am a Boehmist. But to answer you, I cannot do better than to quote a letter from one of the founders of the Quakers, George Fox. This is a letter which he wrote to Friends beyond the sea that had black and Indian slaves, which was circulated through the meeting-houses. He reminds us that God is no respecter of persons, and that He made all nations of one blood and enlightened every man that came into the world, so the gospel is glad tidings to every captivated creature under the whole heavens. The Friends have striven to be guided by this letter, and accordingly, they do not forbid slaves from their meetings. Slavery is the law of the land, and it has been lawful throughout human history, so the Friends do not quarrel with the institution – as I do not – but it is hard to see how any man could find warrant for enslaving souls merely because he owns the bodies they dwell in. The slaves are poor and brutish and ignorant, but they are men and women, so they are brothers and sisters in Christ.'

'You would have interested my father, Mr Tryon. He thought long and deeply on the prompting of Africans towards God, and taught me that there was much scriptural warrant for it. I have wondered about this ban since I came to Barbados.'

'It is policy only, friend Doctor. The planters fear that the slaves, once Christian, would have a warrant to demand their freedom, so they sacrifice the souls of their fellow men to the golden calf of profit.'

Balthasar bade farewell to Tryon and went on his rounds, full of thought. When he got back to the house, he was surprised to find Sibella, blushing and pleased, wearing her embroidered apron, and seated across from her, Lieutenant Palaeologue. The expression on his wife's face smote him; for an instant, he felt a pang of jealous anger that another man could please her so, but the emotion was soon overcome. He could hardly grudge her the pleasure of Palaeologue's company, given the crippling isolation of her life in Bridgetown. He was only too well aware that while Sibella, for her part, despised her neighbours for their vulgarity and pretension to a genteel status hardly any of them possessed, they held her in contempt and scorn for transgressing the ultimate barrier and marrying a mulatto. She tended to conceal her troubles from him, as he concealed his from her, but he knew that their disdain weighed heavily upon her.

'Palaeologue!' he said, coming forward to shake his guest by the hand. 'Well met, my dear fellow. It is too long since we have seen you. You will stay to dinner, I hope?'

'I would be pleased to,' said the Lieutenant. Once Balthasar was seated, Sibella slipped discreetly out, doubtless to turn the kitchen up by the ears, and send Jack running for further delicacies to honour their guest – one of the great advantages of living in town was that the Cheapside market was less than five minutes away. He began to look forward to the meal with pleasant anticipation.

Balthasar kept the Lieutenant sitting as long as he decently could: they usually dined at noon, but it was shortly after one when at last he led him through to their dinner. He was greatly pleased by what he saw: Sibella had spared no expense, and though they lived frugally in the main, he applauded her extravagance in honour of the man who was their chief friend and patron. In addition to the shoulder of goat, chine of pork and fricassee of fowl he had been expecting to see, there was a dish of steamed crabs and sea-eggs, one of palm-hearts, and a fine plateful of fried flying-fish – Sibella had realised, he was glad to see, that a man who lived

215

up-country would relish fish. There had also been a hasty sortie to the pastrycook's by the cathedral, he observed approvingly: there was cheese cake, and a fine custard decorated with preserved fruits. Sibella had also set out anchovies, olives, gherkins and a dish of figs and raisins. Jack, Caesar and Bridget were standing very correctly, Bridget behind her mistress's chair, Caesar poised to attend his master, while Jack waited to look after the honoured guest. All three of the servants wore a distinct air of complacency at this domestic triumph.

They sat down, and Bridget went round pouring the wine. Lieutenant Palaeologue proposed a toast to the bright eyes of his hostess, and dinner began. Their guest praised everything, did full justice to the feast, despite the airless heat of the room, and was particularly appreciative of the fish, which pleased Sibella greatly. The resilience of youth had stood her in good stead, and she had regained much of her London looks since they moved to their own home. In the face of Palaeologue's good-natured rallying, her cheeks were flushed, and her eyes sparkled: she looked happy for the first time since they had come to Barbados.

Once the table had been cleared of broken meats and they were sitting over dessert with their glasses of wine, Palaeologue revealed the reason for his visit.

'There is a question I wanted to open with you,' he said. 'As you know, there are no Caribs left in Barbados. They were not, I think, aboriginal inhabitants of the Antilles, but from what I know, they settled the islands a century or so before we came, seizing the land from the Arawaks, a peaceful people, greatly given to dancing and dreams. The Caribs, on the other hand, were fierce and lordly, though very skilled with their hands, and they are so to this day. I was minded to go across to Dominica, and speak with the Caribs there. My father was most interested in them, and I have time on my hands now. Also, the Governor of Dominica was known to my father, who introduced me to him, and

I think you would improve one another's acquaintance. His name is Thomas Warner, and he is the son of Sir Thomas Warner, who was founder of the English colony in St Kitts. His mother was a Carib lady, and when Sir Thomas died, they were ill-treated by the widow, who considered herself injured by the connection, and declared that he and his mother were mere slaves. She fled with him to her family in Dominica, where he became a notable leader among the Caribs for his strength and courage. Governor Atkins appointed him Governor of his island in 'sixty-four, so he is a great man among both peoples. I wondered if you might care to join me on this venture? We might leave, perhaps, in a week.'

Frantically, Balthasar reviewed his patient-list in his mind. The cancerous lady had died, to her own and her family's relief; Tryon was the most serious case to come his way recently, he was mending, and in any case, if he were not well on the road to recovery after a week, he would not object to seeing Caesar. Balthasar could refuse to take any more patients until after his return. In sum, his affairs were in as good a posture for leaving as they would ever be, and he was greatly desirous of meeting Governor Warner, the first non-white man of consequence he had ever heard of in the Antilles.

'Yes, I will come,' he said firmly. Sibella was looking at him piteously; he would hear of it, after their guest was gone, that much was clear.

'I am glad of it. I would value your company, and I think you would find much to interest you.'

'Lieutenant Palaeologue,' blurted Sibella, 'are they not cannibals? Will they not eat you?'

Palaeologue smiled at her. 'They have the reputation of cannibals, it is true,' he said gently. Balthasar was touched by his care to allay her fears rather than laugh them away, as he might well have done. 'It may be that at some time, or in some places, Caribs have eaten human flesh, but I know nothing of it. They seem not to do it now. In my experience of them, they diet themselves on cassava and pig-meat, for the most part. You need have no fear that we will end our days in a stew-pot, or that we will be forced to an obscene feast. No Carib has ever offered me man's flesh, of that I am certain, and since we would be under the countenance of Indian Warner, there is not the remotest fear that they would offer to eat us, or do us any harm whatsoever. It is true that they keep the brain-pans of their dead enemies by way of trophies of arms, but so did the wild Irish in times gone by, and if Paul the Deacon's *History* is to be believed, so did the Lombards of Italy — you might even say that we do the same, at home in England. Is not the Lord Protector's head on London Bridge to this day? A liking for preserving the heads of one's enemies is not at all the same thing as a craving for human flesh.'

Sibella's face showed clearly that she was not, at heart, convinced, but she thanked him graciously enough, and sipped her wine.

It had been years since Balthasar had let himself think of a holiday, and he looked forward to the excursion as eagerly as a schoolboy, for all Sibella's fears. It seemed almost no time before he and Lieutenant Palaeologue were taking ship for Dominica, accompanied by Caesar and Lady Palaeologue's slave Isaiah, who had been detailed to act as the Lieutenant's personal servant when he was in the Indies.

Barbados, low-lying as it was, disappeared swiftly into the sea. It was only a two-days' sail to Dominica, and so short a journey was very pleasant. There was a fresh breeze off the sea, and the ship ploughed through sparkling blue waters, with silver shoals of flying-fish breaking the surface periodically, glittering like the showers of silver sixpences flung to the people at the Lord Mayor's Show. Their own island seemed hardly out of sight before they sighted St Lucia, though so high were the central peaks, it was long enough before they came anywhere near it. Balthasar leaned on the rail, listening to the waves rustling beneath the keel, and watched the island as it slid by on their eastern flank lit by the setting sun, relinquishing his observation post only when it was too dark to see more. In stark contrast to Barbados's intensively cultivated slopes, St Lucia seemed a tall and rugged rock bursting from the ocean bed, dark-green and shaggy with pristine forest. They passed Martinique on the morning of the second day, another island of the same general form, and a mere thirty miles or so later, came to Dominica, a third.

'It is thought that these islands are the peaks of drowned mountains,' remarked Palaeologue as their ship approached Prince Rupert's Bay. 'It is hard to imagine what cataclysm can have befallen the land to sink them so beneath the waves. My father formed a theory that the Antilles might be the original site of Noah's Flood, though he never could decide which of the great peaks we have passed, and the others which lie before us, might be the true Mount Ararat. The names we have for them now are artificial, and date no further back than the Spaniards, at best.'

When the ship had made safe harbour at Portsmouth, Lieutenant Palaeologue sent word to the Governor's residence, and while they awaited his response, they retired to the upper room of an inn overlooking the harbour to smoke their pipes. An hour or so later, the boy returned with a message. The Governor was from home, and was spending some time in one of the nearby Carib settlements in the mountains further inland.

'Then we shall follow him there,' decreed Palaeologue. 'It was the Caribs we hoped to see.'

They hired horses from a stables near the harbour, where they were also able to find a man to serve as guide and interpreter, who seemed from his features half-negro, half-Carib, and the party of five set off up-country. The dripping green jungle into which they climbed, buzzing with insect life and stealthy movement, was something completely outside Balthasar's experience. The town they were looking for stretched along the bank of a river, and it was some little time before Balthasar realised that they were nearly upon it: the houses of the inhabitants, which were elegantly constructed of wicker, were set reticently back among the trees for the most part, and it was impossible to see how many there were. As they approached, it became clear that they had been under observation for some time; people emerged from their huts, and there was movement in the forest to either side.

Balthasar looked at them with interest as they came more clearly into view. The Caribs were not a tall people and they tended to slightness; their faces wore flat and inexpressive, with narrow dark eyes and high cheekbones. They wore only brief aprons of beads, with more beads decorating neck, wrists and ankles; their noses, lower lips and ears were pierced and adorned with jewellery of metal and bone. Their hair was glossy black and straight, and they seemed to be a brown-skinned people, though it took a look at the shy children peering from behind the trees to be sure of this, since the adults decorated their bodies with a red, oily substance which gave their flesh the colour of a robin's breast.

'Good day to you,' said Palaeologue, removing his hat, 'I am looking for the *acarewana*.'

The interpreter rode forward and repeated the sentence, though Balthasar strongly suspected that more than one of the blank-faced listeners understood him perfectly well. At any rate, they hardly needed a middle-aged fellow with green beads, who for all his nakedness was clearly a person of some consequence, to tell them that he was coming, when they could see perfectly well that a magnificent but surprising figure had emerged from the largest of the huts and was walking towards them at his leisure. Governor Warner wore his own hair, which was as crow-black as any Carib's, abundant, and flowed freely over his shoulders, but he was a head taller than the tallest of the Caribs, broad-shouldered and seemingly strong enough to wrestle an ox. He had narrow black eyes and a somewhat Indian cast of countenance, but in contrast to the Indians, who seemed to grow no hair upon their faces and little enough anywhere else but on the head, he wore a short beard clipped to a point, and moustaches. He was dressed in a European shirt, breeches and shoes, the shirt of finest linen, edged with Mechelin lace at cuffs and band, but his ears were pierced and hung with large, pendant pearls, and his shirt lay open on his hairy, brown-skinned breast, displaying three necklaces of coral, pearls and gold. His forbidding expression lightened as he recognised the Lieutenant.

'Young Palaeologue. You are taller by a head since I saw you last, and you are grown the very image of your father, though you have not his height. Well met, my friend,' he said, as Palaeologue swung lightly off his horse and held out his hand. 'I did not know you were back in the Antilles.'

'I have thrown up my commission to play the part of a son and tend to my mother's interests, Governor – she has been a widow these two years, as you may know. But her affairs are in good order, so I have brought a friend to see you, sir. May I present Balthasar van Overmeer. He is a surgeon and doctor by profession, and by ancestry, the son of a king.'

'I am glad to see you. I bid you both a hearty welcome.' Balthasar dismounted and came forward. The Governor clasped his hand in a powerful grip, and gave him a searching look. 'Where was your father king?'

'He was king of Oyo in Africa, Governor Warner, but he was set aside in some internal dispute, and sold into slavery.'

'It is an old story,' the Governor commented. 'The African kings on the West coast have long been at strife with one another, and the slavers reap the profit on't. There is an exiled king of the Akan people cutting cane in Barbados at this very moment, they tell me, a man called Kofi, who was king of Akwamu. He is greatly respected by his fellows.'

'I did not know that,' said Palaeologue, looking surprised and a little displeased. 'Which plantation is he on?'

Warner shrugged. 'Things come to my ears, my friend, that white men do not generally know, but not necessarily in any detail. We are two hundred miles from Barbados. Ask your servant, not me.'

Palaeologue turned to Isaiah. 'Do you know of this man Kofi?' he demanded.

Isaiah shrugged and looked blank. 'I don' know, massa. Mebbe anudda parish?'

'Well, it is no matter,' said Palaeologue pleasantly. He indicated the Governor's splendid jewels. 'I see you go fine among the Caribs,' he observed.

'Ay, so I do. It answers their notion of greatness, and why should I not, when it adds to my state?'

'Why not, indeed? Rank is rank, however it is shown.' Palaeologue took a deep breath, his face becoming more serious. 'Governor, I have a reason for coming here, and I would like to see what you have to say to it. My father was a scholar, as you may remember, and the great work of his last years was a theory of the universal history of the world. I have been turning over his papers since I came back, and I have found the notes towards a treatise, in which he argues that if the Caribs, and the other peoples of the New World, are fellow to the people of the old world – as they must be, since the Bible tells us there were not two Creations – then the continents must once have been more closely connected. The theory which he came to believe was that the Antilles are the remains of Mount Ararat and the other mountains which, the Bible tells us, border the plain of Shinar, which must now lie beneath the waters of the Atlantic. He sought a proof of this, which is what I have come to discuss with these people of yours.'

'I fail to see what basis there might be for discussion,' said

Warner. What in a lesser man might have been mild dissent came from his lips like the final decision of a judge.

'Language,' said Palaeologue promptly, no whit deterred. 'The authorities are all but agreed that Hebrew is the primaeval language of the human race, for how could it be, if Hebrew was not the language spoken in Paradise, that it is the Jews who have preserved the tradition of God's word? You will find the argument in Postel's *De Originibus.* If there is one human race, one world, and one God, then it follows that at the beginning, there was one language.'

'My old preceptor, Sir Thomas Urquhart, held similar views,' Balthasar said, intrigued. 'In a book of his which I have he says that words are the signs of things, instituted at the first, from which follows, if I understand him, that there was once a perfect language, which has been decayed and corrupted in the course of time. He hoped to bring together the perfections of many several tongues to create a new universal speech.'

'A noble project indeed,' said Palaeologue, 'but my father was more concerned with the question of finding out traces of the pristine or primitive tongue than with recreating it. He began to test his idea here in the Antilles, and he found correspondences between Hebrew and related tongues and the language of the Caribs. He thought, therefore, that this might constitute a proof that the Caribs are descendants direct of the line of Noah, perhaps through Nimrod the mighty hunter, for the Caribs are hunters to this day.'

'Strange, if so,' commented Warner sceptically.

'But the Caribs, and the other American peoples, must come from before the time the earth was divided,' objected Palaeologue. 'Why should they not bear traces of their heritage? I will show you what I mean.' He produced a small notebook from the pocket of his doublet, and consulted its pages. 'Ah, I have it. Would you recognise the word *"liani"*?'

'*Liani*? I cannot be sure of your pronunciation. "His wife"?'

'This is my father's case. "His wife" is "*li hene*", in the Hebrew tongue. I read no Hebrew, but he has written it here.'

'Is it, indeed? Have you further examples?' Warner's face had softened out of its habitual mask of command, and he spoke almost eagerly.

'*Nchiri?*'

By this time, they had an intrigued and curious audience. Governor Warner, manifestly interested himself, explained the nature of the quest, or question, to the headman and the other bystanders, provoking much nodding and quiet exchange; the Caribs, it seemed to Balthasar, were a decorous folk, restrained in their actions as in their expressions.

Warner frowned. '*Nchiri?*' A chorus of interested comment and suggestion broke out, as he tried the word various ways. 'Nose?'

'Aha. Yes, and it matches the Hebrew again, which is "*ncheri*". "*Yene kali*"?'

This provoked much discussion, and eventually Warner said, 'I do not know what you mean.'

'I am sorry to hear it. My father pairs it with "*e'onq ali*", which he writes, means "my necklace". The correspondence seems a close one.'

'Necklace!' Warner plunged into animated conversation with the chief and other leading men: emphatic nodding, at last, suggested consensus. 'We would say, "*yehe hali*". But you must realise, my dear sir, there are dialects among the Caribs.'

Palaeologue's face was, for a moment, perfectly blank, then he laughed a little in irritation. 'I suppose there would be. So much for my father's theories.'

X

The circumstances which distinguish the Koromantyn, or Gold Coast negroes, from all others, are firmness both of body and mind: a ferociousness of disposition, but withal, activity, courage, and a stubbornness, or what an ancient Roman would have deemed an elevation of soul, which prompts them to enterprizes of difficulty and danger.

Bryan Edwards, *History of the West Indies*, 1657

May 1675

Washing was the single most loathsome job in the house, thought Sibella with passion. It was a thought which occurred to her frequently. After two years of housekeeping in the Antilles, she had accustomed herself to inconveniences so appalling that only her iron will kept her from begging Balthasar to take them home, but the laundry remained something which she resented afresh every week.

She was constrained to wash weekly: in the dreadful heat and humidity, they needed to shift linen daily, and they owned only a limited quantity. It was very expensive in Barbados, since every stitch was imported, and moreover, dirty clothes, always damp when they were removed, were desperately vulnerable to insect attack and mildew: the laundry could not safely be left to mount up as it could at home. In London, she had done a big washing only every few weeks, but when she discussed her household with Lady Palaeologue and Cleopatra, they had firmly recommended that in tropical conditions it was better to own less and wash it often. She had seen the point of the advice, of course, but it made a hideous amount of work.

Accordingly, she was in the kitchen with Bridget, Adjaba, and their latest acquisition, Molly the wetnurse, all four of them sweating like so many cheeses: she could see the sweat standing in drops on the other women's faces, while condensation ran down the whitewashed walls; her own smock was saturated and sticking to her skin. The wet linen was safely in the buck-tub; all morning they had been labouring in the yard under the cruel sun, pouring lye through the clothes, stirring and shaking the buck, rubbing and pounding at stained items on a washboard while the caustic lye stung and reddened their hands. Now, the linen was finally clean and rinsed, after bucket after bucket of water had been fetched from the cistern and poured through it, and it was ready to be wrung out, starched and ironed. The kitchen fire was blazing, and the irons stood on the hearth, their faces to the heat, while starch simmered in the biggest of the kitchen pots. Between the midday sun and the heat of the fire, the temperature of the room had climbed to the point where it swelled her feet in her shoes and made her head pound sickeningly. All afternoon, they would haul the heavy, wet linen from the buck, dip it in starch, and iron it. Each piece took an enormous investment of energy in conditions which made it difficult to do anything at all. For her own part, besides problems created by the impossible climate, she still found it hard to stand for any length of time. The birth of her first child had not been easy, and though the baby was now three months old, well-doing and like to live, after a morning on her feet she could feel her womb dragging down, giving her a dull, heavy pain in the small of the back and adding immeasurably to her tiredness.

The baby was asleep upstairs; the nurse did not ordinarily leave her alone, but in the weekly emergency of the laundry, she could not be spared, so Sarah was left to sleep if she would, and fret if she must. I might have known, thought Sibella grimly, hearing a familiar, distant wailing drifting down the stairs. As so often, thinking of her baby seemed somehow to provoke Sarah into wakefulness – or perhaps, she thought suddenly, the waking child herself tugged at some secret cord of sympathy between them. Wearily, she straightened herself, and turned to the wetnurse.

'Molly, you had better go to Sarah and feed her. Please come back down as soon as may be.'

'Yes, ma'am,' said Molly, slipping expeditiously out of the hot kitchen.

Sibella turned back to the others. 'We must get on. Bridget, do you iron the collars in the basket, you have good skill with them. Adjaba, you and I will wring the sheets.'

Washing day crawled on, with more than the usual frustration. The wristband of one of Balthasar's best shirts was torn by the buck-sticks, and had to be put aside for mending; there was a stain on a good damask tablecloth which would not come out, and one of a pair of expensive knitted stockings had been damaged by white-ants while it awaited washing.

When Bridget brought her the stocking to show her how it had suffered, it was the last straw. Sibella sat down suddenly and burst into tears. She found herself often tearish since Sarah's birth, and she detested the slippage of the self-control on which she had once prided herself, with some justice. Bridget put the stocking down hastily, and brought her a drink, the sugared lime-juice and water which she favoured. It was refreshing, even though it was not cold, or even cool.

'Mistress my dear, bear up,' she said solicitously. 'We will be finished soon enough.'

Sibella blotted her eyes with her handkerchief, and blew her nose. 'It will never be finished,' she cried, despairing. 'We slave every week over linen which is but a few hours in wear – I could stand that, I think, but the insects are like the plagues of Egypt. Nothing can even be laid away in safety. The worst of it is, for all that I have suffered, and all that we endure from day to day, we are people of no consequence – I had such hopes of the estate, Bridget, it has gone nigh to breaking my heart. I hate it here, Bridget, I hate and loathe this town, and this island. My life is a waking nightmare.'

It was an outburst of uncontrollable bitterness, such as she had often made: she was too proud to say such things to Balthasar, since she was deeply conscious that it was she who had insisted that they go to the Indies, but she felt safe in relieving her feelings to Bridget, who could be relied upon for murmured endearments and expressions of obscure sympathy which soothed her heart even while she chid her maid for a fool. Disconcerted and vaguely affronted by the silence which ensued, she dabbed her eyes again, and looked up at Bridget, who was standing in front of her with the earthenware jug in her hand, staring at her fixedly as if she had never seen her before.

'Bridget?' she said, beginning to collect herself. When the other woman made no reply, she spoke more sharply. 'Bridget, do you forget yourself?'

'I forget nothing,' said Bridget, a hard tone in her voice which Sibella had never heard before. 'By the living God that made us, I have had enough of you and your vapours. It's enough to make a body cast up to hear you sitting in this grand house, wailing like a baby because you are not the mistress of creation! Bad luck to you and yours, that you inherit a fortune and sit down to cry!'

Sibella's blank astonishment turned abruptly to kindling indignation. 'Bridget!' she snapped.

'No, mistress. Listen to me for this once, then send me to the fields if you like.' She was in deadly earnest, and against her first instinct, Sibella straightened up a little and listened, bewildered by this sudden revolt from the only servant she considered a friend, and yet gripped by sick fascination. She was dimly aware that Adjaba had retreated to the far end of the room, and was watching them warily.

'Mistress Sibella, you have never thought about me,' began Bridget vehemently; her voice was low and even, but it carried such passion that Sibella felt compelled to listen. 'Just a wretch of an indentured servant, some London doxy, oh, yes, I have heard you say so. But I am a Burnell, and you have known my name all this time, and never troubled yourself to wonder at it. Well, I will tell you who I am, my fine madam. The Burnells were Norman knights, and great lords and barons in Ireland. My kin are not mere Irish, they are leaders among those they call the Old English. We were set aside in the time of King Henry, because we stayed strong in the Faith, but we are as English as you are. We have suffered greatly for religion these hundred and fifty years and are come to poverty, but for all that, I am a noblewoman born and bred, and you are the daughter of a squireen and not fit to latch my shoes.

'My family were loyal to the King, mistress, for all the hurt he and his line have done us, and when the country rose against him, my father and my two uncles came over with Lord Byron's troops to pour their good blood forth in his service. When Fairfax and Brereton defeated Byron and forced him to a surrender, they still lived, and they were made honourable prisoners of war, taken in fair fight. My mother brought me and my young brothers over to England after that – she feared to leave us in those bad times, and she hoped to help my father and our other kin. They were in prison in Hull, and one day when she came there, scattering the last of our gold like corn before chickens for so much as the condescension of a sight of them, the Governor told her the Irish were sent to Barbados.

'We waited, and hoped, and starved, mistress. We were gentle-folk reduced to beggary in the King's cause, but they called us Irish, and there was none to help us. My mother went as nurse to a sick woman, and she was able to keep me by her, while the boys were sent away to St Omer's, where we had a cousin who could stand

229

sponsor, and I have never seen them more. After my mother died, I got my living by my hands, and at the last, in despair of my life, I took an indenture to Barbados, thinking at least I might get word of my father and his brothers, that perhaps when the seven years were up, I might hope to live decently with my kin.

'Think of it, mistress! Open your eyes, if you can, to what you see here, and think of what I found! I came here in a worse case than you, looking for news of better men, and when the truth was made plain to me, it was more bitter than death. Your father was a Royalist officer, and he left you a plantation. Mine was another, and he suffered and died in a field-gang, for the abominable crime of loyalty and Irish blood, because when the King came in again, and the Commonwealth went out, Devil an amnesty there was for poor Irish prisoners. King Charles has forgotten many a friend, but he will answer to God for what he did to the Irish. There were noble lords left here to live and die naked among the blacks, without even a priest to see them from the world, and when I think of it, my heart is so hot with gall and bitterness that if this vessel were full to the brim with English blood, I would drink it and be glad.'

Sibella sat staring at her maid, too astonished to speak; the tears had dried on her cheeks. She felt very sick, and her mind was somehow clouded. 'Bridget, is this true?' she asked, helplessly.

'I would scorn to lie to you,' the other woman flung back.

'Oh, Bridget . . . this is more horrible than I can think of.'

'I have had to think of it these many months,' Bridget retorted.

'Bridget, do not provoke me!' she shouted, her voice breaking out of her control. She buried her head in her hands, and wearily massaged her forehead. 'I am sorry. I knew nothing of this, and remember, if you please, it is not I that has injured you. I will not cast you off because you have shown me what is in your heart – do not force me to it with your ungovernable pride.'

Her feelings were turbulent; it was hard for her to put thoughts together. She had been fond of Bridget, had thought that she knew her, but she saw her in a new light now that she knew she was of noble birth; their relationship had necessarily changed. She could not imagine the humiliation her maid and her family had undergone; the picture she had raised was horrible beyond belief.

'Bridget, we must talk further,' she said, getting up and going to the door. 'Molly!' The nursemaid appeared with suspicious alacrity, standing with downcast eyes; Sibella turned to her, and spoke sharply. 'Molly, you and Adjaba must finish with the laundry, for once. There is not so very much more to do, and you can manage perfectly well.' As Molly curtsied and moved silently to do her bidding, she held out a hand to Bridget. 'Come with me.'

She led Bridget upstairs to her own closet. 'Come. I think we would be the better of a glass of wine.' She kept a modest supply of Canary in her private cupboard, having never cultivated a taste for rum, even taken with water. Bridget went to fetch the bottle and poured two glasses. 'Sit here beside me.'

For a minute or two, they sipped their wine in silence. In that welcome period of respite, Sibella found her mind clearing a little. The shock of what she had been told seemed to be forcing her mind to a new clarity, like stirring rennet into milk: as she sat still, it was as if a curdy opacity was settling, leaving clarity behind. 'Bridget,' she said suddenly. 'You had no right to speak to me as you did. You are my maid, or perhaps I should say, my gentlewoman. You have been kindly treated by us, better by far than most of those who came over with you, and for the next five years you have signed away the right to determine matters for yourself.'

Bridget looked at her, catching her lower lip in her teeth; and very soberly, she nodded. She was generally a plain woman, and between her emotion and a day's hard work in the heat, she was plainer than usual, reddened and puffy about the eyes, yet Sibella looked at her face with relief, because she looked merely tired and sad; the bitter rage was gone from it.

'But all the same, I am not sorry to have heard your story,' she persevered, with painful honesty which was somehow a relief to her mind, as if she had taken a purge. 'I am thinking about all that has happened since we came here. All that I hoped for, and how my feelings have altered since England. I am beginning to think that in my heart I am grown frightened of this country, because of how it is changing me. I hate it for the heat and all the things that plague us, of course, but it seems almost as if this is an accursed place, like Circe's island in the old tales. It corrupts the minds of men as surely as it rusts their weapons and rots their linen. You tell me that gentlemen like your father were reduced to the likeness of beasts of the field, that other men may grow rich, and from what I have seen here, I cannot but believe you. The only nobility here is wealth, and the populace worship sugar as its god and idol. I have fallen into the same contagion, hoping to make us great here, and it has been a fool's bargain. Balthasar has been right all along; we can do no better in Barbados than we do now. We should take what we have and be thankful for it, and go home! I long for England, Bridget. Oh, how I long for nights which are cool enough to sleep in. Let us be friends again, and never speak of this more.'

Bridget looked at her for a long moment; Sibella could not read her expression. 'Very well, my lady.'

'Bridget . . .' asked Sibella tentatively, as another thought struck her, 'you have surely made enquiries, if your kinsfolk be alive or no? There are free white servants here in the town – is it possible your father or your uncle may be one of them?'

'I have asked about, my lady. The poor souls that survive their indentures live mostly below the hill, at Hackleton's Cliff, and they do not make common cause with the negroes. But my kin were prisoners of war, not indentured servants. There was no period set to their sufferings, and they worked until they died.'

Sibella sighed, and drained her glass. Silence lay heavy between them, but it was like the aftermath of a thunderstorm, a relief to the mind. 'We must go down again, Bridget. We should help the slaves put the laundry away.'

Balthasar did not come home for dinner on washing day, since the kitchen was entirely given over to wet linen, but dined in one of the Bridgetown taverns. He did not return until after his evening round of visits. She watched him, as he sat in the chair opposite her picking at his supper without appetite. They had been married nearly three years. No great time, but it struck her suddenly that although he was only thirty-five, he had gone from a young man to a middle-aged one since they came to the Indies. The furrow from nose to mouth was notably more pronounced, his cheeks were thinner, and his eyes were set deeper in their sockets, darkly shadowed beneath. He looked extremely tired, and his face bore the marks of constant, unremitting strain. Her heart smote her: he was her husband and master of the house, so of course she ensured that it ran for his convenience and according to his requirements, but because he was a central fact in her life and part of her, she did not habitually reflect on him any more than she reflected on herself. Now, she wondered suddenly if this life in the tropics were not as hard on him as it was on her. He had never complained – but, she thought with sudden compunction, he would not, as long as he thought her set on staying.

'Balthasar?'

'Yes, my darling?'

'I have some strange news – no, it is no cause for alarm,' she added hastily, as his eyebrows rose. 'I was talking with Bridget today, when she fell into a hot fit of passion, and in her heat, told me something which she has been keeping secret.'

'There is not a priest hid on the island?' he asked abruptly, his face darkening.

'No, no such thing. She told me that she is a gentlewoman, a lady even, of an ancient and noble family in Ireland. They were proscribed for their religion, and fell into hard times in the late wars. She came here because her father was exiled here in Cromwell's time, and she found he had been condemned to a field-gang. I can hardly believe such a thing would be allowed.'

'But do you believe her, generally?'

'Yes, I do.'

'I would like to ask Lieutenant Palaeologue what he thinks of the tale,' said Balthasar, 'but he is over in Dominica again, I believe. On the face of it, though her tale is sad, it is far from impossible. I have seen white men in slave gangs, and I know many of them are Irish. The most part of the white hands on this island are Irish Catholics, and since the planters consider them implacably revengeful and murderous in their inclinations, they more often serve in the cane-fields than in gentlemen's houses. Even if her father was all that she says, I fear that his rank would have been no protection. But, Sibella. Is this a difficulty for you? Do you want to sell her indenture?'

'No. We are good friends again. But I wanted to ask you if you would agree to release her from her bond. It was not so very costly, since it was only for seven years. I would have her free to marry: she is a gentlewoman, after all, and in this place, where women of quality are hardly to be found, she may yet make her fortune. Perhaps I should ask Lady Palaeologue to advise us.'

'Well, if you wish, my mouse. I know you would be sorry to lose her, but if you feel you have a duty to her, I will not stand in her way.'

'Thank you, my dearest.'

'But, Sibella. I do warn you. I have no desire to buy another slave. If you let Bridget go, you will have to train Adjaba to stand as your right-hand woman. Her English is greatly improved, and she is a girl of good natural parts. I hope you will manage well enough.'

'Balthasar . . .' Her voice trailed off. He looked at her enquiringly, and in a rush, she added, 'Could we go home?'

He sat up a little in his chair, looking greatly surprised. 'But Sibella, my dearest, I thought you were determined on staying here until we had made somewhat more of our lives. You have said this often enough, and I have heeded you.'

'It was talking to Bridget which has changed my ideas, Balthasar. There is an infection of getting and spending in this island, and I freely own, I have been moved by it. But for all that you can do, and for all that you are the best physician in the island and attend many of the leading men, even Governor Atkins, we will never be anything but people of the middling sort. It is not skill or learning which is valued here, but only sugar. I think sometimes that their minds must be candied with sweetness, and their veins run syrup. They will never elect you to the House of Assembly, not just because you are mulatto, but because you are not the lord of many cane-fields.'

'Well, of course,' said Balthasar, 'but I did not know you knew it.'

'Neither did I. I have been hiding my eyes, I think, but I will hide them no more.'

'Sibella ... you do not imagine, do you, that by returning to Europe, we can fare any better?'

'Of course not. I have spoken for staying in this hellish place, because for long enough, I had the notion that in this little country, we might rise to be people of consequence and make something of our children, but it is not so. I have been deceiving myself. We will never be gentry again – I am quite resigned, and I have let go of my dream. It was my father's only gift to me, so I valued it, but I should have known from the life he gave my mother, it would be a flower with poison in its heart.' Dismayed, she realised that Balthasar was beginning to waver before her eyes; she was on the verge of tears again.

'Please, Sibella. Say no more. You are distressing yourself.' Hastily, he rose and poured her a glass of Canary. 'I am profoundly glad we are so well agreed. I think we should take a little time before making any final decisions, but in principle, I do not think we should stay much longer. We must needs wait until Sarah is weaned, since conditions on shipboard would dry Molly's breasts to all but a certainty, but we are more likely to see her grow to comely womanhood in England. The climate here is hard enough on us, but it is Moloch's oven for tender babies, black or white. The moisture of their infant state complies with that of the air, and breeds worms. Remember, Molly lost her own child. And I have seen too many deaths.'

Sibella sipped her wine with relief flooding her heart. The decision was made. Balthasar's ponderous, methodical habits of mind had irritated her almost beyond endurance when they were first married, but even when she had found him most annoying, she had always had to acknowledge to herself that he was scrupulously just. Now, as she argued for throwing up all that he had achieved at her own instigation, and at a cost to himself she was only now beginning to think about, his unshakeable integrity and sense of fairness seemed to her virtues beyond price. Eyes downcast, she drained her glass, and silently thanked God for the man she had married.

Two or three weeks later, Lieutenant Palaeologue presented himself, jaunty and smiling as ever, and was greeted, as always, with unaffected pleasure and the best that the house could provide. Balthasar was still out, so Sibella took him to her closet, not displeased to have him to herself. 'Well, Mistress Sibella,' he said, after the preliminaries were over, 'you will like to know that I am minded to take a wife.'

'My felicitations, Lieutenant Palaeologue! What lady has captured your heart?' she asked, immediately interested, but somehow a little regretful. He was of an age when it was natural and right that he should establish a household, but she could not but fear that marriage would change him.

'No lady, as yet. It is the principle and theory of wedlock which I have embraced,' he said airily.

'Excuse me a moment – Bridget,' she said to the waiting-woman, who stood by the door, ready to pour their wine. 'We have all we want for the moment. Could you go down to the kitchen, and see how Adjaba and Molly are managing? You have a nicer sense of setting forth a table than either of them.'

'Lieutenant Palaeologue,' she continued eagerly, once the door had shut behind her maid, 'if you are in need of a wife, and you have no lady in your heart, consider my Bridget. We are in process of releasing her from her indenture. She is chaste, well-conducted, and a most excellent housekeeper, and she is a de Burnell, the daughter of Norman lords in Ireland. There can be no better-born lady in Barbados.'

He sat regarding her, his olive-skinned face kindly but distant. 'Mistress Sibella, I am sure she is all that you say she is, and a woman could come with no better recommendation than that she has satisfied you, but for all that, she is not for me. Each to their own, but I would not marry a Catholic, or an Irishwoman, and she is both. The Catholics are not to be trusted, for they are dispensed from keeping any bargain with those they miscall heretics, but above all, the Irish are a nation of infinite treachery, who will never come to good.'

Sibella felt herself flushing. 'But Lieutenant, if you are so nice in your taste, then how will you find yourself a wife who is all you would wish? There are few enough unmarried women in Barbados who are not whores, or the daughters of whores – forgive me. I have misspoken myself, but it was from affection.'

'Forgiven and forgotten, Mistress Sibella, all but the concern for me, which I will keep in my heart. I have decided to look in another direction entirely, and I will marry a princess of the Caribs.'

'A Carib!'

'And why not? The Caribs are chaste, cleanly, comely to look upon, and well adjusted to the climate. I have discussed the matter with Governor Warner in Dominica, and the daughter of a great chief among the Caribs is a person of as long a pedigree as any Norman lady in the world. Governor Warner is speaking for me, for a Carib princess is not even to be looked upon by a stranger like myself. When I next return to Dominica, he will have found me a wife.'

Sibella stared at him, bereft of speech. For a moment, she wondered if he was jesting, but it was clear that he was not. She was deeply relieved when a stir and bustle downstairs heralded Balthasar's return, and she was able to turn the conversation.

A few days after that, when Balthasar was leaving the house on his evening round of visits, a voice spoke to him out of the blackness of the stable-yard, while he waited for Jack to saddle and harness his horse.

'Doctor?'

The voice was familiar, though in the dusk, he could barely discern the dark figure which was standing deep in the shadows. 'Yambo? How come you here?'

Yambo ignored the question. 'Doctor, yuh faduh did Africa man, an' a king. I come tuh tell he son someting.'

'What thing?' asked Balthasar, thoroughly confused.

'June twelve. Da' day, yuh mus stop home wid yuh wife. Dey gwine be a mark pon de door. Ask nuh more, Doctor. I speak de trufe.'

'It is June the sixth,' said Balthasar stupidly, then realised he was speaking to the empty air. Yambo had slipped out through the hole in the fence which had given him his entrance.

Balthasar questioned Jack severely, but he denied all knowledge of Yambo or his secret. He rode off on his rounds in a disturbed frame of mind. It was hard to know what to make of the incident. He thought of going to the Governor, but his sense of honour revolted from breaking a confidence, especially from a man no longer young who must have risked a lashing – not his first – to bring it to him. There was nothing he could say to the Governor without implicating Yambo, a man he valued and respected, and if Yambo were questioned by the authorities, he would certainly be put to the torture. And what justification, after all, had he given for handing him over to the suspicious agents of government? By the time he was going home, Balthasar had decided to let the matter drop, though he gave orders that the fence bordering the yard between the stables and the house should be replaced with a wall of coral-limestone.

When June the twelfth came round, he woke remembering Yambo's injunction. He prepared himself, as usual, for his morning's rounds, but when he was shaved, dressed and ready for the street, he went and looked out of the first-floor window at the front of the house before going down to the stable. As he stood looking out over Bridgetown, trying to make up his mind, he heard the bell of the cathedral begin to toll, and some moments later observed some few of the Barbados militia marching along the street in haste, pikes in hand.

He shut the window with decision and barred the shutters, then went hastily to give directions that all windows and doors must be shut, barred and bolted. No member of the household, white or black, was to leave the house that day. Sibella, alarmed, questioned him closely, but for the first time in their life together, he lost his temper, stood on his authority as a husband, and ordered her to do as she was told and keep her mouth shut. He interrogated the slaves as severely as he could, desisting only when he had assured himself that they were entirely ignorant of what was going on.

For the rest of the interminable day, they all sat idle in the darkened house, trying to make sense of the occasional sounds which filtered through from outside. Sibella, with her admirable discipline, sat knitting a stocking with unfaltering fingers, Sarah asleep in the cradle by her side, while Balthasar sat with a candle and tried without success to concentrate on a book. Bridget busied herself with some darning, her lips faintly moving; Balthasar suspected that she was saying the Rosary, but he affected to ignore it. The slaves sat together in the kitchen, doing odd jobs, then as the day wore on simply sat, talking together circumspectly in hushed voices.

They all went to bed a little earlier than was their habit, then when the next day dawned over a Bridgetown which looked very much as usual, Balthasar ventured out, taking both Caesar and Jack with him. He found his patients almost universally in a state of alarm: something had happened, but nobody seemed to know what it was, or if it was over. The story became clear in the days that followed. A rising had been planned, in considerable detail, and over many years; the instigators were a group of Coromantees, who had laid their plans in the strictest secrecy. They had chosen the old king Kofi, or as the English called him, Cuffee, as their leader, and they had intended to inaugurate him in a throne of state on the twelfth of June, after which there was to be a general rising in which the sugar-cane would be fired and the planters massacred. A woman slave called Fortuna belonging to Judge Hall had overheard some hint of the plans, and had told her master, who had immediately alerted Governor Atkins. The Governor, in turn, had put Barbados under martial law, and appointed a summary court of oyer and terminer to examine the suspects.

Balthasar heard all this in sweating horror. The idea of a general massacre appalled him, and he knew he had been profoundly remiss in not alerting the authorities to his suspicions. The fragility of the society he lived in came fully home to him; the fact that the white masters were so outnumbered by the slaves to whom they denied the ordinary rights of a man that they must needs be brutal in order to be certain of their own lives. But on the whole, though he did not share this thought with either his wife or his attendant, he found the actions of Fortuna harder to understand than those of either the Coromantee or the Governor; he had noticed, with some sadness, the frequent lack of sympathy between field-hands and house-slaves. He was greatly distressed to hear that Yambo was among those who had been arrested. It immediately plunged him into a moral quandary: if he went to speak for the man, he would have to confess what had been said to him, and would stand revealed as a fool at best, or a knave. As a mulatto, and hence a person of suspicious loyalties, he might even find himself in personal danger, which would in turn jeopardise his wife and child.

After a night of painful heart-searching, he awoke with his mind made up. He ordered Jack to saddle the horse, and set the animal on the road to Speightstown, where the court was sitting since it was the nearest settlement to the centre of the disturbance. He intended to present himself, if this was permitted, as a character witness, and make what plea he could on the basis of Yambo's long years of care for his fellow negroes.

Speightstown, as he approached it, was held in an eerie silence. Even the chickens and the dogs seemed subdued, and the breeze brought with it a ghastly odour of corruption and burning. As he trotted towards the central square, the street was empty, though he knew that he was watched. He emerged into the square itself, and took in the scene before him. The militia were drawn up four deep before the courthouse, fully armed. In the middle of the square was a still-smouldering bonfire built round a number of iron stakes; each with a twisted, blackened body standing supported by the chains that bound it. Their arms were raised and their heads flung back, open-mouthed. Bathasar knew abstractly that the bodies would have taken this form as their sinews shrank and contracted in the fire, but he could not make himself believe it. They looked as if they had been pleading for life, or surcease to their torment. More stakes had been erected on either side, topped by severed heads, almost unrecognisable lumps of dark matter concealed beneath a moving blanket of flies, which also clung and clustered to the stakes and the ground beneath them. The stench was terrible, and the silence almost complete, but for the occasional snort and stamp of a restless horse.

'What's your business, sirra?' demanded the captain, riding forward.

Balthasar took off his hat. 'I am a doctor in Bridgetown, sir. I have come to ask if I can speak for Yambo. I believe him to be a man of honour, and he has been of the greatest assistance to me professionally.'

'Too late, Doctor,' said the captain. He jerked a thumb insolently towards the terrible relics standing in the fire. 'There is Yambo. He died bravely enough. The Coromantees all do.'

Balthasar absorbed the information, and bowed his head. Then he put his hat back on, turned his horse, and rode out of Speightstown without a further word.

Angry and sad as he was, he thought he had better call on Lady Palaeologue and see how she had fared in the emergency. He found her in a great taking, distressed almost beyond speech. Lieutenant Palaeologue was with her, he was relieved to see. Both speaking together, their words stumbling across each other, they told him that Quashie had been one of the conspiracy, though so secret in it that even his wife Nanny had not known of it, and Isaiah was also suspected. Quashie's was one of the severed heads that Balthasar had seen that morning in Speightstown; Isaiah was in prison, and would probably be sold off the island, Nanny was lying inconsolable in her hut, and the whole household was set by the ears.

Balthasar prescribed a soothing, gently soporific tisane of soursop and wild cherry leaves, both of which Cleopatra readily produced, despite her own obvious distress – due to the nature of his errand, he was out without his doctor's bag. He was heartsick to remember that it was Yambo who had told him how to use the leaves. The tisane took half an hour to prepare, but once it was administered, it took effect quite rapidly, to his great relief. Lady Palaeologue's pulse improved and slowed, and the look of staring anxiety began to go from her eyes, replaced by decent sadness and exhaustion. He sat with her as long as he dared, letting her have her talk out, and excused himself only when he felt he must: with a curfew in place, he dared not leave it too late to return to Bridgetown.

Lieutenant Palaeologue saw him to his horse. 'I will not forget your care of my poor mother,' he said quietly. His manner was uncharacteristically subdued.

'It is the least I could do,' he said.

'You are a good friend. Take care, and I pray that you reach home safely.'

In the weeks that followed, the life of Barbados gradually resumed its even tenor. More than fifty slaves had been executed, and as many again deported – including Cleopatra's man, Isaiah – or savagely flogged. Martial law was lifted once it was clear that the revolt had been scotched, so except for those directly involved, the alarm faded gradually into the past. For those who had suffered directly, the memory was not so easily dispelled. Sorrow, shame and a kind of bewilderment seemed to have propelled Lady Palaeologue into old age almost overnight. Having lived on kindly terms with her slaves, having known – or so she had thought – and respected Quashie for thirty years, she was unable to accept the idea that he would have been willing to rise against her. She questioned Nanny again and again, unable to refrain, until she contrived to turn the black woman's heartbroken loyalty to sullen anger. The household, once so harmonious, was irreparably damaged; worse than that, Quashie's action had cast into question whether the harmony that appeared on the surface had ever truly existed. Balthasar visited when he could, and so on occasion did Sibella, and sat patiently through long, dreary hours of rambling monologue in which the old lady obsessively revisited the events of the revolt, as if they could somehow be forced to yield an acceptable meaning. One unintended result of these difficult encounters was that Balthasar resumed his work on medicinal plants of the Antilles: it gave him something to think about while he half-listened to Lady Palaeologue, and more importantly, he began to conceive of it as a memorial to Yambo, something permanent salvaged from the wreck and wastage of making such a man a field-slave. It was only much later that it struck him that the work would also have pleased his father.

Lieutenant Palaeologue returned to Dominica to fetch his bride once his mother's health and spirits had recovered a little: he was in no way to be diverted from this strange project. Balthasar had thought Lady Palaeologue would prevent it, but it seemed as if she had been so overset by the misfortune of her household that she had no spirit to oppose him. They did not know when they might hear from him again: Sibella even wondered if he was intending to join his wife's people, which seemed to Balthasar on the whole unlikely. Still, he had sailed to Dominica in a season when shipmasters were increasingly unwilling to trust their vessels to the sea: as July came to an end, the risk of storm increased, and in August and September none would leave harbour if it could be avoided.

Early in August, one rainy night when they were preparing for bed, and the household was locked up for the night, they were alarmed by a thunderous knocking on the door. Hastily wrapping themselves once more in the loose gowns they wore in the evenings, while Jack fumbled with the door, they came down to the hall, candles in hand, to find their household grouped about Lieutenant Palaeologue, who was standing dripping on the floor, and supporting a slender, drooping figure.

'My dear friends, you will forgive my lack of ceremony,' he said wearily, as Balthasar came forward, full of consternation. 'Allow me to present my wife. Her name is Iere.'

They stared at her; she looked back at them mutely, her tiny, masklike face unreadable. She was small, slight and young, dressed in European clothes which seemed to sit so strangely on the slender body that she was all but lost in them.

'Forgive me,' said Balthasar, collecting his scattered wits, 'we are letting you stand, while we stare. You must need rest, a shift of linen. Sibella, my dearest, will you look after Mistress Iere while Bridget fetches candles and refreshments? Lieutenant, does your lady speak English?' The girl nodded mutely, her liquid gaze shifting from face to face. 'Go with my wife, Mistress Iere,' he said with all the kindness he could; the poor creature looked like a trapped animal. 'You are most heartily welcome to my house. Adjaba, run to make sure all is well with the best bedroom, the Lieutenant is weary. My friend, come with me, and I will find you a nightgown. You are wet through.'

The forlorn little figure of Iere traipsed meekly off in Sibella's care. Balthasar and Palaeologue followed them upstairs, and as he came to his friend's side, the light of the candle he was holding caught the other man's face, and he realised that he was in the grip of volcanic fury which he was mastering only by the severest effort of will.

Once Palaeologue was dried and clad in a stuff dressing-gown and a turban, Balthasar conducted him through to the parlour, now ablaze with candles, where an impromptu feast of nuts, anchovies, olives, cheese and cold meats had been assembled by Bridget. The Lieutenant refused food, but was plainly glad of a glass of Malaga wine. A few minutes later, Sibella entered with Iere, almost extinguished in the folds of a loose, flowered chintz gown which on Sibella was attractive and charming, her raven hair hidden in an embroidered linen nightcap which gave her little face an elfin look. She looked swiftly around, and once she saw her husband, subsided primly onto the edge of a chair.

'Will you take a glass of wine, Mistress Palaeologue?' asked Sibella solicitously. Palaeologue repeated the question in Carib, adding, it seemed, an injunction.

''ank you,' said the bride, in a voice hardly louder than a breath. She took the glass Sibella gave her, and held it carefully in both hands, untouched.

'Lieutenant Palaeologue,' said Balthasar, now that his guest had been offered the hospitality of the house, 'you are welcome at any time, of course, but what has blown you to our door at this hour?'

Lieutenant Palaeologue took a long swallow of his wine. His face was set like stone, the lines in it deeply carved. 'Treachery. Governor Warner is murdered.'

'Dead! And who dared kill him?' Balthasar was outraged. Also, following as it did on the death of Yambo, one of the people he had most valued and trusted in the whole of the Indies, the thought that the splendid Governor was no longer in life was distressing to him.

Palaeologue raised his eyebrows, with a touch of his old insouciance, now become a sort of bleak cynicism which hurt Balthasar for its own sake, it seemed so alien to the man he loved and admired. 'Who would dare kill Indian Warner, but his own brother? Philip Warner, the other son of Sir Thomas by the virtuous lady who so resented her husband's bastard she tried to make a slave of him. My friend Warner has been Governor of Dominica these ten years, just as Philip has governed Antigua. He has been a face the English put upon a reality; for they are not strong enough to defeat the Caribs in such a mountain stronghold, and as such, he has served King Charles well. He has been Carib to the Caribs, a man of might and mettle whom they respected, while to the English, he was English enough: as a byblow of Sir Thomas of St Kitts, he was a person of title, however left-handed. But the independent Caribs have been a thorn in the flesh to the planters, and when the Windward Caribs recently attacked Antigua, Philip set forth to subdue them, and asked his brother's help. Warner came to his aid with fighting men and provisions, which he greatly needed. They fought side by side, and when all was done, Colonel Philip invited the Dominicans to an entertainment of thanks on board his ship. When they were deep in their cups, he gave a signal to his own men, and they fell upon them and massacred them, men, women, and children all together.

'I was in the Carib town with my new father-in-law, or I would have defended Indian Warner to my last breath. When the news came to me, I own that I thought to go and try conclusions with the man. But I knew the Caribs would rise, and I had a duty to my bride. I took Iere on the crupper of my horse, and went straight to Portsmouth; I keep rooms there, so I put her into her town clothes, found a skipper known to me, and put my dagger to his throat till he agreed to go to sea. I will go to Governor Atkins tomorrow, to tell him all this, and then let Sir Philip beware. Atkins greatly esteemed Indian Warner. He will avenge my friend, if God or the Caribs do not get there before him.'

As Balthasar listened, he felt the hairs rising on his neck and arms. 'I am truly sorry Governor Warner is dead,' he said, hating his own lack of eloquence, hoping that Palaeologue would discern his sincerity and his affection. 'He seemed to me a kind of hope for the future. But, my dear friend, rest. If you will not eat, then go to bed, and sleep. I will give you a soporific, if you care for one. I feel for all that you say, but I do not want to see you eat your heart out with bitterness. It avails poor Warner nothing, and you have this delicate girl by your side, young and helpless, and in a strange place. Recruit your strength, I beg of you. You have need of it, and so does your wife, and your mother.'

'Sir,' said Palaeologue wearily, 'you speak like my better self. If your wife's woman will but show us to our room, we will go to bed.'

For some time, Palaeologue and his bride continued to stay with Balthasar and Sibella: while Balthasar went about his usual business, Palaeologue went to see Governor Atkins, and subsequently spent his days in the taverns, talking with men from the House of Assembly and the militia, canvassing opinion on the Governor's death; he did not discuss the results of his discussions, but he looked more tired and grim by the day. He was somewhat cheered when the news came that Philip Warner had been captured on Atkins's orders and was on his way to London to stand trial, though it was clear from his few comments that he suspected the trial would be in form only.

Sibella, meanwhile, did all that she could with Iere, who was shy almost to silence. As she rapidly discovered, though the girl was in no way unwilling, she was as clumsy as a child faced with the complexities of Sibella's housekeeping. So mute and bewildered was she, it began to seem a kind of cruelty to ask her to help, even though Sibella was charitably determined to teach her what she would need to know. After a couple of days, she retreated from the struggle, so Iere spent most of her time with the baby, rocking the cradle and singing interminable Carib songs in a breathy little voice which ceased abruptly if she detected any movement in the corridor outside.

When on the fourth night of the Palaeologues' visit they all met at supper and Iere volunteered speech, it seemed a kind of prodigy after so many days of muteness. Balthasar and Sibella looked at her astounded, as if she had been a talking animal. She raised her head, and collected their eyes, then 'Moon,' she said, quite clearly. Holding up one tiny hand, she twirled her forefinger, describing circles. Her eyes were imploring them to understand.

Palaeologue questioned her in his broken Carib; she replied with a musical flood of speech. He shook his head; and urgently, she reached across the table and took his wrist. Allowing her to rouse him, he followed her to the window, shuttered tight against the insects and the night air, and threw it open. The moon was riding high in the sky, with a hazy penumbra of light like a double ring about it. Iere made further attempts to explain, her hands fluttering like captive butterflies.

Palaeologue turned to them, his face grave. 'Iere says there will be a hurricane. My friends, I would recommend believing her. Extinguish all lights, from the top of the house to the bottom, and douse the kitchen fire. We should take flock-beds down to the kitchen, endure the insects as best we can, and rest by the open door. We should shelter while we can, but if the house itself is threatened, we can escape into the yard.'

'Can a hurricane threaten the house?' asked Sibella, horrified.

Palaeologue looked at her gravely. 'It can. Come, Mistress Sibella. Summon your household, and look to your child. The slaves must be called from their quarters and spend the night with us in the kitchen. If the town looks as it does now tomorrow morning, you have my fullest liberty to laugh.'

Sibella set down her glass and rose at once. While Balthasar went to summon the slaves, she took her sleeping child from her cradle and carried her downstairs wrapped in a quilt. Within half an hour, under Palaeologue's direction, they had pallet-beds made on the kitchen floor, and Sarah was sleeping peacefully in one of the kitchen baskets, protected from the mosquitoes by a thin veil of lawn. The men went up and down the house, ensuring that there was no spark of fire anywhere, then they settled down, the slaves on their mats against one wall, Balthasar, Sibella, Bridget and their guests against the other. It was very uncomfortable, especially after the merrywings found them, and very strange to see the stars through the open door.

Balthasar, shifting his aching bones irritably and scratching his bites, found himself increasingly impatient with Palaeologue's fantastical little wife. Sibella was curved round the basket with her baby in it, stoic and uncomplaining. He knew that she was not asleep. But as dawn approached, the still, oppressive night seemed to move as if the island was breathing. A heavy sough, and the palm-trees, their silhouettes growing visible against the sapphire sky, dipped their stately heads. For a moment it was as if the wind was sucked the other way, like the undertow of a wave, then the hurricane was upon them.

Balthasar had never imagined anything like it, and never forgot it. The very air seemed to be screaming, and a deluge of rain hammered into the yard, a solid bulk of water falling from the sky as heavy as sand. Sibella had scrambled to her knees, petrified, arching herself over her child, Balthasar, in turn, tried to set his body between his wife and harm; they clutched one another with a grip like death. After some endless minutes of intolerable noise, all the tiles avalanched from the roof; some of them crashed into the courtyard, exploding in shards of terra-cotta, while others were blown on the wind to do harm in some other place. As the dawn broke, they saw the entire roof of the stable, which had been thatched with palmetto, lift off and blow away. The house rocked like a ship with the force of the wind. It was full light before it began to die down, though the torrential rain continued, by which time their ears were ringing and they were dizzy with the intolerable howling.

Palaeologue looked at them very soberly, once it was possible to speak and make oneself heard. 'I think we have done well to spend the night as we did,' he said.

Too shaken to speak, Balthasar nodded. Sibella rose, and served rum to all of them, slaves and free together. The wind and the rain had left the air very cold. None of them could stop shivering, and the fiery warmth seemed to ease their hearts. Jack bravely ventured out into the flooding rain and picked his way across the ruins of the courtyard to see how the beasts had fared. He came back downcast, to report that a roofbeam had fallen across Balthasar's horse and broken her back.

'I will kill her then, poor beast,' said Palaeologue at once. 'There is a vein in the throat I know. Give me your sharpest knife, Mistress

Sibella, and I will put her from her misery.' He squelched grimly across the courtyard, and returned a little after, soaked to the skin, to report that the job was done.

'My dear sir, you must shift your clothes at once,' said Balthasar. 'From what I can see, it is safe to go upstairs. Make free with my wardrobe, but warm yourself, for the love of God.' As his friend turned wearily to leave the kitchen, he looked at his wife. She was sitting huddled on the flock-bed, clasping their child. Her teeth were chattering, and her face was quite grey. 'My darling Sibella,' he said, 'we are going home just as soon as we can find a ship to take us.'

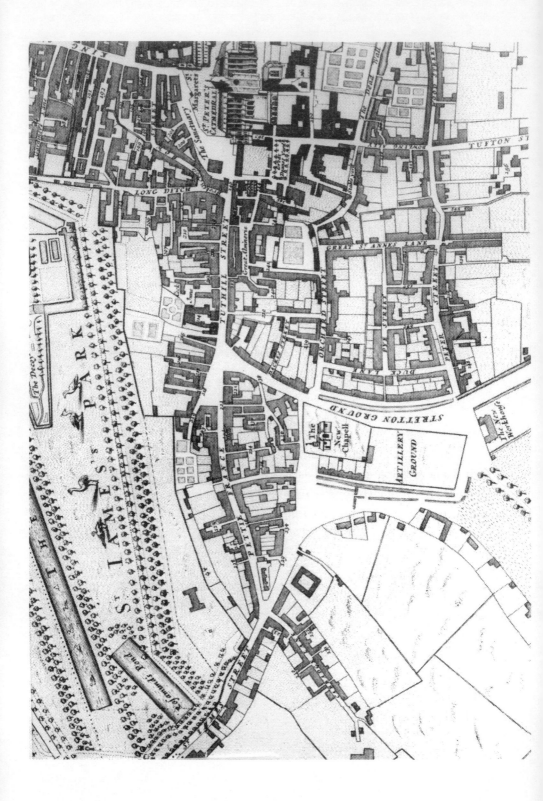

XI

Doth that lewd harlot, that poetic queen,
Fam'd through Whitefriars (you know who I mean)
Mend for reproof, others set up in spight,
To flux, take glisters, vomits, purge, and write.
Long with a sciatica she's beside lame,
Her limbs distortur'd, nerves shrunk up with pain,
And therefore I'll all sharp reflections shun,
Poetry, poverty, pox are plagues enough for one.

'Epistle to [Robert] Julian', London,
British Library Harley 7317, 1684

January 1684

'Oh, I am so glad to have you home,' said Sibella, the moment he opened the door. 'How is it now?'

Balthasar closed the parlour door behind him, and walked straight across to the fire. He stood over it, chafing his numb hands. As the heat encountered the frozen surface of his garments, his breeches and coat began to steam. He glanced over his shoulder to where his wife was sitting like a broody hen, huddled in a quilted jacket with her feet on a warmer – a wooden box holding a terra-cotta pan of smouldering charcoal – with their little daughter beside her, leaning against her knees. She was a pleasant sight, with her face lit by concern for him. 'There are people walking on the Thames,' he said.

'Is the ice so thick!'

'It is a foot or more even by the Bridge, they tell me, a yard thick at least, along the river. They are so sure of it they are even setting up booths on the ice, and people are talking of a frost fair.'

'Oh, Father. Can we go?' said Sarah at once. Balthasar looked at his daughter as she sat tucked up on her stool beside her mother with his usual mixture of love and anxiety. She was pretty, with an olive complexion, hazel eyes and fluffy, light-brown hair, and she had an adventurous spirit, but at nine, advancing towards womanhood, she was also delicate, too thin, and often ill. He worried about her a good deal.

'We will think about it, my mouse. If you wrap up very well, the cold should not be injurious, but the fog is still very bad, and I fear that it might set you coughing again.'

'Is the fog not lifting?' asked Sibella, her voice roughened by exasperation. 'Surely it has gone on long enough. I have never known such a winter.'

'No, and I think now that it will not, until the thaw begins. The exhalations from the sea-coal we burn are, I think, freezing in the air, and not being dispelled by the breeze in the normal fashion. At any rate, something is hindering the ascent of the smoke, and I can only imagine it is the cold. It is lying so thick now that one can scarcely see across the street.'

'I wish you were not out so much,' said Sibella; she was evidently trying to keep a note of complaint from her voice, but not entirely succeeding. 'I am in fear all the time till you return.'

'My dearest wife, there is no help for it,' protested Balthasar. 'The streets are very dangerous, and there is much need for a surgeon's skills. I have never had so many broken limbs in a winter, and the poor souls must be tended. I come home as soon as may be, I assure you, but Squirrel must pick her way on the ice, and it is a slow business. She is a wise-like beast, and her shoes are well roughened – Thomas took her to the farrier's to recut them only yesterday, so she is as sure-footed as any horse in London.'

'I want to walk on the Thames, Father,' said Theodore suddenly, surprising them all. He was a dreamy and unaccountable child, who often seemed barely aware of what was going on around him. He had been curled on the hearth, staring into the fire when his father came in, and had shifted only minimally to allow Balthasar to stand beside him. It would have been hard for his parents to be sure that he had heard a word since his father's return.

Balthasar sat down; the insidious bone-deep chill was beginning to release him, and he was now merely cold. 'Come here, Theodore,' he said.

His son got up obediently, abandoning the mysterious little collection of twigs, marbles, knucklebones and other scraps with which he had been playing, and came to his father. Balthasar lifted the little boy onto his knee, where he sat passively, thin legs dangling, looking gravely up at him.

'Why would you like to walk on the ice, my Theodore?'

The child's lips parted: he looked as if he was listening to someone whispering in his ear. 'Oh ... when we look at the river, I mean, when the ice is gone, we can think, we walked on the water. Like our Lord.'

'Was there ice, when our Lord walked upon the water, Theodore?'

He considered the question, a crease momentarily disturbing the smooth skin between his brows. Solemnly, he shook his head.

'Good boy. Well, on Saturday, we will go on the river, if the weather gets no worse.'

For the next three days, the promised expedition dominated family conversation. The fog and the icy, snowbound streets, congested with all the heavy traffic that normally went by water, presented so many dangers that Sibella and the children were virtually housebound. They seldom even opened a window: apart from the cold, which was hard enough to keep out even with them closed, the flat, oily smell of the fog seemed to catch at Sarah's throat and make her cough. For more than three weeks, when they were not in the kitchen helping the servants, Sibella and her children had spent nearly all their time together in the parlour, which was relatively warm: the children's rocking horse had been moved down from their nursery, and Theodore was allowed to play with tops and balls indoors, normally forbidden for fear of damage to the furniture.

To fill their dreary days, Sibella perseveringly supervised Sarah's work on her sampler, or set her stints of knitting and plain sewing; she had her read and write and cast up figures. They were looking forward to Twelfth Night, which would fall on the following Monday, so for the first time Sibella involved her little daughter in planning the dinner, and making the great cake which was its distinguishing feature; the cake which contained the raw bean which made its lucky recipient King of the Feast; Sarah was still too little to be safe in a kitchen, but it gave her a sense of consequence to stand on a block wrapped in one of her mother's aprons stoning raisins, and in addition, it gave her needed employment.

Theodore, meanwhile, played with his toys, and looked at books. His great delight was Balthasar's own copy of Hooke's *Micrographia*, which he was allowed to look at if he was very careful. For the duration of this time of captivity, it shared the Bible's table of honour by the window. Theodore would kneel for long periods in a chair, his elbows on the table, completely absorbed in its exquisite engravings of magnified seeds, lichens and the other wonders revealed by the microscope, especially the great, fold-out engraving of a flea, which fascinated him. Nobody knew what he saw in the pictures: they had all asked him at one time or another, but he merely looked confused. However, he would stay at his station by the table until he was so cramped and cold his mother had to lift him down. On the whole, though both children had days when they cried, sulked, and went into the pouts, they were very good about their enforced imprisonment. Though Balthasar and Sibella had themselves very little taste for fairs and outings, preferring to stay home, they were agreed that the babies must be indulged this once. They deserved a treat.

The momentous Saturday dawned after a poor night. Both Balthasar and Sibella had feared that Sarah would make herself ill, as she often did, from excitement and would be forced to stay in bed; they were bracing themselves for tears and screams. But she woke bright-eyed, and no worse than usual, the trouble, instead, had come from an unexpected direction. Little Theodore had been visited by one of the terrible nightmares which periodically afflicted him. They were often about things he had seen in pictures, but in this case, for an hour or more after they had wakened him he sat up in bed clinging to his father, weeping in distress and talking incoherently of an old black man who frightened him. Eventually, they had got him off to sleep with a little hot milk fortified by brandy and treacle, and gone back to their own cold sheets. They woke into the darkness of the morning reluctantly, sticky-eyed and tired. But as they all sat at breakfast, the children's eager anticipation – Theodore seemed to have forgotten the terrors of the night – gradually infected their parents, and they began to look forward to the excursion.

Sibella did her utmost to ensure that the children would be warm enough. They each wore two pairs of knitted woollen stockings; Sarah had six petticoats on, one of them quilted, and Theodore wore three shirts, including the knitted one he hated because it was itchy. It took Sibella and Anne, her maid, nearly an hour to make them both ready, after which the children were left to sit, stiff bundles of cloth, strictly enjoined to do nothing at all, while the women hurriedly made their own preparations.

It was still very dark when they left the house. The fog so shrouded the city that the sun only began significantly to penetrate the dun-coloured mists once it was some way up the sky. They clambered awkwardly into a hired hackney-coach, and sat in the dark, fusty interior, the children bouncing a little with anticipation, while the driver made his slow and awkward way to the Temple Stairs, where the fair was thickest.

Once they were out of the coach, they stopped to look down at the scene from the embankment: the fog was beginning to clear, and the view was confused and exciting. Balthasar felt his son's hand stirring in his own, even through their gloves. All along the sides of the river, mounting near as high as the embankment itself, were massive heaps of shovelled snow, and out in the river there were wooden booths, roofed and sided with dingy brown canvas, arranged in two rows as a formal street. Many of them sported flagpoles, but otherwise, seen from above, they seemed dull brown boxes. There were even horses and coaches on the ice; and the children cried and pointed at the sight of a land-yacht, a coachlike vehicle with wheels and a square sail, decorated with enormous flags: since there was no wind to speak of, it lay becalmed in the middle of the ice, flags and sail drooping. Here and there, braziers glowed and open fires twinkled: the largest, at a prudent distance from the street of booths, was a gigantic bonfire, with, as they dimly discerned through the blanketing fog, a gantry over it supporting a roasting ox. The smell of burning beef tallow came up to them, even where they stood. The lively scene faded into invisibility after a mere hundred yards or so, enfolded in fog. They descended the glass-slippery stairs as cautiously as possible, and walked into the fair.

The surface of the ice was scattered with salt and sawdust, so although it was wet and nasty, it was reasonably safe underfoot. They wandered towards the ox-roast, drawn like moths by the warmth and light. It was a marvellous spectacle; the leaping flames were doubled by the slick, glassy black lake around the bonfire where the heat had successfully melted the top inch or so of ice. It kept up a perpetual hissing, and sat in a fuming oval of white steam where the edge of the flame met the ice. The great carcass was extended on a gibbet of trestles, on an enormous spit turned by a cart-wheel, and tended by a gang of half-naked men, their torsos sweating and reddened by the flames.

'Three hours to go, gentles,' shouted one, seeing the family lingering. Balthasar touched his hat in acknowledgement, and they walked on into the main street. In the booths, hucksters sold such things as hot buttered ale, wine both hot and cold, cracknels, coffee, gingerbread, sugar-candy and toys: there was even a booth selling silver plate, and more than one with glassware. He looked down at the round eyes of his children, and took a glove off in order to fumble in his pocket. He gave each of them sixpence, saying 'You may lay it out as you please.' Sarah curtseyed, and Theodore ducked his head; he looked at his new wealth, a silver threepence and three pennies, as if it represented possibilities beyond imagination, then clenched it hard in his mittened fist.

'Look around carefully before you choose,' advised Sibella.

The children nodded solemnly. 'Yes, Mother,' said Sarah, always the speaker for both.

'Keep tight hold,' Sibella warned. 'If you wander away, you might be stolen by the gypsies, and then how would we find you again?' She linked arms with Balthasar, and each with a child held firmly by the other hand, they moved off slowly across the ice, looking from side to side. The whole of London seemed to be there to walk on the river. There were several groups of musicians playing, fiddles and hautboys for the most part, though they could also hear kettledrums and trumpets. The children wanted to invest a halfpenny apiece in a puppet show, so they all stopped to watch Pulchinello; Sarah and Theodore insisted on staying to the end, so as not to waste their money, but for all that the showman had spread sacks on the ice within his booth and laid down duckboards, they all agreed afterwards, stamping their frozen feet, that it had really been too cold to stand still, and resolved to keep moving from then on.

'Look,' said Sarah, pointing. They all followed her, as she tugged her mother towards an intriguing booth from which customers were emerging with pieces of paper, bringing her father and brother along behind like the tail of a kite.

'They are printing here on the ice!' she exclaimed, and it was true. The printer was selling ballads about the fair: there were copies lying about for fourpence a sheet, but they were also printing souvenirs, for sixpence a name.

'Oh, please can we have one,' begged Sarah. 'When all this is quite gone, we can show people we were here.'

'Let us have one, then,' said Balthasar. He spelt out their names for the printer: Balthasar, Sibella, Theodore and Sarah Stuart. On the ship returning from Barbados, he had decided to use his mother's name rather than his father's. After more than twenty years away from Holland, he spoke English like a native, with only a slight, residual trace of accent. He was tired of the suspicion which his Dutch name caused, as well as of the mess which English tongues made of it. When the notion crossed his mind, he had asked Sibella what she thought, and found she was all in favour of the change, so change they had. Now, they stood together, fascinated, watching the man's hand moving as precisely as a machine among the cases of type. The forme was locked, and less than a minute later, Balthasar had handed over four shillings and fourpence and was walking away with a ballad in his pocket, and a quarter-sheet of coarse Dutch paper in his hands, holding it carefully, since it was still rather sticky, just as they had seen other people doing. They went back outside, and the children pored over it, fascinated; the sun had come up, after a fashion, and it was light enough to read. Their names were set forth within a decorative border, and the children eagerly spelled out the legend at the bottom, which said, 'Printed by G. Croom, on the ICE on the River *Thames*, January 2, 1684'. Sarah was good at her books, and read well; Theodore was making progress, when he could be coaxed from his dreams. But he was as delighted as his sister to see their names in print, so Balthasar cherished hopes that he could be persuaded to spell through the ballad in the days that followed. He took it out of his pocket, and glanced through it before giving it to Sibella and the children, and was relieved to find that its sentiments were impeccable: the author concluded that,

> Hard times the good and righteous God has sent
> For our more hardened hearts as punishment;
> From heav'n this scourge is sent us for our pride,
> We're plagu'd with ice because we do backslide.

It might be true, he thought, putting it away. In the last generation, London had been purged by fire, was it now being purged by ice? But the Frost Fair gave no promise of general amendment. Quite the reverse.

'My God, is that the Duke of York incog.? If so, Kate Sedley must look to her nails, he is on the best of terms with that cit and her brats.'

Aphra was standing with a recent acquaintance, Tom Browne, in the Whip and Eggshell, one of the fair's many taverns, near enough the door to see out. Her glance followed his discreetly pointing finger, and her heart missed a beat as she recognised Balthasar van Overmeer. It was easy to understand Tom's mistake; the Dutch doctor, who must now, like herself, be in his mid-forties, had aged considerably, and with the new thinness of his face, the pouches beneath his eyes, and the deep lines scored between nose and mouth, he looked very like the King's brother. Even their colour was similar; as Lord High Admiral, the Duke had acquired a blue-water sailor's permanent tan, and was very dark in the face.

'No,' she said firmly, 'it is some common fellow.' She sipped deliberately at her mug of hot ale, draining it, and turned away. Swathed in shawls and vizarded as she was, she need not fear recognition. All she felt was a remote irritation at the way that a tedious peccadillo of her distant youth had obstinately surfaced yet again – her momentary qualm on seeing him was, she recognised, no more than an habitual reflex. She wondered when he had returned from the West Indies. Until the disastrous amalgamation of London's two theatre companies the previous year, when they still competed for new plays, her name had been plastered on playbills two or three times a year for as much as a fortnight at a time. If he had been in London, he could have seen it on many occasions. On the other hand, if his connection and his practice were not fashionable, it was perfectly possible that such a man, a dull, provincial Puritan, could have escaped knowledge of her entirely. Now, in this new climate, it seemed unlikely that she would ever be heard of again.

'You are right as usual, Aphra,' said Tom, irritating her by his refusal to drop the subject. 'But he is very like. It is passing strange. The first Charles had a quiverful of lawfully begotten brats, and no byblows at all that I ever heard of, unlike his sons, who get lusty boys in every bed but their wives'. This fellow cannot be the Duke's own, unless he swived his wetnurse. There can be ten years between them at best.'

Aphra shrugged. 'Coincidence merely,' she said, dismissing the subject. They returned their mugs to the stallkeeper and strolled on together, Aphra steering their path discreetly away from Balthasar and his family. It took only a few steps to lose them in the shifting crowd.

'It is long enough since I have seen the Duke of York,' observed Tom. 'Not since before he was sent to Scotland. I believe he is in more favour with the King, though the people still hate him for his Papistry. He is not yet forgiven that shipwreck, when he saved his dogs, his priests and his strongbox, and left honest Englishmen to drown. But all the same, it is whispered in Whitehall that he may even get the navy back. I only wish he would give his mind to the players once more. It is the purpose of courts, surely, to keep players and poets, lest their glory depart like Ichabod for want of advertisement. I went to see Algernon Sidney the Republican turned off a fortnight past – he died resolutely, and like a man, proclaiming that he died for the good old cause, and the crowds cheered him. If kings do not act like kings, there may be others beside Sidney who think them expensive cattle to keep. We may fall out of monarchy yet – his majesty grows more absolute by the day, and the charge of his household is such that the people will not bear it, when none benefit but priests, foreign whores, and the King of France. All us poor scribblers will break, if this goes on, perhaps even his high-and-mightiness Dryden. Have you been to visit poor Nat Lee?'

'No, indeed,' said Aphra firmly. 'I could not bear to see one of our old fellowship stripped and whipped in Bedlam for the loobies to gawk at. I am certain it was naught but poverty that drove him out of his wits – is it not a terrible thing to have a playwright made a free show? – he was willing enough to entertain, if he could but earn a guinea or two by it! I tell you, Tom, whenever I go to Dorset Gardens, I cannot pass Bridewell without a shudder, and a moment of thankfulness that I am outside it, and not within.'

'You are not without recourse, I hope? I should hate to see you beating hemp, but I have scarce a shilling to spare myself.'

'I copy still. It is a wretched living, but Robert Julian still needs hands of write for his lampoonists' factory, so I can pay my new landlady three weeks in four. I had to remove from Mr Coggin's in November, which I greatly regret, since he was so convenient for Tonson's. My poor Poll has gone unpaid this six months – she is less a maid now than a companion in misfortune. But I hope not to copy for ever. When the theatres conjoined, I knew it spelt disaster to playwrights, so I conceived the idea of turning to my first profession, translating – there is nothing in Dutch a person of fashion would read, but I learned tolerable good French in my youth.'

'As we have cause to know, Mistress Aphra. Your "Imperfect Enjoyment" was a version after de Cantenac, was it not?'

'Bravo. It was indeed, though there were not many recognised it. Anyway, with this project in mind, I spent the spring of this year in Paris. I was made welcome at the salons and *ruelles*, and met many ladies distinguished for wit and gallantry – the great Ninon de l'Enclos, Madame de Maintenon, and the Sappho of our age, Mademoiselle de Scudéry. I also met many of their votaries, and polished my command of the French tongue. I have found many sprightly tales in French, pretty things that the wits and the misses will want upon their tables, without the trouble of conning over a foreign language. Since there is no market for plays, I will turn my hand to Tallemant, and perhaps Fontenelle.'

'And you had another venture, I think, Aphra? I saw an advertisement some weeks back, before Christmas?'

'Ah. That is another new projection, and it is going well. It is to be called *Love Letters between a Nobleman and his Sister.*'

'That whoremaster Lord Grey, I presume, and Lady Henrietta? How came you by them?'

'My dear friend, I am making 'em up from beginning to end. I have heard often enough from you College wits that Venus freezes without Ceres and Bacchus, but though bread and wine are short enough in my lodgings, I find hunger lends my invention wings. They are the softest, most melting, amorous letters wit can contrive; they would raise a conscious blush on the face of a Vestal, though there is not a line obscene or disgraceful. They will make my fortune, I hope – those who are not seduced by sugared prose will read 'em for the scandal.'

'But do you not fear the King? You did not easily escape prison, after your *Romulus.*'

'By no means,' she retorted. 'Monmouth is not to be traduced. I have learned that lesson – though I meant every word of my Epilogue. But even at his most blindly indulgent, the King must know that his darling bastard surrounded himself with fools and knaves. And I do not think that his majesty cares a straw for Lord Grey.'

'Let us pray for a *succès de scandale*, then, to lift you to Parnassus, far above the sublunary world of landladies and duns.'

'Well, it may be,' said Aphra wearily. 'I will be content enough if it pay my debts and give me licence to run up more. But *Letters* is far from complete. I have my Tallemant translation in hand, which I have hopes of to answer present necessities. There is to be a Twelfth Night gathering at Tonson's; I have promised a twelfth-cake, which I trust will turn out well; I have never been a housewife, and I have not made such a thing since I was a little maid standing by my mother, but Poll will help me, and between us, we should contrive well enough. I will call at the grocer's on the way home for raisins, almonds, sugar and spice. I can ill afford it, but I would rather be liberal among my friends than pinch pennies like a Puritan. No honest man, or woman either, should sleep sober on Twelfth Night.'

'Bravo, Mistress Aphra. I am glad I will see you so soon. I am also going to Tonson's, because Mr Creech will be there. He must return to Wadham after Christmas, or they will expel him from the University, but his heart is in London now. He will be a useful man for you to know, and though he is not the easiest of fellows, you have a good start in acquaintance. I know you admired his Lucretius, and he was pleased by your poem on it. But I happen to know he also has a great facility for extempore translation from Latin; it may be, that you could collaborate most fruitfully. Versions of Ovid from your hand would be worth the reading – *Amores*, perhaps. Or even Horace. There is a good market for Classical translation.'

'It is a kind thought, Tom, and a timely one. I will pay the closest attention to Mr Creech.'

The morning after Twelfth Night, Aphra dressed with what care she could. She was not at her best. The cake had been a complete failure; though she and Poll had compounded it with care, the baker to whom they had taken it had let them down. He had sized her up immediately as an irregular customer, and since most of the good housewives of the neighbourhood had similarly been demanding that he should bake their twelfth-cakes, hers had ended up placed at the extreme edge of his oven, where one side began to burn. Seeing the state it was getting into, he had then compounded his crimes by removing it while the middle was still sad. In her irritation at this expensive disaster – the ingredients had cost a pound and four shillings, for which she had had to sell her squirrel muff – she had drunk too much at Tonson's, slept little, and wakened unrefreshed in her icy room to the sound of Poll's snoring; she and her maid slept together, this vicious winter, for the sake of warmth. But the evening had not been a wasted one. She had indeed met Creech, whose Lucretius she genuinely admired. Drawing on her considerable experience of flattering young University men with literary aspirations, she had, she thought, impressed him. In any case, he had agreed to read her Tallemant translation; and a favourable reaction from a real scholar who was also moderately successful in the Grub Street market might, she hoped, put five pounds on what she could ask from Tonson.

Since the amalgamation of the companies, pawning her clothes had become a regrettable necessity, but even though she owed money in all directions, she still had some finery, without which her life would be unlivable; a two-year-old silk mantua, steel-blue, and still highly presentable, which she had bought with profits from *The City Heiress*. With a linen tucker and her bronze-coloured scarf, it looked very well. Peering into her small mirror, she wished the scarf a rose-colour or carnation: it had suited her when she was in health, but she had not been particularly well for months. Her complexion was winter-dull and mottled, with dark patches beneath the eyes; she needed all the help she could get, and the bronze made her look even yellower than she was.

'You look very well, mistress,' said Poll, putting down the comb and standing back to survey her, huddling her rancid old shawl about her shoulders.

She sighed. 'I do not, Poll, and you know it.' She reached for the pot of carmine, applying it circumspectly to her cheeks and the lobes of her ears with a hare's-foot: as she well knew, paint was a dangerous tool for a woman of her age, since anything more than the merest hint and she would look a raddled old whore. She laid the hare's-foot down and looked in the mirror again. That would have to do; she could hear the rumbling wheels, the clip-clop and jingle as the hackney-coach she had hired to take her to Tonson's drew up outside.

She threw her cloak on, picked up her budget with the precious manuscript in it, and cautiously descended the stairs – cautiously, for under her silk mantua, she was wearing every petticoat she still possessed, and movement of any kind was far from easy.

The coach moved at a snail's pace through the crowded streets; Aphra held back the leather curtain and peered out into the murky morning. On an ordinary day, she could have walked faster, and for so short a journey, eighteen-pence was an absurd price, but as she looked out at the jostling vehicles, the horses, and the pedestrians slipping and sliding in icy slush, she was devoutly thankful to be in the coach. She sank back on the seat, beginning to worry a little. Creech had made it clear that he must catch the Oxford coach or risk being sent down: he would not wait.

They were within sight of Charing Cross, just passing the Pope's Head tavern, when disaster struck. The driver locked wheels with a coal-cart, the horse went down, and after an agonising moment when the coach seemed to be balanced at a drunken tilt, the wheel came off, and the coach itself fell on its side. Aphra was precipitated out as the door burst open; and for a dreadful second, she thought the coach would fall on her and crush her, but she was thrown clear; if clear was the word, sprawled in the half-frozen slush which was already soaking through her clothes, clutching her precious budget in a grip of death; a horse's hooves missed her head by inches. Her driver, swearing, was trying to cut the traces of his own animal as it threshed ineffectually on the ice, struggling to rise; everyone around them seemed to be shouting, some in alarm, some in rage. A good Samaritan risked his own life, dashing in among the carts to help her to her feet before she was run over; she knew her danger, but she was unable to rise, dazed by the fall, and almost immobilised by the layers of sopping, icy garments clinging to her legs. The man dragged her clear of the mêlée and supported her into the Pope's Head.

She collapsed onto a bench, and looked up at her preserver; a rough enough man, he seemed, a carter or a drover perhaps, now nearly as wet as she. 'Thank you, fellow, you have the heart of a trueborn Englishman, and I think you have saved my life. Will you take a brandy with me, to keep out the cold?'

He touched his hat, a ruinous affair of dun-coloured felt. 'That I will, ma'am, and glad of it.'

She intended to reach through the several plackets of her wet skirts to her purse, which like any prudent woman, she kept several layers in from the outer world, but as she moved her right hand, she was jolted by pain which brought tears to her eyes. In the general shock she had sustained, she had not noticed that she had sprained her wrist. She began to sob, helpless to control herself. The pain itself was no more than the last straw, but the direness of her misfortune began to become clear to her. Creech would be away before she could give him the Tallemant translation, her best dress was ruined, and, as her numbed brain began slowly to tell her, she was deprived even of the last resource of copying, for her writing hand was out of use.

*   *   *

Balthasar, coming along Charing Cross, saw the wreck of the coach. With a wheel missing, it was immovable until a wheelwright could be fetched, and the traffic was having to go round it, with all attendant difficulties and loss of temper. It had clearly been a bad accident. Concerned, he turned into the Pope's Head; if anyone had been hurt, they would certainly have been carried in there. He left Squirrel with an ostler, and went through to the public bar, where he stopped a pot-boy.

'Tell me, fellow. Has anyone come in here hurt? I am a surgeon, if one is needed.'

The boy sniffed, wiping his nose with the back of his hand, and shrugged. 'Naught but a decayed town-miss, sir. She was hurt in the hand, that is all. She sat here for a while, till she was recovered, then she called for a coach and went home.'

Balthasar reclaimed Squirrel and rode on through the over-crowded streets. Care and vigilance were needed, but he was too worried to give his full attention to managing the horse. Sarah was back in bed. She had taken no apparent harm from the Frost Fair, but she had got flushed and over-excited merely in anticipation of Twelfth Night, and by the end of the excitements of the evening, the games and the feast, she had been running a fever. Balthasar cursed himself for inadvertently making matters worse; she had been overjoyed by her present. He had bought her a very grand poppet with jointed arms and legs and a silk dress which took off. A ridiculous extravagance; and of course, having spent so much on Sarah, he had had to buy something as good for Theodore, who had thus ended up with a wooden knight on horseback; the horse was on wheels, so the knight could be made to joust, or stood on his own feet to fight with a sword. Sibella had said nothing in the face of the children's ecstasy, but he could sense her disapproval: she was inclined, generally, to think that he indulged the children unduly, in the Dutch manner. Revolving the whole business in his mind, he wondered what had got into him.

The thought of Sarah was becoming more and more painful to him. He was beginning to dread listening to her little, bird-boned chest, as he had that morning; one day, he feared, he would hear more than the crepitus of catarrh in her lungs, there would be the first dull traces of phthisis or consumption. He was deeply reluctant to let the thought so much as enter his head, lest it somehow bring the event, but he was beginning to wonder if they would rear her. He had bought the magnificent doll, he realised suddenly, as a kind of apology to her for the dreadful, inescapable fact that as a professional, he could not shut his eyes to what he plainly saw, and he was beginning to think of her as already marked for death.

From Sarah, his thoughts wandered on to his family more generally. Sarah had started well enough; her troubles had begun on the ship back to England. Two years later, they had had Margaret, who lived less than a week; she had been a sickly child from the first, and Sibella, numbed by milk-fever, had accepted her passing with apathetic depression. A year later, Sibella had suffered a bad miscarriage; the year after that, God had given them Theodore, a dreamer, but healthy. Since his birth, there had been no sign of another one. But Sibella was only in her mid-thirties. He wondered if they would have more. After twelve years of marriage, the bond between them was strongly established. They respected and liked one another, and the early tensions between them had been resolved by time and proximity, but gradually, their relations had become more friendly than passionate. Their days were long and hardworking, and often enough, once they got into bed, both of them were too intent on sleep to think of anything else. Sometimes weeks would go by before he thought of troubling her – perhaps he should make more effort to do his duty, he told himself. A single child was a fragile hope to be extending towards the future.

He shook his head, trying to cast off the thought of children. With Christmas past, it was time to think of the New Year, and what it might bring. The errand of the morning was to Mr Reeve the instrument-maker's: it was high time that he went to turn over his stock, and see if there were any new developments in the tools of his trade. At the very least, he needed a new set of scalpels.

'Mr Tonson, I should really have thought verses of mine worth thirty pound,' said Aphra, a little desperately.

'Mistress Aphra, twenty-five is a good rate, as good as any poet in England is getting,' objected Tonson.

They were sitting together in his shop and drinking sherry, sitting by the empty grate, since the fire was not lit on this fine spring day. Any of the idlers who wandered in and out of the shop would see them established there like two old friends, and perhaps imagine that they were discussing the literature of the day – or its authors. Yet she was achingly conscious of the power he held over her. Since her sprained wrist had kept her from any recourse to copying for the 'secretary to the Muses', Robert Julian, she had got deep into debt. With infinite pains, she and Poll had unpicked the steel-blue mantua, rubbed it with fuller's earth, and moved the worst-damaged breadths of the silk to where they would show the least. It would never look fresh again, but it was just wearable. Almost everything else she owned was in pawn, down to the knives and forks. Twenty-five would just about pay her debts – except to Poll – but with nothing over. Her heart sank at the prospect.

'Dryden got fifty,' she objected at once, smiling at him as charmingly as she could.

'Dryden is Poet Laureate,' he reminded her. 'He commands sales far beyond what any other poet in the land can expect, and he is paid according. Mistress Behn, all London is agreed you are sole empress of the land of wit, but for all that, your verse does not bring a great return.'

'To be sure – though this is quite a different article. Will not Sir Coxcomb and Master Spark want to have the latest thing from France? This should not sell on my name alone, so I hope for great things from it. Mr Tonson, it grieves me to dispute over five pound where I am so obliged, but you cannot think what a pretty thing *The Island of Love* will be, and what a deal of labour I must spend on it. Dear Mr Tonson,' she said coaxingly, longing to throw her wine in his fat face, 'pray, ask your brother to advance the price to just five pound more, it is worth so much to me at this time. I want money extremely, or I would not urge this.' Her tones remained low and conversational, she had no desire to share the knowledge of her desperation with every long-eared ninny in London, but she could not keep her voice from shaking as she appealed to him. 'You know how things stand with the playhouse. This may be my principal earning for this year, and I have been without getting for so long that I am on the very point of breaking.'

'My dear Astrea, I am sorry for it. But the whole of Grub Street is in like case – with your wit and your beauty, you have more recourse than your brothers of the pen,' he said reasonably. 'And if I raise the rate for one, I must raise it for all; such news travels swiftly. It is no favour to the profession, if you bring me down with you. I am still your best interest, as you well know. Twenty-five pound.'

She cast down her eyes, unwilling to show him her fury. She had not whored since the earliest days of her independence, and then, only as a kept-woman; precisely who, she longed to retort, did he think would buy the favours of a woman of forty-five in mediocre health, were she never so witty? 'Can you not ask Dryden for another poem?' she wheedled. 'He wrote one for my *Poems on Several Occasions*, and though it was but an indifferent piece, the work of an hour, I am sure his endorsement sold more copies. We are not on speaking terms, for he did not reply to the letter I sent, but I will go to Will's Coffee-House, and see if I cannot persuade him to a better humour.'

'Oh, Aphra. I did not mean to tell you. He agreed to write, as you know, but in the event, he did not.'

'Whence came the poem?' she asked sharply.

'I took it upon myself. It sold copies, there is no doubt; and he had agreed to do it, so he was not in a position to complain. In any case, even the Poet Laureate cannot afford to quarrel with me indefinitely.' His tone was mild and explanatory, but Aphra felt the warning. She took a deep draught of her sherry, aware that she was blushing with anger and humiliation.

'A little more?' he asked solicitously.

She forced a smile. 'I would be glad of another glass.'

'Twenty-five pound, Aphra.'

'All the more reason to drink up your sherry, Mr Tonson,' she replied blandly. 'I will not be tipsy at my own expense for some little time.'

When Balthasar came home, one day in April, he found Sibella full of excitement. When she heard him come into the house for his dinner, she ran down the stairs to greet him. The spring had brought colour back to her cheeks, and he thought suddenly how pretty she still looked when her face was animated. He had got in the way of taking her looks for granted, but looking at her bright eyes he felt a shock of pleasure of a kind he had almost forgotten.

'Balthasar! There is a letter from Lieutenant Palaeologue.'

'What does he say?'

'He is coming back.'

'One minute,' said Balthasar hastily. He gave his cloak to Anne to hang up, ducked into the kitchen to wash his hands, and joined Sibella in the parlour as soon as he could. She handed him the letter, and he sat at the Bible table by the window to unfold the large, closely written sheet while she stood behind him, leaning over his shoulder. He put a hand up absently to touch her arm. They had formed a habit of being tender with one another since early in the New Year. Around the time of Candlemas, three months previously, Sarah, who had been troubled by a persistent, dry cough, had suddenly begun to spit blood. The fit passed off and had not yet returned, but although they never spoke of it, each of her parents knew that the other was aware that they would probably not see her live to grow up.

Palaeologue's hand was characteristic of him; small, but very masculine, with firm up- and downstrokes, a scholarly hand for a sailor and planter. He must have learned it from his father, thought Balthasar; he makes his e's after the Greek fashion.

'My dear friends,' he wrote:

I am coming back to England. We have heard here that the Duke of York is returning to favour, and like to get the navy back. I would rather take a risk that this is so, than stay where I am. Sir Richard Dutton, who succeeded Sir Jonathan as Governor, has abused his authority in no small measure. He has taken to himself the right to impose sentence without reference to the other powers of the island, which is a threat to all our liberties, he has filled the administration with his relatives and friends, and day by day, he enriches himself through extortion and fraud. Need I say, further, that he has the ear of the King? The planter community is embattled against him, and it may illustrate his methods if I say that he has trumped up a charge against your old patient Col. Codrington (who leads the opposition as you would expect), and claims he is in the King's debt for some 600l. – though the Col. has, for his side, been able to produce written evidence to show that the King owes him twice that. He has ejected half the island's schoolmasters for fear that they are Quakers, and half the clergy for insufficient orthodoxy – as you well know, since no replacements are to be had, this must needs leave the children untaught, and the parishes with none to wed, church or bury their people. I will not trouble you more with pettinesses, though you may be sure, the island talks of nothing else. In such a state of tyranny, it seems to me that it is no good time to be a small planter. His fines and exactions fall on us as a class, but what is a small matter to a Codrington or a Drax is a great one to me.

I must confess, also, that I am tired of this life. My mother broke her heart when Quashie died, and her last years were sad ones. We were not able to set a grandchild on her knee to cheer her; we have been in good hope time after time, but none has lived beyond the first month. We can make nothing more of this plantation than what it is, a sufficiency, and it is not my nature to dream away my days like my father. Had I trusted the Governor, I might have sought a post in the militia, but I would not care to find myself making war on my fellow citizens. We will return to England, therefore, and I will see if I can renew my naval commission; if not, it may be that I will buy a ship with the proceeds of Logue Hall, and set up as a merchant adventurer.

This has been a long letter, but there has been much to tell you. I long to see you once more – my dear doctor, since you left the island, I have found no friend so much to my mind. Mistress Sibella, I hope to see you bonny and blooming, a rose surrounded by hopeful buds. My namesake thrives, I trust. I was greatly flattered that you named one for me, and I look forward to making his acquaintance. Expect to see us within three months of receiving this.

Balthasar finished the letter, then went straight back to the beginning and read it again. He sat back and looked at Sibella.

'I think he has made the right choice,' he said. 'According to the *London Post*, the Duke of York's star is rising now that the King's bastard is so disgraced, and there is no doubt that the Duke sets great store by the navy. We may hope that we can greet him with good news, though I do not think there is a war afoot to bring him prosperity.'

'I am so glad we left Barbados,' said Sibella, 'and doubly glad that the Lieutenant is leaving. It is no place for a gentleman, and what he says is shocking. The planters are detestable Mammon-worshippers, but the King at war with the planters is no better. Why should they not keep their money, when if the King gets it, he will spend it all on light women? There is no justice in that.' She turned away. 'I must finish dressing your dinner, Balthasar. The letter put it from my mind. I was going to make you a dish of collops, to have with the fowl from yesterday. Everything else is ready.' When she had reached the door, she paused with her hand upon the knob. 'I wonder what Mistress Iere is like, now she has been married nigh on ten years?'

Balthasar pushed back his chair, and prepared to follow her to the dining-room. 'We shall have to wait and see.'

XII

I mind not grave asses who idly debate
About right and succession, the trifles of state;
We've got a good king already, and he deserves laughter
That will trouble his head with whom shall come after.
Come, here's to his health, and I wish he may be
As free from all care and all trouble as we.

John Oldham, *The Careless Good Fellow*, 1680

June 1684

The Lieutenant's second letter was a short one, which came in the hands of a messenger who looked like a pot-boy. 'My dear Doctor, when your duties permit, enquire for us at the Town of Ramsgate, near Wapping Old Stairs. We are well and hearty, and look forward to seeing you.' Balthasar tipped the boy an extravagant shilling, sending him off whistling, and went to tell Sibella.

'I have never been to Wapping,' said Sibella, once she had read the letter. 'It is east of the city, is it not? What has led him to go there? Why has he not come to Westminster, when he knows we are here?'

'Do not feel hurt, my dearest. We passed it when we went to Blackwall to take ship for Barbados. I may have pointed it out — do you recall seeing Execution Dock, with the pirates hanging in chains? Well, Wapping is the settlement of new houses behind Execution Dock. As to why the Lieutenant has settled there — if you remember, we had to go and meet the *Penelope* at Blackwall

277

because capital ships do not come far upriver, they draw too much water. Neither do the ships of the line. If a man's business is with the sea, whether naval or mercantile, then he is bound to settle to the east, where he is convenient for deep-water vessels. There are trim, new houses to be had in Wapping, and I imagine he is thinking of buying one when he has had time to look around him. It is almost entirely a seamen's settlement, I believe. It is not as pleasantly situated as Westminster, because the winds blow from the west for nigh on three-quarters of the year, so it gets the sea-coal and stinks of the whole great mass of the city in its air, as we do not. Few people would choose to live there unless they had reason.'

'I am sorry for Mistress Iere, then,' said Sibella. 'It is so hard to get linen clean if there is soot in the air. But however bad the air, it cannot be worse than Barbados. I hope they will be happy. When can we go and see them?'

Balthasar considered. 'I am very busy this week, my mouse. We could go on Sunday, after church, if you were prepared to ride so far – it is a matter of perhaps seven mile to Wapping, probably further if we have to go up to Austin Friars then strike down to the river, and I know you do not enjoy long riding. But remember, the fine for hiring a coach on a Sunday is ten shilling a head.'

'We are certainly not paying two pound,' declared Sibella firmly. 'That is ridiculous. Let us take the horses. I will do well enough. Whitefoot is a good, steady beast. Send to the Lieutenant and tell him so.'

On the following Sunday, Balthasar viewed his family with pride as they assembled in the stable-yard. Caesar and his wife's maid Anne attended service in Westminster Abbey, so they could easily walk, but Balthasar clung to his membership of the Dutch church. Having given up his Dutch name, it was all the more important to him that he sit under a Dutch predikant, lest he forget who he was, and even, perhaps, his native tongue. Sibella, after her years in the Everaerts household, understood Dutch perfectly well, but it was, he knew, a little hard on the children, who had only fragments of the language: they suffered through the service uncomprehendingly in the mornings, and on ordinary Sunday afternoons, Sibella catechised them in English, read them the lesson from the King James's Bible, and told them about the sermon. The break in this weekly routine of boredom perhaps added to their air of festival.

The family kept two horses; Whitefoot was normally used by Caesar when he attended Balthasar on his rounds, but they owned a side-saddle so that Sibella could ride him on Sundays. When they went to church, Sarah sat on a pillion seat behind her mother, clinging to the pleats of her cloak, and Theodore rode on Balthasar's saddlebow. On this day of days, when they were to see the Lieutenant again, Sibella was wearing a new silk mantua, a delicate green trimmed with silver lace which brought out the chestnut tint of her hair, still thick and glossy, a beaver hat with an ostrich plume, and a dove-grey Palatine trimmed with black squirrel. Sarah was in her best blue damask, which Sibella had made for her out of a previous gown of her own, and Theodore had a new suit of tawny velvet which, again, had been cut from one of Sibella's old dresses, rejected and unpicked into breadths before he was even born. They made a handsome and harmonious group; and Balthasar looked at them with pride. He was aware that the transparency of his daughter's complexion and the brightness of her brown eyes boded no good, but they lent a heart-aching, other-worldly prettiness to her little face.

'Well,' he said briskly. 'There's no time to stand and stare. We must get ourselves to church, or the predikant will frown at us. My dear. Let me assist you.' He helped Sibella onto the mounting-block, and she swung herself nimbly onto Whitefoot's back. When she was securely seated, he draped her skirts becomingly and lifted Sarah up to her pillion. Then he stood Theodore on the mounting-block, got up on Squirrel, and pulled his son up in front of him. Clicking his tongue, he set his horse into motion, and as Sibella fell in behind, encouraged him to a sedate trot.

When they were going out of the City past the Tower, having done their duty by the Church, Theodore suddenly spoke. 'Father, is Mr Palaeologue a boy like me?'

'My dearest child, of course not. He is a good, brave man, an officer in the navy. Perhaps you will be as fine a man when you grow up, if you mind your books, and obey your parents.'

'Then why has he got my name?'

'Theodore, it is you that has his name. We named you after him.'

'Am I part of him?'

'No, my son. But I hope you will be good friends.'

Theodore's question stayed with him as they rode into Wapping. He had named the boy in compliment to his dearest friend, but perhaps, it struck him, he had also hoped the child would partake of the Lieutenant's qualities, his quick wits, his charm and his ready address. Looking down at his own Theodore's round, curly head, already, he knew, tangled in secret dreams, nothing seemed less likely.

The Town of Ramsgate was easily found, opposite Wapping Old Stairs on the township's main street. He went into the stable-yard, helped his family down, and ushered them into the saloon, where he enquired for Lieutenant Palaeologue. A rough-spoken but civil maid took them upstairs to a corridor of private rooms, and knocked on one of the doors.

There was an answer from within, and she went in: he heard her say, 'A Doctor Stuart for you, sir.'

Immediately, Palaeologue appeared in the doorway, and took Balthasar by the shoulders. 'My dear old friend, let me look at you.' He himself was considerably changed; there were only a few white hairs in the pointed beard and the sailor's crow's-feet at the corners of his eyes were deeper, but he had lost teeth at the back of the mouth, which hollowed his cheeks and made him look much older. He pulled Balthasar into a strong, uncharacteristic embrace which warmed his heart, then released him. 'And Mistress Sibella. My dear friend, I was expecting to find a comely matron, and what do I see but a mere girl!' As she rose from her curtsey, blushing and pleased, for a moment, it was almost true. 'This must be Sarah. I am pleased to renew your acquaintance, my dear. And this is my namesake.' He squatted easily on his haunches, and Theodore came trustingly forward. Palaeologue put out both his hard, tanned hands, and the child put his own into them.

'Theodore,' he said gently, 'I am not your uncle, and I am not your godfather, because I was on the other side of the world when you were born. But I will always be your friend, if you let me.'

Theodore bit his lip, as if in thought, and looked up at him with large grave eyes. 'I would like you to be my friend.'

'Good boy. Then that is settled. Come in, come in. They will bring us some food in a few minutes, I trust.' He was as brisk as ever, but his gaiety had become a little jerky; it even crossed Balthasar's mind that the children might be afraid of him, but they seemed happy enough.

They followed him into the keeping-room, and there, standing quietly by the hearth, was Iere. In that first moment, Balthasar hardly recognised her. She was a little thicker in the body than she had been, though still, by European standards, very slight. But diamonds flashed in her ears, and she was dressed in carnation silk which flattered both the clear brown of her complexion and the raven gloss of her hair; she was an elegant little lady, and no longer looked as if she were bundled in clothes she did not understand. As his eye fell on her, she dropped him a curtsey, very correctly.

Sibella went over to her, and took her hand. 'My dear, I am so pleased to see you. I hope your journey was not too vile?'

'Thank you. We did very well.' Her reply sounded very unlike the shy, half-wild creature they remembered. Her voice was still soft, but her English had a curious staccato quality, which, he realised, came from her habit of accenting all syllables equally. She was clearly now fluent in English, but it was as if she had left the music of speech behind with her Carib tongue.

'Let me present my children, Mistress Iere. This is Theodore, and this is Sarah.'

Theodore bowed, Sarah curtsied, as they had been taught to do. Iere put out her hands – she was not much taller than Sarah – and they went to her obediently to be kissed. When she straightened up again, her face was completely expressionless, but Balthasar sensed that she was moved.

The door to the bedroom opened, and Cleopatra entered, curseying to the ground; like her mistress, she was a little older and fuller-figured, but she still had the same natural grace, well set off by her simple clothes. Balthasar was delighted to see her; he well remembered the quiet, apparently effortless efficiency with which she had run Lady Palaeologue's household, even once her mistress had deteriorated into a care-distracted and querulous old woman.

'Welcome to England, Cleopatra,' he said, taking her hand and kissing her soft cheek. 'I am very glad to see you again.'

'And so am I,' said Sibella, coming to kiss her in turn. Balthasar saw the glint of a coin; Sibella had given the woman something, probably a guinea. A generous gesture, and gracious. It pleased him that she had thought of it. 'You will want warm things, Cleopatra. Last winter was very hard, and the next may be as bad.'

'Thank you, mistress,' she replied, curtseying, and looking pleased.

There was a knock at the door: the promised dinner had arrived, curtailing further conversation. It was an elaborate one and he could see the delight in his children's faces; among other treats, there was a dish of partridges, a handsome pie, and a magnificent trifle decorated with candied rose-petals and violets. Cleopatra moved to direct the setting of the table, and under cover of the ensuing bustle Balthasar took Lieutenant Palaeologue a little to one side, and stood with him, looking out of the window at the dockyard cranes and the ships in the river.

'Sir. You said in your letter you had had no luck with children, yet it is easy to see that your wife wants nothing better. If I do not intrude, where lies the problem?'

Palaeologue shrugged, but his eyes were wretched. 'She carries well enough, and though she is narrow-made, as you see, she has seldom been in difficulties,' he replied, so quietly that Balthasar could barely hear him. 'Yet one by one, they have all died. We have never had two children in the house together. One lived to four months.'

'Oh, my dear friend. What a cross for your wife to bear. We lost one, between Sarah and Theodore, so I know the pain of it. How many have there been?'

'Five,' Palaeologue replied, with bitter brevity.

'Well, you will see them in Heaven, that is certain. But I will pray that you have posterity to comfort you on earth. And ... I am not a specialist in childbed problems, as you know, but it may be that I can help. If you so wish, I can examine your wife, and prescribe a regimen.'

'Thank you, my dear Doctor. As far as I can tell, we are healthy enough, but we will try anything.' He glanced back into the room, where the two servitors were just finishing setting out the dinner. 'Ha. Let us to table, my friends. My new little friends, let us see how much you can eat. It is all here for you to enjoy.'

'Oh, thank you, sir,' said Sarah, her eyes sparkling. Sibella did not give sweets or rich food to her children, except on feast-days and holidays; so as the inn servants set dish after dish on the table, she had stood mute and round-eyed, with an air of increasing hopefulness. Theodore seemed not to have heard; he had drifted towards the fireplace, which was carved dark oak, and he was running his finger over the smooth contours of a mermaid's smiling face.

'Behold this dreamer!' said Lieutenant Palaeologue, laughing. 'You should have called him Joseph.'

'Theodore, come to table,' ordered Sibella. The child tore himself from his contemplations, and came away obediently.

'Do you have the news, Lieutenant?' asked Balthasar once they were all seated.

'I think I know what directly affects us. The Duke is back on the Privy Council, he has his hands more and more on the reins, and though he has not the name of Lord High Admiral, he has the position. You will be pleased by the Truce of Ratisbon, I imagine?'

'I am, though I grudge King Louis even Strasbourg and Luxembourg. France is big enough. Still, it is little enough of a guerdon for all he has expended these twenty years. But it is poor news for you, I think. With peace in Europe at last, your chance of a command is the lesser, is it not?'

Palaeologue replenished Balthasar's glass. 'That is true enough, on the face of it. But, in confidence, I am not certain that peace will be with us for long. The King is worn out by his debaucheries, he cannot last much longer, I suspect. What do you think? It is you who has the medical knowledge – I go purely on what I have seen of other men who have lived as the King does.'

'You may very well be right. There is talk that he is failing.'

'Well, then. The Duke of York is well enough as Admiral; I have even prayed for him to be reinstated, Catholic or no. But will the nation stand for a Catholic king? He is zealous in his error, and as all the navy knows, he is a man of inconceivable obstinacy and no tact. At least the succession is Protestant – since he has never begotten a child on his Papist wife, the crown will go to his daughter by Anne Hyde and her husband the Stadhouder, and both of them are firm

Protestants. It must irk him grievously. But if he is overly hot for the Pope, then I suspect the nation may rise against him, Dutch William will come over, and we will have a fourth Dutch war. Alternatively, Monmouth may rise against his uncle, and if he does, I think William might support him. Monmouth is estranged from his wife, and will never have a legitimate heir, so William would still come to the throne in the end. The royal bastard is staying with William and Mary in The Hague, you know, on the best of cousinly terms, and who knows what they talk of in the evenings? William has no love for James, any more than for Charles. They betrayed him in 'seventy-two, and he has not forgotten it.'

'You see further than most, Lieutenant,' commented Balthasar admiringly. 'I came prepared to tell you the news out of the old world, but you have made yourself the master of the times in but a few short days.'

Palaeologue laughed. 'Only of certain aspects, I assure you. And it is easy enough done here in Wapping, where news comes in daily with the captains. Tell me, Doctor, does the situation strike you as it does me? I have come back to these tales of Popish James, Bastard Monmouth and Dutch William, and what I find myself thinking is, have we come all this way, for this? A generation of men, ay and women too, suffered, died, fell into poverty and disgrace, for the cause of the King. I was brought up among antique Royalists, and so were you. And for what did our parents suffer? A puppet of King Louis, a doting whoremaster ruled by his – what-ye-will, a man so lacking in principle that he will close the Exchequer, bankrupt his navy, or set Barbados by the ears, that the Duchess of Portsmouth may buy diamonds and change her plenishings four times in a year.'

'I have observed it,' said Balthasar, catching Sibella's expression, and letting a note of warning sound in his voice.

'You are right, sir. This is not the time or the place. Well, my chickens, have you had enough sweet-stuff? Not one tiny spoonful?

Bravo. There's my heroes. Doctor, tell me, has anything worth reading been published these eight years?'

'There is interesting new work in the sciences,' said Balthasar after a little thought. 'In my own field, I have found much of value in the work of Thomas Sydenham, especially on gout, and as a sailor, you will be interested by new developments in chronometrics and the science of measurement. But if you mean the arts, there is nothing in the way of literature written in this age which will outlive it, either in English or Latin. I came across a collection of verses in 'eighty-one which seemed to me to have substance, by a fellow who was Latin secretary to the Commonwealth, but I believe they were written some years since. This is an age of lead.'

'Ay,' said Palaeologue bitterly. 'We are the descendants of great men, but they would not know us – *"nos nequiores, mox daturos progeniem vitiosorem"*, as the poet has it.'

'I do not think so,' objected Balthasar. 'My father's life put him in the way of great events, and he rose greatly to them, whereas mine has not, since it has pleased God to set me in a modest walk of life. But perhaps in His eyes, a man who rules himself and his family well is of no less weight than one who rules a nation, or the very world. There are good men in bad times, my dear sir; I dare avow that you are one, even if you are not emperor of Rome. And I do not see why my son should be a worse man than I am. I hope he will be better.'

'That is the more easily said by a man with hopeful children.'

Balthasar opened his mouth to continue the debate, but shut it again, hearing the pain in his friend's voice.

Lieutenant Palaeologue and Iere bought a pleasant brick house in Wapping High Street, and settled in apparent contentment. The Lieutenant laid regular siege to Admiralty House through the autumn and winter, and was rewarded the following spring with a lieutenancy in the *Bonaventure*, which was being sent to the Mediterranean as part of an operation against the Algerine pirates. He was elated and excited when he came to tell Balthasar and Sibella his good news.

'I shall see my ancestral lands at last. Perhaps even Stamboul, which was once the city of Constantine. I long to see the Golden Horn. It is an ill wind that blows nobody good – the King was rash in the extreme to give up Tangier in the spring. It was part of poor Queen Catherine's dowry, and since it is all the good he ever got of that luckless woman, I should have thought sentiment alone would make him keep it, even if he could not be made to understand his interest. Still, it is of a piece with his folly and idleness generally. Now, of course, the Barbary corsairs and the pirates of Algiers and Tripoli swarm unchecked and prey on shipping, and we no longer have a base of operations. We will have sharp work, to reduce them. The lateen-rig gives their dhows great flexibility and responsiveness; we are not so handy or answerable to the wind.'

'And how will Mistress Iere manage in your absence?' asked Sibella, stemming the flow before he became yet more technical.

'Well enough, I hope. She has made friends in Wapping, two or three pious and worthy ladies, captains' wives, whom she met at St John's. And Cleopatra is a tower of strength – she is a person of the greatest sense and discretion, as you will remember. We have a cook-maid and a good, steady man, who I think may offer for Cleopatra in time, they seem to have a liking for one another. The house is new, and I do not anticipate any emergency beyond her powers. But if she is in difficulties, I hope she may look to you?'

'Of course. I am only sorry we are so far away. With Balthasar so busy, we will not be able to call often,' said Sibella anxiously.

'I know it, my dear. But to know that there are old friends in London who have a care for her interests is a thing beyond price. She is not the bewildered creature she was when you first knew her. In the years of my mother's sad decline, she had perforce to learn what needed to be done, and do it. All that is necessary is that in the event of calamity – *absit omen* – she has a point of recourse in you, and it eases my mind to know that it is so.'

Balthasar and Sibella paid a visit to Wapping after the Lieutenant's departure, and were relieved to find he had spoken no less than the truth. Iere was managing perfectly well. They kept up what contact they could. Palaeologue returned unscathed from his Mediterranean adventures late in the autumn, and when he and Iere rode over to keep Christmas with them, he announced that they were once more in hopes of a child.

July 1686

Something had got into his dream; he was dreaming about sailing up the Walcheren Canal to Middelburg, as he sometimes still did; the sail was flapping, and the boom hit against the side of the boat, thump, thump. And it went on thumping, as if determined to stove in the side. Balthasar scrambled to his feet to shout at the skipper, who turned with his hand still on the rudder to look at him. It was his father who was steering, but his eyes were white and blind like those of a cooked fish. He woke with a start, to realise there was a thunderous knocking at the street door. He scrambled out of bed in his nightshirt, Sibella stirring beside him, and fumbled across the room to open the shutters. Bright moonlight lanced into the room as he leaned out; below, he saw the pale oval of Palaeologue's upturned face.

'Balthasar,' he shouted. Even in his alarm, Balthasar felt a qualm of surprise, to hear him use his first name. 'Come with me, for the love of God. Iere is dying in her pains.'

'Instanter,' he shouted. 'I will meet you in the stable-yard.'

Sibella was sitting up in her nightcap when he turned back to the room.

'I must go to Mistress Iere,' he said. His wife, always reliable in an emergency, did not delay him with questions, but got up and lit a candle while he scrambled into breeches, stockings and coat. Candle in hand, he dashed for his budget. Seized by a sudden thought, he delayed to hunt his shelves for van Roomhuyze and Swammerdam, and with the books under his arm, he clattered down the back-stairs to the stable-yard, where he arrived to find Timothy the groom standing in his shirt, yawning, bleary-eyed and holding a rushlight, while Lieutenant Palaeologue finished saddling up Squirrel with his own hands, and tightened the girth.

'How long has she been in her throes?' he asked.

'Two days and nights. The women kept me out for long enough, but at the end I forced my way in and she begged me to fetch you. It is a transverse lie, they tell me.'

As he spoke, he was swinging himself back onto his own horse. 'God have mercy,' said Balthasar, to no one in particular. Palaeologue was already scouring out of the yard, and Balthasar stuffed books and budget into the saddle-bags, scrambled onto Squirrel's back, and followed suit. They cantered in and out of silvery bars of moonlight falling between the houses; and as they went, with the sound of the horses' hooves echoing in the empty streets, Balthasar desperately reviewed all that he knew, which was not much. Women almost invariably looked to other women for help, and a surgeon was only called in when matters were desperate. The only normal births he had any knowledge of were his own wife's three childbeds. He had once performed a caesarian on a dead woman, in hopes of saving the baby, and he had van Roomhuyze on caesarian section in his bag, if the worst came to the worst. He had performed three embryotomies – the hideous business of extracting a dead child, piecemeal – and he had witnessed two transverse lies, sufficient to make his heart sink at the prospect. The baby was lying cross-ways, not up and down. Typically, the contractions would have forced one arm out of the womb, leaving the child unbirthable. This had been going on for two days! It was already clear the midwife did not know her business; she might be competent in ordinary circumstances, but she must have panicked in the face of this rare calamity. He should have been fetched the day before, if not sooner. It was most unlikely that the child still lived.

They reached Wapping and leaped from their horses in the dark hour before dawn. The house was unmistakable; in the quiet streets, it was the only one clearly set by the ears, with light spilling through the shutters. Balthasar collected his books and his bag, leaving the sweating horse to the care of Palaeologue's servant, and followed his friend up the stairs.

The chamber was all he had expected from previous childbeds. The window was tight shut, the fire leaped in the hearth, making the room suffocatingly hot on this mild summer night; candles in all stages of burning down were stuck in sconces here and there. Cleopatra sat swaying a little on a backless stool, only a telltale darkening and swelling beneath her fine, slanted eyes showing her exhaustion; the midwife sat by the bed, head nodding, and three honest matrons dozed in chairs disposed about the room. The room smelt of sweat, blood, excrement and defeat. The women were slumped like soldiers after battle: awake or asleep, something about them said that they were no longer presiding over a birth, but keeping a dead-watch. He went straight to Iere, who was uttering a repetitive whimper at each breath, like an animal, and at the sudden movement, the women began to wake and collect themselves.

'Cleopatra, water and soap, if you please,' he said. He bent over the bed, and touched Iere's forehead. He felt sick at the sight of her. Her eyes were sunk back in her head, the lips dry and purplish. She was running a fever, but when he removed his hand from her forehead and took her wrist, it was cold, and there was almost no pulse. She seemed not to know he was there; her teeth were locked, like those of a creature in a trap. Cleopatra came up with a basin of water, a towel over her arm. He discarded his coat — unwelcome, in that hot room – and rolled his shirt-sleeves up past the elbow, saying 'Thank you, my dear.' He washed his hands with care; he had a strong feeling that he must approach this ordeal cleansed of all that had gone before.

He turned to the midwife. 'Mrs –?'

'Mrs Cook, if you please,' she said. She was a stoutish woman, an honest, ugly person, with wattled cheeks, and a little, round, red tip to her nose. Now, her eyes were bloodshot with exhaustion, her hair beginning to stray from beneath her cap. Something about her reminded him of Anna, his servant and foster-mother of long ago, a great panicker. He must go carefully, he thought, for all the urgent need of haste, and try not to frighten her.

'What is the situation?' he asked, as gently as he could.

'It is a bad lie, sir. After eight hours, I put my hand up to see how the lady did, and found a little arm sticking out.'

'What did you do?' he asked, praying that she had not followed the practice of the worst of her kind, and cut the arm off at the shoulder.

'Greased my hand with oil of roses, doctor, and pushed the arm back in. Sometimes the lie corrects, with the working of the womb.'

'That is true,' he said gravely. 'You did well.' He wanted to pick her up and shake her till her teeth rattled in her head. She had acted perfectly correctly, but she had not had the skill or knowledge to act further, so she had folded her hands. Iere had spent at least eighteen hours in the tortures of the damned, because this fool of a woman had not the sense to admit defeat! 'But unfortunately, it has not done so.' He tried not to sound censorious, but she flushed. It was clear that she had not wanted him sent for. She was probably able enough in the ordinary way, he thought, looking at her with dislike. The transverse lie was mercifully rare, she might never have had to deal with one.

'Well then, we must resign ourselves!' she burst out. 'What is to be done, but try to turn her? I have seen it done, it is torture beyond endurance, and all for nothing.'

'Let her die in peace,' said the oldest of the ladies in the room, who were now all awake, and standing in a sombre group. 'Poor soul, she has suffered enough. You can see the death in her face. Give her laudanum, and let her go easy.'

'But she is your friend!' protested Balthasar.

'I speak as her friend, sirra. You are a man, you do not understand. I would ask nothing more, if it was me lying there. She's past help, and she has made her peace with God, so don't go meddling. Give her some laudanum, and be done with it.' Balthasar was quelled for a moment by her tone, then he heard a sound from the direction he least expected, a dry whisper. Iere was speaking.

'Doc'or. Cu' 'im out.'

'Mistress Iere, you are very weak. It will kill you, I think.' The details of the procedure crowded to his mind. Cut to the side of the midline. Three layers of muscle, then the fascia, push the bladder out of the way, cut the womb low, and reach for the child's head . . . He knew how it was done, he had done it, but a woman so reduced would not survive.

'Cu'.' He could barely hear her. She was in such pain, so bent on giving birth, she was no longer concerned if she lived or no. But he would not have it. The child was dead, to all but a certainty. He would not sacrifice a living mother to a dead child.

'No,' he said. Before anyone could react, he threw back the bedclothes, and knelt beside her. 'Hold her shoulders,' he directed harshly. Thanking providence that he had inherited his mother's long and fine-boned hands, he put his left hand on the swollen belly, folded the right as narrowly he could, and reached into her body. It was a horrible business. Even with the cervix fully open, introducing his hand was all but impossible. He ignored the wretched whimpering, the involuntary jerking of Iere's body, fiercely concentrated, afraid only that his circulation was so impeded he would lose sensation in his hand. The consternation behind him was extreme, and the room was Bedlam; the midwife and at least one of the matrons were screaming at him to let her alone, some kind of altercation was in process, and at least one person was sobbing hysterically. After a while, he registered that someone was holding poor Iere down – with great efficiency, he noted with a stray fragment of attention, probably Cleopatra, the only woman of sense among the lot of them; where he knelt, he could see nothing but part of the poor girl's belly. Once his hand was fully in, it was a matter of moments only. Groping constrainedly among slimy, rounded forms, he found one tiny foot, then another. Grasping them as firmly as he could, he pushed down with his left hand, and pulled steadily, shoulder muscles cracking. His hand came free, the child's body, then the head. The baby slithered forth in a gush of blood, blue, bruised, quite dead. He was expecting nothing better, but he sagged as he knelt there by the bed, and rested his head on his cleaner hand, overwhelmed with exhaustion.

'Balthasar,' said someone warningly. 'The afterbirth.' He looked up, blearily astonished. It was Sibella, and it had been Sibella all along, sitting to hold Iere, while Cleopatra fended off the outraged midwife.

'What are you doing here?' he said stupidly.

'I came after you. On Whitefoot.' She was corsetless, wearing a loose morning gown and a cloak, her night-plait escaping from beneath a hood. It was an astounding thought, his wife galloping half-dressed and alone through the streets of London, but he had no time for it. He merely thanked God that by a miracle, she was there when she was needed, faithful, staunch and true. Poor, inept Mrs Cook had at least severed the birth-cord and taken the child from between Iere's inert legs, and was washing it. He pulled gently on the cord as it hung, and though Iere was apparently unconscious, he was rewarded after a minute or so with the sight of the afterbirth.

Its appearance, he hoped, would herald an end to her loss of blood. The pulse was threadlike; they could still lose her, if she did not stop bleeding.

But she did stop bleeding. She was lifted unconscious from the bed by Sibella and Cleopatra, and her friends cleansed her and changed the sheets before they put her back. She can hardly weigh more than a child herself, he thought irrelevantly. Someone put a draught of brandy in his hand, so he drank it. There was another cruel task still before him. Mrs Cook had washed the dead child very decently, and dressed him in a linen shirt, which Iere must have hopefully got ready. He took the tiny creature in the crook of his arm, and, drunk with weariness, went to see Lieutenant Palaeologue.

He found him in the room below, with a candle, a bottle and a Bible. It was grey dawn, all but daylight, but he seemed not to know it. He looked up eagerly as Balthasar entered, then his face froze.

'My dear friend,' said Balthasar. 'You still have a wife.'

Palaeologue bowed his head. 'God be thanked,' he said after an interval. 'I had been so sure she was dead. Let me look at it.'

Balthasar laid the child on the table. The Lieutenant brought the candle, in a hand which trembled hardly at all, and together they looked at the blue, secret little face. 'Maid or boy?' he asked, after a time.

'Boy.'

Palaeologue put the candlestick down at the baby's head, with great care. He seemed hardly aware of what he was doing. Balthasar put out his hands, and Palaeologue took them; tears were pouring down his face. Blinking free of them, he raised Balthasar's right hand gently, and looked at it; as if his peculiar sensitivity had somehow discerned a pain which Balthasar himself had barely noticed. He looked at the hand and arm, the bruises which were beginning to discolour, the coating of dried blood.

'Oh, God in heaven, Balthasar, what a business.'

Balthasar took him in his arms, as if he had been his own little son. 'Theodore. God will not forget you.'

Palaeologue bowed his head, and wept in earnest, like a beaten child.

April 1687

'Mistress, what is it?' Poll sat up in bed, thoroughly alarmed. Aphra's breathing was harsh and stertorous, she was propped up on her elbows, fighting for breath. The cords in her neck stood out, and she was grey with pain. 'Is it the aches again?'

Aphra nodded, unable to speak.

'Mistress, you must have a doctor.'

She nodded again. 'Not Fenner,' she whispered harshly, 'not paid.'

'I will go and ask about, mistress, and find someone.' As quickly as she could, Poll huddled on her clothes, and went out to the apothecary's. If all else failed, she thought, she would try and persuade them to give her still more laudanum, though the last time she had asked, they had refused her credit. At the very least, in charity, they might be prepared to tell her where she could find a cheap doctor.

When she reached the apothecary's, she found a black servant waiting at the door, holding two horses. She slipped past him, as furtive as a shabby old rat, and entered the shop. There was a man standing at the counter, speaking to the apothecary.

'Four drachms of rhubarb, if you please, put up in a solutive syrup of roses. Oh, and I will take an ounce of Gascoigne's powder.'

Luck indeed, she reflected. No man would buy such quantities for private use. The fellow must be a doctor. 'Oh, sir,' she said pathetically. As he turned, surprised, she saw that he was a mulatto. 'Are you a doctor?'

'I am,' he said. 'My name is Doctor Stuart.'

'Will you attend my mistress, for the love of God? She is deathly sick.'

'One moment.' He turned back to the apothecary and paid for his purchases. 'Take me to her.'

It was the grim alleys of Salisbury Court that she led them to; an unwholesome warren where debtors and criminals lay in relative security and defiance of the law. Their horses paced slowly behind the grey, scurrying figure, as if at a funeral. When they got to the house, Caesar prepared to wait, while Balthasar jumped down from his horse and handed him the reins.

'You must stay with the horses, or we will never see them again. I will not be long,' he said as discreetly as possible, 'I do not look for payment in a place such as this. I will do what I can for this poor creature, then we will go home to our dinner.'

'Yes, sir,' said Caesar.

Taking his bag from his servant, he followed the maid up three pair of stairs to the attic, as he was more than half expecting to do: poverty rose to the attic, or sank into the cellar. She opened the door, and announced, 'Doctor Stuart.' There was a faint answer from within.

He stepped into the frowsty room, and looked about him with distaste. There was a bed pushed into the corner under the eaves, with a woman in it. It had once had curtains, but the rail was now naked. Otherwise, the room contained an old stool and table, piles of dusty paper, and little else. Some tawdry finery was hung on pegs on the wall, but there was no curtain at the window, only an old, ink-stained apron, tied by its strings. He went to it and hitched it up so as to shed some light on the patient, and turned to look at her. An old whore, he presumed, past her freshness, and living as best she might. She was a woman of about his own age, forty-five to fifty, her thinning brown hair bound in a loose pigtail, dressed in a dingy, sour-smelling smock. Her eyes were shut, and she was breathing light and fast. She has pawned her last change of linen, poor creature, he thought, in remote pity. He had laudanum in his bag, which would ease her pain, and *aqua scordii*, a cordial, which should strengthen her. He mixed her a dose, and raised her a little. 'Swallow this.'

It was a moment before she was able to unclench her teeth, but when she did, she swallowed the dose obediently. He pulled up the stool and sat holding her wrist, examining the action of her pulse, while the drugs took effect. He would give her five minutes, in common charity.

He was thinking of his own affairs, and not looking at her, when a change in her pulse alerted him to the fact that she was awake.

'Well, madam,' he said to the wan face on the greasy pillow, 'I hope you are a little recovered.'

The woman tried to smile. 'We meet at last, Doctor.'

He looked at her as she smiled up at him without understanding her, and at last, he thought he recognised the face, greatly though it had changed. 'Mevrouw Behn?'

'The very same. Thank you for your charity, Doctor van Overmeer. I will not pay you, you know.'

'I did not expect it, mevrouw.'

Her pallid cheeks flushed a little, as if he had angered her. 'I have been liberal all my life, when my circumstances permitted. But I can earn very little now, when I need it the most.'

'So I see,' he said, as gently as he could.

She heaved herself up in the bed, leaning her back against the dirty plaster, until she could look him in the eye.

'You think I am a whore, and I am not. I am a playwright, Doctor. I have wondered, sometimes, that you did not see my name.'

'I went to a play once,' he said frankly. 'It bored me to death, so I never formed the habit of looking at playbills. But what has brought you to this? Why do you not continue in this profession? Surely, wit but increases with the years, till you reach your climacteric?'

'Do you truly not know? There used to be the Duke's and the King's companies in London, and each year they bought twenty or more plays apiece. But in 'eighty-two, they united, and the new company buys four plays a year, if that. It is no longer possible to make a living as a playwright.'

'There are many different Londons, Mevrouw Behn, one for each rank and kind. I know nothing of the world of the stage, so yours and mine have never overlapped. It has been a strange life for a woman, surely, that you have chosen, and it seems to have profited you little. Would you not have been better to stay at home? You were a virtuous wife when I first met you, and you were in better case than this.'

'I will not tell you about Johan Behn, doctor. I do not care to remember him. But in any case, I have lived as I wished. I have valued liberty more than life, and I value fame and honour as much as any man. I did not write my plays for the third-night's profits alone. I have sat in the coffee-houses, a wit among the wits, honoured and praised, and there are few women can say as much. If I am come to poverty at the last – well, few of my brothers of the pen can say aught else, in this generation. Otway died a beggar, Wycherley spent five years prisoned for debt, Nat Lee went mad for want of a guinea. At least I am not in Bedlam or Bridewell.'

'It may be so. Tell me about your sickness.'

'It is gouty, perhaps. I have difficulty in walking, sometimes, and even in writing. And sometimes I have fits of terrible pain in my bones and joints, such as the one which brought you to me. I find I can control the onset, to some extent, by diet, which makes me think it may be gout. I follow the principles of Mr Tryon, and avoid meat and stimulants. I was forced to this course by poverty at the first, but I have come to see the benefits. This outbreak was the first for long enough.'

'I am wrong to think that our lives never overlapped. I knew Tryon in Barbados.'

'How very strange. Did you read his *Way to Health, Long Life and Happiness*?'

'No. When I knew him, he was not a writer, or if he was, he did not say so. But his principles were already formed then – Mevrouw, thinking about your symptoms, is it possible you might have the *lues venerea* again?'

Aphra barked a contemptuous little laugh. 'I have done little enough to earn it, mynheer. I do not pretend a virtue I have not, but a woman on her own cannot risk getting with child. I have loved, certainly. I have kissed and played and towsed, but since I came to England, seldom have I experienced the final enjoyment. In the main, my pleasures have been those of the imagination, an organ more capacious than the sacred instrument of love, for all men boast.'

'That is bad for your health, mevrouw. A passion often raised and not satisfied may bring a *furor uterinus*. Perhaps the humours of the womb, denied fulfilment, have struck in and brought these griefs in their train.'

'What do you mean, Doctor, by passion that is satisfied? I got little enough joy of Johan Behn, I assure you. It is not dunghill coupling that "satisfies" a woman of sensibility.'

'You speak of the Epicureanism of love, mevrouw, of which I know little. But you have neglected the brute needs of the body, while banqueting the mind on imaginary feasts. This cannot but cause harm. But you mention Capitein Behn. It occurs to me that you may possibly be suffering a return of the *lues* of your youth. I thought you a perfect cure, but the disease is a stealthy one. It sometimes has a way of lying hidden for many years, and I fear greatly that your way of life may have encouraged its return.'

'The rewards of chaste marriage, then,' she said sarcastically. 'I would believe that more easily.'

They looked at one another for a time in silence. Balthasar tried to keep the pity from his face, knowing she would resent it.

'I did you an injury, Doctor. I have not forgot it,' she said haughtily.

'Nor have I. Mevrouw, why did you steal my father's books?'

She sighed. 'It is hard to remember now. A decision taken on the moment. I was curious in those days, and the old painter, I forget his name, had whetted my interest – did you know I was an intelligencer for the King? He used to pass my dispatches.'

Balthasar shook his head. She was bringing the past crowding round them, and all that she said cast light on things he had not understood at the time.

'I have no Latin,' she went on, 'so I could not tell if they were of use or not, and I hoped for some advantage. I was mortally weary of my life in Middelburg, and I recall that I was always looking for help towards my independence. But when I took the books to a friend and we read the diary over, I could get nothing from it, except that for the first time in my life, I was inspired to write a play – looking back on it, it would have been a very bad one, though I used some pretty things from it in *Abdelazar*. It was about a lady of great parts, but trusting and with little discretion, who was gulled by a magician into marriage with a black man. It was to be called *The Female Rosicrucian*. But Johan mistook my budget for one of his own, and carried it to Middelburg with your father's things, so even that was lost. Just as well, I suspect, though as a prentice effort, it perhaps made a way for my later work. If you ever care to enquire at 't Schippershuis for your possessions, you will do me a signal favour by throwing it in the fire.'

'When did your husband mistake the budgets?'

'It was the last time I saw him, in the summer of 'sixty-five. We believe he got to Middleburg, but on his way home, he was caught into the Battle of Lowestoft, and *The Good Intent* sent to the bottom. I have never been back to Middelburg to find out.'

Balthasar laughed a little, shaking his head again. 'So my father's books were in Middelburg for seven years, and I did not know it. I left Zeeland in 'seventy-two. I went to 't Schippershuis to enquire, of course, after I found the books gone. Your present made me sure who had taken them.'

'Oh, Doctor. I should blush for my younger self,' said Aphra wearily. 'But I find I do not care any more, and I suspect, neither do you.'

'I care about the unkindness. You were not kind when you were a flourishing young matron in Zeeland, and you are not kind now. But what you are saying is a terrible thought for me. Are you telling me that if I had thought to try again a year later, then your bear of a brother-in-law would have thrust the books into my hand?'

'I think so. I cannot be sure.' She closed her eyes wearily, slumping a little in the bed. Suddenly, she opened them again, and looked at him, pushing herself back up to a sitting position. 'Doctor, I have a great deal on my conscience. Tell me. Have I injured you very greatly?'

'I thought so once. But I think so no longer. Without those books, which might have guided me differently, I have simply had to live my life as myself, a plain Dutch doctor, not a courtier or a man of fashion, but merely a poor fellow who does what good he can in the world, and tries to rear his children in the ways of the Lord. You town wits seem to think that a man who does not set up for a rake must needs be a hypocrite, so you will think me a hypocrite, I am sure. Perhaps you blew away my father's dreams; but looking back, I cannot think that they would have availed me anything. I never felt they belonged to me.'

'I formed some ideas about those dreams, from your father's book. Who are you, Doctor? I guessed, but always wanted to know for certain.'

He shrugged. 'I have seldom spoken of this, but it is all one now. I do not think you will betray my confidence, and it would matter little if you did. I am the son of Omoloju, the *aremo* of Oyo, and Elizabeth, the Queen of Bohemia, and I was born in lawful wedlock.'

'Your father was betrayed into captivity. Mr Jonson's words come back to me. And he was a king.'

'He was.'

'And you are our new King's cousin, on the mother's side. You are very like him, you know.'

Balthasar shrugged.

'Doctor. The Queen is with child, as you must know, and already the people are murmuring against King James. They say there will be a boy, a Catholic heir, even if he has to bring one down the chimney. I do not think his majesty would stoop so low, he is a man of honour. But tell me. You are heir-male of Elizabeth of Bohemia, since all her other sons are dead or Catholic. For a man to have a true claim to be a monarch, he must be begot by a king on a queen, but your father was a king, even if he was black, and you tell me they were truly wed. If King James is put to flight, you have a better claim to the throne of England than King Charles's bastard son or James's daughters. You were born of a secret marriage, but so were Mary and Anne. Your line is the senior one, and you are male. Does your blood rise to it? Would you think to challenge?'

He looked at her in utter astonishment, and laughed. 'Oh, mevrouw. That is a playwright's notion, if ever I heard one. If I had any ambition that way, you scotched it more than twenty years ago. My parents' marriage certificate and the affidavit of my christening are bound into the cover of my father's diary. On account of your late theft, I have no proof of my legitimacy, or even of who I am.'

She seemed to sag a little where she sat. 'God is mocking me,' she said.

'As well He might. Mevrouw, make your peace with Him. Have a care for your soul. I do not care a straw for the throne of England, and nor should you.'

'You betray your mother, Doctor,' sneered Aphra. 'Royal blood declares itself – a true king will make his kingliness felt, be he ever so humble in his circumstances.'

'Mevrouw, you are speaking perfect nonsense. There was a man who would be king when I was in Barbados. A slave, of course, but he was a king in good sooth – men of quality and judgement among the Coromantees knew him. They made a compact to raise him, and take the island for their own.'

'And what happened?'

'What you would expect. They were betrayed, and they met wretched deaths, burned, flogged and tortured, with the perfect coolness of Roman heroes. The Coromantees possess an elevation of soul that enables them to meet their end, however terrible, with fortitude or even indifference. I have never forgotten it, not just for the horror of the executions, but because of the mockery of the planters. They jeered the Coromantees for their dreams, with hateful laughter, as if they thought them no better than monkeys. Your fancy puts me on a white horse in Whitehall, mevrouw, with plumes in my hat. I see myself on a hurdle drawing towards Tower Hill. No, mevrouw. For all the royalty of my blood, your country-men would not even allow me my dignity, if I did any such thing.'

He finished speaking, leaned forward to put his hand on her fore-head, then took her wrist again. 'I think you are much recovered, mevrouw. I will leave you some opium, as a palliative.'

'I must thank you, Doctor.'

He looked at her with cold dislike. 'You must indeed.' There was a loose guinea in his pocket. When he judged himself unob-served, he slipped it into the tumbled bedcovers. A gift of pity, and contempt. There was a bitter satisfaction in doing good in recompense for ill. He was tempted to humiliate her further, but his mind swerved away from it. She would soon be dead, that was clear, and he was not God, to sit in judgement. 'We are perfectly inimical to one another, mevrouw,' he said suddenly. 'I despise your notion of liberty, which seems to reside merely in the inability to govern your passions. True liberty, to my mind, resides in mastery over the self, and the good governance of a household, however small. But I admire the greatness of your spirit.'

'Thank you, Doctor. There are depths to you which I had not suspected. You will not own your blood, but I think it owns you. I wish you well.' She shut her eyes again, apparently in dismissal, and relaxed her supporting arm, allowing her body to slide back to near-horizontal. Her mind seemed to be elsewhere, and Balthasar wondered if she was nearer her end than she had appeared. She was in poor case, but from the state of her pulse, she should not be exhausted merely by a conversation.

He stood up, reaching for his hat, thinking of poor Caesar, who had waited outside all this time, wondering, perhaps, if he had been knocked on the head for his purse. 'Goodbye, mevrouw. God keep you. We will not meet again.'

She did not reply.

'A stroke of luck, mistress,' said Poll, after Aphra had lain with her eyes shut for five minutes or more. 'Are you feeling any better?'

'Be quiet, Poll,' said Aphra, sitting up again and pulling her old shawl round her shoulders. 'The black doctor has done more for me than he knows. Reach me a paper. He has given me an idea for a story, and I may repair our fortunes yet.'